W9-CAF-507

OLDER THAN GOODBYE

A JUDD WHEELER MYSTERY

OLDER THAN GOODBYE

RICHARD HELMS

FIVE STAR
A part of Gale, Cengage Learning

GALE
CENGAGE Learning·

Farmington Hills, Mich • San Francisco • New York • Waterville, Maine
Meriden, Conn • Mason, Ohio • Chicago

GALE
CENGAGE Learning

LIBRARY OF CONGRESS CATALOGING-IN-PUBLICATION DATA

Helms, Richard W., 1955–
    Older than goodbye : a Judd Wheeler mystery / Richard Helms.
        pages cm. — (A Judd Wheeler mystery ; 3)
    ISBN 978-1-4328-2949-0 (hardcover) — ISBN 1-4328-2949-1 (hardcover) — ISBN 978-1-4328-2946-9 (ebook)
    1. Police chiefs—North Carolina—Fiction. 2. Murder—Investigation—Fiction. 3. Mystery fiction. 4. Suspense fiction. I. Title.
PS3608.E466O43 2014
813'.6—dc23   2014020034

First Edition. First Printing: October 2014
Find us on Facebook– https://www.facebook.com/FiveStarCengage
Visit our website– http://www.gale.cengage.com/fivestar/
Contact Five Star™ Publishing at FiveStar@cengage.com

Printed in the United States of America
1 2 3 4 5 6 7 18 17 16 15 14

For Elaine
*For reminding me each day I draw breath to live
as if everything is a miracle.*

CHAPTER ONE

In an obscure honky-tonk near the Louisiana/Texas border, several years back, a Southern blues band played to a house filled with truckers, sharecroppers, weed-dealers, day laborers, and women who had long since traded dreams for expedience. It was a typical night, sweltering and steamy. It was the kind of night when local sheriff's deputies posted themselves in the convenience store parking lot across the street, lying in wait for the inevitable fistfights and gunplay, or to collar the inexorable DUI from the patrons who were in the bar for one reason and one reason only—to ingest as much alcohol in as short a time as possible in hopes of drowning their desperation.

Some people say there was a thunderstorm brewing that evening, but that may be the stuff of legend. What is certain is that the band was hopelessly and pathetically uninspiring. One story says that, at the first break, the lead singer said fuck it all, took to his car, and headed down the highway to an oblivious fate. Others say he suffered from a sudden stomach virus and spent the entire second set in the fetid bathroom. Nobody knows for certain, because that's how stories like this one grow from mere happenstance into myth.

The bartender that night was named Sean Burch. Most everyone called him Shugga, a name he picked up for unknown reasons during five years tending the state highways in an orange jumpsuit with block lettering on the back, either shoveling out hot asphalt with a snow shovel or digging it up with a mattock under the watchful gaze of pockmarked, sunburned, suet-laden gun bulls behind mirrored sunglasses.

Their lead singer gone AWOL, the band prepared to pack it in for the evening. Burch, who had memorized every Southern rock and blues anthem ever written while passing his prison stretch, saw his business for the night disappearing. So, he stepped up and asked if he could fill in.

The only other option being forfeiture of their pay, the band agreed. Shugga Burch took the microphone, told the players which songs he wanted to do, and launched into the set. By the second number, the crowd stopped yapping at one another and gave Shugga their entire attention. By the third number they were two-stepping and line-dancing all over the rough-hewn bar floor. By the end of the evening the band had a new lead singer for keeps. Shugga's voice was a cross between Robert Johnson's Faustian blues and the loping idle of a Top Fuel dragster. It was hypnotic, full of rasping discord, yet every note carried the promise of more, and it was impossible to stop listening.

Burch had done his full bump, and had no parole officer to check with. When the band left town that night, he rode with them.

They changed their name to Deep Creek Redemption, and within months they added "with Shugga Burch." Tour dates picked up, and they began to get record play. Then, the way lightning sometimes strikes, they received a Grammy nomination for their single "Shugga Bugga Shuffle," written by Burch himself. They graduated from dance clubs and honky-tonks to amphitheaters and stadiums and coliseums. They spent a year opening for the top groups, before the lightning struck again and Burch won a CMA award for another of his compositions, "Sweet Sugar Honey," and followed it up with a Grammy. The band changed its name to "Shugga Burch with Deep Creek Redemption." They became the headliners.

Magazine articles heralded Sean Burch, who eventually dropped two letters from his nickname and now went simply by Shug, as a symbol for self-redemption. His story of rising from a prison road worker to the stratospheric regions of the music world became an exemplary parable for all the downtrodden fans who adored him.

There were other stories—dark, fearful whisperings of incidents along the road—that belied Burch's reputation as a changed man. Women who somehow made it through the rings of protective handlers surrounding the great man, often only after Burch had pointed them out, left his tour bus with a strange, otherwordly look in their eyes and a tendency to flinch reflexively at sudden sharp sounds. People who knew the women said they would never describe what happened in the bus, but were forever and terribly changed by the experience.

There was the story, repeatedly squelched by the record company, about the hitchhiker for whom Shug's bus stopped on a lonely stretch of Kansas blacktop, only to deposit him later by the roadside in Missouri, and how he might someday regain the sight in one eye and is rumored to have eventually reacquired the ability to swallow and to speak in simple sentences.

If his previous life of uncertainty had taught Burch anything, it was the importance of not putting all your eggs in one basket. As he accumulated large amounts of wealth, he diversified his holdings. Some went into apartment complexes. Some went into coin laundries or parking lots or dry cleaning shops. With time, music became one of the minor components of Shug's annual income. The whispers started again, vague insinuations that the miniature empire he had forged from his singing career might hide a multitude of financial sins. Some said that shirts and slacks weren't the only items being laundered.

Every time the whispers became too loud, or whenever some enterprising young investigative reporter dared to look too closely at Burch's operations, *things* would happen. It might be an unfortunate accident, or an unexpected arrest for possession of illicit substances, or sometimes people simply vanished. There was no way to backtrack these occurrences directly to Burch. He was too lucky, many said, to ever get caught doing anything not on the up-and-up. So the whisperings remained innuendo and supposition, and Shug Burch got richer with each passing year.

I knew better, of course. Sean Burch and I had a history. You could say, in a sense, that I had set him on the path that led to his success. Perhaps we had been like random asteroids in the years since, revolving slowly and surely in our orbits, ignorant of our separate lives but destined for a cataclysmic and inescapable collision.

One thing was certain. When I learned that he had returned to Bliss County, I knew we were predestined to meet at some point at the dark, tragic end of a lonely country road, a meeting from which only one of us was likely to return.

CHAPTER TWO

"You recognize that face, Chief?" Harvey "Slim" Tackett asked, as he placed a grainy photo on my desk.

"Should I?" I said.

"I got a call from Buddy Hargette, the fellow who owns the car wash over at the shopping center. Says he pulled that off a security camera this morning."

I inspected the picture again. The camera had been set about face height, but the picture quality was pretty poor. The image showed what could have been a face. The person in the picture was wearing a Carolina Pythons cap, so there was a shadow across his face.

"What's his beef?" I asked.

"Says he's being ripped off. The old tape-on-the-dollar trick."

I took a sip of my morning coffee.

It was an old scam. Most places these days, it won't even work anymore. Some, like car washes, have older versions of bill changers that aren't as sensitive to anomalies in dollar bills. With those older machines, you can run a strip of clear cellophane tape right down the middle of each side of a dollar bill, leaving a tail about five inches long. You put the bill into the changer, while holding onto the tape tail, wait for the machine to give you your quarters, and then you pull the bill right back out again. You can do this as many times as you like, until either the tape breaks and you lose your bill, or until the machine runs out of quarters.

Replacing the bill changers with newer, more foolproof versions costs a lot of money, and car washes run on a pretty mean profit margin. Buddy Hargette had decided that it made more sense to put in a security camera, so that anyone contemplating a career of petty bill changer theft would think twice and go somewhere else.

Unless, of course, the master criminal was too stupid to recognize the camera.

I took another look at the picture. "Is that Spud?"

Slim grinned. "That's what I thought."

I took another sip of the coffee. I craved a doughnut to go with it, but as I had nosed over into middle age I found it harder and harder to keep off the excess pounds. In addition, I prided myself on my ability to defy stereotypes.

"Spud Corliss. A bad haircut held up by an imbecile. Last I heard, he was in training school," I said.

"So did I. I called his juvenile probation officer. She said he was sent back to his momma a couple of weeks ago. Good behavior time."

"That's code for 'we're sick of dealing with his whiny little ass.' Didn't take him long to recidivate."

"I'm amazed he wasn't popped his first weekend out. What do you want to do?"

I placed the picture on my desk, and took another sip of coffee. Half of my mind was occupied with Spud Corliss. The other half was debating whether I'd rather have a cream-filled or a cruller.

"Can't let Spud start a damned crime wave in this town," I said. "We let him walk on bill changer theft, the next thing you know he's gonna start selling illegal raffle tickets."

"Can't have that," Slim said.

"Would ruin the entire social fabric in Prosperity. I reckon I'll drive on out to the Corliss place, pay ol' Spud a visit."

"Want me to come with you?"

"For Spud Corliss? I think I can handle him."

"Ten-four, Chief."

Slim left my office. I heard his snakeskin boots clomp all the way down the hall of the police station, until they were joined by the creak of the spring on the screen door leading out to the parking lot.

"Spud," I said to the picture from the car wash, "you are ruining a perfectly good morning for me."

One benefit of being the chief of police in Prosperity, North Carolina, is that I exercise my authority to use the newer patrol car. We only own two, but the one I'd assigned to Slim was three years older than the one I took for myself. Considering that we put somewhere around a hundred thousand miles on a bubbletop each year, and considering that the town council was stuffed with skinflint Republican oligarchs who hated to pay for anything they could get for free, it had taken something on the order of a Biblical edict to get the one new car the department did own. We'd probably have to stretch the older car for at least another year, and then Slim would inherit my car after I leveraged my soul to the council for a replacement.

It was early autumn, which in Prosperity is often referred to as summer, extended. Halloween was only three weeks away, but the trees in my town were still relatively green, edging over toward yellow. The harvest was mostly complete on the remaining farms in my formerly agricultural paradise, which meant that the air was filled with the early scents of decay and elemental entropy. We wouldn't see a frost for at least a couple more weeks, if then, and winter was still a distant prospect.

Spud Corliss had been baptized as Brian, but almost nobody save for his mother called him that. His father had been among the first soldiers killed in Afghanistan, trying to run Osama to ground, back when Spud was not much more than a pup. Spud's mother was still pretty, and barely thirty, so after a decent interval she had begun dating again with something resembling a fury. You'd need more than a football scorecard to keep track of the procession of men who drifted in and out of the Corliss house throughout Spud's short childhood. Without a steady male influence, and with his mother frequently distracted by *affaires du coeur,* Spud's social development had been left more or less to chance.

My first encounter with Spud had come when he was only ten, a couple of years before my wife, Susan, was killed in a head-on crash with a transfer truck on the Morgan Highway bridge over Six Mile Creek. Gwen Tissot, the owner of the Stop and Rob convenience store located between my farm and the City Hall where the police station was housed, had called to complain that some kid was shoplifting stroke books from the rack behind the counter while Gwen was exchanging propane tanks for other customers. She had seen Spud dash around the unsupervised counter through the front window of the store—on two occasions, no less!—before she decided to hand his fate over to the local constabulary.

I set up a stakeout at the store using one of my officers, a young kid named Stu Marbury. Truth be told, it was a waste of a good cop, but I figured it would be learning experience for him. Stu set himself up in the beer cooler, where he had a good view of the front counter, but where nobody in the store could see him.

Spud came into the store and played a couple of video games, until a customer showed up to switch out a used propane tank for a new one. Sure enough, as soon as Gwen stepped outside to complete the swap, Spud dashed around the counter and grabbed a copy of some rag called *Hot Humps,* and tried to stuff it inside his jacket. Considering that I had socks older than

Spud, it's hard to imagine what he expected to do with the magazine, but it did seem to be a source of some fascination for him.

As Spud headed for the door, Stu stepped out of the beer cooler and grabbed him by the arm. Spud was busted.

Like most kids on their first bust, his trip to Juvenile Court landed him on probation. Neither the concept of probation nor the attentions of his Juvenile Court counselor seemed to resonate with Spud, however. Within a month he was back in front of the judge for tossing bricks through a couple of car windows in the Prosperity Glen High School parking lot.

It was more or less at this time that he acquired the nickname *Spud*. It might have been cruel, and maybe even a little inappropriate, but everyone who came into contact with him agreed that Brian Corliss had been born with the brain of a tuber. The nickname started with his Juvenile Court counselor, a thirty-year veteran who had seen his share of dumb kids, but never one the likes of Corliss. He referred to his client as "Spud" in an informal pre-hearing meeting one morning, and like a bad smell (something else for which Spud was famous) the name sort of hung on him.

Spud had gravitated in and out of juvenile courtrooms for several years, until the judge got sick of his face and decided that the kid would benefit from eating state food for a year or so. The last straw came when Spud held up another kid at the high school during a football game, using a three-dollar toy gun he'd stolen from the local Piggly Wiggly. Ironically, he didn't get enough in the heist to even pay for the gun, but armed robbery is armed robbery, and Spud's ass was shipped off to a training school near Asheville.

Now he was back in Prosperity, trying to pull the old tape-on-the-dollar scam at the car wash. It seemed that training school had taught Spud a few new tricks—an iffy proposition under almost any circumstances.

I parked the cruiser in the gravel driveway of the Corliss home, a squat, flat-fronted structure covered in cheap siding, and trudged across the patchy lawn of crabgrass, chickweed, and dirt toward the front door. There was no front porch. A set of three wooden steps led to the extruded aluminum door. I knocked on the storm glass. After a few moments, JoBeth Corliss answered the door. It was already ten in the morning, but she was still dressed in a thin cotton zip-up house robe. She had still been a beauty when first widowed a decade earlier, but years of being the town pump had taken their toll. Her hair was thin and needed to reacquaint itself with shampoo. Her eyes were glassy.

"Chief Wheeler!" she said, before glancing quickly behind her—I presumed to assure that there was no incriminating evidence lying around the living room.

"Ms. Corliss. Is Brian here this morning?"

"What's he done?"

"I need to talk with him, ask a few questions. Is he here, ma'am?"

"Not sure. Have to check. Wait here."

She didn't close the front door, but she did leave me standing on the front steps with the storm door closed. I saw her disappear around the corner into the hallway. After a few seconds, she returned to the front door.

"He's getting out of bed," she said. "Will you come in?"

I stepped directly into the living room. It was dominated by a threadbare, sprung-out thrift store sofa and a fifty-inch flat screen television. There was a heavy smell of grease in the house. A scraggly cat curled in the corner, next to a litter box that cried out for changing.

"Is there a problem, Chief?" JoBeth asked.

I decided to sidestep her question. "How's Brian been doing

since he got out of training school?"

"Oh, he's been great," she said, her voice slightly slurred. "I really think they got through to him up there."

"That's good to hear. Is he in school?"

"Well, Chief, you know he's seventeen now, and he don't have to go to school no more by state law. He's behaving himself, and he's looking for work. He put in an application at the Goodyear store over in Morgan the other day. He's tryin' to pull himself together, you know."

I smiled at her but didn't comment. I figured a mother had a right to believe the best about her child, even if that child had all the social scruples of a water moccasin. A couple of seconds later, Spud shambled around the corner. He wore a black Guns and Roses tee shirt and a pair of knit drawstring pajama pants. His hair was in disarray and he was barefoot. He scratched at an armpit as he looked me up and down.

"Brian. I have a problem," I said. "I was hoping you could help me out with it." I pulled the computer printout from my pocket, crossed the room, and showed him the picture taken at Buddy Hargette's car wash. "Is this you?"

He didn't have to answer. The limited wattage in his brain barely provided enough power to tell the truth, let alone fabricate a reasonable lie.

"The person in this picture," I continued, "used the old tape-on-the-bill trick to steal money from the car wash. Looks a lot like you, doesn't it?"

I glanced at the picture again, and noted that he was still wearing the same tee shirt. Based on the odor arising from it, it hadn't been washed either.

"Kinda," he said.

"Are you still on probation?"

"No. I done all my time."

"Which means that, being seventeen, any crimes you commit

would be covered under the adult criminal system."

I saw some tears start to form at the corners of his eyes.

"You gonna take me to jail, Chief?"

"That depends. How much money did you pull out of the machine?"

I think he wanted to try to lie to me, but again he couldn't think fast enough.

"About thirty dollars, I reckon."

"You spend all of it?"

"Only five or six dollars. I still got the rest back in my bedroom."

"Tell you what. You go get what you have left, and you and I can go visit Mr. Hargette over at the car wash. We'll make restitution and I'll talk with him. Maybe he'll decide not to press charges, under some conditions."

"What kind of conditions?"

"Well, you'll probably have to stay away from the car wash and maybe away from the shopping center altogether. He might want you to work off the rest, first."

"And if he decides to press charges?"

"It would be a misdemeanor, and since you don't have any adult charges you'd probably wind up on probation."

"Just got off probation."

"Beats jail," I said. "Why don't you go change clothes and get that money and we'll go see Mr. Hargette?"

He stared at the floor for a moment, then nodded. Without a word he turned and shuffled back down the hall.

"He's a good boy," JoBeth said. "He makes bad decisions sometimes, but his heart is good."

"I'm not going to lie to you," I told her. "Stealing is a big deal, whether it's thirty dollars or thirty thousand, and Spu— Brian's been at it for a long time. I reckon we can work something out with Mr. Hargette, but this is the last time I go to bat for the boy."

"I appreciate it, Chief."

I heard Spud coming back up the hall, and checked my watch. It was 10:30. If we could get this whole matter squared away by noon, I might call Donna, see if she wanted to meet me for lunch.

When I looked up from my watch, Spud was back in the living room. Instead of a bag of coins, he held a small revolver.

"Ain't gonna go back on probation," he said.

I held up my left hand, more a reflex than a reasoned response, as my right hand instinctively snapped the restraining strap on my service pistol.

Spud jerked the trigger three times. I felt the bullets hit me and, for a second, I imagined I was okay. Then I felt myself slip to the floor. Things went into slow motion. JoBeth Corliss screamed something, but I couldn't tell exactly what it was. Spud ran past me, out the front door.

I tried to reach for the two-way microphone on my left shoulder to call in an *officer down*, but for some reason my hand wouldn't go where I willed it. There was an adrenaline roar in my ears, and my field of vision began to crinkle at the edges. I glanced down and saw a trio of dark stains spread across my uniform shirt and begin to merge with one another, and I moaned a little because the pain caught up with me and a well of fire and sharp, streaky agony shot through my torso like heat lightning.

JoBeth stared at me as I lay on the floor, ruining her frayed carpet, and then she ran to the phone. My visual field whited out and I began to lose my hold on consciousness.

The last two things that went through my mind were tangentially connected images—not exactly phrases or sentences, but more like concepts that included varying degrees of regret and shock.

The first image was of the bulletproof vest sitting in the trunk of my cruiser, instead of under my shirt where it belonged.

The second thought was that—after spending almost ten years on the mean streets of Atlanta, and another ten as the police chief of Prosperity—I'd had my shit scattered by a kid with the brain of a tuber.

And then I didn't think anything at all, for a long, long, time.

CHAPTER THREE

A lot of things happened over the next couple of months.
I don't remember most of them.

CHAPTER FOUR

Many months after the fact . . .

Dr. Kronenfeld had lost a little more hair since I'd last been in his office, and he looked thicker around the belt line. His gaze was still laser-intense.

"So, you believe that was the starting point, where the whole story began?" he said.

"Everything was good until then," I said. "From the moment Spud turned that gun on me, everything seemed to . . . spiral."

"You nearly died."

I held up two fingers. "Did die. Twice. At least my heart stopped, which I guess is as close as you get to going all the way. Stopped once in the ambulance, and once again the second day I was in the hospital."

"You knew what happened, though."

"Not at first. Not for a long time. I was out for quite a while. I didn't wake up for almost a week, and I drifted in and out for a week or so after that. Could have been more. I don't recall most of it. They say I set some kind of record for the number of wires and tubes they had in me. Seems at times I was more machine than man."

"But you survived."

"Barely. Donna says there was this little spark of life that refused to go out. Spent almost a month in recovery. You know what recovery is? That's the place they take you after surgery. Most times, you stay there for a few hours. Sometimes a day. I was there a month. What

22

does that tell you?"

"*It was touch and go.*"

"*More like damn near gone. They were afraid to cart me off to Intensive Care. Scared I might blow a gasket and die all over them on the trip over. So I didn't know much about what happened for a while. Spud shot me three weeks before Halloween. I took my Thanksgiving meal through a tube in the ICU. By Christmas, I was doing a pretty good job feeding myself.*

"*Around New Year's, they put me in a regular room. That's when Slim came by, told me what happened. How Spud went on the run. Holed up in that shanty over near Tulip Springs. Told me about the standoff and what the sheriff's deputies found when they finally stormed the place. You know what?*"

"*What?*"

"*I think that was the worst. All the shit I'd gone through and hearing what Spud did to himself was the worst. I nearly had a relapse right there. I never understood why he shot me in the first place. I believed I'd made it clear to him. We were going to set things right with Buddy Hargette. I don't know what that boy was thinking.*"

"*They didn't call him 'Spud' for nothing.*"

"*I reckon. I don't know what happened to Spud up at the training school, but he must have had his fill of locks and badges. He must have thought I was going to cross him, lock him up again. Hell, I don't know. Who knows what kind of junk goes through the head of a kid that dim?*"

"*But that wasn't the end of it.*"

"*No. Of course not. Whatever gods I pissed off were nowhere near done with me. That was only the beginning. Fact is, I don't know if they're done yet. What do you think? Have I served my penance?*"

"*I'm Jewish, Judd. I don't believe in penance. Atonement, sure.*"

"*So, have I atoned?*"

"*Hell, I don't know. You haven't told me the whole story yet.*"

23

"Sometimes I wonder if it's ever going to get better."

"That one I can answer. You keep working, it will. So, what happened next?"

I rubbed my face. My skin felt dry and hot. I realized I'd shaven carelessly that morning.

"Well," I said, "next, I went home."

CHAPTER FIVE

Somehow, I'd missed winter.

It was a Saturday in the middle of March, that point where the dogwoods and Bradford pears dare to blossom despite the promise of more killing frosts. The smarter trees—the oaks, poplars, and maples that rimmed my hundred-acre farm in Prosperity—knew better. Their branches were still naked and bone-like, and rubbed together in the breeze as if warming themselves from a long, cold slumber.

I sat in a cushioned wicker chair on the fifteen-foot deep front porch of my house, set back a few hundred yards from the Morgan Highway, which ran from Prosperity to the county seat. My legs, still shaky and uncertain of supporting my weight, were covered with a patchwork quilt my grandmother had made sixty years ago. At my side, on a cedar table I'd built twenty years earlier, was a book by a bestselling mystery author. It had lain there for several hours, as I had lounged and stared through the tree trunks at the cars and transfer trucks that sped by on the highway. My son, Craig, had meant well when he'd bought me the book, but I'd had my fill of killing and crime. My eyes glazed over as I read, and eventually I'd simply put it aside for another time.

Inside the house, I could hear Donna Asher humming as she made us a late lunch. Tuna salad. Heavy on the mayo. Steak fries and a chocolate shake. The doctor said I needed to put on more weight, to replace what three months in the hospital had whittled from my hide.

I'd weighed two-twenty on the day Spud shot me, and I'm not bragging when I say that it had been mostly muscle on my six-three frame. I'd trained regularly through my adult life to maintain the athletic body I'd built as a high school and college quarterback. When I got out of the hospital, shortly after the first of the year, I'd morphed into a spindly hundred-fifty pound scarecrow.

Appetite was hard to come by for a while. Nothing tasted the way I expected. My doctor told me that the blood loss might have caused some damage in the parts of my brain where flavor registered. Maybe he was right. All I knew was that forcing food down my gullet was like shoveling boulders up a chimney. My system craved nourishment, but my spirit couldn't muster enthusiasm for eating.

I ate, if only to keep Donna happy. Before I was shot I had believed that poets and philosophers had yet failed to define a relationship the depth of ours. On the other hand, I'd spent our years together as her protector. There were spaces in our devotion, elbow room that allowed us to breathe and move freely, but we still orbited in each other's gravity like binary stars, hopelessly and forever bound to one another by a power that even we could not explain.

I underestimated her. Since coming home, she had become *my* protector and provider. She taught English at Prosperity Glen High from shortly past sunup until late afternoon, but the rest of her life was dedicated to my recuperation. She hadn't slept in her own home since January. She said she didn't feel right being two miles away, not knowing whether I'd fallen on the way to the bathroom, or that I might be lying in bed or on the sofa, hungry, without the will or energy to drag myself into the kitchen for a snack. She said she rested better the closer she was to me.

I saw the lie in it, of course. I'd awakened a dozen times in the night to find her sitting and watching me, as if she were terrified that I might stop breathing if she averted her gaze for even a moment. I had never felt so loved and supported in my life, nor as guilty.

I heard the screen door squeal open on winter-rusted hinges, and slam shut again, and I made a mental note to squirt some graphite on those hinges and replace the hydraulic cylinder the first moment I was able, and then I added those chores to the endless list I'd compiled in my head since returning home.

Donna picked up the novel and placed a tray on the table in its place. She'd bought sweet Hawaiian pretzel rolls at the new bakery in Prosperity—the one I'd never visited, as it had opened since the shooting—and she had layered lettuce and tomatoes on them before dropping on a great scoop of tuna salad. She served my plate, and her own, and she sat in the other wicker chair to eat.

"Damn place is falling down around me," I said. "Old houses need more upkeep than new ones."

"Yes," she said. But she didn't add anything. I think she had become used to my cranky rants.

"When you go to the store next, pick me up a can of graphite spray."

"Go with me, and pick it up yourself."

I couldn't help it. I had to smile. Our conversations had trended this way for weeks.

"Might at that. After lunch, maybe I'll take my cane and walk out to the Morgan Highway to the mailbox, find out what kind of bills I got today."

"Don't need the cane anymore," she said between bites. "Nothing wrong with your legs."

"These wobbly sticks?"

"You're stronger than you think. Your problem isn't with your body now. Have you considered any more about returning to work? Don't look at me like that. I'm serious."

"What would I do? Sit in my office and stare at the walls?"

"You're the police chief. Do chief stuff. Start slow. Be an administrator. Nobody's asking you to chase bad guys right off the bat."

"You've been talking to Kent again."

Kent Kramer is the mayor of Prosperity. Technically, he isn't my boss, since I work for the town council. Kent likes to suck up power the way a sponge does water. He likes to believe that he can order me around. Because he's been one of my closest friends for over a quarter century, and because I love him, I let him revel in his delusion.

Up to a point.

"He dropped by the school the other day."

"Was that before or after he came over here?"

"Couldn't say. The town's short-handed, Judd. Ever since Stu quit the department, Slim's been holding down the fort by himself."

Stu Marbury had been one of my two patrolmen, back before the shooting. While I was laid up in the hospital, he got an offer to join the sheriff's department over in Morgan, under Don Webb. I couldn't blame him. His wife worked for the county tax office there. The county provided better benefits.

"Slim's a good cop," I said.

"One of the best," she agreed. "But he's working alone. Kent told you he's putting out an ad for a new patrolman?"

"He said he wanted to. I told him he couldn't, because he doesn't run the police department or supervise it. Told him if there's going to be any hiring done, I'd do it."

"So?"

"So, I'll get around to it."

"When?"

"Maybe right after I fix that damned screen door."

Donna cleaned up after lunch and then excused herself to go back to the bedroom for a nap. I craved her company, but I did not begrudge her need for rest. Taking care of me had become a second job for her, and I already knew she slept fitfully at best during the night.

I took another run at the novel, but for some reason I couldn't seem to make the pages relate to one another. It was as if each chapter stood by itself, with no connection to the past or the future. I had been told to expect this, another consequence of getting your gray matter scrambled by blood loss. I hadn't driven a car by myself since the shooting. I considered that a gift to the community because God only knew how bad my reflexes might be.

I've been to college. I know things. I recognized the symptoms I experienced without the need for a shrink. I was depressed. Who wouldn't be? Getting your spokes ripped out will do that.

I must have dozed, because I awoke to the clatter of car tires on the gravel drive that wove through hardwoods from the highway to my front porch. I looked up and saw the red and blue lights of the new Prosperity cruiser, the one I had appropriated for myself until my run-in with Spud. Slim had taken it over, and I knew that—soon—I'd have to make a plea to the town council to ditch the old cruiser and replace it with a *new* new cruiser, since the *old* new cruiser would certainly reek of cigarette smoke from the unfiltered Camels Slim insisted on using to poison his system.

Slim stopped at the foot of the porch steps, and pulled himself out of the car the way a fakir's rope climbs toward the sky. He was about my height, but due to some glandular condition he stayed rail-like and lanky. Like a lot of Bliss County folks, he seemed to carry the weight of ten generations in his haggard, prematurely crevassed face and gray eyes. Veins like braided rubber bands stood out on the back of his hands, and ran up his arms like kudzu vines. As always, he had augmented his uniform with the snakeskin boots I had long since given up trying to dissuade him from wearing. I knew how to pick my battles, and the boots didn't bother me enough to fight over, at least not anymore.

He didn't walk up the steps. Instead he leaned against the passenger side of the cruiser, his hands braced against the door.

"Chief," he said.

"Afternoon, Harvey."

I knew he preferred to be called Slim, but sometimes I went ahead and addressed him by his birth name. I'm the chief. I can do that. Not many other people dared.

"You alone?" he asked.

"Donna's taking a nap. Come on up. Take a load off."

He stepped up to the porch and settled into the other chair.

"What brings you out here?" I said.

"Courtesy call. I ticketed some kid from over in Mica Wells doing sixty in a forty-five zone. He got his license last Saturday, along with a new Camaro for his birthday. I wouldn't want to be him when he has to tell his dad later tonight."

"Live and learn."

"Die and forget it all. Don't suppose I can talk you into pinning on your badge anytime soon."

"Give me a few weeks."

"Whenever. Figured since I was in the area I'd kick by to see how you're faring. We need you back, Chief."

"It's Saturday. You're not even supposed to be on duty. Weekend patrols are for the sheriff's department."

"That was fine, until Stu quit. You and I both know that Don Webb's stretched to the limit over in Morgan. Leave it to the sheriff, and we might get a deputy through here once every three or four hours on weekends. The rest of the time it would be open season for the criminal element."

"Such as it is in Prosperity."

" 'All that's necessary for the forces of evil to win in the world is for enough good men to do nothing.' "

"You read that on the back of an Edmund Burke bubble gum card?"

"You're too fast for me, Chief. Figured you'd recognize the saying."

"Only because it's hanging in my office. I suppose you're keeping my seat warm in there."

"I occupy it from time to time to do paperwork. Don't like it much. The room fits you much better."

There was nothing much to say to that, so we lapsed into silence for a minute or two.

Slim had been the first officer I'd hired, a week after the town council had issued me my chief's badge. He'd been an MP in Japan, after serving in Kuwait during the first Gulf War, and he had distinguished himself as a top-flight military cop before mustering out and returning to Prosperity, the way salmon do to their spawning grounds. He'd tried his hand at various trades, but there's something about living life with a badge on your chest and a pistol on your hip that grows on you like a callus that never seems to soften. The day after I posted an advertisement for town officers he showed up in my office dressed in the suit he'd probably worn in his first ill-conceived wedding, with a hand-typed resume and a pleading look in his eyes that told me he wanted to be a cop more than anything else in the world. I hired him that afternoon, and I've never regretted it.

I'm a good cop. I take pride in my work. I learned policing on some of the toughest sidewalks in urban Atlanta. I've never taken a bribe, and I never will. Slim, compared to me, is a *great* cop. In the way that some people pick up a guitar and immediately make it sing, or climb into a racing car for the first time and go out and dust the field, Slim was born to the shield. If he'd gone up the road to the big city of Pooler and joined the force there, he'd have been made a detective long ago. Instead, he remained in Prosperity, patrolling the rural two-lane blacktops and oiled dirt shanty tracks, handing out speeding tickets and taking break-in and vandalism complaints and responding to Friday night domestic squabble calls. I was doing him a disservice, leaving the entire burden of keeping the peace in our little town on his shoulders.

He was right.

I needed to get back on the job.

I live on the farm my family has owned since before the American Revolution. In its prime it covered over a thousand acres, long before Prosperity was incorporated, and dating back to a time when there was no Bliss County or Parker County. When my first Carolina ancestor broke the ground and felled the trees on this land, he'd done so under a land grant from the English king. Over the centuries, the same way it happens in our human bodies, the farm had been decimated by debt and manifest destiny, sold off in bits and chunks, until now I owned only the hundred acres I'd inherited on the day my father had dropped to the ground in the barnyard with an aneurysm a few weeks after I'd returned from Atlanta to help him run the place.

I had never felt the call to the agricultural life. It lay on my shoulders like a poorly tailored suit. I had tried to run the farm myself for a year or so after my father's death, with the help of my wife, Susan, and a few hired Mexican hands, but in the end I found it a tedious and spiritually draining exercise. Somehow, the spark or gene that had driven my father had skipped a generation. When Kent Kramer had approached me with an offer to run the nascent town police department, I'd initially rejected it out of something like family loyalty, but I'd immediately regretted it, and knew that if he came calling again—as I knew he would—I'd eventually relent.

Now, I was a gentleman tenant farmer. The Mexican workers I'd originally hired to help manage the place now rented twenty- and thirty-acre parcels from me, on which they grew soybeans and corn and snap peas and watermelons during the summer, and cabbage, kale, collards, and root vegetables in the fall and winter. Leasing the land provided some extra income, and I liked looking out the back window of my kitchen and seeing life spring from the soil each year.

All of this goes toward explaining why Jorge Hierra appeared on my front porch about a week after Slim's visit.

Hierra was a lean, angular man with muscles like anchor chains running beneath his walnut skin. His hair was shaved to a quarter inch from his scalp, and he covered it in the field with a tattered straw cowboy hat he'd bought for eight dollars off a rack at the Piggly Wiggly. He now held this hat against his chest as he stood at the base of the porch steps.

"Is there a problem, Jorge?" I asked.

"Si, Senor Wheeler. It is my mother. She lives in Spartanburg, and she has to go to the hospital."

"I'm sorry to hear that. Is it serious?"

"She is eighty years old. At that age, any illness . . ." He shrugged.

"How can I help?"

"I need to go to her, to be by her side. My wife, Estrella, will be going with me. There is nobody to tend to the corn."

Jorge was facing a hard decision, choosing between his family and his livelihood. I admired his desire to stand by his mother.

"I wouldn't worry too much. The plants are nothing but

shoots yet. Corn is pretty resilient. As long as we don't have a drought or too much rain, it should be able to handle itself."

"Si. This is true, but I do not know how long I must be away. I need someone to watch the fields, in case anything should happen."

Jorge didn't know what he was asking. I hadn't burdened my tenants with my personal tragedies. I knew that some of them had heard about the shooting, but I hadn't talked with them about it. Jorge's parcel was nearly a half-mile from the house, and the washboard dirt rut that ran alongside the fields was hell on car suspensions. I'd have to walk there every other day to check on his crops.

Jorge was a stalwart. He had been among the first men I'd hired after my father's death. When Susan was killed, his family scraped together the cash to send a flower arrangement to the funeral home. I didn't even wish to guess how it had eaten into their grocery money. He was never late on his lease payments, and he almost always dropped off a bushel of sweet Silver Queen corn after the harvest each fall, even though I'm not a sharecrop landlord and I don't demand percentages from the men who sow my fields.

"Of course," I said. "I'll look after the corn. If you'll leave a telephone number where I can reach you in Spartanburg, I'll let you know if I see any problems."

Jorge thanked me, climbed back into his truck, and headed out the gravel drive toward his home.

I sat for quite a while after he left, watching the afternoon shadows lengthen in the front yard, until they fell across the ancient stone barbecue pit my great-grandfather had constructed shortly after the Civil War. It had lain cold and neglected since September, and I was surprised to find that I longed for some grilled pork chops with turnip greens and pintos and sweet corn muffins. It was the first food craving I'd felt for . . . well, as far back as I could recall since the shooting.

Slowly, I stood and stepped cautiously down the steps to the gravel drive. Walking still felt like a foreign process, but with each step I seemed to gain a little more steadiness.

The diamond steel expanded sheet that served as the barbecue grate had grown a thick coat of rust over the winter. I pulled it from its brick supports and laid it up against the side of the grill. I had three or four more like it in a storage bin in the barn. I had cut them from a larger sheet using an acetylene torch the year before, knowing that they didn't last more than a season or two exposed to the southern elements.

I retrieved the new grate from the barn, and slid it into place. Then I called Donna over at the school, where I knew she was in her office after classes.

"I want pork chops," I told her.

"Really?"

"I was looking at the barbecue pit and I wanted pork chops. I've put the new grate in."

"I can drop by the store on the way home. I'll bet you need charcoal, too."

"And some turnip greens, and some pintos and Jiffy Mix. I'm good for it."

"Oh, yes," she said. "You are."

If I could volunteer to walk the half-mile to Jorge's parcel every day or so, and if I wanted to eat, then it stood to reason that I was hale enough to go back to work. Six months after taking three slugs in the chest, it was time to pin on the badge again.

CHAPTER SIX

I needed an entire new uniform. I was still down a couple dozen pounds from my pre-shooting weight, and my old uniforms hung on my leaner frame like draperies on a sagging curtain rod.

I won't say it was a pleasant experience dressing for work that first day. I had grown unused to starched shirts and razor-creased khaki trousers, and my brogans felt like lead weights at the end of my weakened legs. My Sam Brown belt had hung in the den closet untouched for half a year, and the first time I strapped it on, it felt foreign to me, like new shackles on a Roman galley slave. The night before returning to work, I had carefully stripped my Sig Sauer automatic and meticulously cleaned it. Then I'd assembled it and chucked in a fresh magazine of brand-new .40 caliber hollowpoints. I had visited an indoor shooting range a few days before to see if I could still park a round within five feet of my intended target, and had been pleasantly surprised with my scores. Apparently my eyesight and fine motor coordination were returning.

I finished dressing, and surveyed myself in the mirror. My fresh haircut lay flat against my skull, albeit considerably grayer than it had been the last time I'd suited up. Donna stood behind me, her arms crossed, examining me from head to toe as if she were a finicky drill sergeant.

"You're missing something," she said.

"I'd guess I'm missing a lot of things."

She retreated to the other bedroom, where Craig stayed when he was home from college, and I heard her retrieve something from the closet. She walked back in with a large box in her hand.

I recognized it immediately. The officers in the Prosperity Police Department wear Stetsons instead of the traditional Pershing caps or campaign covers used by most policemen on the East Coast. I had insisted on this when I was hired. My own Stetson had been ruined when I fell to the floor of Spud's trailer and bled all over it.

I opened the box and pulled out the new hat.

"Can't be the good guy without a white hat," Donna said.

"It's cream, and it's terrific."

I ran my fingers around the sweatband, the same way I always had with my old hat, and then I slid it on. It felt stiff and a little heavy, but the fit was tight and sure.

"I like it," I said. "It feels right."

There were a lot of things I wanted to tell her, but none of them seemed able to form themselves into coherent sentences.

"Thank you," I said, finally.

"For the hat?"

"For everything. I know I've been grumpy and depressed and distant, and I haven't said *please* enough the way my father taught me to do, and I know I haven't thanked you near enough for what you've done over the winter."

She took the hat off my head and kissed me, long and deep, the way she used to before my entire world had been rent by Spud Corliss.

"Wow," I said, after we broke lip lock.

"I did what I did because I love you," she said. "I'd do it again and I expect you'd do more for me. And if we keep this up, you are going to be way late for work and my students are going to need a substitute, and that won't do, today of all days.

So, out with you. Go get 'em, tiger."

She walked me to the front door and shoved me out to the porch. Before the screen door eased shut—I had finally gotten around to fixing it—I kissed her again.

"To be continued," I told her.

"Bet your ass, Chief."

I drove my Jeep because I hadn't wanted to hog a cruiser overnight when I wasn't going to use it for official business.

As I pulled up to the station next to the Town Hall, which had actually been built as a local merchant's home in 1903, I couldn't believe my eyes. Someone had stretched a ten-yard long banner across the second floor of the building, reading *WELCOME BACK CHIEF WHEELER!!!* I pulled my Jeep into my marked parking space, and stepped out as Sherry, my civilian office assistant, threw open the front door and flew out to give me a huge bear hug.

"Chief, you look great!" she said. "We've missed you so much!"

Within seconds, people started pouring through the door of the station into the parking lot. The town council—Elzie Phipps, Fred Warfield, and Art Belts—led the way, followed closely by Kent Kramer. Slim slipped through the door but, rather than join the jubilation, he leaned against the front of the building.

Donna's car pulled into the lot seconds later. She must have left the house only a minute or so after I did.

"You knew about this?" I asked as she climbed from her car.

"Of course. Mayor Kramer set it up."

Kent slapped my shoulder with his meaty paw, and threw an arm around my neck.

"Can't tell you how glad I am to see you back in uniform, Judd. I was real worried about you for a while there."

Sherry actually had tears in her eyes, and I think even Kent was getting a little misty.

"Hell," Kent said. "What in hell are we doing hanging out in the parking lot. We got cake and punch inside. Let's have us a party!"

It was noon before I could get down to real work. I was gratified to see that people had missed me, but I'm a modest sort, and to be truthful I was a little embarrassed by all the hoopla.

When things did finally quiet down, and I had a chance to look through the files, I realized that—while he was a top-flight cop—Slim had really screwed the pooch on paperwork. On my desk was a mountain of back administrative billing that had been ignored, and a file half an inch thick of sheriff's transport and custody orders. It would take me hours, if not a couple of days, to wade through it all. It wasn't the thrilling stuff that most cops get into the service for, but it makes up the bulk of a chief's duties.

I plowed in, reluctantly, and was surprised to find that, by lunchtime, I had almost forgotten the ache in my chest and arms and the weakness in my legs. Perhaps sitting on my porch and watching the world pass by had given me too much opportunity to dwell on my infirmities. Work might turn out to be my path to complete recovery.

More than that, I realized by lunchtime that I was hungry. I walked down the hill to the Piggly Wiggly and bought a fried chicken lunch at the deli counter. The manager, Howie Stone, hailed me as I walked up to the checkout.

"Chief, I sure am glad to see you up and about," he said, as he shook my hand. "Don't mind tellin' you, you gave us a scare. How ya holdin' up?"

"Not too shabby," I said. "A little tired, but I think it will pass."

I reached into my pants pocket for my wallet, but Howie stopped me with a hand on my arm.

"Forget it, Chief. Lunch is on me. You let me know if there's anything you need, y'hear?"

"Thank you, Howie. I'll do that. I'd appreciate it if you'd let me pay. It would make me feel like everything's back to normal."

"Maybe next time. Good to see you up and about."

He shook my hand again, and told the checkout girl not to take a penny from me.

I fell asleep at my desk around three that afternoon. I was organizing time sheets for filing, and suddenly it was as if my eyes wouldn't stay open. I leaned back in my desk chair and closed them briefly, figuring that it was only a brief spell of fatigue.

Fifteen minutes later, I woke myself with a snore that, if it was only half as loud as I perceived it, must have rattled the windows.

Embarrassed, I snapped forward in my chair and tried to figure out where I had been in my paperwork. It took me a minute to recall what I had been doing. My mouth felt dry and cottony, so I walked out to the water cooler and took a drink. I snuck a peek down the hallway toward Sherry, who seemed to be heavily invested in avoiding looking my way.

I took another drink, and then decided that I'd had enough administrative fun for one day.

"Think I'll take the cruiser out for an hour or so," I said to Sherry. "Do a quick patrol of the town. What do you think?"

"Sounds like a good idea, Chief. Get your legs back under you."

I grabbed my new hat, closed my office door, and headed out to the new cruiser. As if recognizing that the top dog was back in town, Slim had reverted to the old cruiser that morning. I shuddered as I opened the door, expecting a wave of stale cigarette odor to roll over me. I was surprised to find the interior spotless, the ashtray empty. It was as if I had never been gone. Somehow, Slim had managed to avoid smoking in the car. I knew what a sacrifice that had been for him. I was also touched by his dedication and respect for me, as a non-smoker.

I took a long patrol loop around the town for the first time in months. A few things had changed in my absence. The McMansion developments were beginning to creep farther out from the town center, gobbling up fertile farmland like a malignant cancer. I knew I had my friend Kent Kramer to thank for many of them, but I didn't begrudge him his way of making a living. I only wished he wouldn't destroy the land I'd grown up on while he made it. A couple of the outlying rural roads had new asphalt. Overall, it was the same town. I began to think that settling back into the job might not be so traumatic after all.

I drove up the Ebenezer Church Road, and passed by the house Carl Sussman had built almost entirely by himself. Carl was an ex-con and a recovering sex offender who had probably saved my life a year earlier. His story was a long and tragic one, and his desire to turn his life around and atone for his dark past drove almost every act in which he engaged. On impulse, I turned into his circular driveway and parked at the base of his front porch.

Carl didn't answer the door when I knocked. I had a feeling I knew where I'd find him. I wandered around to a workshop he'd installed after building the house. The two carriage house doors on the workshop were open and I saw Carl inside, laboring over a piece of work with a chisel and a beech mallet. He wore a Carolina Tar Heels tee shirt, and his hair, which fell to nearly the middle of his back, was pulled back and tied in a ponytail. I saw that he was chiseling out the boundaries and waste on mortises he had hogged out at the drill press with a forstner bit. His arms and face glistened with perspiration, and a bead of moisture hung precariously from the tip of his aquiline nose. He was so intent on his work that he didn't hear me approach until I rapped softly on the carriage door.

He jerked up reflexively and raised the chisel in an almost autonomic threat response he'd likely acquired in the joint. Almost immediately, when he saw me, he relaxed, dropped the chisel and the mallet to the workbench, and walked toward me, rubbing his sweat-drenched palms on his jeans.

"Chief!" he said. "Damn, it's good to see you! How are you feeling?"

"Every day in every way, you know," I said, as I shook hands with him.

"I do. When did you start work again?"

"Today."

"I'm not in any trouble, am I? Hope I'm not a priority on your duty list today."

"No, no. I was out on patrol, and I realized I hadn't seen your place since you finished it, being laid up and all. What are you working on here?"

He walked over to the bench and picked up a booklet, which he handed to me.

"It's a Stickley Morris chair," he said, pointing at the picture of a massive, leather-cushioned lolling chair. "Making it out of white oak stock I harvested from a felled tree in the woods out back. Had a fellow bring in a portable sawmill last November to cut the lumber, and I've had it drying here in the shed over the winter."

"Sharon still around?" I asked.

Sharon Counts was a former Bliss County Sheriff's Department CSI, and one of the strangest women I'd ever met. She had a face like a faded photo of a Dust Bowl Okie, nut-brown skin etched with lines that might have been there since infancy, and a thousand-yard stare that made you believe some people can see dimensions of reality denied to the rest of us. For reasons only she could explain, and she certainly wouldn't even if coaxed, she had become attached to Carl in a symbiotic relationship that wasn't quite romantic or erotic. It was as if they had skipped entirely over the infatuation and rutting phase straight into the trust and understanding that couples only attain after decades of marriage. There was a complementarity of needs, none of them physical, in their pairing, and I had never understood it entirely. It seemed to work for them. Carl, who could never again trust his hormonal drives, and Sharon, who was as sexual as a tree stump, seemed to have found a way to fill the empty spaces in their lives with each other.

"She'll be by later for dinner," he said. "We live in separate places. Probably always will. She likes it that way, and it works for me too. Feel like a drink? I could use a soda."

"No, thanks. I wanted to drop by, see how you were doing."

"Glad you did, Chief. You look good. I'm happy to see you back in the saddle."

All in all, it had been a pretty successful first day back on the job. I was feeling satisfied and pleased with myself as I prepared to head back to the station. I should have known better. My life over the previous year had been one long lesson in the concept that no good deed goes unpunished and that sunny days are nothing more than the prelude to soul-shaking storms.

I had just put Prosperity Glen High School in my rearview when I saw a sedan up ahead blow through a stop sign and turn west on the Morgan Highway. I can understand creeping through a stop, and I've even done it myself from time to time after carefully checking each way, but in this case the driver careened through without much more than a passing nod at the brake pedal. It was still ostensibly in the school zone, to boot.

I popped on the lights and stomped the gas to catch up with him. As soon as I was five or six car lengths away I blipped the siren to tell him, *yeah, I'm looking at you.* He hit the turn signal and pulled over to the shoulder.

I was grateful to find that Slim had left a ticket book and an aluminum folder on the front seat. I hadn't checked it before heading out on patrol, another indication that I wasn't completely back up to speed. I made a note of the license tag on the car, and then slid on the Stetson to go have a word with him.

He had his window down as I approached. I reached his rear bumper, and the first wave of panic arced through my midsection. I had done a thousand traffic stops exactly like this one over the years. Maybe ten thousand. You lose track over time. There was no reason for the surge of adrenaline that rushed through my veins like a hotshot bolus. I should have taken it as a warning.

Instead, I tried to ignore it.

"License and registration," I said, standing behind his front window.

"What's the problem, officer?" he asked. He was a porcine guy wearing a tee shirt with a rebel flag on it and a greasy, soiled ball cap with the name of a local towing firm embroidered on the bill. He didn't immediately go for his wallet, which both irritated me and made me wonder what he might be hiding.

"License and registration," I repeated, with a little more authority this time, in case he had a hard time figuring out who was in charge. At the same moment, I became acutely aware of a loud buzzing noise in my ears that seemed to deaden all other sounds in the world, and I realized that I was breathing heavily. I recalled a night over twenty years in the past when I had awakened in the dark, the electricity dead in the house because Hurricane Hugo had rolled up the interstate from Charleston unimpeded by any structure created by man or nature, and how the wind outside my window had roared like a jumbo jet parked in my driveway. That was not entirely unlike the sound I now heard in my head.

"You all right?" he said, as he handed me the license. His name was Boyd Overhultz.

"This license expired six months ago," I told him, trying to concentrate on the reality of the moment instead of my own fears and unbidden emotional turmoil. "I'm going to have to write you up on that after we talk about the way you ignored that stop sign back there."

"You don't look so good," Overhultz said. "You're sweating pretty bad and you look kind of gray. I'm sorry about that stop sign."

"Your registration," I repeated.

He put the wallet on the seat next to him, and reached toward the glove compartment.

Even as he did, I did a quick security tap on my chest to assure that the vest was in place. I knew I had put it on under my shirt that morning, as I had promised Donna that I would do every day for the rest of my working life. Even so, I doubted my own memory and felt the need to double check. Any time a civilian reaches into a glove compartment, you don't know what he's going to pull out. I knew enough not to stand directly alongside his window. I had positioned myself to the rear of his B pillar, the post behind the driver's window, because I knew from experience that it's hard to shoot someone from over your left shoulder.

I watched his right hand carefully as he dug into the glove compartment, through eyes clouded by tunnel vision and crinkly stars of oxygen deprivation that I knew meant I was hyperventilating. At that moment, I was ready to let him drive off rather than continue the process. I wanted nothing more than to escape to my cruiser, turn the air-conditioning to its highest setting, and try to calm my racing heart. Instinctively, I reached down with my own right hand and unclipped the strap securing the Sig Sauer to my holster.

He drew his hand from the compartment, and my hand rested on the butt of my pistol.

Then I saw he had a slip of paper, not the gun I had—probably irrationally—expected.

"My registration," he said, handing it over to me. "Look, about that stop sign . . ."

I didn't hear most of what he said after that. He droned on with some lame excuse as I examined his registration card, though not a word on it made it through the cloud of confusion and dread that possessed my brain. Finally, I told him to sit tight, and I retreated to my cruiser.

My chest ached, but not the way it had from the bullet wounds. Now it was a deep, constricting, squeezing pain accompanied by needle-like stabs like a knife slicing through skin and muscle, or broken glass rubbing against my ribs. I tried to slow my breathing and pulse. I tried to make my body relax.

I saw Overhultz glance at me in his rearview mirror. After a couple of minutes, I pulled myself together enough to write the ticket without my hand trembling uncontrollably. I cited him for a reckless maneuver and driving with an expired license, and slid the Stetson back on my sweating scalp before exiting the car.

"I noticed you live in Mica Wells," I told him as I handed him the ticket.

"Yes, sir."

"Next time you're in Prosperity, you remember the meaning of the word *stop*. Understand?"

"Yes, sir, I surely will. You don't mind me saying so, Officer, you look awful. You got the flu or something?"

"Keep it in the road, Mr. Overhultz. Have a nice day."

I didn't wait for him to make another observation about my physical state. I walked back to my car, as he pulled slowly back onto the Morgan Highway. I sat in the cruiser for five minutes before I could steady my hand enough to find the ignition switch with the car key.

The mayor's office was in the Town Hall, down the hallway from the town council chamber, but I knew I wouldn't find Kent Kramer there. Over a quarter century earlier, Kent and I had been opposing quarterbacks on the high school football field. He had played for Pooler High School up in Parker County, the metro center to the north of Bliss County, at the same time I was the first-string play caller for Prosperity Glen High. Our farm boys kicked the living bejeezus out of the Pooler High team at their homecoming.

By all rights, Kent and I should have been mortal enemies. Life is strange that way, and after the game we found ourselves in the same burger joint near the Parker County line. After glaring at each other for about five minutes he came over, offered to buy me a shake, and we've been fast friends ever since. I have since learned that Kent does not like to find himself staring across a battlefield at a foe if he can charm that enemy to his side.

That's Kent's special ability—to put people at ease. Like Will Rogers, he never met a man he didn't like, or at least didn't want to make like *him*. Kent didn't know the meaning of the word *stranger*, which is probably why he went into the real estate development business. There were a few other words he didn't know, also, like *tradition* and *scruples*, but sometimes you have to overlook the faults in others if you care enough about them.

As I could most times, I found Kent in his real estate office on the other side of the shopping center that comprised the entire business district in Prosperity. As usual, he was on the telephone.

"Now, you listen to me," he said into the receiver as he waved me into his office, "I'm not interested in dicking around with this. You give me your rock bottom dollar amount, and I'll meet it. But, I find out you've been putting it to me and it will be the last time we do business together, *comprende*? I got better things to do than toss money down a hole. I got a deadline to get this new neighborhood up and I got buyers hoppin' on one foot to buy lots there. So, you knock heads with your partner and you come up with a figure today, because I got five other phone numbers on my desk here that I can call in the next five minutes."

Kent and I had gone in different directions in several different ways over the years. I had tried to maintain some semblance of my athletic physique after high school and college, but as soon as Kent got out of college he started to let his body go to suet. He had gone jowly and loose over the years, his skin sallow and porous. He dressed in the finest suits he could find, yet they seemed to fit poorly on his sagging body. His hair was long, and parted shy of halfway up his head, falling in a large sweep over his ears and collar. His smile was beaming and ivory white, thanks to the attentions of his dentist. I hardly ever saw him in his office without a cigar between his fingers and a glass of scotch next to his right hand. His voice sounded like pebbles rotating in a laundry dryer.

"Judd! Come on in! Get you a drink—some water, or juice, or a soda? I know you ain't gonna take a snort while you're in uniform."

"Nothing for me, thanks. We need to talk."

"Town business?"

"You've been saying we need to hire someone to replace Stu."

"So you finally came around on that one, eh? I'm glad to hear it."

"We need two officers."

"That's what I've been saying. With Stu defecting over to Don Webb's department in Morgan, and you on the mend, we've been two short for quite a while now."

"No. We need two new officers. Besides me."

Kent settled back in his chair and surveyed me.

"What are you saying, Judd?"

"I . . . I had a problem today. I went out on patrol—"

"You did *what*? Hell, I'm glad to have you back on the job, but I didn't expect you to hop into your cruiser and go out busting bad guys. You want to *ease* in, buddy!"

"I stopped some guy from over in Mica Wells. It was routine. He blew a stop sign near the high school. As soon as he reached into his glove compartment for his registration, I . . . well, hell, I don't know exactly what happened, to tell you the truth. I . . . panicked."

"Panicked."

"Yeah. Hyperventilating, flop sweat, racing heart, the works. I had the strap off my gun. I was ready to draw down on this poor asshole! Hell, I could have lost it and killed the SOB!"

"But you didn't."

"Of course not. That would be crazy."

"You ain't crazy, are you?"

I stared at him.

"Hell," he said. "I know you're not crazy! Judd, you got half your vitals splattered by a kid only six months ago. It's natural for you to be a little jumpy the first time you hand out a ticket. That Corliss kid, he wasn't a hardened criminal. You had no reason to think he was gonna jump the tracks and gun you down."

"That's the thing. You never see it coming. At least, that's what I hear. I've got the yips, Kent. I'm about a million miles from being ready to put the uniform back on."

"Looks good on you, though. Sure I can't get you something to drink?"

I knew what he meant, and I wasn't about to fall into that cesspool. Kent is like a walking object lesson on the wages of inebriation and the value of sobriety.

"This can go one of two ways," I said. "I can resign, or—"

"Don't go off the deep end, there!"

"I said *or*. The other option is to reorganize the department. I can stay on as chief, but that would still leave us one patrolman short. The town has grown by almost a third in the last five years, and we're still a two-cop operation, in most respects. I spend over half my time shuffling papers and dealing with you and the town council. My suggestion is that I become an administrative chief, the same way they do it up in Pooler. We hire two new officers to do the patrol and process serving work, and I'll fold, spindle, and mutilate myself to distraction in the department office."

"A fourth employee," Kent said, as if trying it out on his tongue.

"That's what I'm thinking."

"Suppose you'd want a third cruiser."

"Not at the moment. We got by with two for years while I was holding down part of the patrol duties. I reckon we can continue that way for a while."

"Still and all, we're talking about an extra fifty grand each year that's not in the current budget. Hell, this plan of yours could mean passing a bond referendum or something."

"I considered that on the way over. We have money on the books covering Stu's absence since the first of the year—salary and benefits we haven't been paying out. The fiscal year ends in June. We can cover the cost of two new officers until then using backlogged funds. You and the council would have three months to figure out how to come up with the rest for next year."

Kent's cigar had gone out in the ashtray as we talked. He stuck it in his mouth and sucked as he fired it up again, all the time looking over the lighter at me.

"You're sure about this," he said. "This isn't first day jitters."

"I wasn't ineffective out there. I was dangerous. I was out of control. I don't need to be on patrol."

He blew a couple of smoke rings in the air, then took a swig of the scotch.

"I been thinking," he said. "Didn't Don Webb offer you a detective position over at the county sheriff's department a couple years back?"

"He did. What about it?"

"Still interested in being a detective?"

"I'm a cop, Kent. What do I know about investigations?"

"You solved that Gypsy Camarena murder. And there was Steve Samples's killing last year."

"I got lucky with Gypsy, and Steve Samples's killer gave himself up."

"But you knew before he gave himself up that he'd done it."

"Not really."

Kent flipped his hand back and forth.

"Let's not argue about it. Me, I don't want to see you out of the uniform. You're a damned fine cop, and while sometimes you bust my balls I think we're fortunate to have you. But—if you're determined to make these changes—I'd like to propose that we give you a dual title. Chief Detective."

"What?"

"Sounds good, don't it? You'd be the police chief, but you'd also be our detective. I don't want a man of your experience sitting in an office all the time signing reports and doing payroll. We got lots of things to keep a detective busy—missing persons cases, assaults, car thefts, murder."

"Don't even *say* murder. Until Gypsy was killed two years ago, there hadn't been a murder here in fifteen years."

"And now there's been six, counting Samples and all those poor folks got buried up on Nate Murray's farm. You solved those, too, if I recall correctly. You said it, Judd. Town's growing. Growing places get growing pains, the way any city does. You agree to take on the investigative work as well as the administrative, and I'll guarantee I'll get your extra patrolman. Might even be able to swing an unmarked car."

"My Jeep's fine for now."

"Hell, what kinda cop drives around in a Jeep?"

I had hoped to put off the discussion, but Donna walked into my house as I was boxing up my uniform to stow it in the hall closet.

"What's this?" she asked.

"Let's eat first. We can talk about it later."

She opened my closet and slid several hangers around.

"Your uniforms are all gone. I don't think this can wait until after dinner."

I knew better than to try to snow her.

"Let's sit down, then."

I led her to the couch, and we sat, and I tried to explain what I'd gone through on patrol. She didn't like the idea that I'd taken the cruiser out any more than Kent had, but at least she let me tell the whole story before she spoke.

"So, I'm hanging up the uniform," I concluded.

"But not the badge."

"No. Kent wants me to keep pulling chief's duties, and also the detective work that comes along from time to time. In return, I get a third patrolman. I'll work in civvies. I can't help thinking that something about the uniform helped bring on the yips."

"Not surprising. You were wearing it when you were shot."

"It didn't feel right from the moment I put it back on. I wanted it to, but wanting wasn't enough."

"Okay. As long as you aren't quitting. I can't imagine you not being a cop, and Prosperity needs you. This panic thing bothers me. I think you need to go see Dr. Kronenfeld."

"I'm way ahead of you. I called him as soon as I got home. Got his answering service. I'll set an appointment when he calls back in the morning."

"Shame about the hat," she said. "It favored you."

"Oh, I'm keeping the hat. Can't be the good guy without a white hat."

"You said it was cream."

I settled back into the couch. For the first time since ticketing Boyd Overhultz, I could feel myself unwinding, like tension releasing from a ratcheted leather band around my chest. There were places in my head Donna could reach, places that I dared not expose to anyone else. She knew how to slap the off switch on my insecurities and anxieties like nobody I'd ever met, even my deceased wife, Susan. I wondered what path my life might have taken if she hadn't been a part of it, but then I dismissed the possibility as too terrible to consider.

"Now, who in hell ever heard of a good guy in a cream hat?" I said.

CHAPTER SEVEN

After he stuffed the ticket in his glove compartment, from which he never expected to retrieve it, and after checking the rearview to assure that he was out of that meddling cop's sight, Boyd Overhultz hammered down the Morgan Highway, his speedometer spinning up over seventy in spots. The man he needed to see in the county seat didn't like to be kept waiting.

He detoured by the county airport, a single asphalt strip a mile long lined with decades-old stamped steel hangars that catered mostly to pleasure fliers and the occasional small business jet. Five stoplights later, he turned into a strip mall that boasted a contract license plate outlet, a Mexican *carniceria* with looped ropes of blood-red chorizo and sides of pork and goat hanging in the painted window, a boot shop with a hand-painted *Going Out For Business-Huge Deal's* sign yellowing and cracking with age and sun exposure in the window, a hot dog joint that proudly displayed its Health Department score of 87 on a placard over the cash register, and—at the very end—a burned out strip joint with an overflowing trash dumpster and five or six white construction trucks clustered in front of it.

Overhultz pulled his junker around the strip joint to the loading bay in the back, killed the engine, and didn't bother locking his door before climbing the concrete steps and entering the rear of the gutted club. The builders were restoring from ass end out, and at the rear of the club the walls were framed, drywalled, and mudded—but not yet painted—and doors to various offices had been installed. Overhultz knocked on the third door and opened it without waiting for a reply.

"You're late," the man inside said.

"Got popped over in Prosperity for blowing a stop sign."

"The idea here is to avoid the police."

"I played it cool. He didn't look so healthy. I even asked him if he was okay. I was real friendly."

"He got your license and registration information."

"Well, yeah, but—"

"What if he gets suspicious, starts wondering what a cretin like you is doing hanging around a place that's about ten times out of your league?"

Overhultz didn't know what the word *cretin* meant, but he had a feeling it wasn't a compliment. As it had for most of his indifferent and largely inconsequential life, the sense that a man was talking down to him raised his hackles and put him in a fighting mood. He stifled the impulse, because he knew two things. First, he had been wrong to ignore the stop sign. Second, the man addressing him wouldn't think twice about snapping his neck, gutting him like a slaughtered deer, and running him through a sausage grinder before bagging him and tossing him into a pigsty on the other side of the county. It would be like taking a leak for most guys.

Dealing with insults was part of the price of admission for breathing this man's air. What Boyd Overhultz stood to gain from this association far outweighed the inconvenience of being treated like a walking virus in a tee shirt with sweat-stained armpits and a hat that might have been used to strain a cesspool.

"Did you deliver my message?" the man behind the desk said.

"Well, that's why I needed to come straight here."

"Please don't tell me you come empty-handed. I would find that distressing."

"I *couldn't*. I got to the house, and the man answered the door. I told him why I was there, how I had come to talk some sense into them, and he took a baseball bat to me."

"He hit you?"

"No, but he waved it around like he wanted to bang my head over the left field fence. I told him you had sent me, but that didn't seem to impress him much."

"You used my *name*?"

"Well, yeah. I figured it would make him shit his pants. He sure as fuck's sake wasn't scared of *me*."

"You weren't there to be intimidating, Boyd. All you had to do was talk sense into—"

"I know! This guy, he told me to get my ass off his front porch, and to tell anyone who'd care to listen that he was finished, out of it. I climbed back in my car and headed straight here, swear to God. That's why I missed that stop sign."

The man behind the desk seemed to focus on a spot behind Overhultz's eyeballs, as if he could read the scant gray matter back there and divine the truth in his words from whatever self-serving fabrications Boyd had used to protect his sorry hide.

"All right," he said, finally.

"What?"

"I didn't realize I mumbled. You run along. I'll call you when I need you again."

"I don't get paid?"

"You didn't do the job."

"But—" Some primordial self-preservation system kicked in from a remote corner of Overhultz's brain that hadn't been poisoned by alcohol and amphetamines, and he shut his mouth before it could turn a bad situation into blood on the walls and a trip through a tree chipper. There were places where Overhultz was dreaded and feared, where he was the swinging dick on the floor. This wasn't one of them.

"You run along, Boyd. Don't worry about this. I'll handle it," the man said.

Overhultz backed through the door because his animal instincts told him what a bad idea it would be to turn his back on the man, and he retreated to his rusted-out car, aware of the pounding of his heart and the urgent sense that the contents of his bowels had liquefied.

CHAPTER EIGHT

My new uniform consisted of pressed, pleated khaki trousers, a blue oxford cloth shirt, and a summer-weight corduroy jacket, under which I wore my pistol on a spring-loaded hip holster clipped to my belt. I kept the brogans, because I was used to them and they felt good on my feet. I also kept the Stetson. My gold-plated chief's badge was pinned to my shirt, under the jacket. I still wore the body armor under my shirt. Even though I didn't plan on patrolling the town, and I had no intentions of mixing with dangerous types or placing myself in positions of risk, I had made a promise to Donna and to myself. I was an administrator with arrest powers if I needed them, but the bulk of my employment—I anticipated—would focus on keeping the wheels of the law enforcement bureaucracy in Prosperity liberally lubricated. Even so, I wasn't about to let my guard down again.

A couple of weeks after I made the transition to desk-rider, Sherry tapped on my office door.

"Chief, we got a call from a fellow over in Prosperity Ponds, says he thinks a couple of his neighbors have gone missing."

"I'll take it."

I picked up the phone and found myself talking to a man named Hal Poplin.

"My wife and I got back from the beach last weekend, and saw that the grass was overgrown at the house next door," he explained. "I called them, to see if they were gonna cut it soon, since we have covenants in this neighborhood, but all I got was an answering machine."

"Maybe they went out of town for a vacation of their own."

"I didn't call him out of nastiness. We're kind of close, sir. I wanted to let him know that the neighborhood association might come down on him if he didn't cut soon. I've known these people for several years, and I think they'd have told us if they were going out of town. We do that, you see. We look after their place when they're gone, and they look after ours when we are."

"These people have names?"

"Sure. The Guthries. Roger and Natalie Guthrie. We haven't seen them in a while. I went ahead and cut their grass for them a couple of days ago—you know, so they wouldn't get in trouble with the neighborhood association over the covenants—and to be sure there wasn't anything wrong I went up and rang their doorbell. I saw their cat jump up and run into the entry hall from the living room. Now who goes off and leaves a cat unattended for days on end?"

"You didn't see anything suspicious through the door glass?"

"No, sir. I'd have gone in—the Guthries and we have keys for each other's houses, you see—but I didn't feel right about it. You understand."

"How would you feel about entering the house if a police officer was with you?"

"Well, I'd sure feel better about it, you bet."

"Okay," I said. "Give me your address, and I'll send a cruiser over your direction in a few minutes. Thanks for calling, Mr. Poplin."

I had Sherry dispatch Slim to the Poplin house, expecting nothing would come of it, and I tried to get my head back into the payroll reports I'd been wrestling with for half the day.

About an hour later, my radio crackled, and Slim's voice

echoed in my office.

"Chief?"

"Loud and clear, Slim. You get that situation settled out?"

"Not exactly. I think your caller might have reason to worry. I was wondering if you'd care to drive out this way, take a look with me?"

"You find something suspicious?"

"Not the kind of thing I care to discuss over the police radio."

I've known Slim for almost a decade. I recognized the caution in his voice. He meant business.

"I'm on my way," I told him. I attached the radio to my belt, and headed for my Jeep.

Prosperity Ponds was one of the developments Kent Kramer hadn't built, which made it no less egregious. I knew the land from my childhood, when it had been the Bennett farm. Two hundred acres of rolling hills and a spring-fed pond where Albert Bennett and his children grew tobacco and corn, mostly. It was rumored that if you dared to walk through the corn rows a week or so before harvest you'd probably find a few tall, leafy plants you'd never encounter at a farmer's market. They always disappeared before the harvesters showed up, but the Bennett kids never seemed to want for much, compared to other farm children. I didn't begrudge them. I knew for a fact that large parcels of my father's corn crops had found their way, from time to time, to the kettles of moonshiners. Farming is a hit-or-miss proposition at best, and a cash crop is a cash crop. Long as people didn't complain, I was of a mind to let sleeping dogs lie.

Albert Bennett had gone to his reward five years before I returned from Atlanta. None of his children seemed inclined to live a life in overalls in the shadow of huge corporate farming conglomerates like Cargill and Archer Daniels Midland. They'd sold to the first developer who approached them, made a killing, and now lived in uptown Pooler in fifteenth floor condos overlooking a landscape of urban sterility. The developer had bulldozed most of the hills, paved over the plowed mule tracks, and had dug out the pond to twice its size, because they weren't stupid and waterfront houses command a higher asking price. My adult's eye saw few traces of the farm where we had joined the Bennetts and other agricultural families for autumn picnics and cookouts to celebrate another successful season. It was now hidden behind the mask of real estate greed.

I spied Slim's cruiser up ahead and steered the Jeep in behind it. Slim and a man I figured to be Hal Poplin stood in the shade of the Guthries' front porch. Poplin had sounded older on the telephone, but as I walked up the drive I saw that he was not much more than forty, if that. His hair was still mostly dark, and there was enough of it. Like a lot of people who had abandoned the big city, he appeared tanned, healthy, and well-tended.

I stepped up to the porch. "Mr. Poplin?"

He took my hand as I offered it.

"I'm Chief Wheeler, Mr. Poplin. Slim thinks there's something here I should look at."

"Do you really need me?" Poplin asked. "I'm not comfortable going back inside that house."

"You said that you and the Guthries are close. You're familiar with their house? Where things usually are?"

Poplin swallowed as he nodded. I could see the anxiety in his eyes. He had tried to be a good neighbor, and now he felt that flying in his face like blowback from a muzzle-loading flintlock.

"Tell you what," I said. "You wait out here while Officer Tackett and I have a look-see. If we have any questions or think the place has been disturbed, we'll ask you to confirm it. How's that rest with you?"

"I'd appreciate that," he said. "I don't think much of going back in there."

I started to open the door, and Slim cleared his throat.

"Uh, Chief, you gonna glove up?"

I saw, for the first time, that Slim already had gloves on. Six months off the job had left me sloppy and out of practice, and I'd forgotten to pack gloves in my Jeep.

"You got nitrile gloves in the cruiser, Slim?"

"Always. Hang tight. I'll be right back."

I again appreciated his native skills as a law enforcement officer. Taking care of a potential crime scene was second nature to him. He returned a minute later with a pair of purple gloves. I wiggled my hands into them and, properly protected from leaving confusing and conflicting evidence, I opened the door.

A black and white longhaired cat had been sitting at the door and mewing, but when it saw strangers walk into the foyer, it ran into the living room to hide under an ottoman.

"I'm betting that cat is hungry," Slim said. "Thirsty too. First time I did a walk-through, I noticed that the food bowl in the kitchen was empty. The water dish was bone dry. There's about a week's worth of mail piled up in the box out front."

"You didn't feed or water the cat?"

"I know better than to fuck up a crime scene, Chief."

"I'd appreciate it if you'd moderate your language when you're wearing the badge."

I said this to Slim a lot. He never seemed to pick up on it.

"You think this is a crime scene?" I added.

"Come look."

He led me to the den, situated at the back of the house, with a full wall of windows that started three inches above the floor and rose nearly all the way to the twelve-foot ceiling, which arched upward to a balcony on the second floor. In the center of the room was a glass door that opened out onto a pressure-treated redwood deck about fifteen feet deep. The hardwood forest the developer had spared backed up almost all the way to the end of the deck. It was a pricey house, with hardwood floors, imported Asian rugs, and it was as sterile as an octogenarian nun.

Slim pointed to the fluted edge molding on the doorway leading from the family room into the kitchen. There was a chest-high, ochre smudge on the white paint.

"Blood?" I said.

"That's my guess. There are some drops on the floor in the kitchen, and another smudge on the granite countertop on the island there. There may be more, but I stopped when I saw them and cleared the scene until I could call you."

"You did right, Slim. Let's take a closer look, but don't touch anything."

My first concern was that the Guthries might still be in the house somewhere, but I didn't smell any decomp, so that was unlikely. There was a strong aroma of ammonia as we carefully climbed the stairs, and when we hit the second floor landing it was compounded by a biting aroma of feces. I followed the smell to a small bath off the bonus room over the garage, where I found a cat box that obviously hadn't been emptied for days.

I checked the bedrooms on the second floor. They were all clean and orderly. The beds were all made, and there was no clutter around, no loose clothes on the floor or magazines or books strewn about, so I guessed that none of them were the master suite.

We returned to the first level, and located the master bedroom through a short hallway off the family room. The door was closed but not locked.

Unlike the rooms upstairs, this one looked lived in. The Guthries had a four-poster king-sized bed. It was turned down and the sheets were rumpled. A couple of pillows in shams that matched the comforter leaned up against the outside wall on the other side of the bed from the door. A converted armoire stood catty-cornered diagonally from the bed, and contained a flat-screen television which was turned on and tuned to a sports network with the sound on mute. Two reporters appeared to be talking with one another about the opening day of major league baseball, judging by the graphics behind them.

Another door led to the master bath, an exercise in near-Romanesque excess. A jetted tub the size of a kids' wading pool jutted out from a Palladian window in the center of the room. Next to it was a shower stall with his-and-hers shower nozzles. There was a long granite-topped vanity with two sinks and a small linen closet set into the wall next to a gold-plated towel rack.

I noticed that the sink on one side of the counter had a toothbrush and an aerosol can of shaving cream next to it, while the one on the other side was cluttered with several bottles of perfume and a jewelry case the size of a cigar box. The case was closed, but I didn't touch it. I'd leave that to the sheriff's department's CSI team if I decided to call them.

I did open the drawers on the feminine side of the vanity.

"Tons of makeup," I noted to Slim. "You ever met a woman who goes on a trip without gobs of makeup in her bags?"

"I'm not exactly an expert on women, Chief. Neither of my marriages lasted much longer than a single NASCAR season."

"Wherever the Guthries are, I'd guess they didn't plan on going there. I think we've seen everything we need to see at this point. I'm satisfied. Let's call in Don Webb's crime scene boys and let them take a whack at this place. First thing I want to know is whether those smudges are blood, and if they're human."

★ ★ ★ ★ ★

It took about ten minutes for the CSIs to determine that someone had bled all over the kitchen and the den. Besides the smudges, there were spots on the baseboards and some on the side of the cabinet holding the double oven. It would be a while before they could tell much more than that, such as blood type and such. They collected hair from brushes in the Guthries' bathroom for a possible DNA match, and they lifted a number of prints from around doorways and the granite counters in the kitchen.

As soon as they cleared the scene and headed back to Morgan, I walked next door to talk with Hal Poplin.

"I'm going to need to borrow your eyes," I told him. "I don't know what's what in that house, but you do. I need you to tell me if anything's missing."

"You think something's happened to Roger and Natalie?"

"It looks like they took off in a hurry. We didn't find any cell phones or wallets or full purses, so that's a good sign, but it's also evident that they haven't been home for quite a while, and made no provision for their cat, which is worrisome. You don't know where they are, and according to what you told me earlier they'd have left you a phone message, if they'd had the time. For the moment, I'm calling it a missing persons' case."

"I'll help any way I can. I don't favor the idea of going back in that house."

"It spooks you?"

"It feels strange. Who knows what went on in there?"

"That's what we're going to try to find out," I told him, as we started toward the Guthries' yard. "What does Roger Guthrie do for a living?"

"He works for one of the banks up in Pooler. He's an account and investments manager."

"Have they lived here long?"

"Roger lived here when we moved into our house about eight years ago, not long after the neighborhood opened. I reckon he was among the first to build here. He was a widower, married Natalie three years ago."

"Does she work?"

"I think she might have some sort of home-based business."

"Why do you say that?"

"My wife, Sandra, stays home. Our kids are grown, so she gets lonely sometimes during the day. She's invited Natalie over for coffee from time to time, but Natalie always seems to have other things planned."

"Maybe she's simply not friendly."

"No, they're very nice people. We've had them over to our house for dinner, and we've eaten at their place several times. We even did a mountain trip together last year. Drove up to Asheville and rented a cabin in Pisgah. They're real fine folks, Roger and Natalie. She just seems to be busy during the day."

I opened the front door of the Guthrie house and gestured for Poplin to walk in ahead of me.

"What I need you to do is walk through the house and check to see if anything obvious is missing or out of place," I told him. "You don't need to rummage through closets or anything, but I'd like you to look for clear differences in the house compared to when you've been here before."

It took us ten minutes to scour the house from top to bottom, but Poplin didn't see anything that concerned him. There was a small office situated off the family room, and he paused in front of a desk and pointed to a couple of framed pictures.

"That's Roger and Natalie," he said. "Sandra took one of those pictures on our mountain trip."

"You have any other pictures of them at home?"

"I don't know. We don't print most of the pictures we take—don't have to now that we have digital cameras. We upload them to our computer and edit them there, and then print the ones we really like at the pharmacy."

"What do you do with the rest?"

"Either save them or erase them."

"I'd appreciate it if you'd check your computer files for any more pictures of the Guthries. You can email them to me."

I handed him my business card, and he stashed it in his wallet. Then, an idea hit me. There was a flat screen computer monitor on the desk. I checked under the desk to see if there was a computer there, and at first I didn't see one, until I realized that the left side of the desk was a cabinet rather than drawers. I opened the cabinet. A false drawer front in the center of the desk folded down to reveal a keyboard which slid out. I clicked the power button for the computer, and it beeped to life. And asked for a password.

"Don't suppose you know the Guthries' login," I said.

"They let us keep an eye on their house and feed their cat. They didn't trust us with everything. Why? What do you expect to find on the computer?"

"Probably nothing useful. Even if I could get in, whatever e-mail program they were using is also password protected. It was worth a try. Is this the only computer?"

"Can't say. It's the only one I've seen. This is worrisome."

"It is a puzzle."

"I'm concerned about Kisa."

"Who?"

"The cat. She's obviously hungry. Do you suppose it would be okay for me to take her to our house until Roger and Natalie return?"

"It would be a big help. My only other option would be to call the Animal Shelter. I think . . . what's her name?"

"Kisa."

"Unusual name for a cat."

"Yes. Seems you never find a pet with a name like Ed or Phyllis, do you?"

"No. In any case, Kisa would likely be happier in her own neighborhood. You can take her food and water bowls with you, and if there's any cat food in the pantry, take that too."

"My wife's allergic to cats, but I've always liked them. Hope Roger and Natalie show up soon. Don't know whether Kisa can stay with us for long."

"Do what you can. Is there anyone else you can think of who might know where the Guthries are? Other friends or relatives who live nearby?"

"Well, Roger isn't from around here. He grew up in Buffalo. He only moved down here because of his business. He might have some folks back in New York, but I couldn't say. Natalie . . ."

I turned to him.

"Yes?"

"There you may have some problems, Chief Wheeler. Natalie wasn't even born in the states."

"Where was she born?"

"I'm not certain, to tell you the truth, but she's Russian."

"Russian. Think that's something you might have wanted to mention earlier?"

"Can't imagine why. Is it important?"

"Everything I don't know is important. When did she emigrate from Russia?"

"Not long before she married Roger, I'd say. Her English was awful when we first met. She got better with time."

I scrutinized the pictures again, and was surprised that I hadn't recognized it the first time. Roger Guthrie was balding, bespectacled, and had a face that looked like he used it to hammer nails. He wasn't ugly in the way that a sideshow oddity is ugly, but he wasn't handsome in any sense of the word. His eyes were deep-set and shadowed and his brow protruded like a porch awning. Natalie, on the other hand, had that *look,* hard to describe, something about the genetic intermixing of western Slavs and eastern Asians. She had a long sharp nose, a slight overbite, and her eyes were almond-shaped and deep blue, in contrast to her straight brown hair. Her high cheekbones and small mouth accentuated her prominent jawline. I had seen her type of face before on grocery store checkout clerks, fashion models, and college students, and each time somehow unconsciously presumed they were Russian immigrants.

Whatever the case, the two faces didn't feel right together. I recall a theory I read in a college sociology class called the matching hypothesis, which states that we all tend to gravitate toward people who have our physical features. What made the movie *10* so funny was gnomish Dudley Moore pursuing a woman who was so clearly out of his league. Tens gravitate toward nines and tens. Threes gravitate toward twos, threes, and fours. Maybe because we recognize how many unsolicited offers we get for romantic entanglements compared to others, we seem to know our relative level of attractiveness to others. People who are more attractive can be more picky. Those who are less attractive are more likely to settle.

But there's more to it than that. There's a price to pay for mating outside your level. A ten who matches with a four may feel with time that she's been shortchanged. A five who marries a ten may feel insecure and unworthy, and begin to suspect her spouse of infidelity, based simply on the belief that there is no way such a person could actually fall for her.

Insecurity and inferiority lead people to desperate acts. If I were into subjective grading of people—which I'm not—I'd probably give Roger Guthrie a grade of four or five. Natalie Guthrie was an easy eight, maybe a nine. That led to another dangerous presumption, but I was fortunate to have someone close by who could confirm my suspicions.

"Mail-order bride?" I asked.

He blushed. "Not my place to say, Chief. But Sandra and I have always thought so."

"How did they meet? Has Roger ever told you?"

"No. She showed up one day, and a month or so later they were married."

"She lived with him between?"

"No. She had her own place."

"Know where it was?"

"Sorry. I was never there. I do recall her leaving each night around eleven. It was strange. I mean, they're adults, right? Who bothers with separate homes if they're planning to get married?"

"People with religious scruples," I said. "People with old-world values. People who really don't plan to get married in the first place." I realized, as I said it, that Donna and I had effectively cohabited for several years now, and I definitely had old-world values.

Exceptions to every rule, I guess.

"But if he . . . wow, I can't believe I'm saying this . . . but if he bought and paid for her," Poplin said, "wouldn't the intent be to get married?"

"You'd think so, wouldn't you? No pictures of the first Mrs. Guthrie lying around. Wonder if he has any in storage."

"I couldn't say. Do you really need me here, Chief? I'm not comfortable sitting here in Roger's study talking with you about his personal life."

"I only have a couple more questions. You said that Roger and Natalie married three years ago."

"Right."

"How was their relationship? Did they fight?"

"You mean argue about things, or hit each other and throw

the dishes around the kitchen?"

"Rate it on a scale from one to ten."

He leaned forward and rested his elbows on his knees, clasping his hands. "Maybe a two. I hardly ever heard her raise her voice. Roger has always been headstrong. He expects other people to do things his way. He can be impatient. He's more likely to use sarcasm and sulking than to get violent. I wouldn't think he's the aggressive type. Assertive, sure, but not aggressive."

"Who has all the power in the marriage?"

Guthrie grinned, even chuckled a little. "Look at the pictures, Chief. Roger is a great guy, but he's no Brad Pitt. That picture of Natalie only shows her face, but she's got a body to match. Who do you think has all the power?"

"She manipulated him? Sexually?"

"Bent him around her finger like a soft pretzel. I don't like to talk about these things, Chief. It feels disrespectful. Have I ever heard them fight—I mean real knock-down drag-out fighting? No. But we hear things next door. I never met Roger's first wife, but I hear she was a good lady, a church-going lady. Salt of the earth. And from what Roger told us before he met Natalie, he loved his first wife. But I don't think there was anything in that marriage that prepared him for Natalie. Back in college, we used to call her type a screamer."

"Really."

"One night, last summer, my wife and I were sitting on the screened-in porch, relaxing before bed. Remember last summer, Chief? It was ungodly hot. Sometimes, in the evening, it cooled off nicely, and we could sit out and get some fresh air. So, Sandra and I were sitting on the screened porch. All the windows were shut tight in the neighborhood, and the air conditioners were running hard enough to bring on a brownout. And we heard them."

"Through the closed windows?"

"Through the windows, through the brick walls, out the chimney. Natalie and Roger were going at it like hello Pete. She was saying stuff you usually only hear on the late-night cable, not that I watch that sort of stuff."

"Of course."

"It was downright embarrassing. Only took us a half-hour before Sandra and I decided to head indoors. You get what I mean?"

He shot me a conspiratorial smirk that made my skin crawl a little, and I felt small and voyeuristic listening to his description of the Guthries' goings-on, and his implication that it had somehow gotten his juices flowing. He claimed embarrassment at recounting the Guthries' wild passion, and having eavesdropped on it, but the expression on his face described an entirely different emotion. I felt a burning ache that flowed from a point a half-inch behind the bridge of my nose and spread across my scalp like an August brushfire. At that moment, I couldn't think of a spot on the known earth where I'd feel far enough away from Hal Poplin.

CHAPTER NINE

That evening, I stopped at the Piggly Wiggly and bought a pound of raw Carolina white shrimp, six fresh translucent diver scallops, a jar of sun dried tomatoes in oil, some artichoke hearts in a can, a pint of porcini mushrooms, and a Vidalia onion. At the bakery, I grabbed a tray of garlic rolls. I already had some pesto and a jar of capers at home. Raking through the possible detritus of the lives of Roger and Natalie Guthrie in the form of their private and personal possessions had been a depressing endeavor, and I needed a release of endorphins the likes of which can only be obtained by one of two routes—a hip shot of Demerol, which I had endured enough during my hospital stay, or a top-shelf Italian dinner.

While waiting for Donna to arrive, I sautéed the shrimp in olive oil, basil and thyme, and garlic salt, and put them aside. Then I chopped the tomatoes, artichokes, and mushrooms, sliced the onions into strings the width of a strand of spaghetti, and sweated them in a pan with minced garlic and oil.

Donna walked in through the front door as I added pesto to the vegetable mix.

"God, it's been ages since we had *gamberini pomodoro*!" she said, as she grabbed me around the chest from behind and planted a wet kiss on the back of my neck. "What's the occasion?"

"I know you love it. I guess I haven't felt much like cooking an elaborate meal since . . . well, you know."

"We have wine?" She opened the pantry and found a bottle of cheap dago table red.

"Might have turned to vinegar already," I said.

She opened the screw top on the jug and poured a glass for each of us. After taking a sip, the corners of her mouth turned up in approval. "Nice," she said. "Okay, so what happened?"

"Don't have a clue what you mean."

"Like hell, Chief. You're making comfort food because something at work either pissed you off or made you sad. I've read this book before, and it's a bad chapter. Give."

"After dinner. I still have to pan sear the scallops and cook the capellini."

She wouldn't let it go. I hadn't ingested a lot of alcohol since my encounter with Spud Corliss, so a glass or two opened me up like a filleted catfish. After clearing the dishes, we sat on the couch and I told her about the missing Guthrie couple.

"How strange," she said. "They simply disappeared?"

"I checked with the other neighbors. Nobody saw them leave. After Poplin took the cat over to his house, I checked the garage. There were two cars in there. Wherever the Guthries went, they rode with someone else. And given the evidence in the house, I'd imagine there was some coercion involved."

"No indication of where they went, no witnesses, no messages scrawled on the wall in blood. How in hell do you work a case like this?"

"I did the usual stuff. Copied the pictures of them I took from their house, issued a BOLO on the state network, filed the missing persons reports. I may have to wait until the forensic reports come back before I can do much else. She might have been a Russian mail-order bride."

That got Donna's attention. "Really?"

"There's reason to think so."

"How exactly does that work?"

"I wondered the same thing. After I got back to the office I did a little on-line research. Would you believe that if you search 'Russian mail-order brides,' you get over two million responses? Seems that there's some sort of land-rush business in matrimonial trafficking out there."

"It's legal?"

"As far as I can tell. I suppose ICE doesn't like it much. These women are recruited in Russia, the Ukraine, the Caucuses, even Thailand and Viet Nam, and basically the prospective groom sponsors their immigration. It's hard to get into the country without some promise of employment. Uncle Sugar isn't interested in opening the doors to future welfare cases. So, the man guarantees employment or some other kind of support, the woman enters the country, and after a respectable period they get married."

"Unless they don't."

"I reckon that happens, too. Not in Roger Guthrie's case. Apparently he and Natalie—whom I'd bet was born with a name like Natalya—lived under separate roofs for a while and then they got married. The neighbor says they didn't fight, but had a whole heap of noisy sex."

"Lucky Roger!"

"Lucky? They may be decomposing in the trunk of a 1972 Monte Carlo in a junkyard somewhere while we're enjoying this delicious beverage. There may be a number of adjectives for Roger and Natalie Guthrie, but my cop's head tells me *lucky* isn't one of the better ones."

At the office the next day, I pulled up the courthouse records of the Guthries' marriage license. I had been right. Her maiden name was Natalya Gromykova. I requisitioned her immigration papers from ICE, and they arrived via fax a half hour later. She had been born in the former Soviet Union, in Lithuania. From what I could gather by looking things up on the Internet, Lithuania fared pretty well after the collapse of communism in the 1990s, but took a nosedive in the middle part of the twenty-aughts when the rest of Europe encountered financial difficulties.

None of this mattered much to Natalya Gromykova, since she'd been chewing on the short end of the stick for years. Her mother died five years after Natalya was born, in a vicious street attack. There was no record of her father. She was raised in a state-supported residential school that, by all accounts, was the type of place that made Dickens write long poignant passages decrying the inhumanity of humans. It would have been difficult under any circumstances, but in the politically centralized atmosphere of the Soviet Union it would have constituted a special manifestation of hell.

I recalled a class I took in college, and a professor I had who ranted for days on end on the futility of socialism. He called the Cold War a sham, an attempt by the military-industrial complex to terrify people into not questioning massive arms races and weapons expenditures. He claimed, given the labyrinthine nature of the Soviet bureaucracy, that even if they did decide in a grouchy moment to push the button, it would take them six weeks to find it. He would climb on a chair and, step by step, disassemble the notion of monolithic communism. He said that there were as many different variants of communistic government among the Soviet republics as there were species of butterflies, and most of them were incapable of talking with one another.

The worst part, he explained, was the concept of a planned economy. Five-year plans determined everything. It didn't matter that modern housing methods made smaller bathtubs more efficient—the factories were tooled to produce an antiquated design, and it wasn't in the five-year plan to change that design, so home builders would have to wait to allow their tenants to bathe in twentieth-century comfort.

This was the world in which Natalya grew up, a Marxist—as in Groucho—version of Freedonia, where the needs of a few raggedy kids in a Lithuanian orphan school carried as much weight as a soap bubble.

The sad thing is that, in all likelihood, she was a lot better off there than she realized. According to ICE records, she left the shelter in her mid-teens, and fell in with a crowd of post-Soviet toughs who became the foundation of the Russian Mafia. It amazed me, as I read page after page of her Lithuanian arrest record, that she might ever have been able to enter the country at all, except that—toward the end—I found a curious sudden change in her behavior. Within a period of six months, she went from the long walk out the gates of a Russian prison after serving a six-month dip for petty theft to a middle-class lifestyle. She took a job in an office, went to school at night, and seems to have changed her entire existence from that of a street tough to become a productive, contributing member of the society.

All of which raised my suspicions. Redemption and recovery are nice, conceptually, but there were inconsistencies I couldn't explain. For instance, I could easily understand a woman of Natalya's upbringing signing up with a mail-order bride outfit in order to escape an intolerable life, but why would she allow herself to be bought and sold so willingly at exactly the point when she seemed to have risen above the tragic circumstances of her childhood?

Something didn't fit.

I've been a cop for more than two decades. I have this cop head thing going on that sometimes even seems cynical to me. Doesn't mean it's wrong. In my skepticism, I could easily imagine a set of circumstances in which a false happy ending to

Natalya's early squalor might be constructed in order to make her a more attractive prospect for a potential husband. Buying a cuddle-buddy from Russia may seem like a jolly idea, but there's always the possibility of bagging a whole set of problems that would make abject loneliness seem like a comparatively lazy float in a warm languid swimming pool.

Not to mention the issues the folks who control the flow of immigrants into our country might have with a woman whose entire existence to that point appeared to have centered on the self-serving manipulation of others and a disorganized lifestyle.

Sometimes, I reasoned, it isn't a bad idea to put lipstick on a pig. If—and again I realized that this was the cynical half of my brain cranking away—what I was reading was true, then Natalya had made a miraculous turnaround in a spectacularly short period of time. There was also the disturbing possibility that the entire spontaneous transformation from vandalizing and thieving urchin into a middle-class working girl was nothing more than a façade, the way you'd erect a fancy columned exterior across the front of a shabby, depressing whorehouse.

Knowing more about Natalie Guthrie didn't help me much in finding out where she and her husband had gone. Mail-order marriage led one to consider an underworld connection. Since Natalie/Natalya was Russian, that suggested the Russian mob. My encounters with those guys had been, thankfully, few and far between.

I knew a few things about them, though. The word *ruthless* would only begin to scratch the surface of their potential for cruelty and violence. The murderous outrage committed by the followers of Al Capone and Murder Incorporated in 1920s Chicago would appear quaint and conservative to these guys. Rumor—okay, many say it's more than that—holds that most of the linchpins in the Russian gangs are former KGB, and not the happy, vodka-guzzling party-guys you see in movies, but rather the hardened Lubyanka-trained inquisitors and torturers who spent years perfecting their craft.

Cops are a fraternity, whether they're American or Irish or Sudanese, and KGB was not much more than a pragmatic Russian version of our own CIA.

CIA, FBI, ICE—they're all basically cops, and therefore part of the Brotherhood. You hear stories in this business, and accounts of things that happened behind the imposing stone walls of the Lubyanka kept me awake at night and left a taste like iron filings in my mouth.

I'm a cop. I like to think that I'm a good cop—even shot up and with a head full of unbidden panics and the startle response of a white-tailed deer. Putting on the badge takes a degree of commitment to making the world a better place that most men can't fathom. Searching for Natalie and Roger Guthrie might take me into proximity of people whose morals and ethics seemed to emanate from a septic tank. If it did, I'd have to deal with it.

Finishing the ICE report and realizing that the information on Natalya Gromykova was probably mostly fabrications—at least the last part of it—left me without many avenues to investigate. Presuming they were lies, and having no immediate way to track down the source Roger used to bring her to the states, I was left with Roger himself. The possibility that their disappearance was linked in some way to his wife's sordid past was a romantic notion, but not necessarily an accurate or productive one.

If I had learned anything in my years in law enforcement, it was that people are almost never what they seem to be. Instead of joining a singles group at the UMC and meeting some nice thirty-something American secretary, Roger Guthrie had chosen to walk on the wild side and deal with shady purveyors in human trafficking to find his spouse. That told me much more about him than it did about Natalya. His pictures made him look soft, timid, benign. I decided to proceed from the assumption that this was the mask he wore to hide a licentious, libertine interior life driven by an intent to acquire the sort of existence that most men only entertained in masturbatory fantasies.

One of my Carolina football teammates, a nimble, lightbulb-shaped black guy named Appleby, was a psych major and a born-again Bible thumper. When exposed to the displays of personal entitlement and profane excesses in which college football stars are prone to engage, he refused to accept any attempt to explain it as "boys will be boys." Instead, he would shake his head and condemn them as hopelessly enslaved to their hormonal desires. He would cite a little known statistical phenomenon called Berg's Deviation Hypothesis, which was intended to apply to test-taking behavior, but which Appleby thought explained the entirety of human cruelty and wanton promiscuity.

"Wheeler," he said, his dark eyes sad and resolved, "deviant people deviate. That's all there is to it. I can talk to you because you're straight-up. You aren't one of those animals. You've got respect for people. Those guys, they're lost. They've been sucked into the cesspool so many times they think it's nothing but a hot tub. Their souls are already forfeit, and the only path they are gonna know for the rest of their lives is deviant. You do wrong in one way, nothing to stop you from doing wrong in all ways."

Most of us discounted Appleby as a holier-than-thou ascetic killjoy. Even so, his words had stuck with me through the years, and I had found some truth in them. I had crossed paths with hundreds of deviant individuals, and I had long since come to agree that there is a piece missing in the heads of some folks, the absence of which assures they will always seek the path of least resistance in the satisfaction of their basest natures. Deviant people deviate. If Roger Guthrie had bought and paid for Natalya Gromykova, anticipating carnal delights, then I had to wonder what other acts he might have committed in secret to satisfy other urges and desires.

CHAPTER TEN

Guthrie was employed with one of the major banks in Pooler, the metropolis from which most of Prosperity's tax refugees emigrated. The next morning found me waiting outside the office of his supervisor, a woman named Harriet Styles.

The office was on the third floor down from the summit of one of the high-rise obelisks of power that had sprouted like giant beanstalks. Through a ten-foot high arched window, I could see for miles, and I was gratified to see that, a short distance beyond the concrete decay of the city center, the landscape appeared filled with trees newly greened by spring, and I enjoyed a moment of hope that perhaps the world wasn't destined to become one huge parking lot.

I probably should have dressed in more businesslike attire for my meeting with Harriet Styles, but I had grown comfortable in my new uniform of khakis and oxford cloth and cord jacket, and I had even decided to keep the Stetson for my visit to civilization. Figured it might give me a homey, approachable touch.

Harriet Styles was younger than I had pictured. I had imagined that—in order to reach a position of great responsibility in a major bank—one would have had to rise slowly and with effort through the ranks. Or maybe it was the name *Harriet* that had thrown me off. She was in her middle thirties, with hair a shade of blonde that suggested it was chemically induced rather than natural. She was tall, slender, and carried herself with the self-assurance I've often seen in people who have never experienced a physical threat to their lives or safety. Overall, she was attractive, and despite my deep and hopelessly committed devotion to Donna, I instinctively glanced at Harriet's left hand, third finger. It must be something that men do out of habit, something residual from our prehistoric past.

We exchanged pleasantries, and I showed her my chief's badge.

"I'm familiar with you," she said.

"We've met?"

"No. But you're fairly well-known. My bank has naming rights to the football stadium, so we take an active interest in the Pythons' activities. You solved the Steve Samples murder last year."

Steve Samples had been a prize defensive draft pick for the Pooler NFL team, until one of his teammates found him face down and naked in the kitchen of his Prosperity home, his head minced by a meat cleaver. I didn't like to think about Samples, or the events precipitated by his death.

"We got lucky on that case," I told her. "I'm not sure how much detective work went into solving it."

"Modest, too? Interesting. How can I help you?"

"I'm here about Roger Guthrie. I believe he works for you."

"He did. We haven't seen Roger for some time now, and he isn't answering phone calls or emails. We're about to the point of administratively terminating him."

"So he didn't indicate that he was going to be absent? No illness or other problems that might explain missing work?"

"No. He was here one day and then he didn't return. Has something happened to him?"

"I'm not sure. He and his wife haven't been seen by their neighbors for over a week. There's a missing persons report on them in Prosperity. We found evidence in the house that suggests they may have left suddenly, and perhaps not of their own volition."

"That's disturbing."

"Could you tell me exactly when Roger Guthrie last worked? It would help me pin down the possible date that he and his wife went missing."

"Of course."

She dialed a four digit number on her phone. "Roger's direct supervisor," she explained, as she waited for an answer. "He should know. Hi, Albert? Harriet Styles. Please tell me the last day Roger Guthrie worked in your department . . . okay, thanks."

She wrote the date on a sticky note and handed it to me.

"He hasn't shown up for almost two weeks," I said.

"That's on the outer boundaries of what we will tolerate, usually. If an employee is gone that long with no explanation, we assume he has voluntarily terminated. We cut him a check for unpaid hours, send it with a certified letter of termination, and put a want ad in the paper."

"And you've made efforts to contact him?"

"I haven't, but his supervisor has tried to reach him several times. No luck. Do you think we should hold off on firing him?"

I suppressed an impulse to tell her that, in all likelihood, if a person is missing without a trace for two weeks, being fired would be the least of his worries. I suspected that Roger and Natalie Guthrie were already dead. I didn't tell Harriet Styles this.

"What can you tell me about Roger?" I asked.

"I don't understand."

"I'm trying to build a picture of him in my mind. All I know about him is his physical appearance. I'd like to understand what he's like as a person."

"I'm the wrong person to ask. Perhaps it would help to get

Albert York up here. He's Roger's direct supervisor."

Albert York was in his midfifties, balding, a coronary-in-waiting. Judging by the burst vessels in his cheeks and the way he wheezed after making the quick trot to Harriet's office, he wouldn't have to wait long.

"This about Roger Guthrie?" he said.

"Why do you ask?" I said.

"Ms. Styles called me about him a few minutes ago. You're the chief of police in Prosperity. Roger lives in Prosperity. I read a lot of crime novels. I put it all together."

He settled back into his chair with a self-satisfied smile, waiting for someone to compliment him on his Sherlockian skills. In reality, if he had read *enough* crime novels, he might have known more about what I was doing than I did. I'm a small-town cop. I mostly hand out traffic tickets and tend to domestic disturbances. Detection, despite my fancy new title, didn't exactly come naturally to me.

"I need this conversation to stay private," I told him. "Roger Guthrie and his wife have gone missing. I'm trying to find them."

"When did they disappear?"

"That's one of the things I'm trying to determine. You told Ms. Styles that Roger last worked two weeks ago."

"That's right. He was here on a Wednesday, and he didn't show up on Thursday. Hasn't shown up since."

"No telephone calls or emails?"

"Nothing. Like he dropped off the face of the earth. I've tried to reach him a number of times."

"What can you tell me about him?"

"Like what kind of worker he is?"

"We can start with that. Is he pretty conscientious?"

York glanced over at Harriet Styles, who seemed to understand his reservations, and she nodded.

"Well, yes and no. When he's on his game, Roger is top-shelf at his job."

"What does he do, exactly? His neighbor seems to think he's some kind of accountant."

"Umm, not exactly. Roger is in our arbitrage department."

"I don't know what that is."

"In its most simple terms, arbitrage is the process of buying and selling money," Harriet Styles said.

"You can buy money?"

"Yes. Have you ever been overseas, Chief Wheeler?"

"Haven't had the pleasure."

"If you had, you'd have discovered that you have to exchange dollars for pounds."

"You know, I do believe I did hear somewhere they don't use American money over there."

She gazed at me dully for a second and then smiled. "Oh. A joke. I get it. Well, now, let's say that you did that exchange, but you didn't wind up spending any of your pounds. You come home, and you don't want to walk around with a bunch of British pounds in your pocket, so you change it back into dollars. That's the way it works for most travelers. Now, let's say that you exchange a hundred dollars for its equivalent in British pounds, at today's exchange rate, which is—" she tapped a few keys on her computer "—point six one three two pounds to the dollar. That means that your hundred dollars would buy you sixty-one pounds and change."

"Okay."

"Now, let's say that *tomorrow* you don't want your pounds anymore. Twenty-four hours from now, the exchange rate has changed and its value, compared to the pound, has increased. Your hundred dollars is now worth sixty pounds even."

"I would get fewer pounds for my hundred dollars today than I did yesterday."

"Exactly. However, let's say you did your exchange yesterday, which means that you already have sixty-one pounds and change. So, you buy back your dollars at today's exchange rate, and you get—" She tapped some more keys on her computer "—one hundred and two dollars and twenty cents."

"I made money."

"Yes, and that's what banks do. We make money. That's what Roger did . . . *does*. His job is to buy and sell money, taking advantage of fluctuations in exchange rates."

"It's like investing," I said. "Buy low and sell high."

"Yes," Albert York chimed in. "And that's what arbitrage is all about. So, in one sense, I suppose that you could say that Roger is involved in accounting, as he does have to keep track of all the comings and goings of the money he buys and sells, but that's only one small part of his job. The other is to keep an eye on the fluctuating rates, and to know when to pounce and buy, when to sell."

"Sounds like it takes a great deal of concentration, like being an air traffic controller."

"It's a good comparison," York said. "Arbitrage specialists track all forms of currency. I might start the day with dollars, then buy Swedish kronor, sell them for Japanese yen, convert those to Italian euros, and wind up with Mexican pesos, and that's before lunch. Roger would spend his day shuffling currency all over the globe, figuratively speaking, with the goal of making money by the end of the day."

"How much money?"

"It depends."

"I only made two dollars on my imaginary exchange. Two percent isn't much."

"Two percent a day is a lot," Harriet Styles said. "If you could do that every day, by the end of the year you could make a profit—without compounding—of about three hundred dollars."

"A four hundred percent profit? And this is legal?"

"Our bank had a profit of almost three billion dollars last year. Most of it came from various investments such as arbitrage. Compared to what we make on loan interest, fees, and other profit centers, arbitrage is a—if you'll pardon the term—gold mine."

I turned to Albert York. "You said Roger Guthrie is good at his job when he's *on his game*. What about other times?"

York fidgeted with the cuff of his suit jacket. "I don't want to malign Roger, especially if something bad has happened to him."

"If something bad has happened to him, I need to know everything I can in order to help him."

York coughed lightly, and then he straightened in his chair. "Roger was distracted. Sometimes. Not every day. He had good days and bad days, but lately the bad days were more frequent. A good arbitrage specialist is like one of those guys you used to see on the Ed Sullivan show, the guys who balanced spinning plates on sticks. It's a constant dash from stick to stick to keep all the plates up in the air and spinning."

"Roger was breaking a lot of plates?"

"Figuratively speaking. Yes. He had days when he was absolutely brilliant, the way he used to be all the time. Then he'd come in one morning looking like he hadn't slept all night, dragging himself into the elevator like a man headed for death row rather than someone who'd make his company a million dollars. I saw him a number of times sitting at his desk, staring at the screen for minutes at a time without moving the mouse or touching the keyboard. It was almost as if he were looking at something else, far away."

"Daydreaming."

"If it was a daydream, it was a bad one. The times I found him like that, I thought he was about to upchuck in his wastebasket."

"Something was worrying him."

"Or scaring him," York said. "I walked by his office three times in ten minutes one day, and he hadn't moved an inch, so I rapped on his door to get his attention, see if he was okay, and I thought he was going to jump out the window. And then there was . . . the other thing."

"What was that?"

"About a week before he stopped coming in, I passed by his office, and he was . . . well, he was crying. Big alligator tears ran down his face, his shoulders heaved up and down. I thought someone had died."

"What did he say? About his crying, I mean."

"He didn't, and I didn't ask. Roger and I aren't really buddies. We'd talk sports or cars from time to time, but I got the feeling that if I had asked him why he was crying, he'd have considered it a violation of his space."

"He's never said anything about personal troubles, problems at home, anything like that?"

"Not to me," York said, and looked over at Harriet Styles, who shook her head.

"What are his interests?" I asked.

"You mean, like hobbies?"

"Sure. You read detective novels. I fish. What did Roger Guthrie like to do in his spare time?"

York eyed me as if I had been speaking Swahili.

"I'm sure I don't know," he said at last. "Now that I think of it, I don't know much at all about Roger, outside of work. He's been a good employee, at least until recently."

"Did he talk much about his wife?"

"He's married? I know he was widowed some years back, but

I had no idea he'd remarried. How strange."

"It was three years ago. Surely he would have taken some time off for the wedding, or maybe a honeymoon."

York shook his head. "He's taken vacation time, sure. I suppose he could have gotten married during one of those breaks, but he never said anything to me about it."

"Did he have any friends here at the bank he might have talked to? Someone in whom he might confide?"

"You need to understand, Chief Wheeler. Roger wasn't antisocial, but he never really made a lot of friends. Actually, that made him very good at his job. He'd come into the office in the morning, hook himself into his computer and work straight through to lunch. A lot of guys take a bathroom break every twenty minutes, or knock off for a few to grab a soda out of the machine, or jaw with some buddies, but not Roger. He was a workhorse. Some people are good with people, some people are good with machines, and some people really kick butt at data crunching. Roger was one of the last group. He was great at what he did, buying and selling money. Beyond that, he—well, he wasn't really here."

"And he was always that way?"

"As long as I've known him. Now that I think of it, I don't know much about him at all. I don't reckon anyone here does."

CHAPTER ELEVEN

As soon as I got back to Prosperity, I headed back over to the Guthrie house. This time, instead of searching the place, I disconnected the computer and placed it carefully in the back of the Jeep. I couldn't get into it without a password, but that didn't mean it couldn't be cracked.

I had asked Albert York to quarantine Guthrie's computer at the bank, and to have it examined by one of their I.T. guys. I didn't think they'd find anything hinky, because Roger Guthrie was one of those guys who lived a life compartmentalized into sectors surrounded by impermeable barriers. If there was something to be found, I had a feeling it would be on his home computer, although for the life of me I had no idea what I was looking for.

I was about to back out of his driveway when I got this feeling of something left undone.

I'm not a computer kind of guy. I don't surf the web and I don't have a social networking account. Sometimes I check the news and I use a search engine from time to time to find information on a case, but my life does not revolve around an electronic umbilical. Even so, I have a desktop computer in my home office and I have another laptop that I transfer from my house to the office most days.

Roger Guthrie's life—at least the career part of it—was spent staring at a screen. I couldn't imagine that he'd only have the one computer in his home office. There had to be another one—or more—elsewhere.

I walked back into Guthrie's house and started a more thorough search.

I started in the master bedroom. The room smelled abandoned. I wondered whether the smell of an empty house wasn't something that was acquired, but rather due to something lost. When we live in a space, we constantly fill it with ourselves— our sloughed off skin cells, our lost hair, even the chemistry of our expelled breaths, the biological byproducts of sweating and belching and farting. When people no longer occupy a dwelling, those things dissipate like flimsy smoke. Biological material eventually settles to the carpet or the corners and deteriorates. The airborne remnants of metabolism are pumped out of the house with the circulation of air, and what remains is the house's own fingerprint—no longer biological but rather structural, the out-gassing of synthetic plastics, the mildew-sweet odor of mortar, the last molecular ghosts of drying paint. Without the humans there to keep it running, houses begin to die.

The smell in the Guthrie house represented its inevitable deterioration. Give it a few more weeks and we'd be wading through cobwebs.

I started with the closet, situated off the master bath and separated into masculine and feminine quarters. Roger's clothes filled the left side of the closet and Natalie's, the right.

I realized that, between the clothes rack and the floor, there was a hidden shelf. I slowly ran my hand underneath the clothing from one end of the closet to the other, feeling for any hidden laptops, but all I found were some odds and ends: wrapping paper and spools of invisible tape and a few random preformed bows. On Roger's side there was a stack of white undershirts and soft-porn mags.

And a gun.

My hand froze as it ran over the cold steel of the automatic pistol. I pulled the hangers to each side. The gun was a Sig Sauer P226, in 9mm Parabellum. I recognized it immediately, since I carried a similar weapon. It was an efficient sidearm, dependable and accurate, but tended to be used mostly by police and military units. That didn't mean the average Joe couldn't own one, but it was unusual to see a Sig sitting on some guy's closet shelf.

Had Roger Guthrie kept the weapon for protection? Prosperity's population was overwhelmingly white and conservative. Most had come to Bliss County to escape the high Parker County property taxes. And yet despite the low crime rate, legal gun ownership in Prosperity was higher than in the surrounding, slightly more centric communities.

However, I wasn't looking at a legally obtained weapon. The serial numbers on the Sig had been filed and the area where they had been filed had been welded and ground down flat again, leaving a flat, uniform surface. This was a black-market weapon, and I couldn't figure out why a guy like Roger Guthrie, who could easily afford all the legitimate registered weapons he might want, would have it in his possession.

The answer was obvious. He worried he might need it to do something he didn't want traced back to him.

If Roger and Natalie had been abducted, it must have happened very quickly. Otherwise, Roger would have accessed the Sig and used it. Other possibilities included a world in which Roger and Natalie had gone off with someone they knew, and then been spirited away elsewhere. Or Roger had done something nasty to Natalie, or vice versa, and the survivor had taken it on the lam and we hadn't found the dead body yet.

That was the problem with disappearances. There were too many unknowns to suss out. Whatever the case, Roger had left this illegal hardware behind. That seemed careless at best, since it was a felony to possess it, and perhaps fatally neglectful at worst. When it comes to guns, it's always better to have one and not need it than to need one and not have it.

I left the pistol in place. I'd come back with an evidence bag and retrieve it later. At the moment I was searching for another computer.

The closet was a dry hole, so one by one I searched the drawers in the twin dressers on each side of the soccer stadium–sized room. As in the closet, one dresser was clearly Roger's personal domain, while the other was Natalie's.

Roger's drawers were organized in the classic male style. Top left drawer was socks and underwear—Roger was a tighty whitey kind of guy—top right, a few pairs of pajamas and a couple of small jewelry cases with the assorted odds and ends that men collect over time. There were some wallet-sized photos, most of them looking too old to be of much importance.

I didn't see a computer in the middle drawers.

Things got interesting when I tossed Natalie's dresser. Two drawers down, I discovered a cache of outfits that could only be described as salacious, the type of garments you'd find in the inner pages of a catalog ostensibly marketed toward women but undeniably inspired by male fantasies. The sheer volume of silk and rayon and lace and ribbons looked like the travel trunk of a Parisian hooker, rather than a rural Carolina housewife.

I deliberated over Roger's possible expectations of his bartered bride. Perhaps he found the outfits arousing and expected that his Baltic beauty should dress to satisfy his own erogenous cravings. Having grown up in a permanent condition of hurt and want, Natalie might have seen these trappings as one more concession endured in order to cling desperately to her lifeline of salvation. Wearing these outfits helped get her husband hard, which provided her with the opportunity to please him in that most animal of ways, and in turn motivated him to heap on the goodies. It was a symbiotic relationship driven by mutual shame and reward.

Or perhaps I overanalyzed it. It was possible that these were simply toys.

This impression was reinforced when I opened the drawer below and discovered an array of devices and articles that made me wish I had double-gloved. Silk and lace had given way to plastic and leather, and even a set of handcuffs so remarkably realistic I was tempted to try my cuff key on them. There were vibrators of different sizes and shapes, some of them anatomic facsimiles of turgid phalluses. I found bottles of flavored and scented lotions and gels. It was like inventorying a back-alley sex shop.

I don't know a lot about sex toys, being a meat-and-potatoes sort of guy, but it appeared that most of the implements in the drawer were intended to pleasure women, or at least a certain type of woman with a certain type of erotic tastes. I recalled Natalie's history and the lessons I'd learned in the academy about criminal personality and psychopathy. A common factor seemed to be the lack of critical brain tissue associated with physiological and emotional arousal. One theory of criminality maintained that the commission of a psychopath's antisocial act was a manifestation of the need to raise the stakes, to push the outer boundaries of human behavior in an attempt to stoke the boilers of stimulation and compensate for a sense of emptiness that rode around on their shoulders like a tormenting harpy.

Whether there was something of value here in determining where the Guthries had gone, I couldn't say. If there wasn't, however, then I was nosily intruding on an intimate part of their lives.

In the next drawer, I found a charging cord for a laptop computer.

I didn't find the computer.

There was, however, a small ochre smudge on the inside of

the drawer, looking as if a finger dipped in paint had slid along the unfinished wood. A large empty space almost a foot square was next to the streak, and I could mentally visualize the computer that had lain there, probably right up to the moment that Roger and Natalie bugged out or were forced out of their home.

I had a feeling I'd find nothing of real use on the computer I'd stowed in my car. The real prize had already been removed from the house long before I'd arrived.

Chapter Twelve

I called the CSI team after finding the empty drawer. Then I drove home, changed into jeans and an Avett Brothers tee shirt, and collapsed into the hammock off the front porch.

Donna woke me some time later. I had no idea how long I'd been out, but the sun was angled low on the fields back of my house and I was aware of a ferrous taste in my mouth and pressure in my bladder.

"Took me long enough to wake you, Judd," she said. "You were out cold."

"Long day."

"Feel up to dinner?"

"I could eat."

She'd dropped by the store and picked up a garlic roasted whole chicken, some green beans with shaved almonds, and a quart of mashed potatoes. I excused myself for the bathroom while she set the table. Minutes later, as I returned to the kitchen, she had precisely carved the chicken into breasts and quarters, and had emptied the vegetables into serving bowls.

"Tough day, huh?" she said as I poured icy glasses of sweet tea.

"Still adjusting. It will get easier."

"Bet you'll be hours getting to sleep tonight, after sacking out in the hammock all afternoon."

"It wasn't *all* afternoon. The better part of it, maybe."

"Sit and eat."

Over dinner I tried to talk about everything except Roger and Natalie Guthrie, but I could see the curiosity in her eyes, and I saw her catch herself a couple of times before blurting out a question she really wanted to ask. I ignored it. She knew I'd broach the subject when I'd gotten it completely straight in my head, and it wasn't there yet.

"Your son called me at my school office today," she said, as I disassembled a thigh and leg quarter.

"Checking up on me?"

"Good guess."

"I'm a chief detective now. I'm good at guessing. He's okay?"

"Sure. Says college is going well, but he still worries about his dad."

"I'll call Craig tonight. He's a good son."

"He is. Are you happy, Judd?"

I stopped chewing and peered up at her. This wasn't the question I'd expected. "I have good days and bad days, but overall I can't complain."

"With me?"

I settled back in my chair and massaged at one of the puckered bullet scars on my chest. I had a feeling I'd done that a lot, mostly without being aware of it. Any time I moved too quickly, it was like hitting the damaged muscles with a branding iron.

"Donna, you are hands-down the best thing in my life. Are you worried about something?"

"So many changes. That's all. You seem different than you were a year ago. You spend a lot of time looking off in the distance, as if you're scared there's something out there waiting for you in the dark."

"I'm recovering," I said. "It will take time. Let's put the dishes away and drive in to Morgan tonight and catch a movie."

"I'd rather stay here and curl up in front of the television."

98

"You always fall asleep on the couch."

"Wake me up, then," she said. "You're going to be up all night, no reason for you to do it alone. We'll find some way to pass the time."

"Oh, yes," I said. "You bet we will."

I was only half surprised when I arrived at the office the next morning to find Jack Cantrell sitting in my waiting room.

Cantrell is a federal agent with the Department of Homeland Security. He's built like a miniature model of an out-of-training defensive tackle. His ears look as if ferrets have chewed them and his nose slopes over toward the right side of his face. His head is shaved clean and gleams like polished soapstone. He hadn't lost the cropped moustache and goatee he'd had the last time we'd talked almost two years ago.

"How's it hangin', Chief?" he said as I let the screen door slam behind me.

"Agent Cantrell. Want some coffee?"

"Sure."

I poured a couple of cups from the machine back near the holding cells, and walked into my office. Cantrell followed closely behind. I placed one of the cups on his side of my desk before taking my chair.

"You put a BOLO out on a Natalie Guthrie the other day," Cantrell said, as he lifted the cup to take a sip.

"Yes."

"What's she done?"

"Why do you want to know?"

"Because Homeland Security is interested in her."

"In what way?"

"Can't tell you."

"So, this is going to be one of *those* conversations."

"National security. The fate of the free world hangs in the

99

balance. You don't need to know. Take your pick."

"Bullshit."

"A little decorum, Chief. What's Natalie done?"

"You mean Natalya Gromykova? I got her file from ICE."

"I know. I cleared it. Ignore it."

"Ignore it?"

"It's a smokescreen. There's not a lot of truth in it."

"Which means there is a *smidgen* of truth in it."

He held up his thumb and forefinger, less than a quarter inch apart. "About that much."

"Was she a criminal in Lithuania?"

Cantrell shrugged.

"If I hit on something true, do you have some kind of poker tell that'll let me know?"

"Doubtful. We Homeland Security guys are great poker players. It's the mirrored sunglasses."

"Always fun talking to you, Cantrell. Drop back by someday when you can actually tell me something."

"I *am* telling you, Chief. The Guthrie case is off your books."

I took a sip of coffee as I collected my thoughts.

"Here's where I am," I said. "I got two missing Prosperity residents whose house has suspicious blood stains. One was becoming increasingly erratic at work, where he handled a great deal of . . . no, wait, an *enormous* amount of money. I have a Russian ex-con mail-order bride who avoided company during the day, had a collection of fetishistic sex paraphernalia that would make a hooker blush and a missing laptop computer, which—I'd guess—would go a long way toward explaining her disappearance. Oh, and I have a Sig Sauer pistol with the serial numbers expertly wiped. Now, in your experience, who carries such weapons?"

"Lots of people, especially those you are allowed to ignore. By the way, I'm going to need that Sig."

"Get a subpoena. It's evidence."

"Do I mumble, Chief? This isn't your case."

"There's a toilet in the back room if you need to freshen up."

"I also need that computer you took from Roger Guthrie's office."

"You want their cat, too? The neighbor's taking care of it."

"You can keep Kisa."

I had to smile. "You even know the cat's name. Gotta hand it to you, Cantrell, you guys are thorough."

"We try. I'm going to say this one more time. Natalie and Roger Guthrie are off your radar. Later today the BOLO will be inactivated. You don't have to do a thing. Ride this one, Chief. I mean it. This is stuff you really don't want to pursue. We'll handle it."

We stared at each other.

"You don't know where they are, either," I said.

"Not your business," he said.

"You know I took three in the chest a few months back."

"I'd heard. You look good, considering."

"I'm still a little slow on the uptake. It suddenly occurred to me that you wouldn't be here if you knew where to find Natalie and Roger Guthrie. If you fed guys had spirited them off to some safe house, I'd never hear from you. My investigation into their disappearance would be a perfect cover for you. You took the time to come here and shove me off the case. That means you're still looking for them, too, and you don't want me to interfere."

He didn't say anything.

"And you said you don't have a tell," I said.

Cantrell walked out of my office thinking he had chased me off the Guthries. Maybe he had. I wasn't certain yet.

I wasn't ready to relinquish the computer or the Sig Sauer. If they were important enough, he'd show up sooner or later with a federal seizure order and maybe a couple of intimidating fullbacks in shiny suits and buzz cuts. No biggie.

The fact that he'd visited was enough to let me know that the Guthries vanishing into the ether wasn't a local crime. They hadn't been kidnapped for ransom, and they hadn't been abducted as part of a robbery. Natalie's supposed status as a store-bought wife from the former Soviet bloc suggested an international angle.

On the other hand, Cantrell had tried the same spiel during our last encounter, when I was trying to figure out who killed Gypsy Camarena. He'd suggested that Gypsy's father, a distant cousin of a notorious dealer of Mexican brown tar heroin, might have been the motivation for the murder. When the dust settled, it turned out she was killed for personal reasons and her murder was home-grown. Cantrell had been wrong before. Maybe he was again.

Then there was the whole jurisdictional thing. I grew up in Prosperity. I'm a hometown boy, and now I run the local cop shop. Maybe it's parochial thinking on my part, the sort of stuff that comes from watching too many episodes of *Gunsmoke* when I was a kid, but I operate on the belief that what happens in my town is my responsibility. When guys like Cantrell blow into my jurisdiction, tossing around their federal weight, it makes me cranky. More than that, it makes me want to push back. It's a masculine thing, I suppose. When the big kid on the playground tries to bully you, you stand your ground or you lose face. You'll even take a black eye or a few scrapes to show you won't be intimidated. Some of that never grows out of you as you age. At least, it hadn't grown out of me.

I picked up the telephone and called Don Webb, the Bliss County sheriff, over in Morgan.

"Don," I said, when he answered the phone, "you have any

top-flight forensic computer experts you can lend me for a few hours? I have a machine I need to crack."

CHAPTER THIRTEEN

A kid named Lee Mathis, who appeared as if he should be cruising the halls of Prosperity Glen High School rather than working for the sheriff as a forensic data expert, dropped by the station a couple of hours later and collected the Guthrie computer I'd secured. He told me he should be able to unlock it quickly, but he had a few other jobs to handle first. He promised he'd get back to me by the first of the week.

Since Sherry wasn't being flooded with calls prompted by my BOLO (which Cantrell would cancel shortly anyway), I decided to tend to a little town business.

First up on the list was hiring two new officers. I drafted an advertisement, had Sherry clean it up, and then I sent it out to neighboring police and sheriff's departments in a ten-county area. I also posted it in a couple of law enforcement newsletters, and for kicks I sent it to the *Morgan Ledger-Telegraph,* the local paper.

I was finishing up when Kent Kramer tapped on my door.

"How's it going?" he asked as he sat across from me.

"Not too shabby. Had a visit from Jack Cantrell this morning."

"I know. He dropped in on me, too."

"Did he try to pressure you to pull me off the Guthrie disappearance?"

"He did."

"You tell him to blow you?"

"I did. I get the impression he hears this a lot."

"Some people never learn. I sent a Guthrie computer to Morgan a little while ago, to see if they can get into it. Might be useful. Probably won't. It looks as if another computer, a laptop, was taken from their bedroom dresser. The one I have wasn't hidden, so I'd imagine anything useful was on the one that was taken."

"You busy Saturday night?"

"Not particularly."

"Want to come over for a cookout?"

Kent Kramer's cookouts were never to be missed. While most of them were a cover for schmoozing some local celebrity or potential business partner, he tended to find the best meat in four states to slap on the grill.

"Sure, if Donna doesn't already have plans. Special occasion?"

"Some potential homebuyers. Big money. You know how it goes. I like introducing them to the local law enforcement. It reinforces their perception of Prosperity as a safe place."

"Prosperity *is* a safe place, Kent."

"Tell it to the Guthries."

I was still twenty-five pounds down from my pre-shooting weight, and none of my stylish casual clothes fit well anymore. Donna dragged me into Morgan for a shopping spree on Saturday afternoon, so I wouldn't embarrass her in front of Kent's guests. She said she wanted me to look "spiffy," but I knew the real reason. My old wardrobe still made me look like a twelve-year-old trying on his dad's suits.

Once I dressed and saw myself in the mirror, I was glad she'd insisted on the new clothes. While I perceived my recovering body as scrawny compared to the way I'd been before Spud Corliss ventilated my hide, I looked nice in duds that were the right size. I would never make male catalog models fret over job security, but it was an improvement.

Donna always gleamed like a movie star. A former professional tennis player who found her career in the dumper by age twenty, she had maintained a regular exercise regimen, and she could still run me into the ground and swim circles around me in a pool. I was a good athlete myself in my prime, having played second-string quarterback for Carolina enough years back that I don't like to admit it. I'd tried to stay in shape since a dumpy cop tends to be a sloppy cop, but I couldn't keep up with her.

I was shaving as she stepped out of the shower, and she nearly took my breath away. She did that a lot.

"Quit gawking," she said. "You make me feel naked."

"You are naked."

"Eyes forward, Chief. You'll cut yourself."

I finished shaving, dried my face with a hand towel, and retreated to the bedroom to dress. She joined me a few minutes later. To my regret, she had slipped into her underwear.

"You know who's coming tonight?" she asked.

"I suppose the councilmen will be there. Seth won't. He's still at Georgia Tech for another several weeks."

Seth was Kent's son and a semi-permanent thorn in my side. He had been endowed with every shred of Kent's athletic ability, to the point where there was little room left for humanity or humility. Kent had meant well in raising Seth, but there's something about growing up as the son of Prosperity's most successful business tycoon that, sooner or later, was bound to have a negative impact on his moral development.

"Fine with me. Kid gives me the creeps," she said.

"He's my best friend's son, Donna."

"Then let him look down *your* shirt."

Kent's trophy wife, Crystal, answered the front door when we arrived, and walked us through the house to the pool area in back.

"How are you doing, Judd?" she asked as we walked.

"Better every day," I said. "I figure I'll be back to light-heavyweight by fall."

"I'm so glad," she said, and her face tried to convey it, but between the plastic surgery–enhanced drumhead skin and Botox, the best she would manage was a sort of half-hearted eye crinkle. "I need to keep an eye on the front door. Make yourselves at home, now, y'hear?"

"She's gone up another cup size," Donna said after Crystal was out of earshot.

"Jealous?"

"Are you kidding? I like myself the way I am. At least I don't have to include 'ability to sit up straight' among my more admirable qualities."

"I like you fine the way you are, too," I said.

We walked through the French doors to the pool patio. Kent had set up a bar near the deep end and was playing bartender to the men assembled around him. A small group of women sat around a table under a huge umbrella at one side of the pool. I recognized the town council members, whose wives were the ones at the table. There was a fourth man standing next to Kent, with his back to me, so I could not immediately see who he was.

Kent saw Donna and me, and placed a highball glass on the table next to him.

"Judd! Glad to see you could make it. Fashionably late again, I see. Come on over here. Got someone I want to introduce."

Donna and I navigated around the pool to the bar. We were halfway there when I realized who the mystery guest was. It had been a long time, but as soon as I saw his face full on, the years fell away like a protective fortress, leaving me bare to assault.

He was tall, maybe two inches taller than me. He had shoulders like an ox yoke, and a round face that he'd tried to elongate with a salt-and-pepper beard that framed his thick mouth and gleaming dental implants. His nose was wide, bulbous, and crisscrossed with spider veins, the tip of it edging on purple. His eyes were lupine, the lightest blue I'd ever seen—like chlorinated pool water—surrounded by lightly jaundiced and bloodshot scleras. His hair was combed straight back and collected with an elastic band at his neck into a ponytail that hung halfway to his belt. His was a face I had not seen in thirty years. It was a face I had hoped I'd never lay eyes on again, even as I had always suspected we were destined to be reunited.

"This is our police chief, Shug," Kent told him. "Judd Wheeler, Donna Asher, I'd like you to meet . . ."

"Sean Burch," I said. I didn't offer my hand. Burch wouldn't have expected me to.

"Judd," Burch said. "Police chief, eh? Guess I'm not surprised at that."

He then took Donna's hand, and she seemed to melt. He had always had that effect on women, even before he became immensely famous. I think the poets call it *animal magnetism.*

"So," Kent said, "you two know each other."

"We go back a way," Burch said. "You look good, Judd."

"Long time," I said.

"Not long enough?" Burch said, and punctuated it with a roaring laugh and a stinging slap on my shoulder. "Good to see you, boy. Great to be home. And what do you do, Donna?"

Donna glanced at me and knew something was wrong. As she told Sean Burch about teaching at Prosperity Glen, and he listened as intently as if she were divulging the combination to the safe holding the Hope Diamond, my memory's eye flashed back several decades, to a time before the urban tax refugees invaded Prosperity, a time when Sean Burch and I had been the closest of buddies.

Talk about an awkward reunion! Kent kept looking at me as if I was trying to rain on his party, while all I could think of was how Sean Burch's return to Prosperity could only be a portent of terrible things.

An hour or so later, as Kent tended to the grill and Donna joined the women to talk about things important to women, I took a moment to hit the bathroom. I splashed water on my face, and wondered how I'd manage to get through the unexpected return of my boyhood friend.

I stepped out of the bathroom and headed back toward the patio, when an all-too-familiar voice, like a backhoe diesel rumbling to life, stopped me.

"Judd," Burch said.

I turned. He leaned against a wall next to the kitchen, holding a bottle of beer wrapped in a paper towel.

"I guess Kramer didn't tell you I was coming," he said. "And why do I get the idea that, if he had, you wouldn't be here?"

"Maybe because you always had street smarts. Why *are* you here, Sean?"

"Haven't you heard? People call me *Shug* now."

"I've heard a lot of things about you. In my head you're still Sean."

"Hell, we've all pissed a few gallons since then, haven't we? Heard you got shot last year. I've taken a couple myself over the years. Hurts like a sumbitch, don't it?"

"You have something you want to say?"

He held up one hand, palm out, and took a long draw on the

beer. "Hell, man, I'm lovin' life here. Looks like you've done well. Sell your dad's farm yet?"

"No. I still live there."

"That's good. I like that. It's so . . . *you*. Ol' stick-in-the-mud Wheeler. I'd have been disappointed if you'd done any other way."

"You're moving back to Bliss County?"

"Looks that way. It's been a long, long road, Judd. Too many years, too many buses, too many honky-tonks, more nameless pussy than any man has a right to. I got all the money I can ever spend, long's I don't go around buying up islands and small countries and shit, and I figured it was time to put down some roots. Where better than the soil from which I was plucked so many years ago?"

"You make it sound like something that was done to you."

"Wasn't it?"

"Brings us back to my question. Why are you here? What is it you really want?"

He grinned, his teeth lined up like brilliant marble tombstones. "You think maybe I've come back for a little revenge?"

He pronounced it *ree-venge*, equal emphasis on both syllables.

"Have you?"

"Boy, you make me out to be some kind of monster! Don't know what you been reading in the magazines or hearing on the radio, but I done turned my life around."

"Where do you figure on living?"

"Now, that's a tough one, ain't it? Kent out there thinks I'm gonna buy one of them big ol' manor houses he's dumping all over the county. Me, though, I kind of miss the quiet of the evening sitting on a front porch looking out over a hundred acres or so of fertile planted fields, sipping a cool one with my arm around some sweet thing who wants nothin' more than to lick the sweat off my chin."

"Are you fantasizing about a home or writing a song lyric?"

He pointed a finger at me, and drained the bottle. "Now you're makin' fun of me, Judd. I want what you got. That Miz Asher, now she's a lovely lady. You're a lucky man. You got it all. Hope you appreciate it. Lots of nights on the road, I dreamed of the life you're leading. 'Course, when I was a kid, it was my daddy working for the kind of man who has what you got. You got you a bunch of sharecroppers over to your place?"

"Sharecropping is immoral. I rent the land to people who farm it. They keep what they make."

"Glad to hear it. Think I might find me a nice farm hereabouts and do the same thing. I hear there's one on the market, ready to rebuild, needs five or six deep holes filled up. You know the one? Used to belong to a guy named Murray?"

The year before, during a sweltering, sun-lashed summer, a crazed itinerant tent preacher had buried five people on Nate Murray's farm, including Nate himself.

"I know the place. I don't want to be impolite, Sean, given our history, but I hope you won't mind me saying that it would be like you to try to profit off the misery and tragedy of others."

Something cold and malignant swept across his face, and then, like the briefest of spring showers, it was replaced again by his façade of geniality and well-being. I'd often seen the same expression on sideshow con men and encyclopedia-selling road agents.

"Why would I mind?" he said. "We go way back, you and me, and I don't doubt you have some ideas about me that are based on events that took place at a time long before we were even old enough to know what sin was about. You can't live thirty years in the past, Judd. I'm sure you wouldn't want to be judged by your own behavior back then, now, would you?"

He was right. I carried my own secret shame over what drove us apart in the last days of our childhood, and I knew that—

whatever he had become—I carried at least partial responsibility for every furtively whispered rumor about Shug Burch that had found its way to my ears over the decades. It wasn't the first time I had inventoried my life and wished that I had a way to go back and do a thing over.

"I'm not a righteous man," I said. "My father's best intentions notwithstanding. What you've done or haven't done over the years is on your shoulders, and whether there is some sort of retributional come-to-Jesus moment in your soul's future is not for me to say. My father told me that a good man is willing to extend even the vilest of creatures the benefit of the doubt, until proven otherwise. I reckon, given what we both know about ourselves, you deserve that."

He seemed to relax a little.

"I appreciate it, Judd. I hope to justify it."

"I'm not finished. Having said that, I want to remind you that I am the law in Prosperity. No matter what happened in our youths, or who you hold responsible for your station in life and in the eyes of whatever deity you hold dear, you step one inch out of line and I'll be there to squash you like a bug. Is there anything I've said that you don't understand?"

He placed the bottle on the kitchen island, and extended his hand. "I'd say we see each other clear. Will you take my hand and seal our new understanding of one another?"

I glanced at his tattooed fingers, the images of love and hate pricked into his skin with a safety pin and ballpoint ink in some dingy, mildewed prison cell in a past so far away that perhaps even he could no longer dredge it accurately from his memory.

I took his hand, and even as I did I saw an image in my head of a picture I'd once run across in a library book telling the story of Gilgamesh and Enkidu battling one another at the gates of Uruk, and I wondered which of us represented the tragically flawed king, and which the wild man created by a

the gods as his physical—if not moral—equal.
I found little comfort in either alternative.

CHAPTER FOURTEEN

I didn't say much on the way home. I was still thinking about Sean Burch, and what his return to Prosperity might mean. Donna, being Donna, picked up on my concerns.

"What is it?" she asked.

"Old stuff. Stuff from years ago."

"You never told me you knew Shug Burch."

"His name's Sean. I never knew Shug, though I'd imagine there isn't a lot of difference between the two. I never told you about a lot of things."

We drove for another half mile or so before she said, "Okay, you know I'm not letting that pass."

"There are missing pieces in his head. He degrades the air by breathing it."

"Wow. You really don't like him."

"I didn't expect to see him again. Ever. It was a shock. I'm still processing it. Let's leave it at this. He's not a nice person. Sean Burch's very existence makes me believe that some people arise from a completely alien genetic strain."

"There's more," she said. "I can feel it."

"There's a lot more. I'm not ready to talk about it yet."

"But you will."

"No guarantees. Some things you bury in the ground ought never be dug back up."

"If you won't tell me about it, will you talk it over with Dr. Kronenfeld?"

"If I won't talk about it with you, why would I discuss it with him?"

"Because if you don't get it out with someone, it's going to rip you to shreds inside."

"Maybe not."

"Don't bullshit me, Chief. I've slept with you for too long. You might want to hit the brakes unless you plan to drive right past your house."

Later—much later—that night, Donna woke and realized I wasn't in bed. She padded into the den, where I sat on the couch, the television on with the sound muted. She didn't ask why I was up. Instead, she sat next to me, lifted my arm, draped it around her shoulders, and settled her head on my chest. It hurt a little, since any pressure where I was shot still ached, but I didn't say anything.

"I was thinking," I said, after a couple of minutes. "Do you believe that separated twins could become moral and spiritual opposites?"

"I believe that sleepless nights fuck you up beyond all recognition."

"When we were kids, Sean and I were friends. Maybe best friends."

"This much I gathered. What changed?"

"Children ignore the inescapable in each other. Farm kids live in isolation. It might be three or four miles to the next child your age. You settle for the friends you're dealt."

"What about Burch?"

"His parents worked a farm down by the south fork of Six Mile Creek. A man named Coleman owned the place. He allowed the Burch family to stay in a mobile home next to one of the cornfields. Sean was an only child, like me. We gravitated to one another out of mutual need, I suppose. You didn't grow up on a farm. It's not much like the old *Lassie* show, with Timmy constantly falling down a well or getting caught in a cave. Farm life means work, and lots of it. After my mother abandoned us, there was more. There was a time when farm couples had seven, eight children in order to assure that there would be a lot of hands to take care of all the chores. Here, it was me and my father, and a hundred acres of toil. The Burches only had Sean. Summers for most kids mean hitting the pool or going on vacation. Around here, it meant working from 'cain't see to cain't see'. Same for the Burches. Time for play, for farm kids, was a luxury, and we'd squeeze every ounce from it we could.

"Sean and I did mostly kid things. We hunted arrowheads in the cornfields, swam and fished in that little pond where you like to skinny-dip—don't give me that look. I've watched you."

"Joined me, too."

"Damn right. Some things are beyond a man's ability to resist. So Sean and I spent a few springs and falls hanging together when there was time. Then we hit puberty, and things started to . . . well, they changed. It was like a mean hormone spigot got turned on in Sean's body. He became cruel, even a little scary."

"I work in a high school. I've seen it happen."

"Not like him, you haven't. When we were eleven or twelve, he caught a hoppy toad out near the pond. I saw him take a piece of twine, tie it around the toad's neck, and tighten it until the toad's tongue rolled out its mouth and its eyes bulged."

"Jesus."

"In the old Prosperity junior high building, the one that was torn down later, the heat was powered by a coal-fired boiler. One day Sean told me to meet him in the basement, where the boiler was. When I showed up, he was there with a bag. He opened it, and pulled out a live rabbit he'd stolen from some backyard pen, and he tossed the rabbit into the furnace to see if it would scream. I don't like to relive that memory."

"And you started to move apart."

"Not then. The image of him tossing the rabbit kept me up at night, but I was only a kid. I knew right from wrong, but I had no conceptualization of depravity. That came later. For a long time I ignored his cruelty because I was afraid of losing one of my few real friends. Despite his capability to destroy, Sean could, on occasion, be generous and kind. It was almost as if he swung from one end of a moral continuum to the other.

"We were fifteen when the split came. There was this girl, Lisa Rae Youngblood. She wasn't from a farm family. Her father owned a tire store over in Morgan, and they had a home like nobody else in Prosperity. I suppose it was this town's first Mc-Mansion. Had a pool in the backyard. You've heard the term *shitkicker*? It was coined to describe kids like Sean and me, who spent most of their time out of school working in our parents' fields after they were fertilized with cow manure. The idea of a pool in your backyard was the stuff we only saw at the moving picture show on the rare Saturday afternoon."

"I've lived here for years," Donna said. "I've never run across anyone named Youngblood."

"Thank Sean Burch for that. Or maybe you can thank me. Time changes our memories of our lives, and maybe the way I recall events has little resemblance to what really happened. Sean claims that he made the first moves on Lisa Rae, but I think she favored me. In any case, shortly before the school year started in the tenth grade, she invited the two of us over to her house for a swim in the pool. It was . . . it was like getting an imperial summons. We showed up, and she let us in the front door, and told us her parents were off to Myrtle Beach for the weekend for a golf tournament. We had the house all to ourselves.

"She led us out to the pool, where she'd put a six-pack of

117

beer in a bucket of ice. She had the stereo playing through outside speakers. It was the biggest house I had ever seen, and the closest neighbor was over a half mile away. We drank beer, and swam around for a while, and after a while Lisa Rae was all glassy-eyed from the alcohol, and she asked us if we'd ever skinny-dipped. Well, of course we had. We were farm kids, and the only place we'd ever gone swimming was in the pond on the farm, where there's no need for modesty. That seemed to excite her, and she said, 'Well, then, what are we waiting for?' And, before we knew it, she had tossed her suit onto a chair near the diving board and jumped in."

"You were fifteen?"

"Yeah, and you know what kids that age are like. We'd seen naked girls in magazines, but here was one in the flesh, and we responded the way you'd expect. I think that excited her even more. We swam, and splashed, and played grab-ass, and after a while the beer worked its way through me so I asked her where the bathroom was, and she told me. I excused myself, leaving them alone, and headed for a pool house across from the main house.

"I walked out of the bathroom into this sort of lounging room, with waterproof furniture and a wet bar, and I looked out the sliding glass doors at the same instant I heard Lisa Rae scream the first time."

"The first time."

"There was a lot of screaming. I don't know what happened while I was in the bathroom, but whatever it was had turned bad. Sean was holding Lisa Rae under the water, and I could tell she was panicking and thrashing around, and I saw this strange look on his face, almost like joy, as if he was getting pleasure from her terror. When he finally let her get back to the surface, she screamed and tried to swim away from him, but he was like a cat playing with some defenseless mouse. She'd get a few feet from the edge of the pool, and he'd grab her by the hair and pull her back, and push her under the water again. Finally, she made it to the ladder, and climbed out of the pool and tried to make a break for the house, but he caught her, and he forced her down onto a chaise and tried to kiss her. She slapped him, which seemed to turn him on even more, and he slapped her back, hard, two or three times, until she couldn't even scream anymore. She sobbed and whimpered, and he turned her over on her belly and yanked her body up at the waist and took her from behind, right there on the chaise."

"And you didn't stop him."

"I didn't know what to do. He was my best—my *only* friend. I felt helpless, and ashamed. Every time I think of that day, the shame rolls over me like a rogue wave. Instead of helping her, I stood in the pool house and watched him rape her in every conceivable way, and when he was done he picked her up and threw her back into the pool. As if some kind of spell had been broken, I found my feet and my voice, and I left the pool house. I demanded to know what he'd done, as if I hadn't witnessed the whole thing. He said it was time to go."

"What about Lisa Rae?"

"She was in the shallow end of the pool, sobbing and wailing and praying. Her face was swollen. Sean had broken her nose, and the blood began to pool around her in the water, mixing with the chlorine, turning the water pink.

" '*We can't leave her!*' I told him.

"He said, 'This is what's going to happen. We're getting out of here. We were never here. She got what she wanted.'

"Then I finally got the stones to do something. I told him he could go if he wanted, but I was going to stay and help her. He pulled me aside and grabbed me by the arms. He was only fifteen, but he was already big and powerful. He said, 'You didn't see anything. Nothing happened here. You do what you want, but you better remember who your friends are.'

"He pulled on his swim trunks and his tee shirt, and he left. It took me a half hour to get Lisa Rae calm enough to get dressed. I only had my learner's permit, but we took her daddy's Buick over to the emergency room in Morgan."

"They called her parents," Donna said.

"And her parents called the sheriff's department when she told them what Sean had done. They picked Sean up a couple of hours later. He was tending to soybeans in his father's fields, still in his filthy tee shirt and overalls. He saw me when he walked into the Morgan station, and he knew I'd sold him out."

"You made a moral choice," Donna said.

"I was fifteen. What in hell does a fifteen-year-old know about moral reasoning? I was scared. I knew there was a chance I might get swept up in Sean's debauchery, and I was in trouble. I saved my own skin. Since Sean was only fifteen, the case stayed in juvie court, but this was back in the day, and the judge was a crotchety old bastard who loved to make examples out of people. He sent Sean to the High Rise."

"What's that?"

"A kiddie prison, up in the foothills. Thirteen floors. You start at the top, and work your way down and out the front door. Or, at least, that's the theory. Most kids sent there stay until their eighteenth birthday. I've visited there a few times in the course of my work. Some of the teenagers you meet there make you grateful for the existence of carbon steel bars."

"Burch didn't make it out the front door."

"Sure he did. On his eighteenth birthday. He came home, and for one week he lived in his parents' single-wide over on the Coleman farm. By then I was the big man on campus at Prosperity Glen, all set to go off to Carolina and set the world on fire. We ran into each other one night at the pizza place over at the shopping center. I was there with a girl I was dating, enjoying a pepperoni pie and some cokes, when he walked in. His head was still shaved from the High Rise. He saw me and his face twisted into something tortured and hateful, and he turned around and walked back out. I followed him into the parking lot, and I tried to say something—anything—to make up for what I'd done.

" 'There's a time for payback,' he said. 'This ain't it. Not yet.' Then he walked up the hill, past the Town Hall, and I never saw him again until this evening."

"He moved away."

"You could say that. He got caught in a stolen car over in Morgan, and went down for his first adult conviction. I figure he spent most of the next ten years in the jug. That was before he became famous, of course."

"You think he still blames you for being locked up."

"If I hadn't testified against him after he raped Lisa Rae Youngblood, he probably would have gotten away with it. This was back before the days of DNA. It would have been one of those he said/she said cases, at a time in the south when a battered and abused woman didn't engender a great deal of public sympathy, especially if a jury got the notion she had led her rapist on. Yeah. He blames me."

"People change."

"Human nature doesn't. You carve a statue out of pine and it doesn't turn into marble. I could see the same malevolence in Sean's eyes tonight that I remember from thirty years ago. He's dangerous, and that means if he moves to Prosperity he's going to be my problem."

CHAPTER FIFTEEN

Burch finished his last beer, said his good nights to Kent and Crystal Kramer, and climbed into his Caddy Escalade for the drive back to Morgan.

He wasn't a particularly introspective man, but the meeting with Prosperity's chief of police had unsettled him. There were parts of his life he believed he had put behind him. Running into Wheeler, even after all these years, and even with the way he perceived himself to have risen above the wastage of his youth, had left him with a strange mix of feelings.

Had the reunion taken place twenty years earlier, it likely would have resulted in blood on the ceiling. In his late forties, Burch had discovered that the fires of his juvenile rage had burned down to smoldering embers, like many of his other passions. Nothing seemed to trip his trigger anymore, not even coming face to face with the man who'd been responsible for years of sweat and toil shoveling asphalt under the cynical eyes of itchy-fingered gun bulls on rural routes in the loneliest parts of the south, where the houses were miles apart and the chief exports were despair and substance abuse.

There was another possibility. Maybe he hadn't gotten worked up because, after all those years, he had become Wheeler's better. Who, after all, had the money, the acclaim, the cars, the women? Wheeler had a tin badge, but Burch had a wall full of Grammys and platinum records. Burch had been on the cover of Billboard—not once, but *four times*. Surely, his old childhood buddy had never stood behind the cheater curtains of some amphitheater, stoked on rock and listening to thousands of fans shout his name over and over—*Shug-GA, Shug-GA, Shug-GA!*

Maybe he hadn't flown off the handle because he was finally content.

That didn't mean there weren't scores to settle. The time would come, and maybe soon, when he would put paid all the accounts owed to him, and Judd Wheeler was right at the top of the list of debtors.

Up ahead, in the headlights, he saw a figure walking by the side of the highway. As he drew closer, he realized it was a woman. Burch liked picking up women hitchhikers. Some of his most pleasurable encounters had been with women he'd found by the side of the road. Their gratitude paired with their disposability made them convenient outlets for his overdriven libido.

He tapped the brake to disengage the cruise, and quickly made a security check of the Airweight hammerless revolver he kept stowed in a Velcro holster attached to the front left side of his seat. Most of the hitchers he'd picked up were docile and compliant enough, but he wasn't a stupid man, and he wasn't about to depart this earth at the hands of some psychopathic bitch who got her rocks off by killing random johns. He'd seen that movie about Aileen Wournos a few years back and, while he knew it was an actress playing a part, that bitch had scared the ever-loving shit out of him.

He slowed, noted that there was no traffic coming up behind him, and pulled up alongside the woman on the side of the road.

"You shouldn't be out here walking the highway in the dark," he said to her. "Your car broken down?"

"Ain't got no car," she said. Her voice was tinged with tobacco and whiskey, and had the lyrical quality common to women who'd trod the stage of the Ryman Auditorium for years. It was a voice born of years of Tennessee back hills and honky-tonks and hard, hot sidewalks, and damned little privilege. Most men would imagine her voice etching glass, but to Burch it was lovely.

"Need a ride? I can take you as far as Morgan."

Many women might have thought twice, out of caution or suspicion. This one didn't hesitate. She opened the door and slid in beside him.

"Right kind of you, sir," she said.

"No probs. Happy to help. Were you headed to Morgan?"

"Are there jobs there?"

"I reckon there are one or two."

"I'm sorry, sir, but have we met? You look like someone I might know." Her drawl sluiced out of her mouth like fine ruby port wine over ice cream.

"Guess I got one of them faces," he said, as he turned and grinned at her. In the light from the dash, he realized that she had a few more years on her than he usually found attractive, but she wore them well, and he had to admit that her face was—if not classically beautiful—very handsome. She wasn't the sort of twenty-year-old twist he preferred banging, especially after a night as emotionally upsetting as this one had been, but she was no older than he, and he had to admit that, on occasion, he had greatly enjoyed the benefits of a woman with experience.

"Sean," he said, as he extended his hand. She took it.

"Lily."

"Pretty name. Haven't met a lot of Lilys."

"All the kids in my family were named after flowers."

"Even the boys?"

"Weren't no boys."

"So you don't own a car, and you weren't intending to head

for Morgan. How'd you wind up walking by the side of the road?"

She didn't answer for a while, and he decided she wasn't interested in divulging.

"Excuse me for prying," he said at last.

"Ain't no bother, sir. I didn't know how I should say it. I was abandoned."

"That sounds like a story."

"Not a long one. I hooked up with a man down in Norcross, and we traveled from town to town for a while, picking up work where we could. I reckon he got tired of me."

"I don't want to sound forward, but I have a hard time imagining that."

"We met five minutes ago. You don't know anything about me. You sure we haven't met up somewheres before?"

"You hungry?" he said. "I left a barbecue at this man's house over in Prosperity a few minutes back, and he meant well, but I've had tastier steaks down Mexico way made from bulls who'd lost a fight."

"Don't know as I could tell a good one from a bad one, as long as it's been. I wish you hadn't mentioned food, sir. It's set my stomach to grumbling."

"When did you eat last?"

"Sometime yesterday."

"I think we need to get you to a restaurant. You don't mind if I buy your dinner?"

"Sir, I don't mean to sound ungrateful, but why would you do that?"

"Been hungry myself, once or twice," he said.

"I just realized who you are," she said. "I wish you'd pull the car over now."

"What? You don't want a ride to Morgan?"

"I figure I've ridden long enough. You're Shug Burch. My

boyfriend had some of your CDs. I couldn't place you at first."

"*Shug* was a name they hung on me years ago. If it makes you more comfortable, call me Sean."

"Would you please pull the car over and let me out? I've heard stories about what happens to people when you pick them up on the road, and I have to tell you, after all the misery I've lived through in the past year, that would break my heart beyond redemption."

The Caddy rose over a hill, into a spill of light from Morgan reflected off the clouds overhead.

"We're almost there," he said. "That light, it comes from the Morgan Mall. There are restaurants all around it."

"I'd as soon walk from here, if it's all the same to you."

He didn't slow the car and he didn't respond. Instead, he turned off the highway onto the feeder road, even as he felt her drawing physically away from him, as if she imagined she might be able to meld with the passenger door upholstery.

He drove the car into the parking lot of a chain steak house, but he didn't turn off the ignition. He put it in park and turned to her, as he reached into his pocket.

"Here," he said, as he pressed several twenties into her palm. "Take this money and get yourself a good meal. And take this, too. It's my card. Some partners and I are opening a music club at that address here in Morgan. There's a Salvation Army shelter on the other side of the mall. You can bunk there for the night. You say you need a job? If you've done any bartending or waiting tables, I think we can give you some work. Come by tomorrow and show the man at the club that card. He'll see to it you go on the payroll."

She didn't say anything. Neither did she toss the money and the card back at him. He flicked a button that unlocked the passenger door, and she slipped out into the spill of the mercury vapor lights of the parking lot. Without saying anything, not

goodbye, or *thank you,* or *drop dead,* she walked around the building toward the front door of the restaurant.

As he watched her disappear, he admired the way her ass
filled the back of her jeans. Then he whispered to himself, "Now
why the fuck's sake did I do that?"

CHAPTER SIXTEEN

Dr. Kronenfeld leaned back in his chair.

"I think I'm going to need a scorecard to keep track of all the complexes you're processing, Judd."

"I'm telling it the way it happened," I said.

"First, your mother abandons you. It wasn't your fault, but you're a kid. What do you know? You blame yourself. Then your wife dies. A delinquent teenager you only wanted to keep out of the system nearly blows you away, and then kills himself in a police standoff. Now you tell me you watched your best friend rape a girl and didn't do anything about it. Then you were responsible for providing the testimony that sent him to prison. I hope you don't mind my observation, Chief, but your life is the stuff of Greek tragedies."

"You go to school a long time to learn that kind of analysis?" I said.

"I don't analyze. That's for Freudians. I deal with stinkin' thinkin', and right now I kind of wish I could walk around the inside of your head with a can of air freshener."

"What's your point?"

Kronenfeld leaned forward and started counting on his fingers.

"One. You weren't responsible for your mother leaving, and you didn't kill your wife. Two. You had no idea when your wife called you when she was dying that it was your last chance to talk to her. Three. You did not kill Spud Corliss. He made a bad decision and that's on him. Four. I don't know five teenagers among all those I've ever met who would have known how to cope with seeing their best friend as-

sault a young girl. You were shocked. You were confused. It took you a
while to work it out, but in the end you did the right thing."

"Betraying his trust?"

"He betrayed yours when he depended on your silence. You hadn't
done anything irretrievably wrong. Now, let's change your story a
little. Let's say you'd done as Burch asked. Let's say you had gone
home with him, leaving that poor girl bleeding and bruised and
violated, and later gave him the alibi he'd demanded. You think you
feel guilty now?"

"I know all of this, rationally," I said. "Doesn't make it any less
difficult."

"Which life would you rather have lived? The one where you stood
up for that girl, or one where you protected a violent and depraved
friend?"

"Seems it all came to the same end, when all was said and done."

"Not necessarily. Why did you become a cop?"

"I don't see where—"

"Answer the question. Look back at your life. Tell me when you
first considered becoming a police officer. You were a farm kid. Your
father owned over a hundred acres of prime arable land. By all
rights, that life should have fallen to you. Hell, Judd, Prosperity
didn't even have a police force until you started it. Where did the idea
pop into your head?"

"I know where you're headed. Yeah. I remember. It was when Sean
was arrested. I'd had almost no dealings with the police in my life to
that point. Sean's arrest and trial gave me a front row seat on police
operations. I was fascinated by . . . well, everything about it. The
uniforms, the badges, the guns."

"The power."

"It's a subject a lot of cops don't want to address, but sure. There
is power attached to being an officer. Some people abuse it."

"Not you."

"I've pushed the outside edge of the envelope once or twice."

"But always in the public interest."

"I like to think so."

"And you've done a lot of good."

"You going somewhere with this?"

"It seems to me that a man who has done as much good for his fellows as you might want to feel a little less willing to carry the cross of guilt around on his shoulders like he's trudging toward Calvary, no matter how he came across the desire to be a good man. What happened between you and Burch was unfortunate, but you weren't responsible for all the aluminum wiring in his head."

"And about what happened later?"

"What did happen later, Judd? You've been a little vague about all that. I suspect it's what you've really wanted to talk about from the beginning."

I checked my watch, despite the fact that there was a clock on the wall, and I knew there was way too much time left in my fifty-minute hour for me to duck the question.

CHAPTER SEVENTEEN

It was a Saturday, maybe a week or so after Sean Burch's return had rocked my world. I had been anticipating something awful to transpire, which is probably why I wasn't completely shocked when it happened.

I had finished cutting the grass in my backyard, a half-acre expanse of Kentucky fescue and Bermuda that runs directly up to a stand of red oak, pecan, and tulip poplar trees that separates my residence from the farm fields my tenants work. It was close to the first of May, and the bluebottles and sweat bees had emerged from their pupal state to become irritants of the first order. Sitting on the front porch, I sipped from my second tall sweet iced tea with lemonade. The condensation collecting on the glass ran down it in rivulets to collect in a pool on the table.

I was musing over a report I'd received a day earlier. Lee Mathis, the barely post-adolescent computer whiz with the Bliss County Sheriff's Department, had finally gotten around to Roger Guthrie's desktop. He'd managed to crack the password using whatever hocus-pocus digitally literate wizards possess, but there was nothing of interest on the hard drive. In fact, the documents section was practically blank, and he was unable to locate any hidden files or programs. He suggested that Guthrie might have been particularly wary of computer hackers or spies, and had kept everything except for the actual programs on a separate drive.

Unfortunately, there are all kinds of storage devices around, from CDs to zip drives, and he had no idea what kind I might be seeking. I had returned to the house, and I'd rummaged through the desk, but I hadn't found anything other than paper clips and staples, and a ream of paper. Not only had Guthrie feared cyber intruders, he wasn't much of a packrat either.

It occurred to me, as I sat cooling down from my yard labors and savoring my tea, that whatever storage devices he might have used had been taken along with the missing laptop and the Guthries themselves. It was even possible that they were completely safe in some witness protection program, and the fact that I had been incapable of finding any real evidence in their house was because they had been transported to safety by Jack Cantrell after serving whatever convoluted purpose the federal government had fabricated for them, and Cantrell had wiped their house clean in the process. Maybe the laptop and the zip drives were sitting in a box somewhere, waiting to be retrieved by someone who would never come.

Not that it mattered much. Cantrell had cancelled the BOLO, and had made it clear that Roger and Natalya were none of my concern. And, since I hadn't learned anything of consequence from Lee Mathis, I was not obligated to share my lack of knowledge with Cantrell, which was fine with me. I'd never liked the son of a bitch anyway.

I drained my glass, took it to the kitchen and placed it in the dishwasher, and headed to the bathroom for a shower.

I was drying myself when my cell phone bleeped. I saw on the screen that it was Slim calling.

"Chief, I hope you weren't preparing a weekend cookout or anything."

I'd heard that tone of his voice before, and I knew I'd gone back on the clock.

"What's up?"

"We got us a DB."

"I hopped out of the shower thirty seconds ago, Slim. Might take me a few minutes to get there. Where are you?"

He gave me the address, and I prepared to go back to my official mode.

We get dead people in Prosperity all the time. Some elderly retiree pops a cerebral artery sitting in front of the TV and isn't found for a day or so, or some drunken good ol' boy bites it on the front end of a semi on the Morgan Highway late at night. I recall one particularly unpleasant case involving an eighty-year-old woman who shattered her hip after slipping on a dryer sheet and crashing to her laundry room floor, where she lay for eight or nine days, according to the coroner's report, waiting for a rescuer who never showed. So, people die in Prosperity, and when they're found I'm the first guy who's called. Any death that wasn't witnessed by others is automatically a suspicious death until I say otherwise, even if over ninety-nine percent of the time it's rapidly apparent that the deceased departed this world in a completely typical fashion.

This was not destined to be one of those days.

As I had instructed, Slim had not yet called the paramedics when I arrived. He had told me that Ramsey William Pressley was most decidedly dead, and I trusted his judgment. I climbed from the Jeep and walked up to him on Pressley's front porch. Pressley lived on the far edge of Prosperity from the police department, in a Victorian-style farmhouse with a deep wraparound porch, columns boasting finely carved corbels, clapboard siding, and a cedar shake roof. A plaque affixed to the wall next to the front door proclaimed that the house had been built for Pressley's great-grandfather in the latter part of the nineteenth century. The Pressleys were among the settlers of Bliss County back before the Revolutionary War, along with other families with names like Craighead, Broome, Whitmire, and—of course—Wheeler. Unlike my ancestors, however, the Pressleys had always put great stock in appearances, and prided themselves on having the best of everything.

"You sure it's Ram-Billy?" I said.

"Sure as I can be, considering."

"Considering?"

"You need to look for yourself."

I gloved up and followed Slim into the house.

We smelled the body before we actually saw it. I'm no forensic expert, but I've smelled rotting meat before, and I figured whoever's remains we would run across had been dead for at least a couple of days. It's amazing how quickly we fall from the top of the food chain to the bottom once our vital processes cease. On a really hot day, I've seen a corpse bloat like a birthday balloon in a matter of hours, and you really don't want to be in the room when they split open like a bratwurst on a hot grill.

We found Ram-Billy sitting, more or less, at a rolltop desk in an office off the family room—though, in his case, perhaps a better word than "family" might have been more suitable, since the idea of someone actually living with him long enough to procreate was laughable.

From the neck down, save for a trail of dried blood and im-mediately unidentifiable gore that cascaded down his back and the front of his shirt, he appeared more or less normal. Above the neck was a different matter. His head had been cloven. Like a log split by a maul, it had been hewn in half, and hung in two large portions to the left and right of his midline, each half of his head resting on one shoulder.

"See what I mean?" Slim said. "I figure it's Ram-Billy, but I'll be damned if I'd swear to it in a court of law."

"Yeah," I said. "This death certainly seems to fall into the category of the unnatural. Let's backtrack and call Don Webb, see how quickly he can get a forensic team over here. Don't know about you, Harvey, but I'm in a little over my head here."

An hour later, the house swarmed with guys in yellow hazmat suits and masks, as Slim and I sat in rockers on the porch chatting with Don Webb.

Like me, Webb had eschewed uniforms. He wore a lightweight wool suit with a yellow silk tie he'd loosened in the late spring heat. I'd known Don for over thirty years. He'd been my history teacher when I attended high school, and had only turned to law enforcement after putting in his time for state retirement. Now close to seventy, he'd been the sheriff in Bliss County for almost a dozen years, and a damned fine one at that.

He settled into the remaining rocking chair after exiting the house, and waved at some troublesome gnats that buzzed around his face.

"Now, that's dead," he said.

"Surprised to see you respond to this call yourself," I said.

"Slow day in Morgan. Besides, how often do you get to run on a nice juicy murder? How'd he get discovered anyway?"

"He had a Brazilian cleaning woman," Slim said. "She's been keeping the place up weekly for five, six years now, and she had a key. Today was her day to clean. She walked in, took one look, walked right back out, and called it in."

"I don't suppose she might be a good suspect."

"Not likely," I said. "She gave us a list of her employers, and she's been working in Pooler for the past several days. We know where to find her if we need to ask some questions."

"What's the story on this guy?"

"Ramsey William Pressley," I said. " 'Bout everyone around here calls him Ram-Billy. He's from an old Prosperity family. He was in his thirties when I was in high school, so I reckon he's somewhere in his early sixties now."

"Sixty-four," Webb said. "One of the techs pulled his wallet and checked the license. What I meant to ask is why someone might want to do . . . you know—*that* to him?"

Slim chimed in. "Hell, Sheriff, you want to put together a list of people held a grudge against Ram-Billy, you might as well grab yourself a telephone book. That's the most hated man in all of Prosperity."

"Why?"

"He's always been as mean as cat shit, pardon my French," Slim continued. "Has more money than God, including the first nickel he ever stole, I reckon."

"He was a thief?" Webb asked.

"Not exactly," I said. "Ram-Billy was born to money. He didn't want for anything most of his life. Acquiring more money became sort of a sport for him. He lived to sue people."

"You mean like in lawsuits?"

"Torts, specifically," I said. "When it comes to pain and suffering, old Ram-Billy appears to have been a sensitive fellow. He'd sue because he found gristle in a restaurant steak. If he hired some poor handyman to do repairs on this lovely house of his and he didn't like the way they turned out, he'd sue the poor guy to get his money back and for additional damages. Lately, I hear, he'd been suing telemarketers. Had his telephone put on the Do Not Call list, and when people did call, he'd trace them back, find out who their agents were, and sue both the telemarketers and their customers."

"You can do that?" Webb asked.

"Seems you can get up to a couple thousand per incident going after telemarketing scofflaws in small claims court."

"How'd you know about that?"

"Overheard it last time I testified in court in Morgan. Of course, that was more than a half year ago. Lord knows what he's found to sue people over lately."

"But it wasn't about the money?"

"It was about winning," I said. "Lawsuits were entertainment

tor roughly half the size of a Louisville Slugger. I recognized the bedroom. More than that, I recognized the woman.

"Well, I'll be damned," I said. "Nice to make your acquaintance, Ms. Guthrie."

"Who?" Webb asked.

"Missing person case here in Prosperity. She's somehow mixed up with Cantrell, that puke from Homeland Security you met a couple of years ago."

"Sleazier and sleazier. So this woman's disappeared?"

"Along with her husband. Don't suppose your boy Lee Mathis is available right now."

Mathis arrived about a half hour after the coroner's office wheeled Ram-Billy out the front door on a gurney and loaded him into a transport. It was a bit of a chore for them, since second rigor had set in, and he made for quite a hump in the body bag.

"Is Carla Powers still the medical examiner in Morgan?" I asked one of them.

"Sure is."

"Tell her I'll get in touch in a day or so to follow up on this case, will you?"

"Sure thing, Chief."

Sheriff Webb and I lounged on the front porch, watching the sun descend behind a copse of box elders and black cherry trees at the outer edge of Ram-Billy's lot, until Mathis drove up. We directed him to the computer. Some of the CSI techs were still processing the site, but the office itself had been completed.

"The deceased was looking at this porn site when he was killed," I told Mathis, pointing at the computer screen. "When we opened it, I found the owner of that computer I had you hack last week."

"No shit."

"Well, actually, I believe that computer belonged to her husband, but yeah, this is the woman who disappeared. I'm trying to figure out what she's doing on this website."

"Looks like masturbation to me," Mathis said.

"Not what she's *doing*. Why is she there? How'd this film of her get on the site? It can't be live—that is, it wasn't live when the victim was killed. This is the bedroom in her house here in Prosperity, and she and her husband haven't been there in almost a month."

"Not surprising," Mathis said. "Some of these sites use live streaming, but all of the films on this site appear to be recorded. In fact, they might have been live streamed at some point, and these are . . . well, reruns."

"Is there any way to find out where the film came from?"

"Why?"

"Because there's another computer missing from their house. I think it was stored in her bedroom dresser, and this was filmed in her bedroom. If she recorded this using her laptop webcam, and we can identify it somehow . . ."

"I get you," Mathis said. "We can look for other activity from that computer and track its location. That's a good idea, Chief!"

"That would make my first one today, I suppose. Can you do it? Find the computer?"

"I can try. You see, every computer hooked to the Internet has a specific IP address."

"You've already lost me."

"It's kind of like a VIN number on an automobile. Like a fingerprint. No two IP addresses are the same. I can do several things here, and any one of them might lead you to her computer. First, I can note the website URL and find out who owns it by going through WHOIS."

"Who is?"

"Yes. It's a way to find out who is registered as the owner of any domain name. That's the URL. Then, I can trace the origin of the particular server from which this site originated. It's possible that these individual frames and films are streaming from other servers. I can get you a list of those IP addresses, and you may be able to track activity on them, even find their physical location . . ."

I had no idea what he was talking about, but he seemed confident, so I let him talk.

"How long will that all take?" I said, after he spouted another half minute of techobabble.

"A few minutes. Maybe a half hour."

"We'll wait," I said.

CHAPTER EIGHTEEN

Shug Burch picked up the shot of George Dickel and dropped it into a mug of Budweiser. He always loved watching the russet liquor flow like liquid smoke into the amber brew. After savoring the anticipation, he raised the Depth Charge and took a long draft.

His dinner club, Shug's Nashville, had opened three days before, and business was predictably brisk, fueled by an advertising campaign that had cost upward of six figures—money from a source that still troubled Burch when he stopped to think about it. The main attraction, of course, was Shug himself. Each evening, he posted up at the bar, ready to greet any fan who dared to walk up and offer a hand and an introduction.

His name had attracted several strong B-list country-pop acts, including a couple of TV reality show runners-up. He'd hired a Cordon Bleu–trained chef to run his kitchen, which produced a menu strongly tilted toward grilled beef and chicken, catering to a crowd that largely wouldn't know which end of a lobster to chew on.

"Life is good," he said, to nobody in particular.

"Need something, boss?" the bartender, a recently minted communications major from N.C. State who had played football there, but had raised zero interest in the NFL draft, asked as Shug's voice rumbled across the bar like thunder rolling over a mountain.

"Me, Bobby? What on earth could I ask for what I don't

already got?"

"Nothing I can think of, sir, but I'm not known for my imagination."

"That's why I hired you, boy. You work hard and don't ask deep questions. Pull yourself a draft on me."

"Thank you, Mr. Burch. Mighty nice of you."

One of the bouncers, another failed football hero from Alabama named Andre Bowman, leaned in toward Shug at the bar.

"Mr. Burch, there's a woman here says you offered her a job." He pointed toward the reservation desk at the front of the house.

Shug checked her out, but didn't recognize her.

"She give you a name?"

"No, but she had a card she said you gave her."

Shug took another look, but still couldn't place her. He pulled himself from the barstool.

"Thanks, Andre. I'll talk to her."

He walked to the front of the restaurant, where the woman stood looking over a menu. As he drew near, he realized that she was Lily, the woman he'd picked up hitching a few nights earlier. It surprised him because he had a hard time reconciling the woman he saw now with the road-worn, prematurely sun-aged and slightly desperate woman he'd let out of the car to get some food.

This woman wore a crisp white blouse tucked into new designer jeans that cinched her waist like a corset, accentuating the curve of her hips and butt and her full bosom. She'd spent some time on her hair and makeup. She reminded him of a woman he'd once seen perform on a triple bill with him in an auditorium in Biloxi, who went on to become the star of a couple of Hollywood movies.

"Miss Lily?" He extended his hand.

She grasped it lightly, but he could feel calluses on her palm and an abrasive roughness in her fingers. This was a woman who had put in more than a day or two of hard work. That was a good sign.

"You remember me?"

"You made an impact on me. I trust you got yourself a good meal?"

"You gave me nearly two hundred dollars," she said. "I don't wish to sound proud, but I don't like sleeping in shelters. I've been robbed in more than one. So I found a cheap motel room for a couple of nights while I considered your offer of employment. The motel was small and needs redecorating, but it was clean and I felt safe there."

"Unlike the way you felt in my car."

She diverted her eyes toward the stage. "I am ashamed of my behavior, sir. I trusted too much in rumors and things I'd read in magazines, and when you were kind enough to give me money and ask nothing in return, I cried myself to sleep thinking of how cruel I had been."

Shug couldn't tell for certain whether she was bullshitting him.

"I don't care to live on handouts," she continued. "I have worked in establishments like this in my life and, if you were serious about helping me find work here, I would like to first work off the money you gave me."

"That's not necessary. I think we can find a place for you. What have you done in the past?"

"Waiting tables. Bartending. Cleaning. Pretty much all of it. I've even done a little cooking, but nothing as fancy as you have on this menu."

Shug leaned against the front desk and surveyed her again.

"Where have you cooked?"

"I spent four months on the line at a Waffle House in Toccoa, Georgia."

"You don't mind me saying, Miss Lily, a woman handsome as you would be wasted behind the kitchen doors here. Come with me."

He led her to the bar, and held up the divider so she could walk behind it. Then he sat on his usual stool.

"Okay," he said. "I have a hankerin' for a top flight margarita. Reckon you can rustle one up for me, quick-like?"

She surveyed the collection of bottles lined up on shelves in front of the mirror, and swiftly selected some Anejo silver tequila, triple sec, and a dark bottle of Grand Marnier. She grabbed a lime sliver and wiped it around the rim of a pint stout glass.

"You didn't say whether you wanted that on the rocks or frozen," she said.

"Rocks. Frozen drinks are for sissies."

"Salt?"

"What's a margarita without salt?"

She dipped the rim of the glass in a small tray of kosher salt, and set it aside. He expected her to start by mixing the tequila and triple sec, but instead she took an aluminum shaker half and dropped in five or six lime quarters and a couple of teaspoons of sugar.

"We got sour mix under the counter," Bobby said.

"The gentleman requested a top-flight margarita," Lily said. "Can't make that with sour mix."

She muddled the lime and sugar together for a few seconds, and then poured in two jiggers of tequila, a half jigger of triple sec, and a little bit of mineral water. She assembled the shaker and mixed the ingredients vigorously, and then strained them into the glass. She topped the drink with a splash of Grand Marnier, garnished the glass with a lime wedge, and slipped a

145

cocktail straw into it before deftly placing in front of Burch.

"Your margarita, sir. I hope it meets with your approval."

He took a sip, and set it back on the bar.

"Where'd you learn to make a margarita like that?"

"New Orleans, sir. I worked in a floating casino for a few months. The master bartender there taught me. They called that a Jackpot Margarita."

"What did they charge for it?"

"I seem to recall it was about ten dollars."

"We'll put it on the menu and charge twelve. You've got yourself a job, if you want it."

For the first time, she dared to smile. Her face brightened like daybreak, and Burch noticed that her eyes were a deep green.

"I do appreciate it, sir, and I hope my work will be satisfying."

"Oh," he said. "I'm certain it will."

CHAPTER NINETEEN

"According to WHOIS, the website is owned by a company named Debuchke, Limited," Mathis said, after a few minutes of checking Ram-Billy's computer.

"Sounds Russian," Don Webb said.

"The missing woman is Russian. Well, Lithuanian, but it's all former Soviet bloc states over there," I said. "Wonder how many of these other women on this site are from Central Asia?"

"Hard to say," Mathis answered. "If you drill down, you'll probably find dozens of pages in here. Could take weeks to track back every ID."

"I'm interested in Natalya," I said. "What about that video? Can you track it?"

"I can try," Mathis said, and he turned back to the screen.

Don and I retreated to the porch. There was still an aroma of corruption in the house to which Mathis, in his concentration, appeared to be immune. Having learned years earlier that all smells are particulate, and realizing that every time I breathed in that house I was pulling little putrefied bits of Ram-Billy into my snorter, made me want to avoid the interior as much as possible. The guy had been insufferable in life. I didn't want to carry microscopic pieces of him in my head for a couple of weeks.

"So, how's my patrolman Stu Marbury working out for you in Morgan?" I asked Webb.

"Great. Of course, he's new, which means he's trying to make a good impression, but I can tell you trained him well. He'll be a good deputy. I hear you're looking for a couple of new people."

"Took myself off the line. I mostly handle the administrative stuff now, and this . . ." I thumbed back toward the house.

"Probably not a bad idea. You're not a pup anymore. Better to leave the heavy lifting to the kids."

"If I hadn't known you for almost thirty years, I'd consider taking that as an insult," I said.

"Unless . . ."

"Go on."

"Judd, I knew you as a boy, and I've known you as a man, and I know how much you love the badge and the uniform. How much did getting shot take out of you?"

"What have you heard?"

"I don't pay attention to gossip."

"People are talking?"

"They always talk. That's what people do."

I watched as a trio of bicyclists paraded in front of Ram-Billy's house. They were dressed in skin-tight spandex and wore helmets that might have been fashioned for alien skulls. The conversation was headed in a direction I had scrupulously avoided for weeks, and I desperately wanted to change the subject. At the same time, the man sitting beside me might be the only person within twenty miles who could truly understand and empathize with my condition—save, perhaps, for my shrink.

Even Dr. Kronenfeld might have a difficult time comprehending what goes through the mind of a lawman when he questions his nerve. He might understand the symptoms of trauma, and the processes by which a person withdraws from that terrible brink, but he can't know the sense of loss that comes when your life cuts an acute corner and you find yourself deep in the unmapped land without clues. Take away Superman's ability to fly and see through walls and leap tall buildings with a single bound, and you're left with a man of noble intentions and heroic aspirations, but few means by which to realize them. When a man of the badge finds himself facing down a bad guy and his heart races and sweat runs down his brow, it signals the loss of the confidence that makes him intimidating and, whether we wish to admit it or not, intimidation is a coin of the realm for cops.

"It was tough," I said. "Still is."

"Not surprising. You almost died."

"I don't recall most of that."

"I do. I visited you several times in the hospital. You were never awake. To tell you the truth, I believed as I watched you lie there, your breath controlled by a wheezing machine next to your bed, that if you lived you'd never pin on the badge again. You surprised me. You surprised a lot of people."

I checked behind me to see whether anyone might be eavesdropping, and then I lowered my voice.

"Can I tell you something, Don?"

"Something you don't want repeated?"

"I'd prefer it that way."

"What is it?"

"I . . . I got the yips. That's why I'm in civvie clothes. I stopped some redneck over near the high school for blowing a stop sign. He was digging in his glove compartment for his registration, and I thought he was going to come out with a gun."

"Every cop's worst fear."

"I panicked. We're talking pounding heart, flop sweat, chest pains, dimming vision, the whole package. I wrote him a ticket and I sent him on his way, and then I almost handed in my badge. The mayor convinced me to stay on as an administrative chief and handle special investigations. Twenty years in the field, and I never felt like that before. You remember last year, when

149

Alvin Cross killed your deputy?"

"Kind of hard to forget."

"It was the middle of a frog strangler thunderstorm. Lightning was flashing right and left. Rain was coming down in buckets, and I was faced off against a career criminal asshole with a twelve-gauge. I look back on that, and I don't remember fear. It's like being afraid wasn't part of the equation. Now, I get dreams at night. Not about Alvin Cross and thunderstorms, but about—other stuff. Everyday cop stuff that turns out bad."

"We deny it, Judd, but we are in a dangerous line of work. Catches up with most cops sooner or later. Stress is a killer."

"Has it caught up with you?"

"I'm an elected official. It's not the same. My job is to run the sheriff's department. You ever see me in a uniform? I don't patrol and I don't arrest, and when all is said and done I hardly ever even lay eyes on a bad guy, except once in a while in the courtroom. You've always been a street cop, a hands-on kind of guy. I recall last year, when that imbecile was holed up in his firetrap shitbox house after trying to kill one of my deputies, and you drove around in your cruiser to pick the deputy up and bring him back to the ambulance. Balls, man. Big fuckin' brass ones. Never saw anything like that in my life outside a TV show. Remember what you told me that day? You'd been talking to that cretin on the phone, and you said you *heard* it in his voice. You said, 'He don't want to die today. I'll be safe.' "

"And, as I recall, I also told you that if he shot me you were to turn his shack and him into a rancid memory."

"I'd have done it. I didn't have to agree to it. You went in knowing we had your back. Must be tough to be you these days, walking around with no backup at all."

"I wouldn't say that."

"Me either. I was being sarcastic. I'm so old now, everything I say sounds that way. You got more people holding you up than most folks deserve. There's Donna and that walking nightmare patrolman of yours, Slim Tackett, and your buddy the mayor. I can't run into a town councilman from Prosperity without him bending my ear and telling me how happy they are you're making such a great recovery."

"What's your point?"

"What difference does it make if you're out of uniform nowadays? Hell, you put in your time. In a lot of places cops retire after a couple of decades on the job. Hire yourself a coupla young, kick-ass kids out of the academy, or maybe with a year or so under their belt, and teach 'em how to do things your way. You got a sweet little town here in Prosperity, and a lot of really bad things haven't happened over the last ten years mostly because you've been around to prevent them. Way I figure it, you've earned some desk time. Let somebody else do the heavy lifting for a change."

Lee Mathis slammed the front screen door and settled into the rocking chair Slim had vacated.

"Now, this is strange," he said. "I did some research on the owners of that shaft-stroker website Ram-Billy was staring at when he got his head split. Like a lot of websites, it's owned by a subsidiary of a larger holding company. This one is registered to some company named Baltic Babes Enterprises."

"Supports the idea that most of the ladies on there are Russian. Or at least Russian-connected," Webb said.

Mathis continued. "The primary address of the company is in Estonia, so nothing much useful there."

"You gonna lay the *strange* on us sometime soon?" I asked.

"Oh, yeah. This is good. They also have an address of an American agent. A lot of foreign countries do that, for legal purposes, establishment of bank accounts, that sort of thing. So I checked this American agent's address, and it's local."

I sat up in my chair. "Here in Prosperity?"

"Here on this porch," Mathis said, grinning. "Ram-Billy, it seems, is—or at least *was*—the American agent for Baltic Babes Enterprises. He was looking at his own website!"

Chapter Twenty

Shug Burch had moved from his seat at the bar to a table near the back of the club—the better, he reasoned, to hear the act he had booked for that evening, a regional rockabilly group who had recently signed a contract with one of the largest recording companies in the country.

As they wrapped their first set, Lily walked over and stood by him.

"Miss Lily," he said. "It occurred to me that I don't even know your last name."

"Holder."

"Lily Holder. Everything working out for you behind the bar? You getting your feet under you?"

"Everything is fine, sir. I wanted to ask if you need anything."

"There was a time when I'd be getting started on the evening's drinking right about now. These days, if I don't put away the hard stuff by nine o'clock, my stomach will have me rolling back and forth in bed all night. Fella I knew in the jug had an awful stomach, used to give him fits. He was a big, fat guy, had a gut like a rain barrel. I still got washboard abs, can do three hundred crunches without breaking half a sweat, and my stomach tells me when it's time to switch to something less volatile."

"What would you like?"

"How about a tall Arnold Palmer? You know how to make it?"

"Half and half, iced tea and lemonade. Want me to make it in the back, in case some of the audience might think you're goin' soft?"

"Got a mouth on you, too, don't you?"

"I apologize if I offended you."

"No, not at all. Tell you what, Lily Holder. You make it out front at the bar, in front o' God and everybody. Like I give a damn what people think anymore."

"I'll be right back with it."

Shug watched her return to the bar. He was acutely aware of two thoughts. One, a curious assessment of how Lily might look without all her fancy new clothes. The other was an unfamiliar sense of embarrassment that he might harbor the notion.

He was still trying to figure out why such strange self-conscious ideas were running through his head when he caught sight of Boyd Overhultz near the door next to the bar that led to Shug's upstairs office. He was disheveled and unwashed as usual, which made Shug glad that he hadn't tried to come directly over to the table. Allowing a lowlife like Boyd Overhultz to walk around a nice place like Shug's Nashville without a leash had to violate some kind of city ordinance, and it sure would be bad for business. Boyd jerked his head back, silently beckoning him. Shug rose from his table, and sauntered over to the bar.

"Miss Lily, I need to have a word with a man up in my office. I'd be obliged if you'd bring that drink up there," he said.

"Right away, sir," she said, but even before the words were out he had turned and headed for the exit.

A few minutes later, he closed the door to block out the sound from the floor below.

"I need to get in touch with the Russian," Boyd said.

"So call him."

"He isn't answering his calls."

"And you think I got some kind of hotline to reach him? You should know better. If he ain't answering his phone, it's because he don't want to talk to you. Have you pissed him off again?"

"I don't know, but bad things are happening. You hear about Ram-Billy?"

"No."

"He's dead! I was out to his place only two days ago. I had to get some money to him today and there was cop cars all over the place and they was wheeling a body out on a stretcher."

"Doesn't mean it's Ram-Billy. Maybe some poor census taker was stupid enough to knock on Ram-Billy's door and got shot for his trouble."

"No, it was him! I watched from the street several houses over, and that cop from Prosperity? The one who pulled me over a few weeks ago? He was on the front porch talking with the sheriff for a long time, and I ain't never seen Ram-Billy nowhere. I tell ya, Shug, he's done got killed!"

"That's too bad if he did."

"So I need to talk with the Russian."

"Can't help you, Boyd."

There was a knock at the door. When Shug opened it, he saw Lily holding a tray with a tall glass of tea and lemonade.

"I'm sorry for the delay," she said. "I've never been up here before and I wasn't sure which room was your office. Here's your drink."

She slipped a napkin on Shug's desk and placed the tea on it. When she straightened up, she glanced through the picture window overlooking the club floor.

"My goodness, Mr. Burch. You can see everything from here."

"Yes, Miss Lily. It's quite a view. If you don't mind, I need to finish my conversation with Mr. Overhultz here."

"Of course, sir. Please let me know if you need anything else."

155

She held the tray under one arm and closed the door as she left.

"Shit-fire, Shug. Where'd you find that one?"

"She's new."

"You get a good look at the tits on her?"

"You're speaking disrespectfully of one of my employees, Boyd."

"I'm sorry. Didn't mean nothin' by it. Didn't know you was tappin' that."

"What?" The menace in Shug's voice was unmistakable.

"Seems like I can't say nothin' right today, and I'm sorry for that. I'm worried that the Russian might have done Ram-Billy, and he might have a go at me, too."

"Why would he do that, except on the general principle of thinning the herd and cleaning the atmosphere?"

"Who else would do it? Kill Ram-Billy, I mean."

"Pretty much anyone who ever met him."

"All I know is that the Russian was really angry at him last week. Then he told me to take this money by Ram-Billy's place today. You think he had Ram-Billy zipped, and then wanted to set me up for it?"

"You been in Ram-Billy's place before?"

"Sure. Lots of times."

"You ever touch anything?"

"I reckon I did."

"Then it don't matter what the Russian does. You'll be hearing from the cops shortly. You got a record, Boyd. Your prints are on file. Soon as they collect all their evidence, I figure you're going to be the first person they pay a call on. Scoot, now. I don't know where the Russian is, and I got a fine band downstairs I want to listen to."

"But what am I gonna do?"

"Like I give a shit? Don't come around here again without

calling first. Your presence in my office makes me want to set off a bug bomb. If I were you, I'd get real scarce until this Ram-Billy thing blows over."

Outside the office, Lily tried not to make much noise as she turned and headed back down the stairs. She hadn't intended to listen to the conversation, but the walls and doors of Shug's office were paper-thin. Now she wished she had minded her own business.

CHAPTER TWENTY-ONE

"Ram-Billy Pressley was a pornographer?" Donna asked, amazed.

"Can't say yet," I said, as I sliced a sweet Vidalia onion to go with the hamburgers I was planning to slap on the grill. "I've run into these holding companies before. Some guy needs to shelter some money, or maybe he wants to invest in something that's going to grow faster than the stock market, so he starts diversifying—you know, Laundromats, car washes, self-serve frozen yogurt places, businesses that take a minimum of supervision with a maximum profit potential. Each business has a different name. Some of them sprout their own diversified businesses. After a while it's as hard to follow as untangling a briar patch. Investors smell an opportunity, and they show up offering to pour money into the ventures. Off flies another subsidiary. From what I hear, Internet porn is big business. I did a web search when I got back to the office this afternoon. Most resources estimate that one in eight websites are porn-based. Gotta be some bucks in it."

"But Ram-Billy must have known what he owned."

"Maybe it didn't matter as long as the money kept pouring in. He was always sort of a bottom-line guy. Where the money came from wasn't as important as the fact that it came."

I staggered the sliced onions on a plate and started to slice an heirloom tomato to stack alongside them. Going back to work had stimulated my appetite, and on the way home I'd found myself fantasizing about a huge juicy burger. I had to be careful. Eating like this would turn me into a rotund southern cop in no time flat.

"Maybe he was killed because of the porn site," Donna said.

"I don't know why he was killed. Could be a coincidence. Ram-Billy pissed off half the county at one time or another. I figure there are plenty of folks around who won't miss him, and a lot of them are going to regret they didn't get a chance to take part in dispatching him to the next life. The thing about Natalya was intriguing."

"That is strange. On the other hand, maybe there is a connection there. A Russian mail-order bride goes missing along with her husband, and a movie about her turns up on a porn site which happens to be partly owned by a man who's been murdered."

I covered the plate with some plastic wrap and placed it in the refrigerator, washed my hands in the kitchen sink, and said, "That, my lovely, is what we refer to in the cop business as clues. Tomorrow, I'll try to find out who Ram-Billy's partners are in Debuchke, Limited."

"You think one of them could have killed him?"

"I think I don't know, and I know that what I don't know is important. You want mayonnaise or mustard on your burger?"

"Mayo. Is the fire ready?"

"I'm using chunk charcoal, and it's been ashing over for about a half hour. Stuff makes for one hot fire. I can put the burgers on any time."

"Will it stay hot for a while?"

"A couple of hours."

She put her arms around my waist and pulled me close. I leaned down and kissed her. Seven years together, and she still made my heart race.

"I'm so glad you've got your appetite back," she said, after coming up for air. "Anything else you have a hankering for?"

Surprising myself, I picked her up in my arms and headed toward the back of the house, where we slept.

"Hell," I said, "it'll only take ten minutes to cook the burgers. I figure the fire can wait for a bit."

I placed her on the bed and kissed her a while longer, as my hands ran across her back and her legs. It was warm enough for her to wear shorts, and I easily slid my hand up her thigh and under her pants. She arched her back a bit to help, as she let a small contented murmur escape her lips. She explored with her hand, tugged at my belt, and quickly had my fly open, and her hand found me and caressed with an urgency I hadn't experienced for a while.

We undressed each other, piece by piece, until there were no clothes to remove. She kissed my neck and my shoulders and then my chest. I allowed my fingers to stroke her. She was wet with anticipation, but something told me she didn't want to rush. She slid her mouth down my stomach, kissing as she went, and then she reached my waist, and she took me in her mouth and grasped me with her fingers, and I believed I might explode right away.

Somehow, I held off, but the pleasure was ecstatic and excruciating at the same time, and then she said, "Now you do me," and I was only too happy to oblige. She writhed on the bed and gasped quietly at first and then more loudly as her excitement grew and she became wetter than I'd felt her in many months.

She grabbed my head and raised it to look into my eyes, and said, "Inside," and that was all she needed to say. A moment later I was deep inside her and she wrapped her legs around my hips and thrust herself against me, her hips bucking as I thrust harder and deeper, and then she cried out and pulled me hard against her and with one hand she held the back of my head and with the other she grabbed my ass and pulled me to her and said, "Don't stop, don't you goddamn stop!"

I didn't stop and few seconds later she moaned and screamed again and it was too much for me and I felt something let loose deep inside and every muscle in my body tensed as my vision turned red and I felt myself spasm and flow into her, and then we rolled over on our sides and held each other so closely that it seemed as if we were one person, as we gasped for air and the sweat that soaked our skin began to cool in the air pushed by the overhead fan.

I could feel the pounding of her heart through her chest, and she buried her face in the place where my shoulder meets my neck and she kissed me again. My breath slowed and I kissed her again and told her how much I loved her and had missed being with her in such a primordial and human way and she laughed a little and said that now I had no excuse and then she said, "I love you," over and over, accenting each with a kiss or a nibble, and after a few moments we both began to drift in that endorphin-driven after-sex languor, but we didn't let go of one another, and we dozed clinging to each other as if our lives depended on it.

After a few minutes, she inhaled deeply, ran her hand down my arm, and said, "Wow."

"Wow," I said, back to her.

"Hot fire."

"Sizzling," I said.

"Scorching. Wanna go again?"

"Ten years ago? Sure."

"I knew I should have gone younger. You know what they say about men. They never grow up. They only wear out."

"I'm not worn out yet."

"Prove it."

"Damn, Donna. I'm not Superman."

"Could have fooled me."

We went on like that for a bit, with a lot of adolescent laughing and some tickling thrown in for spice, and then I promised her a rematch, but first I was famished and the fire would not wait for us forever. We showered together, taking time to assure that soap got *everywhere* and then we dressed and didn't bother drying our hair.

Later, as I flipped the burgers on the grill, where the fire had indeed lasted long enough and was assuredly hot enough, and I glanced over at Donna who sat at the picnic table drinking a limed Corona with condensation streaming down the side of the bottle, and she had this faraway contented dreamy look in her eyes, I realized that I had reached a point in my recovery where I could well and truly claim to be back. It felt good. It felt like coming home.

CHAPTER TWENTY-TWO

Slim was waiting for me when I got to the station the next morning. He and another man sat in the lobby with Sherry. The other man looked like an offensive linebacker with a compulsion for weightlifting, but on second glance I realized that he was much older than your average NFL player. He was black, with hair graying at the temples, and marked crow's-feet surrounding his eyes, which were bloodshot. I had a feeling they were always bloodshot.

"Want you to meet someone," Slim said, before the screen door properly shut. "This here is Delano Sikes, but ever'one calls him Gunny. Gunny, meet Chief Wheeler."

Sikes was on his feet with his hand out in an instant. He had a grasp that felt like I'd slammed my hand in a car door. His hands were rough and calloused.

"Pleasure to meet you," he said, in a voice that put shame to the word *bass*. It was more like distant thunder heard from inside a fifty-gallon drum.

"Some grip," I said.

Sikes seemed embarrassed first, and then stricken.

"Gosh, Chief, I'm sorry. I didn't mean to—"

"It's okay. What can I do for you, Mr. Sikes?"

Slim put a hand on Sikes's shoulder. I think he had to stand on tiptoe to reach.

"I met Gunny about fifteen years ago in Tokyo," he said. "I was an MP, but you already knew that. Gunny was a GI-rine who liked to toss back a few and see how many walls he could knock out of a bar before the roof fell in. Fact is, that's how we ran across one another. He was in the process of dismantling a geisha bar in the Ginza when we got the call to throw a net over him and haul him down to the stockade to sleep it off. Took five of us to wrestle him into the back of a Humvee. That was the first of several encounters. Finally, I caught up with him in a bar one night before he started to get his load on, and we had a heart-to-heart."

"Slim set me straight," Sikes said. "He's a good man. My tour was up in the Crotch, so I decided to change teams. Signed with the Army and Slim got me into the MPs. Finished my twenty there."

"That's why I brought Gunny here today, Chief," Slim added. "After punching out with his military retirement, he went to work with a sheriff's department up in Virginia. He's been a deputy there for a little over a decade now. Seems they elected a new sheriff in those parts, a real asshole—pardon my French— and the new guy decided to clean house. According to Gunny, the new sheriff still thinks it's a shame the North won the Civil War, and he deemed Gunny best suited for bringing him coffee and mowing the lawn. They came to a rapid parting of the ways."

"I could use a job," Sikes said, his reddened eyes locked on my face. "I don't need the money so bad, even if it would help for sure. I'm no kid. I been around the block a few times. I turned fifty last month, and I'm not ready to ride a rocker quite yet. I have a few good years left in me before I punch my ticket and start collecting Social Security and Medicare. I want to keep active. Soldiering and policing are all I know."

Slim said, "I figured, since Stu took off for Don Webb's office over in Morgan, and we ain't exactly been swamped with applications for his slot, maybe you'd consider giving Gunny a trial run as a peace officer here in Prosperity."

I glanced over at Sherry. She'd been sitting in the office with Slim and Sikes for a while, and I imagined she had formed an opinion of Sikes. Sherry doesn't say a lot, but I trust her impressions of people. I saw her give a little nod.

"Tell you what," I said to Sikes. "Let's start this whole thing off using the right procedure. Sherry, why don't you give Mr. Sikes an application to fill out, while I have a little talk with Slim back in my office. Please, have a seat, Mr. Sikes."

"Please," he said. "Call me Gunny. Everyone does."

"All right. Please fill out the application, Gunny. I want to talk with Slim for a bit, and then we'll see what's what."

I led Slim back to my office, and shut the door. As he was in the habit of doing, he waited until I sat at my desk before taking a seat himself. He didn't wait for me to speak.

"He's a good cop, Chief. I know he's a little intimidating."

"He's a fucking Bigfoot," I said.

"Ain't he? His rowdy days are way behind him, though. He'll scare the crap out of the scofflaws, but he's as peaceful as they come. I got him in a program back in Tokyo—you wanna know how hard it is to find an AA meeting in Japan?"

"No."

"It's hard. But we found one, and I got him signed up. He's been clean and sober ever since. Got a twenty-year chip to prove it. Once he got in the MPs, he took to police work like it was his nature. Up until this new sheriff got elected back in his county in Virginia, he had a spotless record."

"Meaning it isn't so spotless now."

"Well, he didn't so much quit as he was asked to leave."

"Asked?"

"That's the official story, yeah. There was some dustup about turning the sheriff's car over on its side."

"His *car?*"

"It sounds worse than it was. It was one of them teeny little cars. A Mini Cooper, if I heard it right, and Gunny had a little help. He's not dangerous. And, the way I hear tell, that sheriff was asking for it."

I leaned back in my chair and stared at the ceiling while I mulled things over. Slim was right. I did need a patrolman. Actually, I needed two, since I wasn't driving a cruiser or wearing the uniform anymore. It would be easy enough to check Sikes's record. Slim was a good cop—actually, he was a *great* cop. If it had been Slim instead of Stu who'd taken off for the Bliss County Sheriff's Department, I probably wouldn't have come back on the job after being shot. I trusted Slim in a way I never had with Stu Marbury. Stu was a good cop and a dependable employee, but he wasn't born to the badge the way Slim was.

"You vouch for this man," I said, without looking away from the ceiling.

"Like I'd vouch for you, Chief."

"You believe he's a good match for this department?"

"A first class match. I think he'll make you proud."

"I suppose I owe you a favor from somewhere along the line."

"I wouldn't go that far," Slim said. "But if you hire Gunny, I'll sure owe *you* one."

"If he can do the job, we'll be jake."

I chewed on it for another minute or so, as Slim sat patiently waiting for my decision. Finally, I stood and walked back out to the lobby. Sikes stood as I rounded the corner. He had the completed application in his hand.

"What do you wear?" I said. "You run about a fifty-two long in a shirt?"

"Fifty-six, sir, but I've been working out. I take a forty-two waist in my khakis."

"So you're in shape."

"Want to hold a pushup contest here in your lobby, Chief?"

"You'd win, I reckon. I'm still recuperating from some injuries."

"So Slim told me. I'm sorry to hear about you getting shot."

I took the application from him and scanned it. It listed three jobs in the previous thirty years, two with the Marines and the Army, and the one as a sheriff's deputy. If nothing else, it pointed to a consistent employment record.

"I need you to study up on the North Carolina General Statutes," I said. "Sherry will give you a copy before you leave. I'll check your work record and give a call to your references, but let's say you'll start tomorrow doing some ride-alongs with Slim, so he can get you acquainted with the area. Would that suit you?"

"It sure would, Chief Wheeler. I won't let you down."

"Slim says you're the real deal," I said. "That's good enough for me. He can tell you where to get your uniforms. We'll reimburse you through the uniform allowance in your first paycheck. We'll say you're on probationary status for now. You have a place to stay?"

"He's bunking at my house for the moment," Slim said.

"All right, then," I said, holding out my hand. "Let's see how things work out. Good to have you on board."

He shook my hand so hard, I thought I heard crunching.

I'd already accomplished one major task, and it was only a little after nine. I decided to check another job off my list for the day.

I placed a call to Cantrell in Pooler.

"You got any problem with me investigating a certain murder here in Prosperity involving a man named Ramsey William Pressley?" I asked, as I stirred some artificial creamer and some no-calorie sweetener into my coffee.

"Why would I have a problem with that?"

"Just checking. I wouldn't want to step on any federal toes, you know."

"You jackin' me off, Chief? Because this feels like you're trying to give me shit over this Natalya Gromykova thing."

"Wouldn't think of it. Consider this a courtesy call. You have a nice day."

I didn't wait for him to answer, and I cradled the receiver.

I leaned back in my chair and sipped my coffee. It wasn't terrible, considering. I'd learned a couple of things from my telephone call. The first was that Cantrell might have a tight lid on the Natalya Guthrie disappearance, but he either didn't know she was moonlighting as an Internet stroke goddess, or he wasn't aware of any connection between her and Ram-Billy.

I'd also learned there was probably a player in this story about whom I wasn't yet aware, which meant that I needed to look a little more closely into this whole Debuchke, Limited business.

Since Ram-Billy was listed as Debuchke's American agent at his address in Prosperity, I figured the company should be listed with the Bliss County Register of Deeds.

I called my contact there, a nice spinster about ten years older than me named Jeannie Klug.

"I've told you before, Judd, you want to ask me out you can't call me at the office."

"Jeannie, if I weren't already taken by the most wonderful woman on earth, you'd be the first I'd call."

"Bullshit," she said, and sniffed.

"Why, Miss Jeannie, how you do talk."

"What can I do for you?" she asked.

"Guess you heard about Ram-Billy Pressley."

"Read it in the paper this morning. Awful thing. Was it terribly gory?"

"Worse."

"Well, good then. I hate to be one to speak ill of the dead, but I never had any use for Ram-Billy. He was always rude and brusque, and the one time I asked him out he laughed at me."

"You do realize that harboring a grudge against him makes you a suspect, right?"

"You'll use up this life and two more interrogating everyone in this county who hated that man," she said. "Give me a call when you get around to me. I'll wait. I know you're not calling me to pass the time of day. What can I do for you?"

"Ram-Billy was the American agent for a Lithuanian holding company named Debuchke, Limited."

"Want to spell that for me?"

I did, and said, "From what I can gather, it's either a straight-out corporation or an LLC. Wanted to check to see if there are any other officers with that company listed with the county."

"You want to hold or should I call you back?"

"Will it take long?"

"Not now that we have computers. I was looking for an excuse to ring you up. Here we go. Debuchke, Limited does list an American office under Ram-Billy's name, and if I drill down a little . . . okay, it seems as if Billy was the only American officer of the company, but it also lists the officers of the Lithuanian home company."

"Can you fax that over to me?"

"Sure. Anything else?"

"Could you do a couple more searches for me?"

"For you, Judd darlin', I got all day."

"I'd like to know what other companies Ram-Billy owned, and I'd also like to know which companies these foreign officers of his companies owned, if they're local."

"No problem. I can search by directors' names. What say I try to get this all to you by lunch?"

I told her that would be terrific.

I might not have years of experience as an investigator, having spent most of my time on the job handing out traffic tickets, leading funeral processions, and responding to domestic disputes, along with the occasional vandalism, creeper, petty theft, or assault call, but I had learned one thing over the previous several years as Prosperity police chief. The difference between solving a case and not solving it typically boils down to the ratio between what you know and what you don't know. The less you don't know, the more likely you are to get your man.

Based on that premise, my next call was to the Bliss County Clerk of Courts office. I reached an adenoidal man named Horace Tate.

"I'm investigating a murder here in Bliss County," I told him. "I need a list of small claims torts filed by a fellow named Ramsey William Pressley over the last six months."

"Ram-Billy?" Tate said. "Heard he got himself killed."

"That's right. So I could use that information as quickly as you can round it up."

"Geez, Chief, pulling every claim made by Ram-Billy could take half a day. Seems he's been in here four times a week long's I can recall."

"Then you might want to get started. Think you can get that to me by, say, right after lunch, Horace?"

"I'll do what I can. Might have to pull in an intern."

"Pull whatever makes you happy," I said.

So, I had covered Ram-Billy's business partners, and the people he'd sued. I was trying to figure out who else might have wanted to plow a furrow in his head when the telephone rang.

"Chief, this is Clint over at the CSI office in Morgan."

I tried to picture Clint, who apparently believed that I knew him on sight. It took a second, but I recalled the image of a gawky red-haired kid with residual adolescent acne.

"Sure, Clint. How are things going on the Pressley case?"

"Sheriff Webb wanted me to call you. We've processed most of the prints we collected in the Pressley house. It's kind of a mess, you know, but we were able to pull several dozen decent latents."

"Any of them interesting?"

"Well, most of them belong to the deceased, of course. I mean, he lived there, right?"

"He did."

"There were some who weren't him. We ran them through AFIS, because the sheriff said he wanted us to put a priority on it. Usually they'd have to wait to be uploaded in the order they came in."

"Tell Sheriff Webb I appreciate the favor. What did you find?"

"There were a lot that weren't in the system. We'll keep them on file. Maybe they'll match to something someday. You never know. We got a hit on a couple of sets. They belong to an ex-con named Boyd Overhultz."

If I had been drinking my coffee, it would have wound up all over my shirt.

"Did you say Boyd *Overhultz*?"

"That's right, Chief. You know him?"

"I've run across him. Looks like I might do so again, real soon. Anything else?"

"Well . . ." he hesitated.

"What is it, Clint?"

"One set apparently raised a red flag up in DC. We got an inquiry back asking why we were looking for that person."

"From who?"

"I couldn't tell you. Sheriff Webb fielded that call. I saw him afterward, and he didn't look none too happy about it."

"I'll give him a buzz. Did you lift any other evidence? Hairs, clothing fibers, anything like that?"

"We did, but that stuff will take days, if not weeks, to process. We're still looking at the head wound, trying to figure what you'd have to hit a guy with to make a crevice that deep. The sheriff told us to let you know as soon as we find anything conclusive."

I thanked him, and filed his face and name in my memory so I'd recognize him the next time we ran across one another at a crime scene. I'd gotten a lot of mileage out of being cordial to the guys who analyzed the evidence over the years.

After hanging up, I called Don Webb.

"What in hell is going on down in Prosperity?" he said, even before saying hello.

"Good question. One of your lab guys told me you got taken to the woodshed by a federal puke."

"Not quite, but you sure pissed in someone's grits up there. Expect they'll call you before the day is out."

"Thanks for the heads-up. Think I'll get out of the office for a few hours. Who called you?"

"I'll give you one guess."

"Cantrell?"

"If you knew, why'd you ask?"

"What did he want?"

"Suppose you heard one of the prints we lifted raised some alarms. He wanted to know where it came from."

"Did you tell him?"

"Sure. I don't need any hassle from DC."

"I already talked with him earlier today. He didn't have any problem with me investigating the Pressley murder."

"Maybe that was before someone from Homeland Security

tied a knot in his dick over the prints."

"Doesn't matter. I have no idea where Natalya Gromykova and her husband are, but I have a no-shit dead body on a table over in Morgan, and Cantrell won't push me off that case. He didn't happen to mention who the prints belonged to, did he?"

"I think the intent of his call was to keep me in the dark about that, Judd."

"I got it. Okay, Don. I really appreciate you fast-tracking the analysis on those prints. I know there isn't much you can do on the DNA testing and such."

"My pleasure, at least until that melon-head Cantrell jumped in my shit."

"First round's on me next time we're out together. How's that?"

"First and second round, and you owe me a steak."

"It's a deal."

I pulled the information on the ticket I'd written Boyd Over-hultz for running the stop sign, and made a note of his address. I was hoping he had skipped his court hearing on the ticket, so I could petition the court for an arrest order, but the date hadn't arrived yet. He lived in Mica Wells, which was out of my jurisdic-tion, but that didn't mean I couldn't drop by and pass the time of day with him, maybe ask him why he'd been fingering things over at Ram-Billy's house, maybe see if he had any alibi for the previous several days.

His prints being in the house meant he was a suspect, and I didn't want to face him down alone. I called Slim on the radio.

"What's up, Chief?"

"I need to talk with a guy who might know how Ram-Billy got killed. It would be nice to have a little backup."

"No problem. You got an address?"

I told him, and he said he'd meet me there.

Since I was planning to face down a man who might have

split Ram-Billy's head in twain, I gave my chest a quick security tap to assure I was still wearing my Kevlar vest.

I climbed into the new cruiser and set the GPS for Overhultz's address. It took me a little over ten minutes to reach Mica Wells over the backcountry roads, and a couple more to find the house Overhultz—probably reluctantly—called home. Slim was parked out front when I arrived. As I pulled up behind him, I noticed that some of the neighbors had stepped out into their yards to see what was going on.

Overhultz's house was old, and not well-kept. The roof had a bow in it, and the front porch canted a touch downhill to the left. Paint was peeling from the Masonite siding. The only thing missing was a lethargic tick hound lazing on the front stoop. There was no car parked in the drive.

Slim stepped out of his cruiser and walked over to my window.

"Seen anyone in the house?" I asked.

"Nope. You want me to walk around back, make sure nobody tries to bolt?"

"Good idea."

As Slim headed toward the rear of the house, I slipped on my Stetson, and made a security check on the pistol on my hip, then slid from the car and walked up to Overhultz's front door.

As I walked, I could feel my chest constrict, and a tremble in my hands. I took a deep breath, trying to relax. The panic wasn't as bad as it had been when I stopped Overhultz several weeks earlier, but I disliked it all the same.

I made a cursory knock, and then another. Nobody came to the door. No sounds emanated from inside the house. I toggled the mike on my shoulder.

"Don't think he's home, Slim."

"Nothing back here, either."

I scribbled a note on one of my office cards asking Overhultz to give me a call when he got a chance, and stuck it in the jamb. As I climbed back into the cruiser, I noticed my anxiety flowing away, and I wondered how long it would be before I'd be comfortable confronting bad guys again.

For the moment, I had run out of people to call, and nobody seemed keen on dropping by to the station to confess, so I cut Slim loose and decided to take a short trip out to Niley Baughess Circle. I had discovered some time back that revisiting the scene of a crime after the first exposure had worn off gave me a perspective on things I might have missed the first time around.

I pulled the crime scene tape off the door and let myself in. Immediately, I heard the buzz of the blowflies that had taken over the house after feasting and reproducing on Ram-Billy's body. The air-conditioning was still running, which was a blessing, as it had pulled most of the smell out of the house.

The pool of blood that had collected around the base of Ram-Billy's chair had turned dark brown, but I could see maggots crawling around in it, which was kind of repulsive. After changing the password, Lee Mathis had removed the computer for further investigation back at the sheriff's department's forensic lab.

I had the presence of mind to glove up before re-entering the house, and I walked about pulling open drawers and cabinets, looking for nothing in particular save for anything that might be out of place or strange.

Besides being a Class A asshole, Ram-Billy seemed to have led something of an ascetic life. There was no beer in the fridge. I couldn't find a liquor cabinet or a wine rack anywhere. The freezer contained mostly box meals. The veggie crisper and the meat tray in his refrigerator were nearly empty, as was the dishwasher.

There were exactly eight place settings of everything in his kitchen cabinets, as if he had bought them all at one time. Eight dinner plates, eight saucers, eight salad plates, eight coffee cups, and when I checked his flatware drawer I found eight dinner forks, salad forks, teaspoons, and eight table knives. Everything was clean and well organized. I would have been shocked to discover that he had to take out more than one of any given implement on any regular basis. Most people wanted to avoid Ram-Billy altogether, and I had a hard time imagining what form of human might wish to sit down to dinner with him.

He had an old thirty-five inch cathode ray tube TV, the kind you can't even buy anymore, let alone get repaired. Despite the fact that he was probably one of Prosperity's most affluent residents, his sofa was worn and dilapidated. Seemed that Ram-Billy had a problem letting go of things.

The rest of the house was similar. Utilitarian, maybe even a little shabby with time, and unexpected for a person with the resources Ram-Billy was known to possess.

I took two tours through, in case I had missed anything the first time around, but nothing jumped out at me. Everything of any use in divining who had put a cleft in Pressley's head had already been spirited away by the lab boys.

I stepped back out onto the porch, and reset the crime tape. As I did, a lawnmower barked into life next door, and a lanky, balding man in a tee shirt and jeans shorts started to cut his grass.

Ram-Billy had erected a fence between the two yards, so I pulled the cruiser around to the neighbor's house. He saw me pull myself from the car and killed the mower.

"Help you?" he said.

"I'm Chief Wheeler, Prosperity police," I said, as I extended my hand.

"You're not in a police uniform."

I pointed to the car, and pulled my jacket lapel aside to show him my badge. "That's one of the perks of being chief. Greater opportunity for sartorial self-expression."

"Huh?"

"I get to wear what I want. You heard about your neighbor?" I pointed toward Ram-Billy's house.

"Saw it on the news last night. Awful thing. You know who did it?"

"Not yet. What's your name?"

"Sam Kincaid."

"Mr. Kincaid, you might be able to help me a little. Did you know Mr. Pressley well?"

"We talked from time to time, but we weren't buddies or anything. He borrowed some tools from me once. Said he needed to do some repairs on his house, didn't own what he needed, and didn't want to get ripped off by contractors."

"Did he get a lot of visitors? Maybe more lately?"

"I really couldn't say. I've been in and out a lot lately myself. Retired from the state last year, and I've been traveling. In fact, I'm headed to the beach again this evening, soon's I get the grass cut."

He had pulled the lawn mower from the garage, and had left the door open. I could see a fancy European cabinetmaker's bench and a wall full of tools.

"You a woodworker?" I asked.

He glanced back at the garage. "Not a serious one. Bought that workbench at an estate auction a few years ago. I'll head out to the garage and bang a few nails from time to time, but it isn't a passion for me."

I saw a band saw in good shape, and a well-tended table saw. A large wood lathe stood in a corner, gathering spider webs. Kincaid, or perhaps a previous owner, had installed cabinets on the garage walls, and pegboards to hang hand tools. There were even outlines drawn around the wire hangers on the pegboards to indicate which tool hung in each space. The whole place seemed almost fussily organized.

"I know a man who's a really serious woodworker. His shop looks a lot like yours."

"Lucky guy, especially if he has the time to devote to it. Was there anything else I can do for you, Chief Wheeler? I'd like to get on the road before the traffic to the beach gets heavy."

"Only another question or two. You recall seeing a shabby brown Buick Riviera in Mr. Pressley's driveway sometime over the last week? It has a peeling vinyl roof and a couple of decent dings in the fenders."

"Now that you mention it, I do recall that car. One of the old Rivieras, with the ducktail fastback. I noticed it because I like cars, and that was one of the first American-made front wheel drives back in the day. Of course, most of them are, now."

"When did you see it here last?"

"Must have been in the last week. Maybe last Friday."

"Not in the last two or three days?"

"Not that I recall, but that doesn't mean it wasn't here. Like I said, I'm in and out a lot lately. You think that car might have something to do with Ram-Billy getting killed?"

"Tying some loose ends. Appreciate your time, Mr. Kincaid."

He yanked the cord to restart the mower, and I returned to the cruiser.

I knew Overhultz had been in the house, and based on what Kincaid had told me, he'd been there within the last week, but I couldn't figure out what confluence of happenstance might bring a lowlife like Overhultz together with Ram-Billy.

I was halfway back to the station when my cell phone chirped. It was Sherry.

"Where are you, Chief?"

"I'm passing the Stop and Rob. What's up?"

"Carla Powers called from Morgan. Says she's finished with

178

the autopsy. She wondered if you could drop by."

"Sure. Have I gotten some faxes from either the Register of Deeds or the Clerk of Courts?"

"Nope. I'll keep an eye out for them. When they come in I'll drop them on your desk."

I pulled a U-turn and headed to Morgan.

Bliss County didn't have enough revenue income to fund a separate medical examiner's office, so they rented space in the basement of Bliss Regional Hospital. In North Carolina, the coroner is an elected official, and doesn't have to be a doctor. Ours was a short rotund moron named Billy Wade, who owned a tire company in Morgan and kept getting reelected every four years mostly because he knew barely enough to keep a low profile and not make waves.

While anyone can run for coroner, the local medical examiner has to be a doctor. For the last several years that had been Carla Powers. She was in her mid-to-late thirties, smart as a whipcrack, real easy on the eyes and, if I hadn't already been hopelessly enamored of Donna Asher, I might have given her a tumble. I suspect she knew this, in that phenomenal way women have, and harbored hopes that I might one day come to my senses and make a move on her. I made a point of not leading her on.

I found her sitting at the front desk of the ME office, chewing on a sandwich and reading a copy of *Cosmo*. As soon as I walked through the door, she hopped to her feet.

"Hot . . . *damn*, Chief. Look at you!"

I took off my Stetson, being in the presence of a lady, and placed it on the hat rack. She walked over and eyed me from head to toe.

"I heard you'd ditched the uniform," she said. "I like the look."

She reached out and fingered the lapel of my cord jacket, and her knuckles brushed against my chest and stopped. A quizzical look crossed her face, and she rapped once or twice on my vest.

"Body armor just to visit li'l ol' me?" she said, her eyes dancing. "I'm flattered."

I felt my cheeks redden a little. Carla doesn't take much effort to look at and, while I am completely devoted to Donna, I can't help being a man.

"I was out looking for someone who might be a bad guy," I said. "I figured getting shot three times in one year is plenty."

"I'd say. I can't tell you how happy I am you made it. You had all of us pretty worried. How's the recovery?"

"The body's coming along nicely. I lost over fifty pounds in the hospital. Put about half of it back on."

"Don't gain much more. I like the slimmer you. Your clothes hang better. You don't look so much like a washed-up quarterback. You here about Ram-Billy?"

"Sherry told me you called the station, said the autopsy was completed."

"Yep. Slam dunk. Avulsive blunt-force head trauma."

"I saw him at the house. Never realized a human head could do something like that."

"It was pretty gross, all right. I've seen similar injuries on people who've been in car crashes. Once you cleave the skull, and break the connection between the first cervical vertebra and the foramen magnum—that's the hole in the skull the spinal cord enters—there isn't much to hold a head upright."

"Ram-Billy wasn't in a car. Any idea what kind of object a man could wield that would carry that much force?"

"Not a clue. It would have to be heavy. I don't know whether an ax could get the job done. Maybe if it was really, really sharp."

"Any other issues with the body?"

"Only one of interest. Your murderer did Ram-Billy a favor."

"How so?" I asked.

"The old bastard didn't have a lot of time left, and what he had wasn't going to be much of a party. He had metastatic pancreatic cancer, a particularly nasty type. Based on the number of tumors I found, I'd imagine he had maybe a month or so left, and he was going to hurt. Bad. Probably already had symptoms, but he might have been ignoring them. Never a good idea."

"Could it have progressed that far without him knowing about it?"

"Sure. Lots of people get this far along before they go to the doctor. It's a terribly fast-growing disease, and many people aren't symptomatic before they're terminal. He may have been experiencing some pain already, like I said. There wasn't much food in his stomach. Eating might have begun to cause him distress, and he might have been avoiding food to relieve his symptoms, thinking he had an ulcer or something."

"His refrigerator was practically empty. There were some frozen dinners in the freezer, but not many."

"Sounds about right."

I considered what she had told me. "Okay, then," I said. "That doesn't help me much. I still need to find out who drove a wedge through his head. Dying or not, it wasn't the disease that killed him."

"Wish I had more for you," Carla said. "I sent off some samples for toxicology, but I won't get that back for days— maybe weeks. The labs are backed up something awful."

I thanked her and retrieved my hat.

On the way back to Prosperity, I reviewed what I knew, and what I didn't. The *didn't* column was a lot longer.

For sure, Boyd Overhultz had been in Ram-Billy's house, and he had visited often enough for Sam Kincaid to notice the car. Ram-Billy had been part owner of a porn site featuring a woman

181

who had been missing for several weeks. The porn site was based in Lithuania, and the name of the company that owned it sounded Russian—and what in hell did *debuchke* mean in Russian, anyway? I made a mental note to look it up online when I got back to the office. Another set of prints raised a lot of red flags with the Department of Homeland Security, which had to mean something. I'd already been warned off Natalya Gromykova Guthrie by Cantrell. Was it possible that the mystery fingerprints belonged to her?

There were also all those unidentified prints Clint had found in the house. As they fell into that *don't know* part of the case that made the difference between solving and not solving it, they bothered me. Ram-Billy, being something of an iconoclast, couldn't have had that many people traipsing through his digs. Someone had been there often enough to leave a lot of prints. I wondered who it was.

When I arrived back at the office I put out a BOLO on Boyd Overhultz and his car, as a "person of interest" in the case. If I couldn't find him, maybe I could bring him to me.

Then I opened a search engine and entered the word DEBUCHKE. I didn't get any hits, so I logged onto a translation site. Within seconds, it told me that the word meant "girl."

Well, that was helpful. A porn site featuring videos of girls was owned by a company whose name meant "girl."

Some detective.

Then I gave it a little more reflection.

Natalya Gromykova was a Russian mail-order bride. After arriving in the States, she somehow became wrapped up in an online sex site with a Russian name that was owned by someone in a former Soviet republic.

What if the marriage site that led her to America and the porn site were owned by the same company?

I wrote a note on my legal pad to look into this, at least until

Cantrell caught me sniffing around and slapped my wrist again.

As I finished making the note, the fax machine out in the lobby came alive and started printing pages. It spit out about thirty pages before shutting down. This batch was from Horace Tate at the Clerk of Courts office. It listed every tort filed by Ram-Billy for the previous year. They were all Small Claims Court filings, which made sense.

In North Carolina, the home county of the plaintiff is considered to be the location of an offense, even if the malefactor is hundreds of miles away. Say you're on the Do Not Call list, and you get a blatant sales robocall from Chicago. The person actually committed the offense in Illinois, but you were the aggrieved person in Bliss County, so you get to file there. I'd imagine Ram-Billy actually saw the inside of a courtroom on one out of every ten or twenty filings, since it was too big a hassle for defendants to travel all the way to North Carolina to plead their case. Instead, they'd contact Ram-Billy with a settlement offer to make him go away. He would probably make a counteroffer, jacking up his price by fifty percent, and the deal would be struck. He'd get a check in the mail and inform the Clerk of Courts office that the charges were dropped, and that would be the end of it.

Ram-Billy, as I had heard, had been focusing on violators of the Telephone Consumer Protection Act with his lawsuits, but there were a few in the list that were filed against locals. He'd claimed in one that a restaurant in Morgan had served him tainted meat that gave him the shits, and asked for five thousand dollars for pain and suffering. In another, he'd claimed that a car repairman had overcharged him for a valve job and hadn't done the work correctly, which led to damage to his engine. There was one lawsuit against a landscaping company whom he claimed had not adequately ensured that his trees would not be eaten up by Japanese beetles. That one was filed for two thousand.

Most of the closed cases I found in the filings had been settled out of court, and not for a large amount of money, which reinforced my impression that, for Ram-Billy, suing people was as much about sport as it was for monetary gain or even satisfaction of a grudge. I think he got off on making people uncomfortable.

It was a pretty safe bet that he hadn't been murdered by an out-of-state telemarketing company. His lawsuits, for them, had been largely nuisances and probably eventually written off as one of the costs of doing business. I culled those from the stack and place them aside as "improbables."

I made a second stack of complaints against local businesses, and ordered them by ranking from highest to lowest claim amount. I figured nobody was going to split Ram-Billy from hairline to collarbone over a five-hundred dollar beef. The limit for small claims courts in North Carolina is five thousand dollars, and I noted that he had made almost all of his filings in that jurisdiction. I had a hard time imagining killing someone over five grand, either, but with some people you can never tell. In any case, Ram-Billy's murder had the look of a personal grudge, and I wasn't sure that a business being sued would go to those lengths, unless they were truly desperate.

That left the personal claims, torts filed against individuals who had somehow crossed Ram-Billy's path and raised his dander. There were only four of those, but they were all for the maximum amount. There was one settled case, and three open cases. While I might be upset with someone after paying out to him in a lawsuit, I'd be more likely to lick my wounds and get on with my life than take matters to a much more lethal level. On the other hand, if I anticipated that losing as much as five thousand dollars to a malcontent like Ram-Billy for something I really didn't think was wrong would put me in dire financial straits, then I might try to dissuade him from pursuing legal action. If Ram-Billy were dead, he couldn't prosecute his tort.

Logically, those open cases were the suspects that made the most sense. I assigned them the highest priority, and decided I'd interview them first.

Chapter Twenty-Three

Shug opened the door of his office to find Lily standing outside. She held a bar rag in her hands.

"Miss Lily?"

"I've been standing here tryin' to decide whether to knock," she said.

"Have you made up your mind?"

"I wish a moment of your time, if you don't mind."

"Come on in."

He led her inside and pointed at the chair across from his desk. Instead of taking his office seat, he plopped down on a love seat on the wall perpendicular to her. She stared at the floor, as if trying to decide what to say.

Shug waited, but his mind worked as she deliberated. He liked her—had liked her from the instant she'd climbed into his car on the Morgan Highway—but he had no idea why. Other than their conversation that first evening, they had spoken of nothing but business since she had started work at the club. She had proven to be an industrious and dependable worker, unlike many of the drifters he had encountered in his life.

And there was the other thing. She cleaned up well. He couldn't deny that he felt a physical attraction to her. Despite having a few more years on her than he typically found desirable, he had to admit that, at least to the extent that he could discern, she was well-kept. She always wore her white shirts buttoned to the neck, but he believed that the swell of her bosom was natural, and that if he ever had the opportunity to talk her out of her clothes he would discover them rounded and full. Her jeans fit in a way that left no argument about her flat belly and the curve of her ass. His experience with women left him with the impression that she was made for marathon bedroom romps and sexual abandon.

Yet, he had made no moves on her, and he wasn't certain why. It wasn't her age. While his list of conquests, which he estimated must now number in the hundreds, easily had an average age in the lower twenties, he had enjoyed more than his share of middle-aged women, and had found to his satisfaction that maturity carried with it a level of knowledge and—often—a lack of insecurities and inhibitions that made for some mind-blowing, finest-kind encounters.

There was something about Lily Holder that rode his brakes and held him back. He was even perplexed that, when talking with her, the words *darlin'* and *sweetheart* did not fall easily from his lips the way they did with most girls and women. He had never referred to her as anything other than her given name, and more often *Miss* Lily than not. He recalled a time, deep in his past, when his father had attempted to beat respect into him, and had told him that there are women who must be regarded with honor and respect. He had not understood that reasoning at the time, and in his adult life had run across few women who even remotely elicited the sort of feelings that might lead him to treat them with deference.

There had been one in Georgia, the wife of a preacher who had invited him to dinner, no doubt with intent to sway him off the path of his wicked ways. The man had been a fool, but his wife—so kind, so placid, so reverent—had stirred some forgotten lesson from his childhood, and he had called her *ma'am* without exception throughout the evening, as if uttering her name might somehow constitute a blasphemy, even in the house

187

of a man he considered little more than an imbecile. Meeting her had troubled him for some weeks after, though he continued to travel his debauched road as if nothing had happened. With time, his memory of her had faded, except for a faint impression that the preacher had married way above his spiritual station, with no more awareness of it than he might have of a mosquito on his window screen, and Shug's own self-deprecating belief that he could never be deserving of a creature of such grace.

That was how Lily made him feel. In her presence, he seemed inconsequential. Picking her up on the Morgan Highway, and cutting her loose with money and the promise of a job, had started as a testosterone and alcohol driven opportunistic conquest, and had ended as some sort of involuntary act of kindness born of an instinctive understanding that he was in the presence of a human who existed on a moral and idealistic plane which he could only imagine. That awareness had not faded as he had gotten to know her. Providing her with employment had seemed less an act of charity than penance. Giving her a place to work was the same kind of self-purifying act that led people in other cultures to drop coins in the bowls of filthy, ragged holy men. It was like buying a shard of redemption.

For her part, Lily seemed oblivious to his intents and his feelings, both in general and now, as she sat in his office wringing her hands. He noted that, in the week or so since she had arrived, her torn, shredded, and grit-worn nails had begun to grow back, and she'd applied nail polish. It made her hands look softer and more feminine.

"I don't know how to approach you with this matter," she said. "I like my job here. I like feeling clean, and having some folding money in my purse for a change. You have been so kind to me, but I fear that if I tell you what I've learned, it will drive you into a fury, and I don't believe I could bear to be the cause of that."

"Can I get you a drink?" he said, pointing toward his private liquor cabinet.

"No, sir. With respect, I don't imbibe. I appreciate your offer."

"Then what's bothering you?"

She had not yet met his eyes. A tear rolled to the tip of her nose, and hung for a second before dropping to the carpet.

"Has someone upset you?" he asked.

"Not me. I feel I have an obligation to let you know, as my employer, when you are being cheated. Not to do so would be ungrateful in light of what you've done for me."

"I'm being cheated? How?"

For almost half a minute, she said nothing. She bobbed her head, staring at the floor. He pulled a box of tissues from his desk, and handed one to her. She dabbed at her eyes, and finally raised her head to face him.

"Bobby is stealing from you," she said, and punctuated it with a sob, as if the catharsis of revealing her secret had broken the dam of her fears. Her tears flowed freely now, and Shug could not resist the urge to move to the couch and place his arm around her shoulders to comfort her. She cried some more for a bit, and then seemed to regain her composure.

"Now, what's this about Bobby?" he said.

"He has friends, and they come to the bar to see the shows. They're hard-looking men. They look as if they live paycheck to paycheck. They buy drinks, and sometimes they pay in cash. I've seen Bobby take half the money and stuff it in his jeans pocket. Once he took all of it. He thinks I haven't seen him, but I don't think he would care if I did. I think he believes that he has a right to the money, and that somehow I am obligated to keep his secret."

She began to cry again. Her weight shifted, and she leaned in toward him, placing her head on his shoulder. He had little experience with comforting women, and it seemed best to simply allow her to cry until she stopped herself.

"What are you going to do?" she asked, as her jag wound down.

"You did the right thing," he said. "We're not going to jump to conclusions here, but I'm not going to let one of my employees rob me. You take a few minutes to pull yourself together, and return to work. I'm not saying I don't believe you, but I want to see for myself whether Bobby is abusing my hospitality. You understand?"

She wiped at her eyes with the tissue.

"Whatever happens, I promise you nobody will ever know you told me about this," he said. "And I'll remember. I take care of folks who do me a solid, you understand?"

"No," she said.

"That's all right. You will. Now, go use my private bathroom and freshen yourself up. We don't want Bobby getting suspicious."

After Lily returned to work, Shug picked up the phone and called Boyd Overhultz's number.

"Whassup?" Boyd asked.

"Got a job for you. How fast can you make it over to the club?"

"Don't know as I care to come there at all. Last time I was there you said you wanted to fumigate your office after I left. Shit like that hurts a guy's feelings."

"You ought to try changing your underwear once a year, and get reacquainted with a bar of soap and a razor."

"Nice talkin' to you, Mr. Burch. Call again sometime."

"Wait! Okay. I'm sorry. I need your help. There's a couple

hundred in it for you."

"I'm eating at the fried chicken place right down the block. How's fifteen minutes sound?"

"That will do fine."

It actually took twenty minutes before Overhultz appeared in Shug's office doorway.

"Come on in," Shug said. "Have a seat."

He pulled a roll of bills from his pocket, and a pen from his desk drawer. He slipped three twenties from the roll, and circled the serial numbers with the pen. Then he copied the serial numbers onto the pad next to his telephone.

"I got a bartender who might be skimming cash customers," he told Overhultz. "Don't take this the wrong way, Boyd, but you look like the kind of guy wouldn't know which end of a credit card you use to wipe your ass. I need you to go downstairs, sit at the end of the bar so you can see the register clearly, and see what's what."

"Which one is it? The one with the monster tits? Hell, I'd let her skim just so's I could watch her all day."

"You're talking about a valued employee, Boyd, and a woman whose air you'd defile by breathing it. I'll ask you not to talk disrespectfully about her again. I'm concerned about Bobby, the college boy."

"The jock?"

"Yeah. Watch him real close. He might be slicker than I think. Buy some drinks and pay for them with these bills. I want to know whether he pockets any of them. Can you do that?"

"You bet. What if he is skimmin'?"

"Don't do a thing. Watch what he does. Then come back up and tell me. Got it?"

"Sure thing."

★ ★ ★ ★ ★

"You got a problem," Overhultz told Shug an hour later. "Bobby's takin' you to the cleaners."

"He palmed the money?"

"Two of the bills went right into his pocket. He put the other into the till, but he pulled a ten out before he closed it. He's got fast hands. I almost missed the slip, but they're in his jeans. I'd swear to it on a stack of Bibles."

"Okay. Thanks. Here's two hundred for your trouble."

"Weren't no trouble, Mr. Burch. I got three drinks out of the deal."

"Good, then. You haven't heard anything from Chief Wheeler over in Prosperity, have you?"

"No, but I'm keeping things on the down low. I'm not staying at my place over in Mica Wells. If they're looking for me on this Ram-Billy thing, they're gonna have to look a lot harder than they have so far."

Shug waited until after the club was closed, and Bobby and Lily and the other staff were shutting down the house, before he made his move. He walked downstairs and found Lily stacking glasses into plastic dishwasher racks and Bobby tallying up the till. "Lemme see how we did tonight," he said to Bobby, who handed the register tray over to him.

"It was busy," Bobby said, without a trace of suspicion in his voice. "Rodeo's in town this weekend, over at the Agricultural Fairgrounds. You really pull in the cowboy crowd."

"Good to hear," Shug said absently, as he shuffled through the stack of twenties in the till. He found one of the three bills he had marked, but only one.

"Got the bank bag?" he asked, and Bobby handed it to him from under the bar. Shug filled it with the bills, placed the credit receipts in his pocket, and placed the bag back under the bar. "Fire inspector's giving me shit about how close the dumpster out back is to the exit door. Says if there's a fire it might prevent people from getting out. I need to roll it about five feet." He pulled a foot-and-a-half long flashlight from under the counter. "Give me a hand?"

"No problem," Bobby said, and followed Shug toward the rear of the building.

Lily saw Shug wink at her as he walked by. There was something dark and troubling in his face. She waited until she was certain he and Bobby had left the building, and then she followed, stopping at the rear exit. The door was propped open with a wooden wedge. In the alley, she could hear them straining to move the dumpster. She pushed the door open wide enough to see them through the crack at the jamb.

"Don't think we can move it," Bobby said. "Too damned heavy."

"All right, then," Shug said. "I'll get the trash folks to do it tomorrow. We got something else to discuss anyway. I need you to empty your pocket, Bobby."

There was a pause, and then Bobby said, "What?"

"Hand over the cash in your hip pocket. I need to get a look at it."

Through the crack, Lily could see Bobby hesitate. He glanced around as if looking for an escape route. Then, slowly, he reached into his pocket.

"This all of it?" Shug asked.

"All I got. What's this about? You don't need a loan, do you, Shug?"

"I've asked you not to call me that. See these two bills, here? I gave them to a good ol' boy earlier this evening to use at the bar. Before I gave them to him, I marked the serial numbers, and I wrote the numbers on a slip of paper up in my office." He pulled something from his pocket. "This slip of paper, as it happens. See? The numbers are the same. You want to explain to me how these bills wound up in your pocket?"

"Them's tips," Bobby said.

Shug slapped him, twice. The sound echoed off the concrete block walls like gunshots.

"Don't lie to me, boy!" he said. "My guy paid for each drink with a different twenty, and watched you put them in your pocket before making his change. I can't abide a liar."

Bobby started to stammer out an excuse, but Shug slapped him again. Bobby's face recoiled like a shotgun butt.

"In the old days, I'd have ripped you to shreds," Shug growled. "We've come to a parting of the ways. Don't bother coming to work anymore. In fact, if I ever see you around this place again, I'll see to it you piss blood for a month and I'll bust your kneecaps to pieces. Is there anything I've said to you that isn't clear? Now get your sorry sack of shit carcass off my property."

He turned to walk back into the bar.

"You had to be so smart," Bobby said. "Couldn't leave good enough alone. Nobody was gonna miss that small amount of money. Everybody skims a little. I bet that hot little blonde twist Lily is robbing you silly, and you can't see it because her jugs are blinding you to the truth. You think I don't know what's goin' on ever' time she brings you a drink in your office? You're bangin' her. I'll bet she drops to her knees soon's she gets in your door, and blows the hell out of you. Mebbe I oughta look her up myself, get me a little taste of my own."

Shug stopped, and in the light from the mercury lamp overhead, Lily could see his face darken. He kept his back to Bobby, as if he were purposefully restraining himself from launching an attack. "I'd stop talking now if I were you," he said, his voice tense with anger. "Nothing you say from this point forward is going to make things go better for you."

"Hell, you piece of shit, you could have fired me, sent me packin'," Bobby shouted, spittle flying from his mouth. "But you had to prove what a fuckin' big man you were, slappin' on me like I was some kind of hound. You're gonna regret that. You're gonna regret it a lot."

From the doorway, Lily saw Bobby reach behind his back and bare his teeth in a disagreeable grin.

"But you ain't gonna regret it for *long*," he said.

He pulled a large Swiss army knife from his pocket and opened the blade. He raised it and made a run at Shug.

"Mr. Burch!" Lily yelled.

He seemed to have been waiting for Bobby's attack. He whirled about with a speed Lily had not imagined him capable of, and swung the heavy flashlight, catching Bobby's arm at the elbow. Somehow, Bobby held onto the knife. Shug swung the flashlight again. This time it connected with Bobby's shoulder, and Bobby dropped the knife.

Then, things seemed to happen very quickly.

Shug rose on one foot, then swung his other foot in space. There was a slapping sound, and Bobby's head snapped back. He stumbled two steps, seemed to recover, and with a howl he charged.

Then he seemed to stop, as if held back by a blurry force. Almost more quickly than Lily could follow, Shug pounded his fists into Bobby's midsection, his throat, and his nose. Each punch was accented by a whipcrack of skin on bone.

Bobby grabbed his throat and fell to his knees. Shug pivoted on one foot again, and flat-footed Bobby onto his back. Before Bobby could attempt to right himself, Shug jumped onto Bobby's chest, and started beating him across the face, over and over.

Lily left the doorway and ran toward them. Bobby's eyes were glazed, his mouth hung open. Blood ran from his nose, from a cut at the corner of his mouth, and it had begun to trickle from one ear.

"He's done!" Lily yelled. "Stop it, Mr. Burch!"

With his fists, Shug kept whaling on Bobby's swelling face. Lily grabbed him by the shoulders. "He's out! Stop hitting him!"

Shug ignored her. She tried to grab one of his arms, but he shook her away and pounded again at Bobby's head.

Lily knelt next to him, and placed both hands on his shoulders. "Sean!" she cried. "Stop it! You have to stop! *You're killing him!*"

Instantly, the spell seemed to break. Shug's arms dropped to his side. His head fell forward and he huffed for breath.

Bobby groaned, before his head slumped to one side.

Lily pulled gently at Shug's shoulders. He pushed himself up from Bobby's prostrate body and stared down at the man. He didn't say a word. His barrel chest heaved from the effort. His jacket was torn at the armpits, and at some point the pocket of his shirt had ripped. His knuckles dripped blood.

"Call an ambulance," he said. "I don't want that little shit to lie out behind my place all night."

"You're bleeding," she said. "Come inside and wash off your hands, and we'll call an ambulance for Bobby."

"It's like Mr. Burch said," Lily told the Morgan police officer who had responded to the call along with the ambulance. "Bobby was stealing from the club. When Mr. Burch took him out back to fire him, Bobby pulled a knife. Mr. Burch was only defending himself."

"Did you see Bobby steal money?" the officer asked.

"I did. I was the one told Mr. Burch about it."

The officer finished writing and flipped the duty pad closed. "All right then," he said. "I don't expect Bobby's going to be filing any assault charges. Looks like Shug beat him up something awful, though."

"Please, sir," Lily said, "Mr. Burch prefers not to be called by that name."

"That a fact? I had no idea. Do you suppose he's planning to file charges against Bobby for theft?"

"I believe you would want to ask him about that yourself. I'm certain I have no idea."

The officer thanked her, and left to speak with Mr. Burch, who sat at the far end of the bar, nursing a shot of tequila. They talked for a couple of minutes, and Mr. Burch offered his bandaged hand. The officer asked something. Mr. Burch grinned and signed a cocktail napkin for him. They shook again, and the officer headed for the door.

Mr. Burch pounded back the shot of tequila, and walked over to Lily's table.

"Long night," he said, as he sat.

"Was it necessary? Beating on Bobby like that?"

"At the time, necessary didn't enter into the equation. It was two brutes goin' at it in a back alley. Not my first ride at that rodeo, Miss Lily. Besides, I wasn't going to let him talk trash about you that way. You heard what he said?"

"I did."

"It was disrespectful. I would not have him saying those things."

She tried to see his face clearly in the dim light. His skin was wrinkled and leather tough. His beard was scattered with silver whiskers, and his almost transparent blue eyes were rimmed with red. He wheezed when he breathed through his nose, which she suspected had been broken more than once.

"You beat him because of what he said about me?" she said. "Not because he was stealing from you?"

"I fired him for stealing from me. Sure, I slapped him around a little, but that was to make my point. When he called you those names and made those accusations about you, I tried to walk away. It was wrong of him to say those things and they angered me, but I turned my back and tried to let him be. When he pulled that knife, I felt obliged to teach him some manners he will never forget."

"You damn near killed him!"

"He's a football player. He's taken hits upside the head for years. Probably why he was stupid enough to think he could get away with skimming money from me. Wait, don't walk away. You are correct. I did lose control. My head was filled with a red mist and in my imagination I saw myself ripping the little bastard to shreds. I regret that you had to witness that."

She didn't reply. Instead, she rose, walked over to the bar, and picked up her sweater. She started for the door, but stopped several feet from it. "I believe the stories I have heard about you over the years are true," she said. "I believe you are capable of great violence against others. You have been kind to me, and I do not wish you to think I am unappreciative. I also think you are capable of noble acts and generous intentions, but I wonder whether you have any awareness of that capacity in yourself. I think I should go home now."

"Miss Lily, it's past two in the morning. I don't care for the idea of you walking home at this late hour. May I give you a ride to your motel?"

"I'd be much obliged, sir," she said.

CHAPTER TWENTY-FOUR

The first of the three unsettled personal lawsuits Ram-Billy had filed was against a reporter at the *Morgan Ledger-Telegraph,* the local paper. Her name was Sue Ellen Fornoro. This reporter had mentioned Ram-Billy in an article on the Small Claims Court, and had referred to him as a "serial plaintiff." Ram-Billy had considered this defamation of character and—totally ignoring that doing so proved her point—had filed for damages to his "personal reputation."

I had not met Ms. Fornoro. Most of my dealings with the local rag had been with a cheeky kid in his mid-twenties named Cory True, who seemed to have been assigned to the "Chief Wheeler Beat."

I signed in at the front desk at the paper and navigated my way around the city room until I found her. My first impression as I rapped on the side of her cube was that I was wasting my time.

"Yes?" she said, as she whirled around in her wheelchair. She was rotund and fleshy. Her face was moon-like, her skin stretched tight over subcutaneous fat until it had acquired a polished shine. She wore quarter-inch thick eyeglasses, and judging by the way her eyes were magnified behind them, I assumed that she was severely farsighted.

I flashed my ID and asked if I could sit. She pointed toward a chair, her hand bound in a strapped leather glove of some kind.

"I'm investigating the murder of Ramsey Pressley," I told her.

"Oh, my. Ghastly business. How can I help?"

"I'm not sure, really. This whole process mostly involves ruling out possible suspects, at least at this stage. We hope that forensic evidence might provide us with some additional leads, but for the moment we're going for the obvious."

"Obvious."

"You know. If a woman is murdered the obvious prime suspect is her husband. That sort of thing. You wrote an article some months back labeling Mr. Pressley as a—"

"Serial plaintiff. Yes, I know. And you're here because he's suing me for defamation."

"Well . . ."

"Oh, don't dither, Chief. I've been expecting you ever since I heard about the old coot getting killed. He was suing me for the maximum amount the Small Claims Court allows. And, whether you are aware of it or not, he was going to lose. His own history and the newspaper's lawyers were going to see to it. In any case, I'd already been assured that—on the off chance he might win the suit—the newspaper would pick up the damages."

"Really."

"Part of the cost of doing business. Reporters are sued all the time. Sometimes people don't like what we print about them and they decide to get even. They seldom win, and when they do, they don't win much."

"I see."

"Besides, even if I wanted to harm Mr. Pressley, I'm not in much of a position to do so. Multiple sclerosis. I was diagnosed ten years ago and it's progressive. I can barely wheel myself down to the ladies' rest room, let along wield a bludgeon. I'm afraid your trip here was almost entirely a waste of time."

"Almost?"

"Perhaps you can provide me with some information on the

case I can use in a story."

"I can't comment about an ongoing investigation," I said.

"And I wouldn't dream of asking you to. On the other hand, you can give me some more background on Mr. Pressley, and I can't imagine it would violate any confidentiality issues if you were to answer a few general hypothetical questions about how such an investigation might proceed, would it?"

I answered her questions and scratched her off my list.

The next person on the list was a man named Thomas Schramm. According to Ram-Billy's filing, Mr. Schramm had sold a used car to him through a private advertisement placed in an on-line website. Mr. Schramm claimed that the car had only thirty thousand miles and change on it, a number confirmed by the odometer.

However, almost six months after buying the car, Ram-Billy was fishing through the papers in the glove compartment and came across a service receipt from a local oil-change shop that indicated the car had been serviced at over fifty thousand miles.

Changing an odometer in North Carolina is illegal, but ratting Schramm out to the authorities wouldn't have put a penny in Ram-Billy's pocket. The civil penalty for such a fraud in this state is five thousand dollars, which happened to be the limit for a small claims case. Ram-Billy was in his element. He filed a complaint against Schramm, claiming to have been defrauded out of at least part of the purchase price of the car, and asked for damages.

Schramm lived in a trailer park over in an old part of Prosperity. There was a time, back when I was young, when you could obtain anything you wanted in that neck of the woods. Moonshine, teenaged whores, drugs, guns, and maybe even a store-bought ass-whipping.

Suburban sprawl hadn't yet reached the confines of this little inbred slice of heaven. As a result, both Slim and I had become intimately familiar with the area and its inhabitants, largely matriarchal families populated by folk who made the kid with the banjo in *Deliverance* look like a Rhodes Scholar.

I pulled up in the gravel lot next to Schramm's doublewide— itself a sign of relative affluence—and stepped from the car. As I did, the door swung open and a woman stepped down a set of rickety stairs to the yard. She looked about seventy. She wore a shapeless housedress that she may have owned since the Kennedy administration. Her pewter hair was wiry and poked in hundreds of different directions at once. Her lips collapsed inward, as if she had left what teeth she possessed in a glass by her bedside. She held a lighted cigarette in fingers that terminated in yellowed claws.

"He'p you, sir?" she asked.

"Chief Judd Wheeler, Prosperity Police," I said. "Wondering whether Mr. Schramm might be around today?"

"What'cha want with him?"

"Need to talk with him about a car he sold some time back."

"Somethin' wrong with it?"

"Is Mr. Schramm here, ma'am? My business is really with him."

"You want to see Tommy, you can find him over to the Olive Branch Primitive Baptist Church yard."

"You're saying he's passed?"

"Month ago this coming Friday. Had a stroke. Keeled over at the dinner table. One minute he was chewin' on a piece of pork gristle, and the next he went nose-down in his smashed taters."

"I'm sorry, ma'am. I didn't know."

"Asshole didn't leave me the time of day. So what's this about some car he sold? 'Cause, if someone got a problem with it, it ain't no concern of mine. He can take it up with Tommy in the afterlife."

I crossed Schramm off the list of high priority suspects. As I drove away, I wondered whether Ram-Billy had located Tommy Schramm on whatever side of grace they had earned in the afterlife, and whether they were still scrapping over the mileage on some damned car.

The last name on my short list of potential killers was Lyle Zinsser. Ram-Billy was dragging him into Small Claims Court over a fender bender in the parking lot over at the Morgan Mall. Seems Zinsser was out driving with his sixteen-year-old daughter, in preparation for her license test, when she came to the end of a row of parked cars and didn't brake in time before hitting the perpendicular lane. She was unlucky enough to encounter six inches of Ram-Billy's rear fender as he was on his way to a sub shop for a sandwich, leaving behind a scratch that you might have been able to see from ten feet away if you used the Hubble Telescope.

Ram-Billy was a known cheapskate and tightass, and he had the barest-boned insurance policy sold outside a third-world country. His policy didn't pay for a rental car while he had his in the shop—again, the least expensive place he could find, which took almost three weeks to make repairs—and Zinsser's insurance only covered five hundred dollars worth of rental. Ram-Billy was suing for the rest, along with a rider for pain, suffering, and deprivation of his wheels. The total request to the court, which did not surprise me in the least, came to the maximum allowable five thousand dollars.

What made Zinsser's case interesting was a note on the court files recording he had been issued service of the lawsuit only a week before somebody plowed a furrow in Ram-Billy's cranium.

Zinsser lived in an older part of Prosperity, one which had been built long before Kent Kramer and his fellow developers had descended on the town like ravenous locusts. The houses were largely single-story, post-war brick ramblers, maybe a thousand square feet, on healthy lots that had cost maybe a hundred dollars an acre when I was a boy. Zinsser's house was typical of the area, with a neatly trimmed front yard that could have doubled as a putting green. It wasn't a palace, as so many houses in Prosperity now aspired to be, but Zinsser treated it like one.

I found him sitting on the front porch, sipping a lemonade. He wore khaki shorts, a wife-beater undershirt, and sandals. He was losing his hair and had already begun to compensate for it with the start of a bad comb-over. He was badly sunburned, save for a patch around his eyes that probably came from wearing sunglasses. He watched warily as I pulled into his asphalt driveway, probably hoping I was using it to turn around, rather than cut the engine.

"Afternoon," I said. I introduced myself and showed him my badge. "I'm looking for Lyle Zinsser."

"That's me," he said. "Is there a problem?"

"Some routine questions. Can you verify your whereabouts over the last—say—four or five days and nights?"

"I reckon I can. Why?"

"I'm investigating an incident and I'm trying to rule out people with any known connection."

"What kind of incident?"

"I'm sorry to be a bother, sir, but could you tell me where you've been for the last week?"

"You said four or five days."

"Okay, let's start with that."

"Easy. I was in the mountains with my family. We went up there for a bluegrass festival. Got back last night. Mind if I ask again what this is about?"

"Would you be able to provide some proof that you were in the mountains?"

"Sure. I have the motel receipt inside. We were at the Smoky Mountain Resort, near Hendersonville."

"Anybody else there with you besides your family?"

"My wife's sister came along, too. She's a widow woman. Lost her husband last year. No kids. We figured she'd like to come along. Give her something to do besides sit around the house and mope. She's still here, if you want to talk with her."

"No need. You're familiar with Ramsey Pressley?"

"I reckon I am. Hope I never run across the like of him again. The sour old bastard wants to make a federal case out of a minor scrape on his damn bumper. Wants to haul me into Small Claims. I got a good mind to hire me a hot lawyer to put him in his place."

"I hate to disillusion you, Mr. Zinsser, but there aren't any lawyers in Small Claims."

"Kinda like on *People's Court*, huh?"

"Maybe not as colorful," I said. "I'd appreciate it if you could get that motel receipt for me."

He pulled himself to his feet and disappeared into the house, before returning with a slip of paper. The receipt was in his name, and it covered all the likely dates of the killing. Having been over a hundred miles away, and surrounded by family, he would have had to be a criminal genius to pull off Ram-Billy's killing.

"I'd ask you to hold on to this paper," I said, handing it back. "You should know that Mr. Pressley is deceased."

"Dead?"

"Yes."

"And you thought I killed him?"

"Not really. I have to run down every possibility. You aren't a person of interest in this case anymore."

"What about the court hearing in Morgan?"

"I'm not a lawyer," I said, "but I'd be surprised if anyone will show up to tell Mr. Pressley's side of the story. You show up for the hearing, ready to tell your part, and when nobody is there to speak for the plaintiff I feel certain the court will drop the lawsuit."

"I'll do that, Chief. I don't like to see anyone get killed, being a born-again Christian man, but I am happy not to have to worry about losing that money in court. We did everything we could to make right by Mr. Pressley, and it seemed he was itching to fight. You ever known anybody like that? Like he had venom in his veins instead of blood?"

"You take care, Mr. Zinsser," I said, turning toward the cruiser. Before pulling out of the drive, I scratched through the last name on my list of high priority suspects.

Sherry handed me a sheaf of papers as I walked into the station.

"Came over the fax about an hour ago. Knew you'd want to see them right away," she said.

I thanked her and headed for my office to look through the faxes from the Register of Deeds Office in Morgan.

Right on top were the incorporation papers that named Ram-Billy as the American agent for Debuchke, Limited. As I expected, it listed his home address as the office of record. There were some other papers that outlined the foreign officers, none of whom were familiar to me.

Then, I noted that there was one other officer in this country. The papers listed a man named Bernard Kovalenko, and even more surprising was his address. He lived in Bliss County. Apparently, while Ram-Billy served as Debuchke's American agent, Kovalenko was the true face of Debuchke in the United States. I wasn't surprised he wanted to keep a low profile. The porn sites and possible involvement with marriage brokers smelled of Russian mob. Whoever this Kovalenko fellow was, he wasn't interested in getting a lot of attention.

Jeannie Klug in the deeds office had been thorough. According to the papers, in addition to his hobby filing lawsuits, Ram-Billy had signed on to a number of international businesses as an American agent. Several of them had names that sounded at least vaguely Russian, and four of them also listed Mr. Kovalenko as a principle partner.

She had also provided me with information on other business concerns owned or operated by the principles in every company Ram-Billy agented, and she'd been courteous enough to collate them by name.

Bernard Kovalenko, besides his dealings with Ram-Billy Pressley, was involved in a number of companies. One of them popped off the page as soon as I scanned it—ShuggaBugga Enterprises, which listed as its primary holding a restaurant and nightclub in Morgan, Shug's Nashville.

Now what was a Russian—and a potential gangster—doing wrapped up with the likes of Sean Burch? However it shook out, it couldn't mean anything good.

Then I found another link, one that troubled me greatly.

Mayor Kent Kramer sat at his desk, reading the newspaper from up in Pooler, when I walked into his office.

"Have a seat," he said. "Want a drink?"

"I know it's hard to tell now that I'm not wearing the uniform, but I'm on duty," I said.

"Hell, Judd, I always know when you're on duty. You never wear that damned Stetson off the job. Think I care if you're working? I closed a sweet little deal a couple of hours ago, and I feel like bending an elbow to celebrate. C'mon, join me."

"Sorry, but I'm gonna take a pass on that. You go ahead. I need to ask you about one of your business partners."

Kent pulled himself up and walked, somewhat unsteadily,

toward the bar. "Which one?" he asked.

"Bernard Kovalenko."

He had already grabbed a bottle of Glenlivet, and was about to uncap it, but he froze. He placed the bottle down and returned to his chair.

"Where did you hear I was in business with Kovalenko?"

"You know Ram-Billy got killed."

"I did hear that."

"He was an American agent for one of Kovalenko's companies, a cybersex website called Debuchke, Limited. I've been chasing down a lot of leads in his death, including his business ties, and one thing led to another. There's paper out there that says Kovalenko's invested in your development outfit."

"I have a lot of investors, Judd. Not as many as before the recession, but there are still people willing to put money into a growing concern. While I'm not building and selling as many houses as I did a decade ago, the home sales here in the 'burbs are still pretty healthy. People still want to get away to the country after a hard day's work."

"It's possible that Kovalenko is linked to Russian mobs."

"Sounds a little dramatic to me."

"Who else runs porn sites on the computer featuring Slavic women? I'm still chasing down all of Kovalenko's dealings, but I wouldn't be shocked to discover that he's also selling Russian mail-order brides."

"I wouldn't know anything about that, but so far as I do know, it's a legal business."

"Could be. There's a missing woman here in Prosperity. She was selected by her husband through one of those Russian bride sites. She's also shown up playing with herself on one of Kovalenko's porn sites. Now, if he's brokering sham marriages to bring women over here to market them as meat, that sounds suspiciously close to human trafficking. What do you think?"

"Are you suggesting that I might be involved in his other business ventures? I sell real estate. I don't know anything about pornographic websites."

"I'm not accusing you, Kent. I want to get a handle on this guy. What's he like?"

Kent ran his index finger around the rim of his highball glass. He licked his lips, and I could tell he really wanted a snort. I didn't care. I wasn't stopping him.

"You thinking of paying Kovalenko a visit?" he said.

"Probably. He was involved with a murder victim. He might have material information."

"You're wasting your time. Maybe he'll see you. Maybe he won't. Maybe he'll set the dogs on you. See, it's not like he and I are close. We don't hang together. He approached me with an offer at a time when pickings were slim. Fact is, my development business was on the ropes. He pumped some cash into the system, and he got me through a tough patch. It was good for me. Hell, it was good for *him*. He's made a lot of money off of me."

"He could be using you to launder mob money."

"If he is, then he's doing a good job of it. Until you walked into my office today, I had no true idea that Kovalenko might be involved in . . . unsavory business dealings. Sure, I was a little apprehensive about dealing with Russians. Ever since the fall of the Soviet bloc, these guys have gotten a rep for being the true swingin' dicks on the block. I debated long and hard about taking his money, but I was a little desperate at the time, so I decided I'd use his money and keep my personal distance. He seemed happy with that. Our connection is all about dollars and cents, and I had no idea where those dollars and cents originated. Honest to God, Judd."

"What's he like?"

"He's like anyone else. Maybe he's mobbed up. From what

you tell me, he probably has at least some connection with Russian gangs. That doesn't make him the Godfather, you know. To me, he was like any other investor. He had some money he wanted to grow, and I had the green thumb. I've had him out to the house exactly once, for dinner, shortly after we made our deal. After that, it's all been handled through our lawyers. We're not buddies."

"He's also involved with Sean Burch."

"So?"

"Burch is bad news. He and I go way back. Is Burch also investing with you?"

"Why do you ask?"

"Kovalenko is a primary backer of Burch's nightclub. You tossed a big old party a few weeks back to show off Sean Burch to your friends. I know you like a brother. You don't get off on glad-handing celebrities and dropping names. It's all about the bottom line for you."

"Okay! Burch has put a little money into my development business. Not a lot. And yes, he was referred to me by Kovalenko. What was I supposed to do? Kovalenko took my head out of the noose. I'm supposed to reward him by telling Burch to go put his money elsewhere?"

I shook my head and sighed a little, since I tend to do that when I discover close friends in bad situations.

"You're getting played," I said. "This is the way the gangs work. They get you hooked on money, and then they start pulling your strings. For all you know, Kovalenko is funneling money through Sean, washing it twice to make it look legal. Shug's Nashville may be another front for him. If he's in league with the Russian mob, I'd be extremely careful. You might want to divest yourself of him before he decides to involve you in something I can't help you with."

"Or maybe you're wrong," Kent said. "Could be you've built

this guy up to be some kind of criminal simply because he runs porn sites."

"One of his models, a Russian internet bride, is missing and his American agent got his head split in half. That's a lot of smoke not to have some fire behind it." I stood and picked up my hat from his desk. "I won't tell you how to run your business. But if I were you, I'd reconsider the kind of people you're snuggled with. Maybe nothing bad has happened yet. Doesn't mean it can't. Keep it in the road, Kent."

For a guy who loved to have the last word, Kent was strangely silent. I let myself out.

Chapter Twenty-Five

Bernard Kovalenko lived in the closest thing I've seen to a fortress in Bliss County. His compound was a mile beyond the Prosperity town limits. It was outside my jurisdiction, but I didn't plan to make any arrests. Based on the twelve-foot high stucco fence that ran the perimeter of his property, I estimated his entire estate to run somewhere in the ten-acre range, which was sizable even in an area where town charters mandated minimum lot sizes of one acre each.

I located the drive, which wound through an arbor of red oaks and poplars, onto which a number of *No Trespassing* signs had been tacked. At the end was a wrought iron gate—which was, predictably, closed—and an intercom on a post. I pushed the button to call the house.

"You are on private property," said someone in a tinny voice.

"I'm Chief of Police Wheeler, from Prosperity. I'd like to talk with Mr. Kovalenko."

"We are not in Prosperity."

"I'm investigating a crime in Prosperity, and Mr. Kovalenko may be able to help me."

The voice didn't answer and I began to think I was getting the brush-off. Then, with barely a whisper, the gate swung open from the center on well-lubricated hinges.

"Please drive to the house and park at the front steps," the voice in the box said.

Beyond the gate, the tree canopy again took over as I drove

through the copse for another quarter mile. Eventually, I broke through the forest and saw Kovalenko's house for the first time. It was modeled after a plantation cottage taken to gargantuan proportions. The front façade was three stories, with a twenty-foot deep gallery that wound around the front and sides of the structure. Six massive columns supported the gallery balusters. Potted hanging plants were spaced every six feet on the soffit across the hundred-foot front of the house, and five ceiling fans hung from a tongue and groove beaded ceiling.

The front doors stood at least ten feet high, with cut-glass windows on each side and above the entryway. From the drive, I had to climb six marble steps to the gallery. I had the same sort of feeling standing in the shadow of this mansion that I had experienced walking the streets surrounding the National Mall in Washington. This was a house intended to intimidate, purposefully larger than life. It was a statement to any visitor—*I am more important than you.*

I rang the doorbell and removed my hat, the way my father had taught me to when entering the home of a stranger. Almost as soon as I pressed the button, the right-hand door swung open. I was greeted by a man who wore an expensive pullover sports shirt, the seams of which strained to contain his bulging biceps. He wore expensive sunglasses, which he didn't remove.

"Mr. Kovalenko?" I asked, when he didn't immediately identify himself.

"You are the policeman?"

As if anyone else had come calling in the last ten minutes. I searched his voice for any trace of a foreign accent, but didn't find one. His accent was not local. He sounded like people I had run across in New Orleans, who sounded as if they had come there by way of Brooklyn.

"Chief Wheeler, Prosperity Police," I said.

"Please come in. Mr. Kovalenko asked me to bring you to the pool."

I followed him through the house. The first floor had twelve-foot ceilings, with the exception of the foyer, which rose almost thirty feet or more to a massive Palladian window over the front door. A chandelier, which must have weighed at least a ton, hung from the foyer ceiling framed by the window the way a beacon is framed by a lighthouse.

The floor was fine Italian marble, covered here and there with incredibly ornate Persian wool rugs, which seemed to delineate specific areas of the main floor. Columns rimmed the walkway from the front door to the pool. On the left side was a dining room capable of seating a small army. On the right a massive fireplace and a sitting area containing no fewer than six sofas, with accompanying side chairs and coffee tables. The place seemed more like a fancy hotel lobby than a home.

The man who had answered the door didn't look back at me as he led me through the French doors to the pool. There, I found myself in a setting more commonly seen in old gladiator movies.

On the other side of the French doors was a lanai, perhaps twenty-five feet deep and forty feet across. It had been furnished like an interior room, with sofas, chairs, and a dining table the size of my entire kitchen. On one end of the lanai stood a stone fireplace. On the other was a mahogany bar. Behind the bar stood another young man wearing a similar pullover shirt to the one worn by my guide. Some sort of uniform?

Beyond the lanai was a pool about half Olympic-size. It appeared that I had interrupted a party. Lounging on chaises around the pool were ten or twelve women, mostly naked or near so. A few men, mercifully clothed in swim trunks, also lay by the pool, and from what I could tell it was the women's job to lionize them. I might visualize this scene in a Playboy mansion.

I was led to a table shaded by a huge umbrella. My escort turned and left without offering an invitation, but there was only one person seated at the table.

"Chief . . . *Wheeler,* is it?" the man said, as he placed a book aside and stood to greet me. He appeared in his early fifties, of average height, certainly not more than five-ten. He had a prematurely craggy face that showed the permanent remnants of severe teenaged acne. His hair, which appeared artificially dark, was worn in long waves that fell over his collar and ears. He wore square horn-rimmed glasses two sizes too large for his face, and they rested on a slightly bulbous nose that had pores you could lose a nickel in.

He spoke with a British accent.

"That's right," I said. "You're Mr. Kovalenko?"

"Please, call me Bunny. Everyone does."

"Bunny?"

"A childhood nickname. My sister, five years younger, couldn't manage a word as challenging as 'Bernard.' It kept coming out like 'Bunny,' and it stuck. I really don't mind. I would gladly offer you a drink, but I believe you are here on business and therefore on duty."

"Second time I've had to turn one down today."

"It must be tiresome. Perhaps some iced tea? I've only recently developed a taste for it, and now I can't seem to get enough."

"Iced tea would be neighborly," I said.

Kovalenko glanced toward the bar, where the man there had already begun preparing my tea, then turned his gaze back toward me.

"I seem to have interrupted a party," I said. "I apologize for barging in."

"This?" Kovalenko waved a hand toward the pool. "This isn't a party. These people, or ones like them, are here all the time. I hear it's part of the trappings of being a man of my wealth. On the other hand, I have learned in my brief time here that discussing money is impolite, so I will not mention it again. Do these hangers-on irritate you? I could send them away."

"Don't bother on my account. I won't be here long."

The man from the bar placed a napkin in front of me, along with a tall glass of tea. I picked it up, a little hesitantly. Kovalenko noted my expression, and laughed.

"Oh, please, Chief! It isn't poisoned, and it isn't drugged. What you must think of me!"

I took a sip. It was excellent, with a hint of peach nectar overlaying the sugar and lemon.

"Your man makes a mean glass of tea, sir," I said.

"And now to the purpose of your visit. No doubt you are here to discuss my late business partner, Ramsey Pressley."

"As a matter of fact."

"Yes. Facts. Very sad, terribly tragic. I've expected your visit ever since I heard about Ramsey's killing."

"You could have saved me the trip out here and dropped by the police station. We'd have let you in."

"But getting out might be another matter? In fact, I must say that I am not unfamiliar with you, Chief. You made a bit of a splash when you tracked down that horrible serial killer—what was his name?"

"He had a lot of them."

"Outstanding police work."

"I got lucky."

"And you are possessed by modesty. So refreshing. I am so happy you dropped by today. Tell me. Am I a suspect in your current investigation?"

"We'll call you a 'person of interest'."

216

"Because Ramsey Pressley was the American agent for one of my companies?"

"That's a good place to start. I don't suppose you can account for your whereabouts over the last couple of weeks?"

"Do I have an alibi? Is that what you mean? Well, of course I do. I haven't left my house in days, and I've been surrounded by these sycophants the entire time. I'll let you in on a little secret. I sometimes wish they'd go away. I could use some private time. On the other hand, if they did, I'd be at your mercy, now wouldn't I?"

"I think you're toying with me, Mr. Kovalenko."

"Bunny! Please."

"With your indulgence, I think we'll keep things on a professional level for the time being. We regard murder as a serious business in Prosperity. I accept that you should be able to cobble together some witnesses who will attest to your being in their presence, no matter when the murder took place. It isn't really an issue. After all, I don't think you killed Ram-Billy yourself."

"Ram-Billy? You mean Mr. Pressley? What a wonderful nickname."

"Were you associated with him for long?"

Kovalenko took a sip from his glass, and placed a finger to his chin. "I first approached Mr. Pressley about three years ago. We met playing golf. In the course of our conversation, I ascertained that he was of independent means. That's important in my business. I like a man who keeps to himself, doesn't have a lot of unnecessary business ties. It's inconvenient for my business to become wrapped up in someone else's. I'm sure you understand."

"Not really, but we'll get back to it. What did Ram-Billy do for you, exactly?"

"Not a great deal. We needed an American face. He filed certain papers of incorporation on our behalf. When there were complaints against one of my businesses, he provided the interface. He was a barrier between me and my business, and people whom I prefer to avoid."

"How much is a person like that worth?"

"I'm sure you will eventually get a court order for his bank records, but—if memory serves—I paid him approximately one hundred fifty thousand dollars last year."

"It's good to be an agent," I said.

"It has its advantages."

"And I suppose, being your American agent, Ram-Billy had access to information about your business dealings."

"He was our trusted representative."

"Our?"

"Come now, Chief. The fact that you are here means that you've already accessed our corporate records and know I do not operate as a sole proprietor."

"Your buddies back in Russia."

"Among other places."

"You'll forgive me for saying it, I hope. You don't sound very Russian to me."

"Because I'm not, at least not by birth. My parents escaped during one of Stalin's awful purges. They moved to England, where one of my uncles was already living. I was born there. Being first generation British in a Russian-speaking family, I learned both languages concurrently, and I'm still fluent. I also speak French, German, and a smattering of Cantonese."

"That doesn't explain your Russian buddies."

"I attended some distinguished private schools in England, then matriculated at Oxford."

"Impressive."

"Thank you. I studied economics and finance. I spent some time working in banking in London, until the old Soviet Union fell to pieces. I won't mince words with you, Chief, because I wish to be totally transparent. I saw an opportunity."

"With the Communists no longer in control, you took advantage of the chaos."

"Personally? Not at all. People already on the scene were way ahead of me. I had connections that were beneficial to them, however, and I was sort of a hometown boy, given that I was fluent in the language. I made certain connections, and I offered my expertise."

"You became a bag man for the Russian mob."

Something dark and malevolent crossed Kovalenko's face. I think he believed I didn't see it, but I did. "I suppose you could say that. I have a feeling the word 'bag man' is a bit colloquial for my tastes. I acted as a conduit. Russia was ripe for picking, but the pickings were slim after eighty years of Soviet rule. The people were unaccustomed to such raw, naked capitalism. Still aren't, which is why so many of them are beginning to yearn for the good old days of socialist security. The new businesses in Russia and its former territories quickly saw the need to diversify and internationalize their operations. I was already familiar with western business practices. It was a good fit—" he waved his hand around, as if showing off his palatial dwelling "—as I'm sure you can see. Capitalism! It's a great system, don't you think?"

"Why here in Bliss County? Why not New York? Los Angeles?"

He drained his drink. Before he placed it on the table, the barman arrived with a fresh one and whisked away the empty glass.

"As is often the case," Kovalenko said, "there was a woman."

"Was?"

"My wife. I met her—in New York—shortly after arriving in the country. This was over ten years ago. She was from North Carolina. So gentle, so refined. Would you agree, Chief, that women from the south are bred to grace and beauty?"

"I've never had any complaints."

"We married, and she wanted to return to her home state. We lived in Pooler for a while, in one of those uptown high-rise condos. The penthouse, of course, but it was still communal living. Ours overlooked the Pythons' stadium. I had front-row seats on my balcony for all the games. She became bored and longed to live outside the city, but I had businesses to maintain in Pooler. Your lovely county seemed a nice compromise."

"You aren't still married?"

"It seems she has a short attention span when it comes to men, even men of means such as myself. She became restless. I discovered she was engaging in affairs, which I could not tolerate, so I filed for divorce. She lives in Pooler now, on a very liberal settlement. Would you believe that we've become close friends since the divorce?"

"It happens."

"Indeed it does. By then, I'd discovered that I truly enjoyed living in this little paradise. Except for the middle of summer. It does get hot, doesn't it?"

I pulled the picture of Natalya Gromykova from my jacket pocket, and slid it across the table to him.

"Do you recognize this woman?"

He glanced at the picture. "No. Should I?"

"She's from Prosperity. Her name is Natalie Guthrie, but it was originally Natalya Gromykova when she lived in Lithuania. She and her husband have gone missing."

"I'm sorry to hear that."

"She turned up on one of your porn sites operated by Debuchke, Limited, the company you hired Ram-Billy to agent."

"What a coincidence."

"I'm a logical man, Mr. Kovalenko. I don't like coincidences. I don't trust them. Ram-Billy was looking at the page when he was murdered."

"He was a lonely man."

"Natalya Gromykova was a Russian mail-order bride. Do you own any websites offering women for marriage?"

"I certainly do, with my partners. Russian women are a prized commodity these days."

"Somehow, I have a difficult time thinking of people as commodities," I said, with more of an edge in my voice than I had intended.

"A poor choice of words. I apologize. Women in the former Soviet bloc are born into a different culture than American women. They do not have the same independent spirit that women in the United States have. Some men find that independent spirit threatening. They yearn for a marriage built on more traditional standards. Some men of limited attractiveness have a difficult time building a relationship with women who meet their cultural standards of beauty. Marriage brokers provide a way for men to meet and marry women more to their tastes."

"There were a lot of women on that website," I said. "A lot of them had what I'd call Slavic features. If I were to locate them, how many would I discover had come to this country by way of one of your marriage broker sites?"

"I have no idea. Why? Do you think it would be a great many?"

"You're toying with me again. I find it highly suspicious that Natalya Gromykova was brought to this country as a mail-order wife, and then wound up cavorting with dildos and vibrators on one of your websites. No real problem there, of course. After all, live and let live, as they say. What bothers me is that both she and her husband have gone missing. Prior to their disappearance, people at her husband's bank say he was troubled. His work had deteriorated."

"It's a sad story."

"Tell me, Mr. Kovalenko. What did you do in the banking

business in London?"

"I was in arbitrage."

"The buying and selling of money."

"Precisely. I'm impressed, Chief."

"I have my moments. Roger Guthrie was in arbitrage."

Kovalenko started to say something, then clamped his mouth shut.

"Yes," I said. "Another coincidence. That's what you were about to say, wasn't it?"

"What are you implying?"

"As I said before, I don't like coincidences. One here or there might be random chance. When they start to pile up, they form a pattern. Patterns are important when I'm investigating a murder."

"So we're back to the late Mr. Pressley. You think I murdered him, or had him murdered?"

"I'd entertained the notion. Thinking and proving are two different things."

"For which I am grateful. I've already told you that I want to be completely transparent with you, Chief Wheeler, though I have no legal obligation to do so. By rights, I should have my attorney here barricading your access to me. However, I do not wish to be distracted by the hot spotlights of your suspicions. I shall tell you directly. I had nothing to do with Mr. Pressley's death."

"And here I was thinking how easy you could make my life by confessing."

"No such luck. I have done many unsavory things in my career. I see little advantage in admitting to those I have not done."

"What's your connection with Sean Burch?" I asked.

"Why? Is it somehow related to this murder?"

"I don't know. I've frequently discovered that things I don't

222

know are important."

"I'll make a deal with you. You somehow relate my business dealings with Mr. Burch to the murder, and I'll gladly tell you all about them. I wish to be transparent, but I'm not interested in divulging all my dealings."

"Sean Burch is a sadist and a profligate. His morals emanate from a black place in his soul that makes a sewage treatment plant inviting. The path he walks is scorched earth."

"How colorful."

"I want you to understand the man you've embraced. He is not to be trusted."

I picked up my hat and prepared to leave.

"I appreciate your transparency," I said. "I do expect that I will have more questions to ask you at a later time."

"In the interest of justice, you are always welcome, Chief Wheeler."

I started to let myself out, but I had one more question. I'd waited to ask it, because I wanted to catch Kovalenko off balance, thinking he had rid himself of the troublesome, meddling cop.

"One more thing," I said, as I turned back to him and settled the Stetson in place. "Do you know a man named Boyd Over-hultz?"

That staggered him. He had been reaching for the book, but his hand stopped in midair, and a puzzled look crossed his face. "Overhultz," he said. "Yes. Of course. He has done some work for me."

"Do you know how I can get in touch with him?"

"I can give you his telephone number."

"Already have it. He's not answering. What kind of work does he do?"

"Odd jobs. I sometimes have need for a local to do . . . *local* things."

"Now, *that's* transparent as hell," I said.

"Why do you ask about Boyd Overhultz?"

I had Kovalenko on the ropes. I could tell he didn't like it.

"Glad you asked," I said. "I'm trying to figure out why his fingerprints were all over Ramsey Pressley's house."

"I'm sure I don't know."

"Yeah," I said. "Pressley worked for you. Overhultz works for you. Overhultz's fingerprints are plastered around the murder scene. Another one of those coincidences. A pleasure meeting you, Mr. Kovalenko. I suspect we'll talk again."

I let myself out, and realized I had dug my hands deep into the hip pockets of my khakis, so that Kovalenko couldn't see them shaking. I had learned a lot in our labyrinthine conversation, but I'd paid the price in anxiety. I began to wonder whether I'd ever regain the nerve I'd had a year earlier.

Donna found me a couple of hours later sitting on the front porch, nursing a beer and sulking.

"Got another one?"

"In the fridge."

She returned a few seconds later, twisted the cap off her bottle, and sat in the wicker chair next to the loveseat.

"Keeping your distance?" I said.

"Avoiding shrapnel. Looks like you're going to explode any minute."

"I talked with a very bad man today. I'm eighty percent certain he's responsible for killing Ram-Billy."

"Responsible. Meaning he didn't do it himself."

"People like him don't get messy. They hand that job to underlings. He's connected to Ram-Billy in too many directions to be innocent."

"But you don't have proof."

"No."

That hung between us like a flaccid clothesline. She understood my frustration. She'd seen it before. She knew there were times when I needed to let things cook in my head. We shared our comfortable silence and sipped our beers. When I'd drained mine, I headed for the door.

"Want another?" I asked.

"No. You go ahead. I think I'll go lie in the hammock and snooze while you ruminate."

When I returned to the porch, she was swinging in the hammock I'd hung between two pecan trees near the stone barbecue. She held the beer bottle on her belly, pointed skyward, looking like an abandoned chimney. Half of me wanted to join her, swing in the breeze, and feel the late afternoon sunlight on my face. I knew I wouldn't do that, though. I was not comforting company.

It takes a special combination of personality factors to make someone want to be cop. Among them must be some sort of acetic self-denial, the kind of sentiment that led men in earlier times to take up hair shirts and enter monastic lives of penury and silence. Few people get wealthy wearing a tin badge, and those who do are largely accounted for by guys on the take. The best officers I had known in my life had been those who were driven by internal needs for self-satisfaction. They were rewarded by a sense of doing the job well, and occasionally seeing it result in justice meted. They were too humble to call it nobility, but in a sense it was just that—a willingness to place their own prejudices and hubris aside and tend to the needs of others.

Back when I was in college, my psychology professor lectured about personality traits. He said there were cardinal traits, which comprised a single set of factors that seemed to sum up a man's entire character, and were rarely encountered because most people were understood in terms of the interaction of multiple factors, which he called central traits. Then, there were second-ary traits, which most of us possess to one degree or another, but almost never find an opportunity to display. Heroism, for instance. I have a belief that many of the heroes who charged into the Twin Towers on that day in September were possessed of deep reserves of courage and selflessness they never imagined. They were good and great cops and firefighters. For a brief mo-ment in time they tossed off fears for their own safety, ignored the threat to their lives, and plunged into an unimaginable hell for the sole purpose of saving others. How can you not admire people of that streak?

I had never considered myself a hero. I was a cop, doing a job, the way I believed the job should be done.

Like most cops, I had also encountered temptation. Every lawman eventually experiences moment of doubt. Some miscre-ant with a heart of dross and a laundry list of sins believes he can sidestep karma by purchasing a policeman's silence. Cops have to pay bills like anyone else. Cash is always tight for the average guy on the beat. Taking a couple of bills to look the other way for an all-important minute or two, knowing that the money will go to a good cause, is a tantalizing incentive. I'd known men who, weakened by momentary greed, had lived for years with the shame that inevitably followed. I'd watched their dishonor consume them from the inside like a malignancy, their husks a walking object lesson on the price of submitting to im-mediate gratification.

Two years earlier, a man I'd considered a friend had at-tempted to bribe me so he could skip the country to avoid a murder rap. The carrot on his stick had been my home, which he told me was the target of a conspiracy by politicians to seize and turn into a public park. Give him time to flee, he said, and he would squash the plans. My farm has been in my family since before the American Revolution. It's as much a part of me as my parents and my son.

I was tempted. I stared over the precipice and calculated the equation of my own soul against all I held dear in this world, and it didn't balance. I slapped on the cuffs and decided I'd deal with crooked politicians another day.

Meeting with Kovalenko had tickled my avaricious bones once again. I've always considered myself content with the simple pleasures of my farm and my family—including Donna— and seldom did I wonder what it would be like to live a life where money was a foregone conclusion and I could get anything I wanted by wishing.

That was the life Kovalenko lived. Walking through the immense palace he called a home, I was put in mind of a story I had heard once, about a great duke in Venice who had been given unlimited power. He lived in a Byzantine paradise of a castle, where he could sleep in a different room every night and never hit the same one twice in a year. Anything he wanted could be brought before him simply by snapping his fingers and commanding it.

There was a catch. There always is in stories like this. As powerful as this duke was, he could never leave his palace without the consent of the other rulers of his island nation. He was as much a prisoner of his riches as a man on death row is of his sins.

I had no doubt Kovalenko had told me the truth about his whereabouts the night Ram-Billy died. In fact, I suspected that he seldom set foot beyond the walls of his grand estate. An obvious man of intellect with a soul so shallow you could measure it in thimbles, he had bartered redemption for the masquerade of omnipotence. He owed everything in his sight to men who would not think twice of stuffing him through a sausage grinder. He did not command his own destiny, but someday he would be brought to accounts for his shortcomings.

I knew a thing or two about crime syndicates, and one thing I had learned was the unlimited depth of their greed. Once they had their talons in you, like a falcon with a field mouse, your soul belonged to them.

I might have envied Kovalenko's wordly pleasure dome, but I would not have spent a second sharing his fate. It irked me that he thought his opulence made him better than me, more powerful, more brilliant. When he fell, I realized, there certainly would be brilliance—the blinding illumination of a falling star.

If I could prove that he had ordered the death of Ram-Billy Pressley, a man in his own way every bit as detestable as "Bunny" Kovalenko, I was determined to help that heavenly descent come as quickly as possible.

I only hoped my rage against men like Kovalenko wasn't my own fatal weakness.

CHAPTER TWENTY-SIX

Once a week, usually on Friday night, Shug Burch took to his own stage at Shug's Nashville to do a set of his greatest hits, accompanied by the house country blues band. It was, inevitably, a huge draw. Every time he performed there was a measurable increase in the cash register receipts at the end of the night.

His weekly strut across his own stage also served to stoke his need for applause and approval. He was not an ignorant man, unaware of his own internal drives and needs for attention. He knew the meaning of the word "narcissism," and had even deliberated on occasion the extent to which the word applied to him. Contrary to what he believed others thought of him, he did harbor regrets. He had spent many contemplative hours rewinding the tape of his own life. There were moments he wished he could erase, and the older he became the more those moments multiplied.

There was a weakness in him he could neither deny nor overcome. His father had referred to it as laziness, but Burch had always considered himself expedient. He did not wish to wait for the good things in life to come to him, and frequently he had manipulated events to his favor—for instance, the night he had spiked that lead singer's beer with ipecac so many years ago in a honky-tonk in Louisiana. The event that launched what he perceived as his personal legend had been engineered to allow him to take the singer's place. An opportunity to rise above his lowly bartender's stratum had presented itself. The singer had no talent, save perhaps for manual labor or subservient clerical employment. Burch had rationalized poisoning him as an act of mercy, delivering him from a life of disappointment and failure at a career for which he was ill equipped and sorely suited.

It was a lie, as all rationalizations are, and Burch knew it at the time, as he did now, years later.

Yet, here he was, a southern country blues legend, belting out twelve-bar ballads in a voice like pebbles trapped in a hubcap on a car driving down an oiled dirt road, on the main stage in a nightclub bearing his own name on the marquee. On his office wall upstairs hung framed gold and platinum records, testaments to the Darwinian nature of his rise to stardom, and the competition he'd left devastated in his wake along the way.

The years had flown, many of them now dim and blurred memories. Clubs and amphitheaters and outdoor arenas. State fairs and big-city music halls. Nights on the road in party buses pounding down silent dark highways from one gig to the next, passing the time with pot and bourbon and smack and downers to help him block out the world long enough to sleep, and uppers to help drag himself out of bed in the morning. Rehabs between tours, going cold turkey so he could function long enough to get into the studio and cut one more single or another gold album.

The women.

Hundreds of them, over the years, now mostly faceless fleshy snapshot memories. One, two, even three at a time. One of the perks of stardom. *Hey, Sparky, tell that one over there to come to my bus after the show. See if she wants a little bit of the ol' Shugga Bugga.* They always came. Nobody refused Shug Burch. Who could reject the opportunity to romp with a superstar?

He had read a book once postulating that, among the billions of humans on earth, there were only a hundred thousand completely real people. Everyone else served as background noise. The hundred thousand made the earth move. They created the works of art, and drove the wheels of industry, and commanded great armies. Sometimes they passed their lives in relative anonymity, even as that passage appeared to others as somehow richer, fuller, more productive, and more meaningful than their peers' existences. The book said you could always know if you were one of the hundred thousand because no matter where you went in the world, you always managed to run across someone you already knew.

If that were true, then Shug Burch believed he must surely be one of the hundred thousand.

He pulled the microphone from its stand as the audience burst into another accolade. He scanned the tables in the room. Any woman in the house was now his for the asking. They sat with their dusty-booted farmhand boyfriends, chowing down on his beef and pounding back his liquor, and he knew he owned them. Later that night, as they writhed desperately on the soiled sheets in their doublewide trailers, trying to grab some shred of pleasure from the drudgery of their meaningless lives, he would be in their heads. They would fantasize they were with Shug Burch. If they played their cards right, one or two might even get a shot at the real thing.

He launched in with a ballad he'd written for his last album.

> "You say that my face
> Looks familiar to you
> You say that you know it
> But you just don't know who I am 'cause it
> happened so fast
> I was gone in a flash
> It's not easy to be
> Last Week's Front Page News."

He felt the tension build as he worked through the first verse, and as he reached the title line, the house burst into shouts and screams.

This is power. This is what it is to control people.

As the band vamped over the applause and the cheers, he glanced toward the bar. Lily worked there, along with a new kid he'd hired to replace Bobby. Lily was the head bartender now. Bobby would likely go home from the hospital in a day or so, and if he was smart he'd tear up asphalt getting out of town. Whether he knew it or not, Bobby had become another stitch in the fabric of Shug Burch's legend.

As he waited for the vamp to come back around, he tried to catch Lily's eye. She did not look his way.

"Got a key to the city
Had lunch with the mayor
Made the cover of People
And Vanity Fair
I was tops in the pops
Now it's all in the past
It's not easy to be
Last Week's Front Page News."

He had them now. Several couples had left their table and had started doing the Texas two-step on the peanut-shell littered floor. He loved this moment, being the center of attention, the reason for the audience's very breathing.

Lily wasn't behind the bar anymore. She had disappeared, leaving the new kid to fend for himself.

Burch had tried to talk with her the day after he'd fired Bobby and beat him to a bloody mass of skin and bone in the alley behind the club. She had acknowledged him, but he had found no warmth in her voice or acceptance in her features. He had justified her original fear of him, and now he wondered whether he could redeem himself in her eyes.

> "I did something so cool
> No one did it before
> You'd think I'd invented
> A new cancer cure
> Celebrity's fleeting
> Now I'm last season's shoes
> It's not easy to be
> Last Week's Front Page News."

Why in hell would he be concerned about the opinion of an individual woman, when he could easily possess every other female in the house? What made Lily different?

She mattered because he did not enchant her. What made every other woman he encountered accessible was the fact that he already lived in her fantasies. Lily was different. There was a place behind her eyes where he did not automatically reside. He knew he had disappointed her by pummeling Bobby. It didn't matter that Bobby was a thief who'd deserved a pounding. He had unleashed the brute inside of him, and she had been repelled by its visage.

> "Had my moment of glory
> My time in the sun
> Got a lifetime ahead
> But the best is all done
> Had a shot at the gold
> Now all I got is the blues
> It's not easy to be
> Last Week's Front Page News."

He glanced toward the bar. Lily had returned, and was pulling beers for a group of college boys who had entered the club. As the tap flowed, she glanced in his direction for the first time. Her face was tight. She didn't smile. Momentarily, her eyes met his, and he pointed in her direction, as he had during concerts for years, to establish a sense of direct contact. Usually, women he pointed at squealed and giggled.

She turned away from him, and forced a smile to one of the college boys as she passed him the mug.

Whatever I did, I need to undo.

> "People I meet
> Say 'Aren't you Old So-And-So?
> Man, you were so big
> Where in hell did you go?'
> I thank them politely
> Toss back some more booze
> It's not easy to be
> Last Week's Front Page News."

The crowd in the club stood and cheered again. Many, knowing the song by heart, recognized the closing refrain. They stamped and whistled and clapped in rhythm.

"Thanks, y'all!" Shug shouted into the microphone. "Tell you what. This ol' cowboy needs to take a break. Y'all dance for while, and if you buy enough food and beer and booze, maybe ol' Shug'll come back out and do another set later on, y'hear?"

He replaced the microphone and stepped out the stage's side door. He knew better than to try and wade through the room. Too many people wanted a chance to glad-hand and have a word with the great Shugga Bugga.

He took the back steps to his office, splashed some water on his face at the sink, and mopped the back of his neck with a towel. He sat at his desk and dialed a couple of digits on the house phone. Lily answered at the bar.

"Can you bring up a schooner of beer and a plate of the deluxe nachos?" he said.

"Yes, sir. I'll have it up there in five or ten minutes."

He didn't hear any recognizable emotion in her voice. She sounded flat, almost drugged, even as he knew she didn't use recreational chemicals or even alcohol. He suspected, though she had not confirmed it, that she had been in a program at some point. Maintaining a clear and sober head seemed important to her, which seemed incongruous with a career that entailed purveying the last openly legal and publicly accessible recreational drug.

Shortly, she placed a tray in front of him. "You need anything else, sir?"

"Yes. Have a seat."

"I need to get back to the bar. Steve is all alone down there."

"Steve has worked bars all over the state for years. He's okay on his own. Please. Take a seat."

She sat stiffly on the loveseat across from his desk.

"I think I owe you an apology," he said.

She did not respond.

"I acted rashly the other evening. I lost my temper, and I behaved in a way that may have frightened you. My actions toward Bobby were uncalled for under the circumstances. He did start it, first by stealing from the club, and then by disparaging you, but I think I could have found a better way of dealing with it. With him."

She turned toward the wall where the records hung, as if she were afraid to look him in the eye. A tear rolled down her left cheek.

"I wish I had some idea how else I could make up to you what I've done," Burch said.

She pulled a tissue from her pocket and dabbed at her eyes. "I do not believe you care for me," she said. "I enjoy this job, and I wish to continue working here, but I feel I have failed you in some horrible way.

"The other night you said you wailed on Bobby because he said awful things about me, and you said it again a few seconds ago. I opened my heart to you, and told you how I believed you were capable of great acts of charity and kindness, even if you did not believe so yourself."

"I heard you, Miss Lily. Nothing you said was lost to me."

"Who is the Russian?"

For a few seconds, Shug couldn't speak. "Where did you hear about the Russian?" he finally said, and heard the stress in his voice.

"That awful man you sent to spy on Bobby and trick him into exposing his thieving ways. He also visited you several days before, and he asked if you had heard from the Russian. I was outside your office and I overheard what he said about some man getting killed."

"You shouldn't have listened to that conversation."

"I wish I hadn't. I've had bad dreams about it, night after night. That man in your office thought the Russian had killed someone named Ram-Billy. I recall the name because it was so strange. He said the Russian killed this man, and was trying to blame it on him."

"The man in my office is named Overhultz. He has brains made of sewage. If smarts was dynamite, he couldn't blow his nose. He imagines things that aren't true."

"Like when he made disgusting comments about my body and accused you of doing me like a cheap whore, and you didn't take him to the woodshed?"

"I corrected him. If you heard the conversation, you'll remember that."

"What are you involved in, Mr. Burch?"

"Please. Call me Sean. Or Shug, if you want. I don't cotton to that name, but I'll allow you to use it."

"I don't know that I wish to be on familiar terms with you. I don't know whether you are a good man or a bad one. You say things and do things that confuse me."

He walked around the desk and sat next to her on the loveseat. She knotted the tissue in her hands, and it began to shred into ribbons.

"Miss Lily, the Russian helped pay for this club. I have no reason to tell you that, except to show you that I trust you with this information. He is an investor. I suspect his money is tainted with blood and with evil, but I can't prove that. The Russian is a polite and cultured man, but he is ruthless and violent. I can't tell you whether he killed Ram-Billy. I have no knowledge of it. Overhultz told me *he* didn't, and he may have a sewage trap in his head, but he is too simple to be an artful liar, so I believe him. Overhultz works for the Russian, and he works for me on occasion, and I reckon he'll do work of about any type for any lowlife who'll push a hundred bucks in his hip pocket. I have never hired him to hurt anyone. Have I hurt people in the past? Sure. Will I do it again? Possibly. A man cannot change overnight. But Lily, I'm trying."

She wiped at her eyes. Her nose had become reddened and swollen, and yet Shug thought she was the most beautiful thing he had seen all day. He could feel the emotional barrier between them, and he knew if he tried to pull her to him at that moment she would be repulsed and she would run screaming from the room. So he settled back toward the arm of the loveseat, and gave her the space he felt she wanted.

"I need to think," she said. "You are a frightening man and I believe you are involved in things that could bring great tragedy in your life. A person should not stand in the shadow of an oak in an electrical storm, lest they be struck by lightning. I fear that people close to you have caught a great deal of your shrapnel. I feel tired now and my head hurts. I like working here, but I don't believe I will be of much service to you anymore this evening. With your indulgence, I would like to go home and think about what I should do."

Shug's cell phone buzzed. He glanced at the name on the screen.

"Go ahead. It's all right. Head on home now," he said to Lily. "Your job here is safe. Get some sleep and come back tomorrow."

She pulled the door shut when she left, and Shug picked up the phone.

"Yeah, Bunny," he said. "That could be a problem. What do you want to do about it?"

CHAPTER TWENTY-SEVEN

When I got to the station the next morning, I found Department of Homeland Security Federal Agent Jack Cantrell sitting on the bench outside, thumbing through a newspaper.

"You keep odd hours, Chief," he said, without looking up.

"You were lucky to catch me. Most Saturdays I don't come in at all. I had some paperwork to do. You're going to keep me from it, aren't you?"

He followed me into my office. I had picked up a tall coffee at the Stop and Rob on the way in. I didn't offer to brew any in the office pot for Cantrell. I hoped he recognized this as a subtle hint.

"It's a sad state of affairs when I have to haul my ass out to the sticks on a Saturday to jerk a knot in your ass, Chief," he said.

"I'm sure you could have put it off until Monday. Isn't that your knot-jerking day?"

"Our failure to communicate has been a major disappointment to me."

I stared at him. Contributing to the conversation at this point felt a lot like enabling.

"In case your memory is clouded, Chief, I made it clear. The Natalya Gromykova case is off your radar. Want to explain to me why you were harassing Bernard Kovalenko the other day?"

I scanned his face. "You want to tell me whose fingerprints we found in Ram-Billy's house? The ones that compelled you to

239

call Sheriff Webb and try to scare him away?"

"If I didn't tell the chief law enforcement officer of an entire county, what makes you think I'll tell you?"

"You want to be on the side of the angels."

"Fat chance. Why are you hassling Kovalenko?"

"You know Bunny?" I asked.

"Don't fuck around with me, Wheeler."

"*Chief* Wheeler in my office. You have a point to make? I'm kind of busy here."

"DHS is taking a particular interest in Kovalenko. I was not happy to hear you pissed in his grits."

"Did I?"

"You as good as walked into his house and accused him of murder."

"You got a plant in Kovalenko's place? Please tell me it's not the bartender. Boy makes a mean glass of iced tea. You should try it sometime."

"I have."

"Worth a return trip, isn't it?"

"Not for you. I need you to keep your paws off him."

"Can't do it."

"Why?"

"Because he really is a suspect in a murder that took place here in Prosperity. Because he is linked to so many bad things happening in my town that I think it would be a good idea, in the interest of the public welfare, to make him a distant memory around here. Mostly, I can't because rattling his chain makes you so red in the face, and I am not proud of the secret joy that affords me. You need directions back to Pooler, Jack? We got maps in the front office."

"I don't think you understand what you're messing with. Kovalenko is bad news. He's hooked up with people you don't want tramping around this bucolic paradise. He's like a copperhead snake living under a log. Walk on by, don't disturb him, and nobody gets hurt. Turn over the log, and all hell breaks loose. The kind of hell you and your one patrolman are in no way prepared to cope with."

"We plan to add personnel shortly. You think this Kovalenko is such poison, do me a favor and bust him. Seems neither of us wants him around."

"I can't. I can't tell you why, either. I'm saying to lay off."

I took a sip of the coffee. "Not a lot of people around here liked Ram-Billy Pressley," I said. "I imagine they won't have to bring in a lot of chairs for his graveside service tomorrow. Some people seem to pass through this life leaving nothing but a solid trail of stench behind them. Someone like Ram-Billy gets his head split in two, there are people around who think of that as suburban renewal, like taking down ugly highway signs and planting flowers around an interstate cloverleaf. That doesn't mean we give his killer a pass. I happen to believe that Bunny Kovalenko had Ram-Billy murdered. Can't prove it yet, but I'm building a case. When I have enough evidence, I plan to march down to his big ugly house and drag him out of it by his balls. Actually, it will be Sheriff Webb doing the marching, but I plan to do the dragging."

"You're deluded. Kovalenko isn't scared of a shit-kicker cop from a wide spot in the highway between Pooler and the state line."

"Now you're being rude. And we were getting along so well."

"Maybe I should discuss this with your higher-ups."

"They'd be on my side. They don't like killings in Prosperity any more than I do. Maybe you could help in another way. What's the connection between Kovalenko and Natalya Gromykova? I mean, besides the obvious. You have her and Roger in a nice safe house somewhere waiting for the opportunity to testify against Kovalenko?"

I could see the color rise in his face, and I would love to have heard what he had to say, but we were interrupted by the two-way radio on my desk.

"Prosperity Two to Prosperity One. Got your ears on, Chief?" Slim called.

I toggled the radio. "What's up, Slim?"

"Hope you weren't planning a picnic today. We got a situation you need to see." He gave me an address off of Boone Ridge Road, on the far side of town.

"I'm coming," Cantrell said.

"The hell you are. This is town business. Nice talking with you. Gotta lock up the station."

He followed me out to the parking lot and watched impotently as I climbed into the new cruiser to go meet Slim.

Slim had parked his cruiser on a cul-de-sac of fresh asphalt, in a new development. The builders had only put in the road. There were no houses around yet. At the head of the cul-de-sac was a dirt path leading down and around a hill toward a pond.

A yellow pickup truck was parked on the street. A couple of boys in their late teens sat inside. I saw some tackle boxes and rods in the truck bed. The boys in the truck looked frightened. I tipped my Stetson at them as I walked by.

Slim stood by his cruiser, smoking a cigarette. When I walked up, he stubbed it on the heel of his boot and tossed it into the weeds.

"What'd they do?" I asked, nodding toward the boys.

"Them? Nothing. Well, they went fishing, which is when they found the car." He turned toward the truck. "You boys stay put, y'hear? I'm gonna show the chief what you found."

We walked down the path, and I noted some tire tracks in the dirt. There were several of them, all different makes.

"Boys told me they been coming to this pond to fish for

about a year. Said one of them found it when he brought his girl up here to make out one night. According to their story, the pond is stocked with bream and brook trout, and a few bass."

"We here to talk fish?"

"No," Slim said, as we rounded the bend at the bottom of the hill. "We're here about this."

Ahead of us, parked on a narrow levee between the pond and a drainage ditch, was a Buick Riviera with a tattered vinyl roof.

"Aw, shit," I said. "I know this car."

Boyd Overhultz still sat in the front seat. The driver's side window was rolled down. Two small ribbons of dried blood ran down his neck from somewhere in his hairline behind and above his left ear.

"I ran the plates," Slim said. "This the guy we tried to talk to the other day?"

"It's him. Two behind the ear. Professional."

"I ain't seen a lot of hits, but yeah. I came to that same conclusion. What in hell are we dealing with here, Chief?"

"I don't know yet," I said. "But I will."

Clark Ulrich, Don Webb's senior crime scene tech, answered the call when we phoned in a request for assistance. I'd worked with Clark before. He was very good at collecting evidence. As soon as he arrived, he told us to stay wide of any tire tracks long enough for his techs to take some photos and make some casts of the deeper ones that had been made in mud.

"Can't say for certain until the medical examiner gets here," Clark said, "but I'd guess small caliber. Probably a twenty-two. Certainly no bigger than a twenty-five. Round like that goes in, usually stays in, bounces around a little to Swiss cheese the brain. I've seen a couple of these with guys mixed up with the meth gangs. Anything seem strange to you about this, Chief?"

"Yeah," I said. "Hits like this usually take place by surprise.

Guy's sitting in his car, maybe listening to the radio, and the killer walks up alongside and parks two behind the guy's ear. Gun like a twenty-two barely makes enough of a pop to hear over the street noise. Boyd here wasn't parked at a curb. He made a point of coming here."

"That was my thought. It's hard to sneak up on someone out here in the boonies. My guess is the guy who zagged him was a passenger. They came out together."

"Or, given the number of tracks up the hill, maybe they came in two cars—Boyd in one and the killer, or killers, in the other."

"We'll work up the car once they get this good ol' boy out," Clark said. "In any case, I'd guess he knew the guy who popped him. That should narrow your list of suspects a little."

"We have a pretty good estimate of time, too. The boys who found him fished in the pond on Thursday afternoon, so he was killed between then and this morning."

"I'm not a medical examiner, but I've seen a lot of dead guys. This one looks relatively fresh. Might have been killed as recently as this morning. You know who he is?"

"A suspect in that Ram-Billy murder."

"Sounds like someone's trying to cover up some tracks."

"It does. Take your time, Clark. Do this one right."

He headed down the hill, and I pulled out my cell phone. This was one call I really hated to make. Jack Cantrell answered on the second ring.

"What's up, Chief?"

"Maybe you should have ridden on that call with me after all. It gives me no pleasure to say this, but I got a DB. It's a guy who works for Kovalenko, named Boyd Overhultz. His prints were all over Ram-Billy Pressley's house. I sort of goaded Kovalenko with him the other day."

"You might have gone and got that boy killed, Chief."

"I know. I'm not walking away from this case. This makes

two killings in Prosperity, and I'm not handing them over to the feds. You want to pitch in on them?"

"No."

"Why?"

"Because you didn't use the magic word."

I swallowed hard. I take pride in my work. While I'm not averse to asking for help when I need it, with some people it's harder than others.

"Please. I could use some assistance on this."

"Lemme sleep on it," Cantrell said. "I'll get back with you. Try not to get anyone else whacked down there before I do, okay?"

I didn't get home until after five o'clock. I found Donna on the front porch, sipping homemade lemonade and reading a novel. I kissed her and went inside to put away my gun and hat. On the way back out, I grabbed a glass.

"This used to be such a quiet little town," I said, as I collapsed in the loveseat beside her.

"I already hate this conversation."

"Got another murder. I think I might have pushed this one along a little."

"Maybe you should explain that."

I told her about Kovalenko, who seemed to have his fingers in every business in town and a few in Morgan. I told her about my visit to him, and how I'd surprised him by mentioning the late Boyd Overhultz. Then I told her that Overhultz had been the victim of a professional hit.

"You're feeling guilty," she said. "You think asking about this Overhultz man got him killed."

"More puzzled than guilty. If asking about him was enough to kill him, he probably knew or did something that made him worth killing. Given that his prints were all over Ram-Billy's house, I'm guessing it was something he did, and my prime suspect didn't want him talking."

"Which makes your prime suspect a dangerous person."

"One worth keeping an eye on at all times. Every lead I get in this Ram-Billy case traces back to Kovalenko. He's got his fingers in Kent, in Sean Burch, and in Lord knows what else in this county. There are even connections between him and that couple who disappeared last month. Too much smoke."

"You'll get him," she said.

I took a sip of the lemonade. "You think?"

"It's what you do, Judd. You're like an old hound dog. You've got this Russian bastard's scent in your head now. That's bad for him. He's zeroed in, and it's only a matter of time before you drop the hammer on him."

"For Ram-Billy?"

"For something. They got Al Capone on income tax evasion. You'll find a reason to take Kovalenko off the board, if only to make Bliss County a better place to live. He may not go down for killing Ram-Billy, but he's going down."

I finished the lemonade and crunched a piece of ice between my teeth. Somehow, we'd edged over into May. The days were hot, but as the sun settled behind the poplars and red oaks that separated my yard from the farm fields, a crisp chill quickly fell over the front yard. My favorite season of the year was autumn, but that climatic boundary between spring and summer in early May tailed it by inches.

"Don't feel like cooking tonight," I said.

"Don't feel like going hungry, either."

"What say we forget about this murder business for an evening? I'll take you into Morgan, take you anyplace you want to go."

"You know where I'd like to go?"

"Name it."

"I've heard a lot about Shug Burch's club. I think I'd like to see it. Never been to an upscale honky-tonk before. Think you could stand being in his place for a couple of hours?"

There were two or three circles of Hell I'd rather visit, but this was the woman who had stood by my side for months while I lingered between life and death.

"Let me grab a shower and put on some two-step boots," I said.

CHAPTER TWENTY-EIGHT

We got to Shug's bar a little after eight, as a guest band from Atlanta was warming up. The hostess showed us to a table in the middle of the hall, and we ordered beers so we would fit in with the crowds around us.

"Pretty high class for Morgan," Donna nearly shouted at me over the din.

"Kovalenko's money apparently buys the best."

She pouted. "You said no talk of bad guys tonight."

"You're right. Let's relax and enjoy the music."

The Atlanta band built its set around a mix of Charlie Daniels–style fiddle fire and the kind of stuff you heard back in the eighties by groups like The Doobie Brothers and The Marshall Tucker Band. It wasn't bad—which, at my age, meant it didn't make my ears bleed—and by the middle of the first set Donna coaxed me out on the floor to step lively for a song or two. I hadn't danced in years, in truth since before my first wife, Susan, died. Given that I was still in recovery from a near-death experience, I kept up the best I could, but it was a lost cause. After a couple of fast numbers I was winded and foot-tied. We turned back to our table, and right into the path of Sean Burch.

"Well, I'll be damned!" Burch thundered. "Prosperity's finest! How ya doin', bro?"

He held out a rough paw. It would have been impolite to ignore him in his own place, so I shook reluctantly.

"Donna wanted to take a look at your club," I said, trying to hold eye contact. Even as kids, Burch had enjoyed intimidating people with his stare. I had learned years earlier to return it in kind.

"Be my guest!" he said, raising his hands and turning as if showing the room. "In fact, I mean that. Whatever you want tonight, it's on me."

"No need," I said. "We can pay."

"I wouldn't think of it. Your money's no good here, and I'm instructing the wait staff not to bring you a bill. My way of showing my appreciation for the good work you do down in my hometown. If something isn't up to your standards, you let me know personally, and I'll take care of it." He turned to Donna. "I know we met at the Kramer house a while back, but I am embarrassed to say I can't recall your name immediately."

"I'm Donna," she said, as he grabbed her hand and smothered it between both of his the way you'd slip a hamburger into a bun.

"Donna. I won't forget it again. I always knew Judd was smart, but I didn't know he was lucky too. Are you enjoying yourself tonight?"

"Maybe we should go," I said.

"Please!" Burch rumbled. "Don't do that. We really didn't have much of a chance to talk at that party. I believe you harbor ideas about me that simply aren't true. Believe me when I say you are perfectly welcome at Shug's Nashville. I hope this old man didn't wear you out on the floor, Miss Donna, because I was hoping you'd honor me with the privilege of a dance."

It was an awkward moment. On the one hand I could have pushed him aside, grabbed Donna, and hustled out the door. I didn't because that might have given the impression of capitulation, and I know how Donna hates to be patronized. If she thought I was trying to protect her from the likes of Shug Burch, she'd be angrier at me for thinking she needed it.

"Sure," she said, taking the decision from me. "One number would be fine."

I watched as Burch led her back out to the floor. I knew she could handle herself, but I resented him all the same. I sat back in my chair, perhaps a bit more solidly than I intended, and I took a long draw from my beer mug. The pounding of the band's back beat seemed to fade into the distance as I watched him lead her through a series of two-step routines with a couple of twirls. I resolved to shoot him if he attempted to dip her.

When the song was over he led her back to the table.

"She's a beauty and a fine dancer," he said, as he held her chair for her. "I was right, Judd. You are a lucky man."

He held up a hand, and gestured to a blonde woman behind the bar. Without hesitation, she crossed the floor to join us. She was buxom and round in all the right places, and filled her skinny jeans and shirt in a way that any reasonable man could only describe as ample and admirable.

"This is Miss Lily," he said. "She's the head bartender tonight. Miss Lily, I'd like to introduce you to the chief of police over in Prosperity, a fellow I knew when we were sprouts, back in the Dark Ages. This is Judd Wheeler, and his lovely companion, Donna."

Lily shook both our hands.

"It's a pleasure to meet you," she said, in a voice that might have come from a road-weary Tammy Wynette. Her eyes captured my attention. They were much older than a woman her age should possess, and expressed an inner sadness that defied description.

"You said the chief of police?" she said to Burch.

"That's right, honey, but don't you worry none. Morgan's out of his jurisdiction. He's here tonight for fun, right, Judd? I have some other business to attend to—gotta work the room, you know, shake the bucks out of the customers—but I want you to take real good care of these two. It's all on me. Understand?"

"Yes. I'll see to it."

He patted her on the shoulder, which seemed uncharacteristic to me, and made me wonder whether he had something more than lascivious feelings for her. The Sean Burch I knew would have slapped her on the ass, and maybe even copped a quick squeeze. Then he winked at us, and turned to "work the room."

"You heard the man," Lily said to us. "What can I get for you?"

We left after the second set. I didn't say anything for most of the trip back to Prosperity, until Donna broke the silence.

"Well, that was fun."

"Maybe next time I'll take you to a dog fight."

"I think I saw the start of one tonight. Did you always bristle when Burch was around?"

"It's a complicated relationship."

"Think he's sleeping with that bartender? Lily?"

"The idea occurred to me. Why?"

"Curiosity. She looks like the type a man like Burch would go for."

"How so?"

"Earthy, built, a little shopworn. Looks like she's been around the block once or twice. Looks like she'd know what to do in a dark room."

"Geez. You passed five words with the woman all night, and you've already pigeonholed her into a cultural stereotype. What do you make of Sean?"

"Good on his feet. Don't like his eyes much. They remind me of a wolf's eyes. Feral. You notice how he constantly scans

251

the room? Like maybe he's afraid someone is going to jump him."

"I hear prison does that to you. The textbooks call it hyper-vigilance. The kind of thing cats do when they're eating. You don't keep a close eye on everyone in the joint, sometimes you never leave. That kind of habit sticks with a man. Might lead him to strike out preemptively if he feels threatened."

"Hence the Shugga Bugga legend."

"Such as it is."

"You hate him that much?"

"I loved him, once. Maybe I resent what he did to our friend-ship more than I actually hate him. Maybe I'm still angry at him for what he did to Lisa Rae, and what he forced me to do, ratting him out. It was a long time before I felt comfortable be-ing best friends with a man again."

"Until Kent came along."

"Yeah, I guess. Kent and I have been best buddies for over a quarter century, some of it covering rough road."

"You said he's bound up with this man Kovalenko. What if you found out he was doing something illegal? Could you turn Kent in?"

I had to think about that one. "Things seem more polarized when you're a teenager," I said. "Everything is neatly catego-rized. Black and white. Up and down. Good and bad. The divid-ing lines blur as you get older. You find yourself doing things you'd never imagined. You let things slide, because maybe it serves a greater good to let a little bad go unpunished. Before you know it, you recognize your own feet of clay. Morality starts to shift. Kent's done a lot of good in this world. He supports kids' programs. He raises money for charities, and tosses in a not inconsiderable amount of his own. He's a blowhard, though, full of himself. In some ways he's a lot like Sean, which may be why I was drawn to him at first, like he was some kind of Sean surrogate. I don't know. It was a long time ago. If I were to discover tomorrow that he was actually laundering money for Kovalenko, I might look the other way, at least as long as I could stand to. Maybe I'd take Kovalenko out to save him."

"Take him out?"

"You know what I mean. Don't make me say it."

From the corner of my eye, I saw her shudder a little.

"The big fish," I said. "It's important to keep your eye on the important stuff. Kent told me Kovalenko saved the land business by injecting cash. We both know Kent. He's all about today's problem, doesn't look too far into the future. His desire to save his business in the most expedient way might have opened him up to exploitation by the bigger fish. You know what a bust-out is?"

"No."

"Something the mobs do. They invest in your business, get a little piece of it. Then, little by little, they nibble away at your cash flow. After a while, when you get a little tight, they invest again, take a larger chunk of the pie. Soon they own the larger share. They push you to borrow against your assets, hock yourself right up to the chin. When there's nothing left to borrow against, and they've squeezed every cent out of you they can, they move on to the next sucker, and you're left holding the bag. There's only one way out—bankruptcy. Something like that would kill Kent. Take away his status as the king of the hill, you might as well gut him. If I found out someone was doing that to him, I think I'd have to stop it."

"By any means necessary."

"You do that for people you love."

We drove another mile or so before she spoke again.

"And what about your soul?"

"What?"

"If you let that moral compass swing too far in saving your

friend, what happens if you lose your own humanity in the process?"

"You mean, if I felt compelled to—take out Kovalenko."

"Sure. Let's use that example."

I considered the question. "I've been lucky," I said. "I've always found a way not to let things go that far. I came close, a couple of years ago—"

"To protect me."

"That's right. Maybe I'd have done it, too, if things had swung an inch in the other direction. Sometimes we get lucky," I said.

CHAPTER TWENTY-NINE

I received a call from Clark Ulrich on Sunday morning, shortly after breakfast.

"Sorry to disturb you on the weekend, Chief," he said.

"If you're working, I'm working."

"We processed Boyd Overhultz's car. Found about eleventy-seven parking and speeding tickets in his glove compartment, along with a grody hash pipe and baggie of skunk weed."

"So the highways are safer today for his passing."

"I'd say. There was something else. One of the parking tickets was written by a Morgan PD patrolman the night before we found the body."

That got my attention. "Really."

"Sure thing. Overhultz seems to have enjoyed ignoring parking meters. I mean, why not? If you never intend to pay the fines, why feed the machines, right? Anyway, he got a ticket on Friday night in the thirty-seven hundred block of Hamilton Street in downtown Morgan. There's more. I found a receipt from a tavern, also dated Friday night, and guess what?"

"It's in the thirty-seven hundred block of Hamilton Street?"

"You kinda stepped on my punch line there, Chief. But, yeah. The place is called Smitty's. They're basically a beer and burger joint. Given a choice I'd skip the food. The parking ticket was written at nine-seventeen. The receipt was time-stamped at nine-forty-two."

"Meaning Overhultz was probably in Smitty's when he got

the parking ticket."

"And he probably left around quarter to ten. If I was a police detective instead of a lowly crime scene tech, my next question would be—"

"Did he leave alone?"

"Bingo."

"Think maybe I should drop by Smitty's, see if anyone there remembers Overhultz hanging around on Friday night."

"You'll need to wait a few hours."

"Oh, right. They can't open until one o'clock. The blue laws. That will give me time to pull together some other information I need. Looks like a working Sunday for me. Thanks for the information. I'd be obliged if you'd write it all up and send me a copy first thing tomorrow morning."

I apologized to Donna for depriving her of me on a weekend, and drove the Jeep over to the station. I already had Overhultz's address, since Slim and I had tried to find him there a few days earlier. What I didn't know was whether Overhultz owned or rented the shack. Usually, I'd have called the Register of Deeds office to get the information, but they were closed, so I had to do my own legwork. Luckily, Bliss County had installed an online property tax system a couple of years earlier, which was linked to a database that anyone could access.

It only took a few minutes to find that it was a rental, owned by a man named Leo Tompkins. I jotted down his address and phone number and gave him a call. He didn't sound terribly upset when I told him his tenant was dead.

"Guess I'll have to clean the place out then. He lived there alone."

"Don't do that yet. Mr. Overhultz wasn't killed in the house, but there may be evidence there that can help us find his murderer. With your permission, I'd like to search the place later this afternoon."

"Sure. But make it after three o'clock. I got church this morning and we're having a picnic after the service. Don't want to miss all the food."

"Can you tell me anything about Mr. Overhultz?"

"Like what?"

"Well, what kind of tenant was he?"

"A deadbeat. I threatened to evict him several times for not paying his rent. He wouldn't keep up the yard. He probably cut the grass, what there is of it, once in a blue moon. He was always calling me to complain about one thing or another. The hot water heater would break, or the cable would go out. Gripe, gripe, gripe. Yet, when I needed his rent money, he'd act like I was trying to extort him."

I stifled the impulse to note that the house was little more than a shanty and probably prone to breakdowns, but I didn't want to piss him off.

"Why don't we plan to meet at the house at three?" I said. "I'll probably have one of my patrolmen there to help search the place."

"I'll do you one better. You don't need me there, do you?"

"Not that I can think of."

"I'll drop off a key on the way to church. There's an old wooden bucket on the front porch. I'll put the key under the bucket. You can leave it there when you go. You find anything in that house you need, take it. I'll probably have to gut it anyway, after renting to Overhultz for five years. Not to speak ill of the dead on the Lord's day, but I'm glad to finally be shut of him."

Smitty's smelled like old grease, cigarette smoke, and stale beer, and that was about the best you could say for it. The owner felt so fortunate to have received a Sanitation Grade C certificate from the Health Department, he displayed it prominently over the men's room door. If it enjoyed a Sunday after-church rush, they must have all eaten and left before I got there at one forty-five, because the place was almost empty. A couple of guys who looked two nickels away from homeless sat in a booth in the back. They gnawed on gristly burgers and dipped shoestring fries into ketchup and vinegar.

A man sporting a freshly sutured cut on his forehead sat behind the counter, watching a NASCAR race on a black and white TV mounted over the cash register. "Pick any seat you want," he said.

I pulled back my jacket lapel and flashed my badge.

"This is Morgan," the man said. "Badge says Prosperity. You want something to eat? Won't be on the house."

I slid onto an ancient cracked-leather stool at the bar and rested my forearms on the Formica top.

"I'm investigating a murder. You know a man named Boyd Overhultz?"

"Not by name. You got a picture?"

As it happened, I did. Boyd had been arrested a time or two in his forty years, mostly for low-rent beefs, and I had downloaded and printed a copy of his most recent mug shot. I placed it on the bar.

"Deadbeat," the man said. He wore a striped shirt with an oval patch that said *Lowe*.

"That your name?" I said, pointing at it. "Lowe?"

"What about it?"

"Name's Wheeler. I am the chief of police in Prosperity which, as you've noted, is not Morgan. I don't have authority in Morgan. I am, however, a good friend of the sheriff, Don Webb. Right now we're having a friendly little chat. I happen to know that Sheriff Webb is enjoying a pleasant Sunday afternoon at home. He would not like to be disturbed, but I don't mind disrupting his day if I need to. So, for the duration of our short time together, why don't we pretend that you have to answer my questions? That gonna work for you, Lowe?"

He shrugged. "Sure. Whatever."

"You're the second person to call Mr. Overhultz a deadbeat today."

"You keep asking people, I won't be the last."

"Why do you say that?"

"I don't know this guy by name, but I know his face. He comes in once or twice a week. Always orders the same thing. Cheeseburger with rings and a Bud. Never leaves a tip. Always says he only has enough to pay for the food, but no more. Fuckin' deadbeat."

"At least he paid for the food."

"Yeah, hot shit. So who'd he kill?"

"Seen him around lately? Like, maybe this past Friday night?"

"He's been in here three, four times in the past week. Friday? Yeah, I do seem to recollect he was in here."

"Would have been between eight and ten o'clock."

"Sure. He was here then. With the other guy."

"Other guy?"

"Yeah, the rough-looking one. Your guy sat in that booth over there, under the Coors sign. There was another guy with him. The other guy was rough."

"By rough, you mean . . . ?"

"Like he'd been shoved under a steamroller. Someone had worked him over, but good."

"He'd been beaten?"

"Like with a baseball bat. He had bruises all over his face and his cheeks were swollen. Both his eyes were black and he had a couple of stitches in his chin. If I felt the way he looked, I wouldn't be walkin' the streets. I'd be home in bed with a bag of ice on my face."

"Did Overhultz and this guy come in together?"

"Don't rightly recall, but they left together. Now that I think on it, I don't believe they did come in at the same time, on account of the fact that my waitress that night had to take two orders at that booth, and your guy paid both of 'em. I think maybe your guy sat down first, and the messed-up dude came in later, but I wouldn't swear to it in court."

"Did you know the other man with Overhultz?"

"Might. Might not. Bad as he was beaten, he might have been my cousin and I wouldn't recognize him."

I dropped my card on the bar top. "You see the guy with the beat-up face, you give me a call. Understand?"

"Sure. Whatever."

CHAPTER THIRTY

It was a warm spring Sunday, and Donna decided she'd grade her English students' papers on the front porch. She wore a pair of jeans cut off high on the thigh, and an old seersucker shirt unbuttoned halfway down with the tails tied under her breasts. She was barefoot.

She finished grading the papers, stashed them back inside the house, grabbed a novel she'd bookmarked about two-thirds of the way through, and returned to the porch with a glass of iced tea and lemonade to read.

A few minutes later, a black Caddy Escalade turned into the drive, crunching gravel under its massive tires as it snaked its way through the trees. It stopped in front of the steps. Sean Burch hopped from the driver's seat.

"Miss Donna," he said, from the drive. He stayed by the Escalade.

"Mr. Burch. Something I can do for you?"

"I was of a mind to call on Judd. Don't suppose he's around."

"You missed him. I expect he'll be back around suppertime. Anything you want me to tell him?"

Burch leaned against the car and crossed his arms. "I get the impression you don't like me, ma'am."

"You're mistaken. I don't know you."

"You're a mighty fine dancer. I enjoyed seeing you last night. Would you mind if I had a seat? Couple of things I'd like to talk over with you."

"Come on up."

Donna had taken the wicker loveseat. She dropped the book next to her, as if to indicate the space was taken. Burch sat in the chair perpendicular to her.

"I reckon Judd has told you a lot of things about me," he said. "Some of them likely weren't so nice."

"He told me you tossed a live rabbit into an incinerator, and you raped a young girl who showed kindness to you by inviting you to her house for a swim. Would you mind not staring at me like that? The way you look at me makes me want to wear a burka."

He worried at a hangnail.

"I apologize if I've offended you, but you're a handsome woman, and easy on the eyes, if you don't mind me saying it. I done all them things, and a lot more. That's sort of what I wanted to talk over with Judd. He and I haven't laid eyes on each other for thirty years or more. I'm sure he told you we were close, a long time ago. I think maybe he believes I hold a grudge against him for testifying against me in that rape trial, and that part of coming back here was about settling some old scores."

"I think this is none of my business, and the sort of thing you should discuss with Judd, not me."

"Maybe you can pass the word along to him, so he'll be a little more receptive the next time we talk. I saw the way he stared at me last night in the bar, and I can tell he resents me coming back home. He didn't like me dancing with you, and to tell you the truth I didn't think twice about asking you to take a turn, but my bartender Lily told me later that I was intruding on you by doing it, and I'm sorry if I stepped out of line."

"You spend a lot of time apologizing," Donna said. "My guess is you're troubled by a guilty conscience."

"You aren't the first to suggest it. I don't imagine Judd knows the tenth of all the bad stuff I've done in my life. I reckon if the good Lord chose to smite me today, there wouldn't be much left behind to mark my passing, save for a few records and a bank account. I don't have a family or children. You and Judd aren't married?"

"No."

"Did he ever get married?"

"He did. A woman named Susan. She died in a car crash on the Morgan Highway over Six Mile Creek ten years ago."

"I'm sorry to hear it. And children?"

"One. A boy, Craig. He's off at college."

"A son. And a college boy at that. He is a lucky man, like I said. I don't have none of that, and to tell you the truth there ain't a really huge pile of money in the bank. Seems I keep spending it as quick as I get it. Been lucky on that account, since it seems to keep coming in. But that's not what I'm talking about. The money and the gold records and the club— they're mostly stuff I use to make myself feel good. Been that way for nigh on to twenty years now. Man reaches a point in his life when he realizes he's got a lot more good road behind him than he does ahead, and he starts to take stock of what the meaning of his life has been all along."

He stopped talking, and looked back up at her for the first time in a while.

"Listen to me, gabbing on the way I am, and here we have barely been properly introduced. I think I was prepared to have this talk with Judd, tell him things I've been thinking about for a long time, stuff that's been bubbling under the surface, looking for a way out. You aren't interested in all this. You have a nice day, Miss Donna. I'll catch up with Judd another time."

He stepped back down to the gravel drive, and placed his hand on the Escalade door handle.

"Mr. Burch," she said.

He turned back to her. "Ma'am?"

"You'll discover that Judd is a traditionally minded man. He has clear ideas of the difference between right and wrong, but he isn't a saint. He's made mistakes of his own. He's paid for a lot of them. Have you made amends for all your errors?"

"Remains to be seen, Miss Donna. I'm trying. Problem is, I seem to keep making new ones to take their place. But I aim to do better. I surely do. I appreciate your time."

He climbed into the car and started the engine. "I'm happy to see you weren't terrified of bad ol' Shugga Bugga," he called through the open passenger side window.

She pulled a nine-millimeter automatic from between the cushions on the loveseat, and laid it in her lap. "A serial murderer stood out on the Morgan Highway and took pictures of me sitting on this porch a year or so ago," she said. "He intended to do great harm to me. I determined that I would never be caught unaware. I can't say that I find you pleasant company, Mr. Burch, but I had good reason not to fear you. Have yourself a nice day, now."

CHAPTER THIRTY-ONE

I found the key to Boyd Overhultz's house under the bucket on the front porch, exactly where Tompkins had said he'd leave it.

"We need to glove up?" Slim asked from the base of the porch steps. "After all, Overhultz wasn't killed here. Doesn't seem to be a crime scene."

"Let's presume it is," I said, as I pulled purple nitrile gloves from my jacket pocket. "Could be Overhultz was murdered because of something in the house. Besides, having met the man, we might consider wearing hazmat suits. Everyone I've spoken to seems to regard him as some kind of walking virus."

I opened the door, and Slim followed me inside. I flipped a switch on the wall and a ceiling light illuminated the room. The place was surprisingly clean, or perhaps it simply wasn't as filthy as I had imagined it. Everything seemed to be in order. There was a forty-inch flat screen TV sitting on a table about ten feet in front of a worn green sofa. The coffee table between them had been dusted recently. There were some neatly stacked car magazines on the coffee table, along with a couple of remote controls. The heart pine floors were beaten up by decades of hard-soled shoes, but they were clean, as was a wool area rug in the living room.

The kitchen was neat. No dishes in the sink or pots on the stove. A quick check of the refrigerator revealed nothing out of the ordinary. Boyd Overhultz might have been a slob in other areas of his life, but he had kept an unexpectedly orderly home.

I pulled out drawers in the kitchen and found an unloaded, snub-nosed, thirty-two revolver. I bagged it to do ballistics tests on, since it might be related to an unsolved crime.

I was about to consign the place to the status of a dry hole when I heard Slim whoop from the back of the house.

"Ho-ly shit, Chief. You gotta see this. Looks like we hit the honey hole."

I found him in a second bedroom at the back rear corner of the place. He had opened a sliding closet door, and stood staring into it. It appeared as if someone had wrapped fifty or sixty bricks in aluminum foil and stacked them in the back of the closet.

"I smelled it before I opened the door," Slim said. "Smell that strong is hard to mistake."

I recognized the odor too, from drug busts back when I was an Atlanta street cop. From what I could see, Overhultz must have hoarded forty or fifty pounds of processed marijuana in his home.

"Think it's enough for a distribution beef?" Slim asked, smiling.

"It'll do. Shame the guy's dead. It would have been fun to run him in on this one. Good job, Slim. We'll need to get a set of scales in here and catalog everything. Maybe put a call in to DEA, see if they can handle the disposition."

"Or we can sell it and retire to Tahiti."

I laughed then said, "Wait a minute." I was about three feet behind Slim and had a better view of the closet. There was a cardboard box on the shelf over the clothes rack. "What's this?"

I pulled the box down, and opened it carefully on the bed.

There was a laptop computer inside. I turned it on. The battery was charged and the computer booted in about half a minute. The desktop had a large photo of a couple grinning at the camera with the mile-high swinging bridge from Grandfather Mountain behind them.

"Well," I said, "Pleased to meet you, Mr. and Mrs. Guthrie. I was wondering where you'd been keeping yourselves."

"What's that?" Slim asked.

"That missing couple from a few weeks back. This appears to be their other computer, the one I couldn't find in their house. Looks as if our pal Overhultz has been a very bad boy."

Leo Tompkins showed up at the house he'd rented to Overhultz around six. By that time, we'd been joined by a couple of DEA agents from Pooler, and a drug dog courtesy of Don Webb over in Morgan. Besides the stash in the back bedroom, the dog had discovered two more caches of pot secreted in a cardboard box on a shelf over the washer and dryer in the storage room and under the bed in the master bedroom. I'd also located two more guns.

In addition to the drug dog, Sheriff Webb had rousted Lee Mathis, the computer tech, to come out to the house and see what he could make of the laptop I'd found.

"The IP address matches up with the Guthries," Mathis said. "How'd it wind up in this dump?"

"Overhultz worked for a man named Kovalenko, who runs a bunch of internet porn sites. Natalie Guthrie—Natalya Gromykova originally—was a model for one of those sites. So, in a sense, she was working for Kovalenko too. My guess is this computer contains information Kovalenko didn't want going public, so either he had the Guthries disposed of, maybe by Overhultz, or once they disappeared he had Overhultz steal the computer. Either way, Kovalenko is implicated by association."

"That's pretty slim," Mathis said. "Might not fly in court."

"It's a start," I said. "The camel's nose under the tent flap. Maybe I can use it against Kovalenko somehow."

As we had been talking, Mathis had been cruising files in the computer.

"Whoa," he said. "This is strange. There's a folder labeled Home Business, but it's huge. When I clicked on it, I found dozens of flash files."

"What's a flash file?"

"It's a way of compressing motion pictures. Look."

He clicked on one of the files, a frame opened on the screen, and Natalie Guthrie stepped into the picture, wearing a lace robe through which we could see a black bra and panties. She also wore stiletto heels, which she kept on as she lounged on her bed and opened the robe.

"No need to keep running it," I said. "I've seen this story before."

"Could be a clue," Mathis said, his gaze glued to the screen.

"Close it up," I said. "For all you know, that woman is in a couple of hundred decomposing pieces all over the county, along with her husband. Seems a little disrespectful to gawk at her like that."

"Guess you're right," Mathis said, closing the laptop. "Want me to analyze this computer the way I did the other one from the Guthries' house?"

"No," I said. "This time I want you to find something I can use besides skin flicks."

I watched him bag the computer and sign the evidence receipt. Then I stepped into the front yard. Slim was already there, smoking a cigarette.

"I believe I have advised you in the past about smoking in uniform," I said.

"Indeed you have, Chief. However, in this case I am smoking in the line of duty."

"You want to explain that?"

"Smoking helps me think. I have a nervous condition that

makes me want to move a lot. Smoking gives me something to do with my hands and allows my brain to work on other issues."

"Let's say I buy this rationalization. What great notions are you working on in there?"

"Mostly stuff I imagine you've already considered."

"Try me."

"Kovalenko told you Overhultz worked for him."

"That's right."

"You think Kovalenko is a sort of glorified pimp, selling sex over the internet for the Russian mob, and is little more than a white slaver because of his wife-dealing business."

"I think you are being charitable to the man, Slim."

"You may be right. We've discovered over a hundred pounds of weed in this house. I figure that qualifies as distribution anywhere you go."

"Okay."

"You know what a pound of weed goes for these days?"

"No, and I'm not sure I'd be happy to discover that you do."

"Want me to piss in a cup, Chief? Any time, any place."

"Maybe later. What's your point?"

"It's a lot. A pound of prime skunk costs several thousand dollars. Look around you. This look like the kind of place a guy slangin' herb in this kind of volume might live if he was taking the profits for himself?"

I surveyed the shack again. "He's a middleman, taking a cut," I said.

"And likely a pretty skinny one at that. Someone is running him. Someone else is making the big bucks."

"Kovalenko."

"Sounds like he'd be a good place to start. And since we know Ram-Billy also worked for Kovalenko, I have to wonder what we might find if we take a closer look at his place."

I chewed on that one for a minute or two. "Have yourself

another smoke, Slim," I said. "And you keep right on thinking. Seems you have a talent for it."

I walked over to the sheriff's department K-9 car, where the officer stood next to the German shepherd. He'd poured water from a bottle into a metal bowl next to the front tire, and the dog lay next to it, panting lightly.

"Think Sheriff Webb can spare you for another house call?" I asked.

"Long as I get home in time for dinner. Wife's making pot roast. She hates to see it go dry."

CHAPTER THIRTY-TWO

The K-9 deputy followed me up Ram-Billy's driveway. The crime scene tape over the front door was untouched. As I stepped out of the car, I heard a thudding sound next door, and saw Sam Kincaid, the neighbor, hunched over the Swedish cabinetmaker's bench in his garage, hitting something with a beechwood mallet. I kind of wished I could trade places with him and live the relaxed retired life without the pressure to be the force against evil in Prosperity.

We gloved up, and I cleared the tape and unlocked the front door. As soon as I opened it, the shepherd started to strain at the halter. The deputy released it, and the dog dashed into the house and around the corner toward the hallway.

We followed behind, and found the dog in the bedroom, pawing at a bedside table. The table had three drawers. The dog wanted something inside the middle one.

"Strange," I said.

"Not really," the deputy said. "She always acts that way when she finds contraband."

"It's not that. We checked the bedroom when we found the body. I'm certain we inspected those drawers."

"My dog can smell particulates of three or four parts per trillion. She doesn't make mistakes. There's something in that drawer."

The drawer was filled mostly with books and a few legal pads. The books were law books. I pulled one out and leafed through

271

it. It was a text on torts, which wasn't surprising, since Ram-Billy had made most of his disposable income in small claims courts. I held the book out to the dog. She ignored it, buried her muzzle in the drawer, reached one paw in and scratched at the books.

I pulled them out, one by one, and checked them. The fifth book I pulled out felt light.

"I'll be damned," I said, as I opened it. Most of the book had been hollowed out. From the outside, it seemed like any other law text. Inside, there was a gaping hole, apparently cut laboriously, page by page, with a razor knife. In the hollowed space was a baggie with about two ounces of sticky buds, a small hash pipe, and a disposable lighter.

"Never took Ram-Billy for a toker," I said.

"Takes all kinds," the deputy said.

I bagged the contents and set them aside. With Ram-Billy's stash secured, the dog settled down. "If there were drugs anywhere else in the house, would the dog be that relaxed?" I asked.

"Hard to say. The stuff you found could be masking other scents. Let's trot her around a little, see if she picks up anything else. C'mon, Sheba!"

He led the dog from the bedroom, and slowly allowed her to explore the rest of the house. She didn't get noticeably excited.

"Appears we got everything," he said.

"Wasn't much."

"Enough for a felony bust, if the owner was still alive."

"Yeah, but only felony possession. I was sort of hoping we'd discover that Ram-Billy was involved in distribution."

"Pretty harsh, Chief. The man's dead."

"It's not that. The fellow whose house we raided this afternoon and Ram-Billy worked for the same person. We're after the big fish. If both Overhultz and Ram-Billy were dealing, we'd have a stronger case for probable cause to raid their boss. Tell me: If the dog is inside the house, could she smell weed outside?"

"Depends. The AC is still running in here. That might create a problem. She's looking a little anxious. Couldn't hurt to let her take a little run in the back."

As soon as I opened the door, Sheba's ears perked up, and she pulled against the leash. The deputy released her, and she ran down the back steps into the fenced yard. Before we could clear the back door, we heard her barking.

We found her at the rear of the yard, her face pressed against the chain-link fence. On the other side, perhaps ten feet beyond the fence, a wild rabbit nibbled at some barley shoots, ignoring the frenzied baying from the dog. I lobbed a dirt clod at the rabbit, which bolted into the high grass a few yards farther away.

Sheba immediately sat, as if waiting for a command. The deputy walked her around the perimeter of the yard, until she stopped, cocked her head, then yanked away. She stopped at a garden shed, stood on her hind legs, and began scratching at the door as she whimpered.

The shed was made of particle board with Masonite siding painted a dark brown. The stout plywood door was secured by a keyed lock in a strong metal hasp. I didn't have a key, and I hadn't seen one in the house. I walked around the house to my car, pulled a pry bar from the trunk, and used it to break the hasp. As soon as I opened the door, Sheba bounded into the shed and started circling and scratching at a red sheet metal tool chest, the kind I'd seen in auto mechanics' shops.

"Well, now," I said, as I opened the top of the chest and pulled out a brick wrapped in tin foil, one of six. "I think I owe Sheba a stew bone."

273

★ ★ ★ ★ ★

I arrived at the station the next morning, and settled at my desk with my breakfast. I'd stopped by the Piggly Wiggly down the hill to grab a ham and egg biscuit, a Styrofoam cup full of buttered slow-cooked grits, and a cup of coffee. I spread it out on my desk, and was about to dig in when Agent Cantrell from Homeland Security walked in the front door. Sherry tried to screen him, but he walked right past her and into my office. He sniffed, walked back out again, and returned with a cup of coffee from the percolator I kept on a file cabinet outside the holding cells.

"Did you leave a quarter in the cigar box on the cabinet?" I asked.

"You charge a quarter for this swill?"

"If it were good, we'd charge fifty cents. I had a pleasant dinner last evening and a good night's sleep. If you're here to jerk a knot in my ass, I may object, and I might be forced to shoot you."

He sipped from the coffee without taking his eyes off me, almost as if he took me seriously. Then he said, "My . . . supervisor has asked me to cooperate with your investigation of Bunny Kovalenko."

I set my cup on the desk. "And how do you feel about that?"

"How in hell do you think I feel?"

"In truth, I couldn't care less. Why the change of heart?"

"Seems he got a call from Sheriff Webb over in Morgan early this morning."

I glanced at my watch. "Must have been *real* early."

"Early enough to aggravate his ulcer. He was already mean as a snake when I got in. He gave me the condensed version of the searches you made yesterday. Sounds like both your murder victims had connections to one another."

"I tried to tell you that the other day."

"Tell me again. The expanded version this time. Tell me the stuff my boss doesn't know."

I held up my hand and started counting points on my fingers. "Ram-Billy worked for Kovalenko as an American agent. Boyd Overhultz worked for Kovalenko doing God knows what—probably dealing and the occasional muscle work. We found about a hundred pounds of high-content weed, wrapped in one-pound bricks, stashed all over Overhultz's house. We found about ten more pounds in Ram-Billy's garden shed. We found Overhultz's fingerprints in Ram-Billy's house. I suspect that Ram-Billy and Overhultz were in cahoots, working for a larger weed distributor."

"Kovalenko."

"He's the most likely player I've found so far. We know he's tied in with the Russian mob. We know the Russian mob has tried to horn in on about everything illegal they run across. If they're distributing weed around Bliss County, Kovalenko seems the perfect conduit. I talked it over with Don Webb last night, and we decided to pay Kovalenko a visit today. Might take along this nice drug-sniffing German shepherd named Sheba I met yesterday. Could be fun to see what she uncovers. You in?"

"I suppose I am."

"Anything you'd like to tell me about Kovalenko I might not already know? In the interest of interagency cooperation?"

"I don't like you that much. Let's see what happens."

CHAPTER THIRTY-THREE

Bunny Kovalenko fumed as he stared at Shug Burch from the couch in Burch's office.

"What in hell happened?" he demanded. "I want to know who killed Overhultz!"

"You're saying you think I did it?"

"I called you about him the other night, and the next thing I know, he's dead."

"So? Problem solved."

"You think I meant for him to be killed?"

"Doesn't matter," Shug said. "That sorry sack of shit was a liability. He'd fuck his own mama for a beer. You think he would have lasted ten minutes in an interrogation room, if the cops found him? Now he can't finger you. You should be happy."

"Two men in Prosperity who worked for me have been murdered. Today, maybe tomorrow, that police chief from down there is going to come to my house again. I am not happy about that. For all I know, the police have already been to Overhultz's house. What if they find the product stashed there?"

"If they go there, they won't be able to miss it. But what if they do find it? Overhultz worked for you. Sometimes he worked for me. I heard he's done some muling for the Vulcans motorcycle gang. There ain't nothing that can tie him or that crap in his house directly back to you. There's something else I want to discuss with you."

"I don't think we're finished with this subject yet."

"Far as I'm concerned we are. Don't waltz into my office and accuse me of killing people unless you're damned sure I did. People get fucked up pulling that kind of shit. Here's the deal. I want to buy you out."

Kovalenko's mouth opened and closed, as if he were trying to say something, but nothing came out. It took him a few seconds to pull himself together.

"What do you mean, buy me out?"

"The club. You fronted me a half million to help get it off the ground, and I'm appreciative. The club's a success, full every night, we're making money hand over fist. I also got a fat residual check from my record company a day or two ago. I figure I can buy your stake in the place for double what you paid. That's a hundred percent profit."

"I'm a fucking accountant! I know what the profit is. Out of the question!"

"Nothing is out of the question. I checked that contract we drew up. It says I can buy your share back within the first year of operation, at no penalty. I'm a fair man. You did me a solid, and I figure you should get something for that. I'm offering a million. You want to negotiate?"

"I'm not interested in selling."

"No. That's not exactly right. What you're not interested in is losing this underground expressway you got for pipelining weed. The way things are going, you're gonna be real popular with the *federales* in a few days. That's not a party I'm interesting in attending. So, the shipments stop. Your knuckle-walker friends show up here with a truck tonight, or tomorrow, or the next day, I'll tell 'em to take it to your place. I'm out of the storage business."

"You don't want to do this," Kovalenko said. "The people I represent—"

"Are people, like any others. You ever deal with the Aryan

Brotherhood in prison? Or the Mara Salvatrucha crowd? I survived years locked up with monsters that make your Russian buddies look like pussies."

Shug pulled an envelope from his desk drawer.

"There's a stop-option contract in here. You sign it and there'll be a cashier's check in your mailbox for a cool million the next day. I'm tired of the fast life, Bunny. I'm old and I'm sore and I'm ready to slow things down and savor the years I have left. More than anything else, I got no place in my life for the likes of you anymore. Take the envelope. Sign the papers. You can always find another lowlife to hustle. I want out."

"Maybe I'll go to the police. Maybe I'll suggest to them your role in Boyd Overhultz's unfortunate passing."

"And maybe I'll tell them all about your weed business. What we got here is a version of what they used to call mutually assured destruction in the old Cold War days. We both know too much about each other. Better to make it a clean break. Signing that contract severs our ties, and gives me a convenient case of amnesia where you're concerned. You're a smart guy, certainly smarter than me. A smart guy recognizes a good deal when it lands in his lap."

Kovalenko reached out and fingered the envelope, then lifted it from the table and tapped it against his knuckles.

"I have a condition," he said.

"I'm open to negotiate."

"This police chief in Prosperity, the one who invaded my home."

"Wheeler. I know him. We go way back."

"Can you convince him to back off?"

Shug drummed the top of his desk with his fingertips. "I don't know. Judd's a hard guy to dissuade, once he gets his head around something."

"Then you can scare him."

Shug tossed back his head and laughed. "Fat chance, Bunny! I haven't seen the man in thirty years, but I know a guy who don't scare easy when I see one. If I could scare him, he wouldn't have put me in the joint back when we were teens."

"Then talk to him like an old friend. Reason with him. Help him to see the advantages of looking the other way. I've known a lot of crooked cops—"

"And Judd ain't one of them. Tell you what. In the interest of sealing our deal, I'll have a set-down with him, face to face. Maybe I can get him to slow down a little, maybe provide a little diversion, give you some time to set up an escape route."

"A what?"

"You think I don't know what you're planning? These guys you work for don't like a lot of light shone their way. You start tossing back tea and scones with the cops, and they're gonna get nervous. I reckon you have a real stash squirreled away in Lord knows how many offshore accounts, not to mention the million you'll get for turning over your share of Shug's Nashville. I'd also bet you know how to disappear, if it comes to that. All you need is the time to set it up."

Kovalenko slipped the envelope into his jacket pocket. "I'll take your offer under consideration," he said.

"Be quick about it, Bunny. I'd like an answer within the next twenty-four, y'hear?"

Lily Holder sat stiffly in the passenger seat of Shug's Escalade as he crossed over a twin pair of railroad tracks on the Morgan Highway and turned down an oiled dirt and gravel road that wended its way back through a copse of pines and hardwood trees. The threat of storms over the weekend had blown away during the day, and the brilliant sun, angled low over the ragged fields, cut sharp shadows across the ditches on each side of the track.

"Where are we going?" she asked.

"Want to show you something."

The Escalade broke through the trees, revealing a middle twentieth-century two-story farmhouse, the front yard overgrown with barley and wiregrass and clover. Shug pulled the car around in a circle, and shut it down several yards from the front porch. He walked around the car and held her door open for her.

"It looks like a farm," she said, as she stepped out.

"Because it is one—or at least it was. Gone a little to seed over the last year or so. The owner died. To put it rightly, he was murdered. Didn't have a family, so the property reverted to the state. I've made some inquiries, and they're sellin' it for the back taxes."

"You're thinking of buying this place?"

"I told you I grew up in Prosperity. I came home for a reason. I have done bad things. It may be true that I have been a bad person. They don't put people in prison without good reason. That was twenty years ago. I got out and I was wild, and drunk, and I done my share of drugs, and I've bedded more women than any man has a right to in one lifetime, and I'm not saying this to brag. No, don't walk away. I'm trying to make a point here. Yes. I've been bad. For years I had a streak of the devil running through me, and I lived only for my own basest desires."

"You are confusing me more."

"Please listen. I lived here until I was almost seventeen. I tilled acreage and planted crops and picked cotton and tobacco and corn and pretty much anything else that grows above or below the dirt. For the first sixteen years of my life, home was nothing more than one shack or another, or a single-wide trailer at the edge of a soybean field. We were the folks the poor folks spat on. Until I was twelve I had no idea what the inside of a church looked like, and truth to tell it still is not a familiar sight for me. But a moment comes in your life when you look at what you've made of the time you've been given, and you have to determine its value. I won't tell you the circumstances of that moment in my life, because they are too sordid to relate. I came back here because it's home. It's the place where I veered off the path and where my life went wrong. I came back here to try to start over, and make the life I should have had all along."

"You blame people here for taking that from you?"

"There were people who did not stand by me the way they should have, and for a long time I yearned to make that right. When push comes to shove, you have nobody to blame for your troubles but yourself. This is what I'm trying to say, and what I hoped to say the other night, but failed at miserably. I'm trying. I can't do no more than that. I'm working on building a life I never had with no plans and no tools, and only a suspicion of what it would look like if I had it. You said I was capable of charity and kindness. You may be the only person in my life who's thought that—me included—and it's important to me that you know how much that means. I came back to Prosperity to settle, Miss Lily. This farm is the kind of place that feels like home. What do you think?"

"It needs work. A lot of it. Paint's peeling off the house, and the barn's beginning to sag. Deserted places begin to decay quickly."

"I can have it back in shape in a few weeks. All it takes is a barrel of elbow grease and a buttload of money. I figure I can get my hands on both pretty easy. What color should I paint the house?"

"Why do you ask me these things?"

"I value your opinion. Come on, I got a key from the tax office. Let's have a look inside."

He unlocked the front door and held the door for her to enter first. The house smelled musty and there were spider webs in every corner of the main room.

"Hope you ain't afraid of spiders," he said.

"Only the bad ones. A broom will get rid of the webs. Place needs an airing out."

"I'll bring in a cleaning crew, and they'll have it smelling like a spring day in no time."

"So, you've already decided to buy it?"

"I'm ninety percent certain. I've been out here a couple of times already. The building is sound. The foundation is strong. It needs a couple of weeks of hard work and some love, but otherwise it's what I'm looking for."

"Yes," she said. "I see."

She turned and dashed back out to the front porch. Shug found her in one of the ancient rocking chairs, bent over at the waist, staring at the weathered hardwood planks. There were tears streaming down her face.

"Please go back inside," she said. "I am embarrassing myself."

"I don't understand. Have I said something to upset you?"

"Everything you say and do unsettles me greatly. I have seldom met a man as disturbing as you. I dearly wish you hadn't brought me out here."

"Why?"

"You show me a side of you I have no desire to see, and a future you envision for yourself that I do not believe I will ever enjoy. I may be envious of what you want, since I believe I can never have it. I fear you are flaunting your good fortune at my expense. Does that explain it to you?"

Shug settled into the rocker next to her. "No," he said. "Now I'm more confused. You don't like the place?"

"It's . . . not . . . the place," she sobbed.

"What, then?"

"Oh, for God's sake! Can you not give me a minute's peace?" she cried, and stomped down the steps to the barn.

He sat on the porch, trying to figure out what he had said or done, without success, until she reappeared at the steps. Her eyes were red, her face swollen as if stung by honeybees.

"I apologize for my display," she said. "It was rude and impolite. I beg your forgiveness."

She stepped back up to the porch, and took her seat in the rocker again. "I have one chance to say this," she said, "and I want to get it right. I tried to tell you the other night, but somehow I couldn't get the words out. I do not believe you care for me or for my feelings."

"I do recall you saying that the other night, but I thought you were talking about the way I beat up Bobby."

"That was part of it. After the police left that night, I told you that I believed you were capable of noble emotions. I opened my heart to you."

"I recall exactly what you said, Miss Lily. It had a great impact on me."

"And then you offered to drive me home."

"I did. It was my privilege."

"And that was all."

Slowly, Shug began to understand.

"You anticipated that I was taking you home for . . . to take you to bed?"

"I did." She started to weep again. "And you let me out of the car and waited for me to go through the door and then you drove away. I cried myself to sleep. I got up the next morning intending to call and quit. I did not wish to continue working where I was not wanted. By you, that is."

"I believed I had frightened you," Shug said. "It seemed wrong to . . . I didn't think it would be right to try to . . . I felt it would be taking advantage."

"I wish you had."

"Why did you come back to work?"

"I need the money," she said. "This is a good job. I pondered on it and I decided, even if you harbored no desire for me, I could continue to be a good employee. I've located a nice little rental house over near the elementary school, and I believe that I would like to stay in this town for a spell. If you wish me to continue working here, that is."

Shug stroked his beard and scratched at his cheek. This woman was an unending series of surprises for him. They sat and rocked for a minute, as she gathered herself together again, and he worked through all the things he wanted to say. Tentatively, he placed his hand over hers.

"I feel like we have been talking past one another," he said. "There is something different about you, Miss Lily. I can't tell you what it is, but it's there and I don't completely understand it. I believe you may be a decent human being, a species I've encountered all too seldom in my life. I think, perhaps, there was a reason I picked you up on the road that night. I have not led a proper life. You know I was in prison. Hell, *everyone* knows I was in prison. I have deceived people and I've been cruel and there have been times in my life when I contemplated the possibility that I had no soul at all."

"I do not believe that to be the case," she said.

"Sometimes I think I'm missing fundamental parts that cannot be replaced. There was a man in rehab once who talked to me. He seemed to have insight. He encouraged me to read. He told me that I was seeking a balm for an open wound in my life, and I kept stabbing hyssop into it instead. I had no idea what he meant. I looked up the word *hyssop*, and found it was the spiny plant they dipped in vinegar to slake Jesus' thirst on the cross. I told him he was full of shit, but I was young then, and I had no idea that everything I had done to that point in my life was the equivalent of splashing kerosene on my soul and lighting matches.

"When I found success and became famous, I thought I had found my balm. I was wrong. Found Jesus a couple of times in rehab, but I misplaced him later. Always hoped on the road that I'd find what I was looking for over the next hill or in the next town. Finally gave up and came home. Thought maybe I could start over, make something useful out of my life."

"How's that working for you so far?"

"Fits and starts. I wish to be completely honest with you. When I picked you up by the side of the road, I figured you were gonna be nothing more than another quick easy piece. I've done my share of hitchhikers. I was angry and discontent with my life, and you were gonna carry my water for the night."

"Do you charm all the women this way?"

"I haven't gotten there yet. First time I took in your eyes, I saw all the way back to the point where my road branched off to Shit City. There was more pain and loss in your eyes than I had ever seen in another human other than myself. I think we have much more in common than either of us has dared to say. I think you saw that, too, and I think that's why you took up my offer of work. I think you came here looking for a damned sight more than a paycheck. Could be you're my balm, finally shown up to fill my empty places."

"You think way too much of me. It occurs to me that we know nothing about each other," she said. "At least, other than what we suspect. What do we do about that?"

Shug walked over to the rail overlooking the front yard, and he considered what had transpired since returning to Bliss County. Business was good. He was pleased with what the club had become. For once, maybe he had built something of value. He wasn't completely certain, but he imagined that this must be what pride felt like.

"Seems like we got started off heading in different directions, Miss Lily. I think we should start over."

"You want me to head out to the road, walk the highway so you can pick me up again?"

"I'll take you home," he said without turning around. "Skip your shift at the club tonight. Get yourself a good night's sleep. I'm moving Carl to the night shift after today. Starting at ten tomorrow morning, you're the day manager."

"I don't understand."

"Ain't a decent place in this town to go out to eat after midnight, after you finish work." He turned around. "If I'm gonna court you proper, you're gonna have to work days."

"What about tonight?" she asked. "Steve would be by himself at the bar. He can't run it alone."

"Hell, I'll run it. Did I ever tell you I was a bartender before I became a star? Let's go. I'm taking you home. We'll figure out the rest tomorrow."

For the first time since he'd asked her to come out to the farm with him, she dared to smile. She had a nice smile.

CHAPTER THIRTY-FOUR

Don Webb, Cantrell, and I took a sheriff's department cruiser to Kovalenko's place. The K-9 deputy, a guy named Wells, had Sheba in a separate car behind us.

As the politically elected sheriff of Bliss County, Webb had the right to wear a uniform. Like me, however, he had elected to keep to civvies, in this case a nice business suit, albeit one with a prominent bulge under his left lapel courtesy of the Glock he wore in a shoulder rig there. I was not as elegantly decked out, having opted for my usual brown cord jacket, a pair of khakis, a blue oxford cloth shirt, and my Stetson. I had accessorized my ensemble with my Kevlar vest under my shirt, and my own Sig 229 clipped to my belt.

Based on the pot found in Overhultz's and Ram-Billy's homes, and Kovalenko's own admission that he had employed both of them, we had managed to get a limited search warrant for Kovalenko's manse. The warrant said we could turn Sheba loose and collect anything that revved her up, but it ended there.

We pulled up to the gate, and Sheriff Webb punched the button on the intercom.

"*Deez eez privyet prupperty,*" a metallic voice replied.

"And this is Donald Webb, the sheriff of Bliss County. I have a duly authorized search warrant. You want to open this gate, and do it quick. You copy?"

There was an abrupt click and Don turned toward me. "Not

287

a lot of perks to this job, but I do love jerking an asshole's chain once in a while."

The gate opened with an almost silent hiss, and we followed the quarter-mile drive through the trees. When we pulled up to the front door and stepped out of the car, a burly man wearing a black tee shirt that strained against his bulging biceps stood in the doorway, holding an assault rifle. Reflexively, Don, Cantrell and I all had our weapons out and pointed at the man's greatest body mass.

"You want to lower the ordnance," Webb demanded.

"Your bedgez, please," the man said.

Webb turned toward me. "What in hell did he say? Bedgez?"

"I think he wants to see our badges," Cantrell said from behind the car.

"Oh! Badges. Sure. We got badges," Don said, as he pulled his wallet from the breast pocket of his dress jacket with his free hand and flashed it at the man. Cantrell and I did the same, and the man lowered the rifle.

"Lowering it isn't enough," I said. "Drop it on the chair and step away."

"I apologize," the man said. "Meezter Kovalenko prefers to maintain strict security. You will understand."

He gently placed the weapon on a chair, and stepped back toward the front door.

Wells clipped a leash onto Sheba's harness, and let her to the front steps. Cantrell stepped forward and showed his ID again.

"Cantrell, Homeland Security. Got your passport on you, Ivan?"

"My name not Ivan. I am Fyodor."

"Doesn't matter, Fyodor, I'm fuckin' with you anyway. Maybe we'll check your bona fides later in the day, after we toss this place. Me being Homeland Security should tell you that this is serious business. The sheriff here has a search warrant that will allow this pooch to go anywhere on the property she wants. We need to see Bernard Kovalenko, too."

"Meezter Kovalenko eez away."

"Not too far away, I hope."

"He should return shortly."

Sheriff Webb pulled the warrant from his jacket and placed it in Fyodor's hand. "You are duly served. Please step aside and allow us to conduct our search."

Fyodor allowed the double doors to swing open, and we stepped into the columned marble foyer. I glanced at Sheba to see if anything excited her right off the bat, but she stood obediently at Wells's side.

Fyodor stowed the HK in a closet near the front door. "You weel forgeeve me," he said. "I have taken liberty of contacting Meezter Kovalenko's attorney, and I am attempting to contact Meezter Kovalenko heemzelf."

"You can call anyone you want," Webb said. "We'll start upstairs and work our way down. If there are any locked doors up there, you might want to go unlock them."

"Meezter Kovalenko has guests. Some of them may be sleeping."

"Then wake 'em and tell 'em it's time to rise and shine," Cantrell said. "God damn, Fyodor, it's almost noon."

"Agent Cantrell," Don interrupted. "We're here on official business. We'll treat the people here with respect, and remind ourselves that in this country people are presumed innocent until proven otherwise." He turned to Fyodor. "Having said that, we will need to check all the rooms upstairs. Anyone sleeping up there might want to move so we don't inconvenience them. We'll give you a couple of minutes to advise them."

Fyodor nodded and headed up the stairs.

"You know he's probably with the Russian mob," Cantrell growled.

"No doubt," Webb said. "And should you come here with a federal warrant, you can rough him up all you want. This is a county warrant and is being served under my jurisdiction. I'll decide how we conduct the search."

"What is this?" a voice said behind us.

We turned to find Kovalenko standing in the doorway, his car keys still dangling from his fingers. His eyes were wide behind his oversized glasses.

I didn't know whether Cantrell had ever met him, and I knew Don Webb hadn't, so I took the initiative and stepped forward.

"Mr. Kovalenko, this is Bliss County Sheriff Don Webb, and Homeland Security Agent Jack Cantrell. We are executing a duly authorized search warrant of your home, signed by District Court Judge Jubal Early."

"Wheeler," he said, as if he'd recognized me for the first time—and, given his shock, that might have been the case. "A search? For what?"

"At this point, drugs," Webb said. "I served the warrant on your . . . associate, Fyodor. He has it in his jacket pocket. I have another copy on me, if you'd like to look it over."

"I'm sure my attorney will."

"Fyodor has already contacted him."

"I insist that you cease this intrusion until he arrives."

"Sorry," Cantrell said. "Can't do that. Don't have to, in fact. Your attorney can gripe all he wants, but the warrant is signed by a judge. Unless he can get a restraining order from an appellate court, this house belongs to us for the next couple of hours. I suggest you make yourself comfortable."

"I protest!" Kovalenko said. "In the strongest possible terms!"

"That's your right," Webb replied. "Please don't get in our way."

Fyodor walked down the stairs and winced when he saw Kovalenko standing in the foyer. He started to talk even before he hit the floor.

"I apologize, Meezter Kovalenko. These polizemen arrived weeth a warrant. I had to let them in. I called lawyer and told guests of search."

Kovalenko turned to me. "This is your doing, Wheeler."

"Not mine alone, but I certainly helped. You've admitted to me that both Boyd Overhultz and Ram-Billy Pressley were employed by you. Within the last day, we've discovered a couple hundred thousand dollars' worth of marijuana in the shack where Overhultz lived. You do know he's dead, right?"

"I heard this morning. It's tragic, but has nothing to do with me."

"Time will tell. We also discovered another ten grand or so of marijuana stashed in Ram-Billy Pressley's garden shed. The techs at the crime lab are examining samples to see if they are the same strain and whether there are connections between the packaging, but I have to tell you it looks like Overhultz and Ram-Billy were both engaged in the distribution of a controlled substance. Since they both worked for you—well, I think you see our concern."

"This is preposterous!"

"I'm not a lawyer," I said, "and, quite frankly, as far as I'm concerned you're free to run off at the mouth all you want. Sheriff Webb here is processing a drug investigation, but I have two murders in my town. Both victims worked for you, and both were clearly distributing drugs. You knew I was trying to find Overhultz, because I told you so, and two days later he's found dead, in what looks like a professional hit. What am I supposed to think?"

"And what about this Homeland Security agent?"

"John C. Cantrell, at your service, Mr. Kovalenko," Cantrell said with a smirk.

"Are you suggesting that I am somehow engaged in terrorist

activities? Are you adding that to the list of your absurd suspicions?"

"Aw, hell," Cantrell said. "I'm along for the ride. You know, most people think all we do at Homeland Security is look out for Al Qaeda pukes and hassle people in airports. In fact, thanks to the Patriot Act, we have our fingers in more or less all illegal activity engaged in by foreigners. You're still on a British passport, aren't you?"

Kovalenko was about to explode. His ears had turned scarlet, and he ground his teeth. He didn't reply, having figured out that silence was his best friend. He turned and stamped across the foyer, through the living room, and straight to the lanai, where he sat heavily in a lounge chair. The guy who made the great iced tea appeared instantaneously at his side, and Kovalenko barked out an order I couldn't hear clearly from that distance, but I had a strong suspicion he was asking for something a damned sight more powerful than lemonade.

The ride back to Morgan was quiet for the first couple of miles, until Don Webb sighed. "Two joints and a gram of coke. We're some big-time crime busters, aren't we?"

"I think the warrants were worth more than what we found," Cantrell said.

"Pisses me off that I'm going to have to go to court over that piddling shit," Webb said.

"Doesn't mean squat," I said. "I'd have been surprised if we'd found anything massive. Kovalenko's smart. He knows you don't shit where you eat. That's why he stored his junk at Overhultz's and Ram-Billy's places. Probably has one or two more hidey-holes scattered around the county. Stuff we found was likely brought in by his 'guests,' and he didn't know anything about it."

"So why'd you ask for the warrants and the raid?" Webb

asked. "I was under the impression you expected to make a big haul."

"Shaking the trees," I said. "Taking Kovalenko by surprise put him off kilter. It rattled him. Maybe it will make him go off his playbook, start to improvise. Improvisation in the crime business is a bad idea. You start making it up as you go along, and there are a lot of opportunities to stumble."

"Tell you what," Webb said, "next time you feel like rattling some bad boy, let me in on the joke. I hate getting a stiffie over the prospect of taking down a major felon, just to wind up with blue balls."

CHAPTER THIRTY-FIVE

Bunny Kovalenko sat fuming in his living room. Things had begun to spin apart and he had no idea how to pull them back together. It was as if someone was conspiring against him, setting plays into motion with the specific intent of fucking up his life. Every time he thought he had a handle on the situation, another component would disintegrate.

Fyodor appeared in the vestibule. He was carrying the rifle, but slung around so that it rode the small of his back.

"Mister Kovalenko. You have a visitor."

"I don't wish to see anyone," Kovalenko said.

"Of course. But this man insists he can help solve your problems with the nightclub."

That got Kovalenko's attention. "Okay, bring him in."

A few minutes later, Fyodor ushered in a tall, muscular man who might have been anywhere between twenty and fifty. It was hard to tell from the lumps and bruises that covered his face. He looked as if a car had rolled over his head. One eye was still shot through with broken blood vessels, and when he turned his head the eye had a demonic cast.

"I hear you lost a valued employee recently," the man said. "Fellow named Overhultz."

"He worked for me, on occasion," Kovalenko said. "Valued? Hardly. He did more or less what he was told and he didn't ask for a lot of money in return. He was a means to an end. What concern is this of yours?"

"Losing Overhultz leaves a hole in your organization. I also understand you have a large interest in Shug's Nashville."

"This is not an issue which I wish to discuss. Fyodor, please escort this man out."

"I can help you!" the man said. "I know—*things* about Shug Burch. I know his comings and goings. I can help you gain complete control of the club. I know you funnel weed through the club and you'd like that to continue."

"I'm not happy that you seem to know so much about my business, and I find you distasteful. If you know so much, you know the people for whom I work. You already know that Fyodor is armed. What you've said is sufficient for me to have him . . . dispose of you."

"If I take Shug out of the picture, that would be worth something, wouldn't it? I wouldn't even want to get paid for it, not directly."

Kovalenko laced his fingers on his stomach and took a fresh look at the man. "Why would you want to help me achieve that? What's in it for you?"

"A debt must be paid. He owes me. I intend to collect. Once that's done, I figure you'd be appreciative. Perhaps I could take Overhultz's place, do the things he used to do for you."

"You may be too smart to take on Mr. Overhultz's duties. He was not only a blunt object, but also a rather dull one. You don't strike me as dull. You may even be keen enough to be a threat to my interests."

"I'm ambitious, and that's a fact. You give me the opportunity and I can produce for you."

Shug Burch's demand to buy out his share of Shug's Nashville was a major inconvenience, Bunny thought, especially since the police had discovered the stash in Overhultz's hovel. Two distribution points had been eliminated and, while he had a few more scattered around the county, the impact on his cash flow had already made itself felt. He hadn't signed the papers yet, and if somehow Burch were no longer in the picture, his share of the club would enable him to take it over lock, stock, and barrel.

"I think it's premature to talk about long-term plans," he said. "What you are offering is of interest to me. However, I obviously can't condone or sanction any violent act you might be bent on committing. It's possible I can offer you some part-time work, should you prove worthy. I trust we hear each other clearly?"

"Well, sir," the man said, "there is still some residual ringing in my ears, but I believe we understand one another well enough."

"How satisfying. And what should I call you? You didn't bother to introduce yourself when Fyodor brought you in."

The man stepped forward, and extended his hand. "Name's Bobby Spurlock. I'm right glad to know you."

CHAPTER THIRTY-SIX

I was about to close up shop at the station and head home for a nice dinner with Donna, when I heard a knock on my door, and a buxom blonde woman appeared in my doorway.

"I recognize you," I said. "You're the bartender at Shug's Nashville. Lily, right?"

"It's Lily Holder, sir."

"Please, come in and have a seat, Ms. Holder. What can I do for you?"

She pulled a folded scrap of newsprint from her purse, and slid it across the desktop to me. It was a copy of the *Ledger-Telegraph* story about discovering Boyd Overhultz's body in his car. "I saw that in the newspaper this morning," she said. "It's troubled me the entire day."

Her voice sounded like mint caramel cascading down praline ice cream, with a hint of fear and dread. I'd heard voices like hers in trailer parks and drunk tanks and low-rent honky-tonks my entire life. Something about her didn't seem to fit those stereotypes.

"You have some information about this murder?"

"I know the man in that picture."

"Boyd Overhultz. Mind telling me how you know him?"

"He's done some work for Mr. Burch."

That got my attention. To that point, I'd only known about Overhultz working for Kovalenko. "Mind me asking what kind of work?"

"Mr. Burch asked him to help root out an employee who was stealing from the club."

"How exactly did he do that?"

She described how Burch had used Overhultz as a plant to smoke out the bartender who had been skimming on cash sales.

"This man who died was coarse and rude," she said. "I overheard him saying disgusting things about me to Mr. Burch."

"How did Mr. Burch take that?"

"He was displeased, and he told this man to stop talking that way. May I ask you something, sir? Who is 'the Russian'?"

That rocked me a little. "Where did you hear about a Russian?"

"That man, Overhultz. The first time I met him, he was shut in Mr. Burch's office. He asked Mr. Burch how he could contact the Russian, because he was afraid someone was trying to make it look as if he had killed a man. He was scared. I could hear it in his voice. He said someone had gotten killed, and he was afraid people were going to blame it on him."

"Did he say who was killed?"

"He did, sir. He said it was a man with a strange name. Billy Goat or something."

"Ram-Billy?"

"That's it."

"What else did Overhultz say?"

"He told Mr. Burch that this man, the Russian, was angry at Ram-Billy, and had told him to take some money to his house, and that was when Overhultz found out this man Ram-Billy had been killed. Overhultz told Mr. Burch that he believed the Russian had killed the man, and Overhultz thought he might be next."

"Did he say why he thought the Russian killed Ram-Billy?"

"He said that he was angry at him. He didn't say why."

"What did Mr. Burch tell Overhultz?"

"He said he couldn't help him. Told him the best thing he could do was go hide somewhere the Russian couldn't find him."

"Have you discussed this with Mr. Burch?"

"I have, sir. I asked him a few nights later who the Russian was. He explained that the Russian was a man who helped raise the money to open Shug's Nashville."

"Did he tell you the Russian's name?"

"No. He said the Russian was a polite and cultured man, but a very violent one as well. I have to tell you, Chief Wheeler, that frightened me."

"Ms. Holder, it's obvious that you care for Mr. Burch. If you don't mind me asking, why did you come here today?"

"I wanted you to know that Mr. Burch didn't have anything to do with this killing stuff. He outright told me he had no idea who killed this man Ram-Billy, and the papers say Overhultz was killed at night this past Friday, and I can tell you Mr. Burch was at the club until three in the morning, and he was with me for another half hour. He drove me home after we tallied up the cash register receipts for the night. We talked for a brief bit in the car, and then he went home and I went to bed."

"I see. Is there anything else you wanted to tell me?"

She fretted with her hands, then pulled a tissue from her handbag. "Mr. Wheeler, I know you and Mr. Burch have a history together. I understand that you and he were once close friends, many years ago. I don't know what regard you have for him today, but I can tell you that he is trying to make his life over. I know he has been a violent man and that he has hurt a lot of people, and I have seen with my own eyes the violence of which he is capable, but we have talked about it on several occasions and I truly believe that he is trying to change."

"Wait," I said. "What kind of violence have you seen him do?"

Tears formed at the corner of her eyes. "That man who was stealing from us? Bobby? Mr. Burch fired him at the end of the night. Took him out to the alleyway behind the club. Bobby became enraged, and he pulled a knife on Mr. Burch. So it was self-defense, you see."

"What was self-defense?"

"Mr. Burch tore Bobby apart. Beat him to within an inch of his life. I watched it, and if I hadn't pulled him away I believe Mr. Burch would have killed Bobby. They had to cart him off in an ambulance. The police came, and they determined that Mr. Burch had no choice. Like I said, it was self-defense."

"And you said Boyd Overhultz helped Sean figure out that Bobby was stealing from the till?"

"That's right, sir."

A piece of the puzzle fell into place in my head. "Ms. Holder, can you tell me a little bit more about this Bobby fellow?"

"I don't recall his last name. Everyone just called him Bobby, but I'm sure Mr. Burch has records of it. And there's the police report and the hospital records. I'm certain you can find everything you need to know about him there. But that's not why I came to see you today, sir. I came here because I know that Mr. Burch was acquainted with both these dead men, and I wanted to be certain you knew he didn't have anything to do with their deaths. Mr. Burch is trying to turn his life around. He's told me as much more than once. He's buying a farm and he wants to put down roots. Doesn't that sound like a man who's putting his life on the mend?"

"Do you believe her?" Donna asked over dinner that night.

"Damned if I know. She works for Sean, after all. He can be charismatic when he wants to. It's part of his lore. For all I know, she's sleeping with him and wants to protect him. One thing she said did twang a string. She mentioned this guy

Bobby, who Sean supposedly beat to a greasy spot a while back. Apparently my dead guy, Overhultz, helped finger Bobby for stealing from Sean at the club. The bartender at Smitty's told me there was a man who appeared pretty beaten up eating with Overhultz the night before the killing."

"You think this man Bobby killed Overhultz?"

"I've seen stranger things."

"Why would Overhultz be eating with a man he set up for a first class ass-kicking?"

"Overhultz was dealing pot. Judging by the amount of the stash we found in his house, he likely was pretty well-known among the user population. The fellow at Smitty's said Overhultz came in and sat down, and the other man came in after him and joined him at the booth. What if that man was this Bobby guy, but so beat up and disfigured that Overhultz didn't recognize him? He could have given a fake name, said he wanted to make a buy. Overhultz wouldn't suspect a guy that messed up to be a cop."

"So maybe it went like this. Bobby makes arrangements to purchase some weed—maybe a lot of weed, like a brick or two. He arranges to meet Overhultz down by the pond. Overhultz gets there first. Bobby shows up a few minutes later, and parks behind Overhultz's car. He walks up from behind, on the driver's side, pulls a gun, sticks it behind Overhultz's head, lights out, and Overhultz is nothing more than a rancid memory."

"For revenge?"

"It's one of the classics."

"But you know what that means, don't you? If it is Bobby, then he's already killed once. Overhultz fingered him for stealing, but it was Shug Burch who lit him up in the alleyway. I don't think I'd be satisfied with killing the man who tricked me. I'd want a little bit of the man who messed me up, too."

"Leaves me with a problem, doesn't it?"

"No. You need to warn him."

"I do?"

"Absolutely. It's your duty. Forget all that crap that happened between you and Burch thirty years ago. If Lily is right, he's making an attempt to turn things around. Hell, I wish I'd known about this when he came by yesterday. I'd have told him myself."

I nearly dropped my fork. "What? Sean came here yesterday?"

"While I was on the porch, reading."

"Why didn't you tell me?"

"Because every time someone mentions Burch you act like they fed you a maggot burger. That man is riding your back, and he has been ever since he showed back up in this county."

"He's dangerous."

"I had it covered. I never sit out alone here without that pistol you gave me. I had it in the cushions of the wicker couch. I don't think I needed it. There was something about Burch. He was respectful, and he kept his distance, but there was something else. He was looking for you."

"I'll bet he was."

"You want to park the attitude? When it comes to Burch it's like you have a blind spot. He wanted to talk. I could see it in his eyes, hear it in his voice. I felt like he wanted to get something off his chest."

"He's a psychopath," I said. "Charm and sympathy are his stock in trade. He was running a game on you."

"I don't think so," she said, as she picked up her empty plate and carried it into the kitchen. "I work with teenagers every day of the week. They know head tricks that would make any psychopath proud. After all these years, I know shuck and jive from genuine, and my gut tells me Burch wanted to get right with you."

I carried my plate and the glasses to the sink. Donna stared out the window at the rays of setting sunlight streaming through the dust from the trees in the woods at the edge of the yard. I could see the reflection glint off a tear at the corner of her eye.

"You have trust problems," she said.

That stopped me. I waited for her to continue.

"Ever since Spud shot you. Things are different for you now. You always took the police work seriously, but you also believed in the good in people. If you didn't, you never would have walked into the Corliss house without a vest on. You considered Spud eight flavors of idiot, but you didn't fear him. You believed he'd hear you and make the right decision, instead of pulling a gun on you. Now you question everyone. You question Kent's loyalty to you, even though there isn't a man alive who loves you more. You believe Sean Burch is the same person he was when you were kids together. You question me."

"Never you."

"You questioned me only a minute ago. I told you my impression of a man with whom I have no history at all, and you chose to ignore it. You went with your preconceptions. I bought you that hat because it seemed like the kind of thing the good guy would wear, and that's how I regarded you. Way you've been acting sometimes lately, I wonder whether I ought to take it back and drop it on the returns counter. I think I should go home now, before I say something I truly regret."

"Please. Don't."

"I think it's best. I'm hot, and I don't see this conversation going in a cool direction. Before I go, I'm going to tell you what you should do, and then you need to make a decision. Whatever Sean Burch did when he was a teenager, and whatever he's done since, you've heard from two different people today that he seems to want to make a change. If you're right about this Bobby, and if you take your job seriously, then you need to warn Sean about what might be coming. It's the decent thing to do. I'm not making that a condition of patching up this little spat we're having, because I know it's a passing thing and will blow over by morning. Right now, you have more pressing matters to deal with than me, and me being here is keeping you from doing what you need to do. So I'm going. I'll talk to you tomorrow."

She stood on tiptoe, kissed me on the cheek, as if to reassure me that, like a spring thunderstorm, the noise and fury of our evening would dissipate, and then she walked out the front door. I heard her car crank, and stood motionless as I listened to her tires crunch the gravel.

She was right, of course. I had a moral obligation, not only as a law enforcement officer, but as a human being, to let Sean know a man might be gunning for him.

Before I could do that, I needed some more information. Ten minutes after Donna marched out of the house, I sat in my office at the police station. I dialed the sheriff's department in Morgan, and asked for the records division. A woman named Frieda answered the phone.

"I'm looking for an arrest record," I said. "I don't know the last name of the perpetrator, but his first name is probably Robert, or Bobby."

"That's not much help, Chief."

"It was a fight, over behind Shug's Nashville a couple of weeks ago."

"You mean that boy Shug Burch kicked to a crisp?"

"You heard about it?"

"It was quite a topic of discussion around here. Shug Burch is a celebrity, and from what I hear he wields a mean tire iron to boot."

"He beat this boy with a tire iron?"

"Hell, I don't know. These stories tend to take on a life of their own. Give me a couple of minutes to track down some specifics, and I'll call you right back."

It took her a little over fifteen minutes. I picked up the phone on the first ring.

"His name is Robert Spurlock, height six-two, weight two-ten, brown and blue. No priors. They charged him with assault."

"So he started the fight."

"Police report says he came at Burch with a knife."

That jibed with the story Lily Holder had told me. "Can you fax me a copy of the report?"

"Sure thing, Sugar. How's the recovery going?"

"Recovery?"

"You know. Getting shot and all. I hear you're back on your feet."

"I'm feeling much better, thanks."

"We're all glad to hear it. You had us all pretty worried for a while. Gimme a call if you need any more information, y'hear?"

Frieda was nothing if not efficient. A few minutes after hanging up, my fax machine whirred to life and started spitting out pages.

The officers who had responded to the fight at Shug's Nashville had been thorough. There were statements from Sean and from Lily. According to the reports, Spurlock had been transported to Bliss Regional Medical Center. I called them next, and reached a woman I know in Medical Records.

"I'm trying to locate a patient," I said, "and I don't know whether he's been released. From what I've heard, he was pretty badly injured. Can you tell me if he's still there?"

"Sure, Chief. Give me his name."

"Robert Spurlock." I also gave her his date of birth. I heard her tapping on her computer keyboard over the telephone.

"He's gone, Chief. They let him go last week. Seems he

305

looked a lot worse than he was actually hurt."

"How's that?"

"You know. Facial injuries. There are lots of vessels in the face, and they bleed like crazy. You can get bruised up in the face without having a lot of real damage—broken cheeks, fractured orbits, that sort of thing. They kept Spurlock for a couple of days, mostly to make sure he didn't have any significant concussion, and then bumped him to the curb."

"What was his release date?"

She told me. It was three days before Overhultz met with the man at Smitty's.

Plenty of time to formulate some plans for revenge.

I figured I'd call Tom Larabee, the police chief over in Morgan, to give him a head's up about Spurlock, but I was interrupted by a knock on my door. I glanced up to find Kent Kramer standing there. I almost didn't recognize him without the stogie and a glass of scotch in his hand.

"Was working late," he said. "Saw your light."

He didn't look healthy. I'd been so focused on my own condition for months that I might have missed some changes in him. "You okay? You look a little sick."

"I need to talk to you."

"Have a seat."

He sat, but didn't talk immediately. He seemed to let something percolate in his head. I waited. We'd had conversations like this from time to time over the years. Kent had a way of letting his words put themselves together when he had something important to say.

"There's a problem," he said finally.

"Can I help?"

"Jesus, I wish you could, and I hate like a sumbitch to put you on the spot."

"You can't. You know that, right?"

"This time . . ." He shrugged.

"What is it?"

"I had a visitor this afternoon. A few of them, actually. Bunny Kovalenko and a couple of his friends."

"Russians."

"Yeah. Bunny was angry. Said you and Don Webb and that puke from Homeland Security tossed his house."

"I can't talk much about that, but yeah, we sort of did. We had a warrant."

"I heard. Is Bunny in real trouble?"

"I'd suspect his problems extend much further than what I can drop on him," I said. "But we didn't help him much by adding the legal issues. We've talked about this already. Kovalenko is tied in with dangerous people. The worst kind. I was distressed to hear he had a stake in your business."

"Yes. That's the thing, isn't it? He's got me by the balls. I needed his money, and I'm not stout enough yet to buy him out. This damned housing crisis."

"Tell me what he wanted."

Kent leaned forward and rubbed his face with his massive hands. I could see his eyes were more bloodshot than normal.

"He wants me to make you back off."

"Investigating him?"

"Yeah."

"You know I can't do that, and you know you can't make me."

"Oh, you've made that perfectly clear. Many times. Maybe you should have copied Kovalenko on the memo, because he seems to think I can control you."

"He's not simply asking for a favor, is he?"

"How do you know?"

"You look like shit. Whatever he has on you, it scares you. Did he threaten you?"

Kent shook his head, even as he said, "Yeah. Sort of."

"Financially?"

"Partly. Look, Judd, if I'd known who he was and who he worked for, I never woulda taken his money. Now he says he has to get you off his back, and he's demanding that I put pressure on you."

"Or he'll demand his money back."

"That's part of it."

"He made physical threats? That's why he had the muscle with him?"

"Not exactly."

I slammed my palm down on my desktop. It sounded like a pistol shot in the room.

"Damn it, Kent! Quit dancing around it! I've known you for thirty years, and we can talk to one another. Out with it! What did he say?"

"He's going to kill you," Kent blurted, and followed it immediately with something that, had it not been Kent Kramer, might have been a sob. He covered his eyes with his hand. "He's going to ruin me and he's going to kill you, if you don't stop butting into his business."

I sat back, a little shocked.

Kent ran his hands through his hair, and tried to pull himself together.

"Everybody works for someone else," he said, his voice trembling. "Even if they own their business, everyone is beholden to somebody. It's the way the world works. Right now I owe Kovalenko. He works for the Russian mob. I don't know what he does for them, but I've dealt with businessmen for years, and I can smell the stink of fear. He's screwed the pooch with whatever it is you have on him. His bosses are pissed, and he's in damage control mode. The only way he can take the heat off himself is to get you to back off your investigation."

"I can't do that," I said.

"You *have* to!"

"I couldn't if I wanted to. It's too big now. Don Webb's in on it. So's Cantrell. There are murders involved, and . . . other stuff. No matter what I do, Kovalenko's circling the drain."

"He'll take us both down with him!" Kent cried. "I know it. I can tell. Leave him to Cantrell and Don Webb. *You* back off. That's all I'm asking."

Kent was egotistical and self-serving, but he wasn't cowardly. For the first time in our lives together, I saw him terrified—for himself, for me, and for everything he held dear.

I owed him. It had been Kent's idea to hire me as Prosperity police chief. When Susan was killed on that horrible day a decade earlier, Kent stayed at my house for two straight nights as I wallowed in shock and grief. He'd helped pick out the dress for her to wear in the coffin. Hell, he'd picked out the coffin, and he paid for it out of his own pocket.

After I was shot, Kent visited me every day—every damned day, rain or shine—as I lingered between life and death in Surgical Recovery. Beyond all that, I owed him for thirty years of unwavering friendship. He'd never asked me for anything, and now he asked me to do a simple thing for him. All I had to do was step back and let other lawmen take the lead with Kovalenko. Justice would still be done. Bunny would get his day in court, if his Russian bosses let him get that far.

It was a simple thing I could give him. With a word, I could wipe the terror from his face and he'd sleep easily that night, confident that the violence had passed him by as surely as the angel of death had foregone doorways smeared with lambs' blood in ancient Egypt.

I hesitated. I weighed all the options.

Then I pulled out a legal pad and a pen.

"Write it down," I said. "Write down everything Kovalenko

said, exactly the way he said it. If he threatened you, tell me exactly what he threatened. If he threatened *me,* write that down, too. Write down how he invested in your business, and exactly how much money he gave you, and tell me how you came in contact with him. Write it all down as if you were writing a story, from the first time you heard of Kovalenko until he left your office this evening."

Kent stared at the paper and pen. "Why?"

"It's an affidavit. Obstruction of justice is a felony in this state. With Cantrell involved, it might also be a federal offense. You write it all down and I'll take it to the DA in Morgan and we'll have a grand jury indictment by tomorrow morning. It doesn't matter what else Kovalenko might or might not have done. When he tried to force you to take me off the case, he screwed himself."

"You really want to do this?"

"You know how they finally got Al Capone back in Chicago? Tax evasion. The FBI couldn't scratch him. Elliot Ness and the Untouchables couldn't stop him. He was too slick. He had too good an organization, too many palms greased in high places at City Hall. Then, a skinny guy on Ness's team realized they could get him for not paying taxes on all his bootlegging income. And that was it. Capone got hauled off to prison and that was the end of his criminal career. From what you tell me, Bunny's bosses aren't the real threat here. It's Bunny. He's running scared himself. He's getting desperate and he's starting to crack. To protect himself from his controllers, he's making mistakes, and the biggest one he made was coming to you. You write down everything you know, and I'll have him in a cell this time tomorrow night."

"I don't know."

"Damn it, Kent! Listen to me. We have him. He made one wrong step and we can take him down now. It's fourth quarter, we're down by six, and we have the ball on his twenty with a minute left. You know what to do. You did it a hundred times. Pull the trigger on this bastard."

His hands trembled as he reached for the pad.

CHAPTER THIRTY-SEVEN

The ADA on duty in Morgan that evening was a kid fresh out of law school named Marvin Sattrick. He was tall and broad and pudgy, with a squashed nose and eyes that peeked from sockets indented half an inch into his face. He still had residual adolescent acne. While driving to his office, Don Webb assured me he was good, and that was enough for me.

"It's thin," he said, as he read over the affidavit Kent had written and signed. "The elements of conspiracy are here, more or less, but it would really be nice if we had a little corroboration—a witness maybe, or some kind of recording."

"Kent doesn't have any recording devices in his office," I said.

"That's a shame. Like I said, the elements are here, and that's a good thing. I'll call the DA, talk it over with him. If he likes it, we can take it to the grand jury tomorrow morning, and maybe have a bill of indictment by lunch."

"That would be great."

"I said *maybe*. Don't get your hopes too high. This is compelling reading, and the DA might consider filing charges unilaterally based on it, but convincing a grand jury could be a different matter. I'll call you tomorrow morning, maybe eleven o'clock."

Don and I thanked him, and Sattrick headed back to the courthouse to do his paperwork.

"You know he won't be in long," Don said. "Guy like

Kovalenko probably has his lawyer on speed dial. Worse, his attorney is Minor Levine."

"Scumbag," I said.

"I do believe that is his official title, yes."

"Maybe I can hold Levine at bay for a while. Kovalenko threatened Kent in Prosperity, which makes it our case. If you can give us a little backup, we can arrest him and put him in the holding cell at the Prosperity PD. Sherry is due a little time off. I'll call her tonight and let her know she can take a couple of paid days off."

"The three of you, having to maintain law and order for the entire town," Webb said. "Seems too much to ask. Any reasonable person would understand if you weren't around when they come a-calling."

"We are spread a little thin. Levine might show up with a writ to release Kovalenko, but if there's nobody there to serve it on, what's a guy to do? He won't wait in the parking lot forever."

"You're playing a little fast and loose here, aren't you? If there's nobody to keep an eye on Kovalenko in your jail, there's nobody watching the henhouse, either. Seems like a ripe opportunity for some fox to spring your chicken."

"I didn't say nobody would be watching the station. We'll be around, only not inside."

"Who knows what kind of miscreant might show up at your door if he thinks you're away?"

"My impression all along is that Kovalenko is the big fish in this deal. Who knows? Maybe he isn't. Might land a whopper by dangling Kovalenko as bait."

Webb clapped me on the shoulder. "Even when you were a student in my history class, you were a bright kid," he said.

"Jury's still out on that one. I need to talk with Tom Larabee before I head back to Prosperity. I'll call you tomorrow as soon as I hear from Sattrick about the grand jury indictment."

Don Webb and I weren't the only law enforcement officials keeping late hours. I found Tom Larabee chatting with a desk sergeant in the Morgan Police Department next to the courthouse. He was a rotund man with silver hair and untamed eyebrows that grew every which way like a gorgon's hair. He and I had crossed paths from time to time, but Morgan crime rarely intersected with Prosperity crime. We weren't exactly drinking buddies.

I showed him the information I'd received on Bobby Spurlock.

"This the guy Shug Burch turned inside out?" he said.

"The same. I think the beating he took might have propelled him off the rez. The guy who fingered him to Burch turned up dead a couple of days ago down in Prosperity. According to a guy over at Smitty's, the dead fellow had dinner the night he was killed with a man who looked as if someone had rearranged his features with a jackhammer."

"You suspect it was a revenge killing?"

"It makes sense. Thing is, the dead guy, fellow named Overhultz, also worked for a suspect in another killing down in Prosperity."

"Boyd Overhultz?"

"That's right."

"Been kind of busy of late. Hadn't heard Boyd was dead."

"So you knew him?"

"Small time lowlife. Lots of petty theft, some drug dealing, once in a while he'd rough up a guy if you paid him enough. Can't think of three people who'd give his passing more than a minute's thought. If Spurlock did kill Overhultz, he probably did the county a favor."

"Doesn't mean he gets to slide on it."

"No. Suppose it don't. Tell you what—I'll distribute a detention order on Spurlock to my patrol officers. If they see him, they'll bring him in."

"There's something else. If Spurlock did kill Overhultz because of the beating he took from Burch—"

"We already have the occasional officer watching the parking lot at Shug's Nashville looking for potential drunk drivers. Maybe I'll beef up that patrol, and have them keep an eye out for Spurlock."

"Thanks, Tom," I said. "I might make it to bed sometime tonight."

"Busy evening?"

I slid on the Stetson and said, "Got one more stop to make. Need to talk with an old buddy."

Lily wasn't behind the bar when I walked into Shug's Nashville. Instead, there was some college kid slinging beers and mixing hard liquor drinks. I stepped to the bar and flashed my badge.

"Need to talk to Mr. Burch," I said.

"He ain't here, sir."

"When do you expect him?"

"He went out to dinner a couple of hours ago. I reckon he'll be back shortly. Can't remember the last time he wasn't in the house by ten o'clock. He likes to be around for closing, so he can handle the cash bags himself."

I checked my watch. It was nine forty-five.

"Can I get you something to drink?" The boy behind the bar pointed to the beer taps.

"On the job," I said. "How about a sweet tea?"

"Coming up."

I had the tea down to the lemon slice and the ice cubes about the same time Sean walked in with Lily Holder on his arm.

Sean looked like he'd been handed a Grammy. His face darkened a bit as he saw me, and he leaned over and whispered something in Lily's ear. She took a seat at the nearest empty table. A waitress appeared so quickly at her side I figured the word had gotten out that she was the boss's gal. She acted a little uncomfortable at the attention.

Sean sat on the stool next to me.

"Judd."

"Sean."

"You might be one of three people in this world who still call me that automatically."

"I never knew this Shug guy. I have a couple of messages for you. First, you need to keep an eye out for Bobby Spurlock. He's a prime suspect in the murder of Boyd Overhultz, and I think it all stems from that night you turned him into an alley burger out back. If he did kill Overhultz, he might be gunning for you."

"Bobby doesn't scare me. If he comes at me straight on, he'll lose again. If he ambushes me, ain't much I can do about it anyway."

"Second item. You have some kind of beef, you work it out with me directly. I was not happy to hear you'd dropped in on Donna the other day."

"Well, Judd, truth be told, I was looking for you. There are some things I think we should discuss."

"Maybe once this whole crime wave business in Prosperity is over. For now, if I hear about you hassling Donna again, I'm going to take your head off at the shoulders and stick it on a pike. Is there anything I'm saying that doesn't register with you?"

"I think you've made your position perfectly clear. I bear you no ill will, Judd. Like that old movie guy out in Hollywood said, we've all passed a lot of water since that day back when we were teenagers."

"We'll leave that discussion for another time. One more thing. I understand you're wrapped up in Bunny Kovalenko's business somehow. It would be in your best interests to disentangle yourself. Kovalenko's headed down a cobble road barefoot, and you don't want him dragging you behind him."

"My, my, Judd, you do care after all."

"Don't think I'm advising you of this out of some kind of affection. I want to keep matters as un-messy as possible. Warning you is part of that agenda. I gotta boogie. Remember what I said about Donna."

I dropped a couple of bucks on the bar for the tea, and headed for the door.

"Judd!" Sean called after me. I turned to face him. "Really love your hat. Know where I can get one?"

"You want to wear this hat, you gotta back up about thirty years and choose a different path for your life. Keep it in the road, Sean."

At three o'clock in the morning I was awakened by the jangling of my telephone. I was pretty certain it wasn't business, since those calls usually came over my two-way. I glanced at the caller ID. Donna.

"You know this is the first night we've slept apart since I got out of the hospital?" I said, before even saying hello.

"I know. I feel awful."

"Does that mean you aren't mad at me anymore?"

"Of course."

"You want me to come over there, or are you coming here?"

"Neither. It's too late. We'll make up tomorrow night."

"I talked with Sean."

"I'm glad."

317

"He doesn't seem fearful of Bobby Spurlock."

"I'd suspect not. You and he are from the same mold. If you weren't so pig-headed, you'd recognize that."

"Are we fighting again?"

"No way."

I paused for a few seconds to think of a way to tell her what had happened since she had stormed out of my house.

"We're probably taking Kovalenko down tomorrow," I said, finally.

"How?"

"He made a huge mistake. He tried to get me off his case by pressuring Kent. He didn't realize the loyalty Kent and I have for each other."

Another long silence.

"He threatened Kent?" she said.

"He threatened me, through Kent. That's obstruction, and it's a felony beef. The DA is taking Kent's affidavit before the grand jury tomorrow morning. We should have Kovalenko in lockup by lunchtime. We're hoping we can sweat a confession out of him on the Ram-Billy murder and the disappearance of the Guthries."

"And that will end it?"

"It should tie up all the loose ends, if it works out that way. Things can get back to normal around here."

"Good. I like normal," she said. "Normal feels good."

"Let's make a deal," I said. "I'll try to be less of an asshole, and we don't sleep apart again. There's a you-shaped hole in this bed that I find disagreeable."

"Sounds like time for a new mattress."

"Makeup sex would be a lot easier if you weren't two miles away."

"Tomorrow night we'll go out for dinner, my treat. Then we'll come back to your place."

CHAPTER THIRTY-EIGHT

I sat at my desk the next morning, fidgeting and waiting for some word about the indictment and futilely trying to get some paperwork done at the same time, when the telephone rang.

"Saddle up," Don Webb said. "Grand jury bit on it. We can go get Kovalenko."

"Is Cantrell coming?"

"Phoned him five minutes ago. He's on the way to your office. I'm putting together an arrest team of deputies here."

"I'll call in Slim and Gunny."

"Gunny?"

"My new patrolman. Slim's been showing him the ropes."

"Gunny Sikes?"

"That's right."

"He tell you about trashing his sheriff's car up in Virginia?"

"It came up in his job interview. From what I hear, the sheriff asked for it."

"Gunny's sort of a legend up around those parts. Seems he had a real talent for kicking ass and taking names. Got yourself a real tiger there."

"We'll see how he works out. This will be his first big bust."

We discussed logistics, then he headed off to round up his posse. I called Slim and Gunny over the two-way and asked them to head for the barn so we could coordinate the arrest and our plans for the follow-up surveillance, once Kovalenko was in the Prosperity lockup.

Cantrell swaggered into the station a few minutes before noon. "Excited about taking Kovalenko out?" he asked.

"Sure. One less asshole in my town is always welcome news."

"You've got some kind of ogre sitting in the outer office? Someone gave it a badge."

"My new patrolman. We keep him around to intimidate the undesirables. Got time to answer a few questions?"

"To the left, and Capricorn."

"Not those kind of questions. You didn't get a hard-on for Kovalenko until I sent in those prints from Ram-Billy's house. Someone up the line tore you a new one. Don't look at me like that. I could tell when you dragged ass into my office afterward. You were ready to chew the paint off my holding cell bars. Even so, when I asked you about the Guthries, you almost blew a gasket. This whole thing actually revolves around Roger and Natalya Guthrie, doesn't it?"

"Barkin' up the wrong tree, Chief."

"Yeah, I can see how unconcerned you are. After we take Kovalenko down today, I think you owe me an explanation."

"Go ahead. Hold your breath. I think blue would look real nice under that cream cowboy hat."

I stared him down, hoping I might intimidate him into answering. When I realized that wasn't going to happen, I took another direction.

"Drove by the Guthries' house the other day," I said. "Noticed the grass was cut and someone had watered the flowers. I dropped in on their neighbor, Hal Poplin. He said a lawn service comes out once a week and keeps the place tidy. Asked after their cat, Kisa. Poplin seemed bewildered. Told me a man showed up a week after he first called in the disappearance. The man told Poplin he was a detective with the Prosperity police, and he wanted to take Kisa off their hands. Poplin didn't think to call me at the time, since I was the only person who knew he had the cat. Except that I wasn't. I mentioned Kisa to you the first day you dropped in to warn me off the Guthrie disappearance. Told me I could keep Kisa. You knew her name and everything. Couple of days later someone drops in on the Poplins and relieves them of the cat."

"You're asking me to talk about things you don't have clearance to know," Cantrell said. He seemed a little smug about it.

"I don't suppose it matters," I said. "The penalty for obstruction in this state is pretty stiff. That should give you plenty of time to prep the Guthries to testify against Kovalenko for the really big stuff. Sure would like to know what it is they have on him."

"Don't have a clue what you're talking about."

"Let's see. Roger Guthrie was in arbitrage. Bunny Kovalenko was in arbitrage. Roger met Natalya through Kovalenko's mail-order bride company, and somehow she winds up hootchy-kootchying all over Kovalenko's porn websites. I can easily imagine a scenario in which a man desperate to get his wife's snatch off a ton of computer screens might be willing to do almost anything."

"Time to go yet, Chief?" Cantrell said, glancing at his watch.

"Roger's boss at the bank over in Pooler, Harriet Styles, gave me a crash course in arbitrage a while back. Buying and selling money. Buy low, sell high. Of course, it could also work the other way. You could always buy high and sell a little lower—not enough to take a real bath, but certainly enough that nobody would get suspicious. Sounds like money laundering to me, and from what I hear, Roger Guthrie was emotionally unstable enough to volunteer to engage in all kinds of nefarious money-laundering schemes for Natalya's boss. Albert York, Roger's direct supervisor at the bank, told me he came across Roger crying at this desk a few days before he disappeared. I think that's where he made his mistake—mixing his illegitimate business with his actual job. Seems likely to me he got caught, and by the time York saw him sobbing his lunch hour away, you guys already had your hooks in him."

I could tell by the crimson in Cantrell's ears that I was on the right track.

"I've seen that look before," I said. "You were sitting right where you are now, and I asked whether you had the Guthries stashed in a safe house somewhere. You never got to answer because we got that call to go out to the pond where Boyd Overhultz took two for the team, but I could tell I'd hit a nerve."

As if on cue, the phone rang. It was the sheriff department's central switchboard number. "Ready to roll," Don Webb said. "What say we convene outside Kovalenko's front gate at one-fifteen sharp?"

"I'll have my patrolmen there. How many deputies are you bringing?"

"I have four men lined up, with two cruisers. Don't forget your vest, Judd. I'd hate to see you get shot up twice in one year."

I racked the receiver and walked over to the gun safe in the corner of my office.

"It's roll time," I said, as I unlocked the safe and took out my shotgun. I started loading shells into the pump feeder.

"Got another one?" Cantrell asked.

"Nope. But I bet you have plenty of firepower in the trunk of your car, along with a vest you should be putting on right about now. Oh, one more thing before you head out. I called Harriet Styles at the bank over in Pooler this morning. Remember, she was the VP in charge of Roger Guthrie's department? Asked her whether they'd replaced him yet. Strangely enough, she told me he hasn't been discharged, despite the fact he hasn't shown up for work in almost a month. What do you make of that? You okay, Cantrell? You look like you're about to have a stroke."

I gave Don Webb and his deputies a ten-minute head start, since they were driving in from Morgan, and then we headed out. I tossed the keys to the old cruiser to Gunny Sikes and informed Slim that he'd been upgraded to the newer car. I took my Jeep and Cantrell followed in his Ford. Since we weren't in pursuit, and didn't want to give Kovalenko a lot of advance warning, we drove without lights or sirens.

The sheriff's department cars fell in behind us. I called ahead to Slim, who led our contingent, and suggested we pull over and let Don pass. Kovalenko lived right outside the Prosperity town line, which made this bust officially a Bliss County operation. I knew Don wanted to take Kovalenko down as badly as I did, and I didn't intend to steal his thunder.

We pulled over and let them pass, but Cantrell drove on by and placed his car between the two groups of local cops. That pissed me off. He was, more or less, an invited guest to this party, and he was trying to make himself a player. Par for the course, I figured.

We didn't pull up directly to Kovalenko's gate. Instead, we formed a cordon around it, in case someone had leaked news about the indictment to Kovalenko, and he had planned some kind of dangerous welcome.

I noted that one of the deputies was my old patrolman, Stu Marbury. I waved at him as he stepped out of the car.

"Chief," he said. "You look great. Glad to see you've recovered."

"Enjoying your new job?"

"I am today," he said, grinning.

Don stepped out of his car and sauntered over to the intercom. I'd known him for over thirty years, all the way back to when he was my high school history teacher, and I'd never seen him swagger quite the way he did now. I could tell he was digging this bust.

He pressed on the button, and waited for someone to answer. Seconds passed in silence. Don pushed it again. No response.

On the off chance someone was paying attention inside, he pushed it a third time, then leaned over and said, "This is Bliss County Sheriff Donald Webb. I am executing a duly authorized arrest warrant for Bernard Kovalenko. If this gate isn't opened in thirty seconds, we'll tear it down and drive in regardless. If I were you, I'd take this the easy way."

Thirty seconds passed like thirty years, but nobody responded. I already had the winch line on my Jeep loosened, and the hook ready to attach to the gate. Don nodded, and I latched on, hopped back into the driver's seat, and punched the winch button. The braided steel cable pulled taut, the gate groaned, and then it flew open with a snap that sounded like a pistol shot. Don told us to drive in single file, guns ready in case of an ambush from the woods, and form a semicircle around the front door.

We followed him in, and after we were in position he climbed the steps to the front porch, rang the doorbell, then stepped quickly to one side and held up a hand.

"It's open," he said.

"Unlocked?" I called.

"No, open. The door's cracked about a quarter inch. I'm going to swing it in."

He stretched his leg and kicked the door gently. It swung inward on well-oiled hinges. From the drive, I could see light streaming through the house from the lanai and the pool. I didn't see any people.

In case the intercom had malfunctioned, Don called through the door and repeated his announcement. Nobody replied.

I was a little surprised that I felt as good as I did. Ever since the shooting, I'd felt waves of near-crippling anxiety every time I was in the company of some miscreant. Now I felt a little wired, but not in an unpleasant way. Maybe my old instincts were returning.

Don stepped back down to the drive to consult with me and Cantrell.

"Seems kind of silly to storm the place if it's empty," I said. "Send a deputy around back, see if anybody's near the pool. From what I've seen so far, I think we have a dry hole."

"I don't like this," Cantrell said. "If Kovalenko has bugged out, it means somebody warned him about this raid. That means there's a leak somewhere."

"The indictment was sealed," Don said. "Minor Levine, Kovalenko's attorney, wasn't in the hearing. Can't imagine who might have warned him."

"Someone from the DA's office," I said. "They prepared the indictment. Has to be from there."

"We'll deal with that later," Don said. He called Stu over and told him to reconnoiter the rear of the house.

"Nobody around the pool," Stu reported. "I don't see any signs of anybody anywhere. I think the place is empty."

Don Webb swore quietly, stroked his chin, and examined the open front door again.

"How do you want to play it?" I asked. "This is your show, Sheriff."

"We don't storm it. For all we know, Kovalenko left behind booby traps. Motion activated explosives, or God knows what."

"I don't think the asshole's that industrious," Cantrell said. "Fuck this. I'm going in."

"The hell you are!" Don grabbed Cantrell's arm.

Cantrell shook him off and walked up the steps to the front door. He peered in briefly, and then crossed the threshold. We held our collective breath.

Nothing exploded. Nothing happened at all for a few minutes, and then Cantrell reappeared in the doorway. "You guys can come inside," he said. "Kovalenko left us something."

Cantrell was halfway through the house, toward the lanai. He stood over a body that had been hidden from our view by a column attached to a knee wall.

"I was right," I said, as we stared down at the bullet-pocked corpse.

"How's that?" Cantrell asked.

"The bartender, the guy who made that great iced tea? Looks like he was your plant. They found out about him, and decided to put him out of the picture before they hightailed it."

"His name was Barclay," Cantrell said. "And whatever they did to him, I'm doing double to Kovalenko. You can clear out. Barclay was a federal agent. That makes this a federal crime scene. I'm taking this one over. Go on home, boys. I'm in charge here now."

I sat on my porch, sipping a Corona with a slice of lime, and considering all the different twists this case had taken. Jack Cantrell had been a sandspur in my shorts for years, and if I were being honest with myself I'd have to admit that I enjoyed sticking the barb in him and twisting. I was certain now that he had the Guthries hidden somewhere safely, waiting to testify against Kovalenko. I'd also seen the look on Cantrell's face as he stood vigil over the body of his colleague. Wherever Kovalenko had flown, it would be a good idea for him to keep flying because I had no doubt that Cantrell wanted to feed him inch by inch, toes first, into a blast furnace.

In any case, it was off my plate. Killing Barclay had put Kovalenko in a whole new class of assholes. If he supposed he had problems dealing with a small town police chief, he was going to find being chased by Homeland Security and the FBI a special brand of hell I wouldn't wish on a rabid dog. If he was smart, Kovalenko was lounging on a beach somewhere in the Caribbean and plotting his ultimate escape to some dot of land in the middle of the Indian Ocean. Even then, I didn't think he could consider himself safe. I suspected his real problems were with his Russian handlers, and somewhere along the line he had screwed the pooch with them. His ham-handed attempts to kill the loose links in his crime chain, and to intimidate Kent, smelled more of desperation than design. He was running scared.

I had a couple of steaks marinating in Worcestershire sauce and kosher salt and coarse pepper in the refrigerator. I'd cleaned off the stone barbeque and stacked a pyramid of chunk charcoal in it, ready to light. Donna was coming over after she finished her work at school, and I figured I had a lot of making-up to do.

A dilapidated, twenty-year-old pickup turned off the highway and headed through the trees toward me. It pulled up in front of the steps, and Jorge Hierra stepped out. I hadn't seen him in weeks, since he'd gone to Spartanburg to visit his ailing mother.

"Afternoon, Jorge," I said. "Something I can do for you?"

His face was drawn, his eyes darker than ever. The veins in his sinewy arms ran under the skin like high tension wires. "I have sad news," he said.

"Your mother?"

"She passed early this morning. I received a telephone call from my sister."

"Come on up. Can I get you something to drink?"

He thanked me and sat on the top step, his back resting against the brick pedestal for the pyramid pillar. He was welcome to have a seat in one of the chairs, and he knew it. I think he was more comfortable on the hardwood planking of the deck. He asked for a Coke. I got him one from the fridge.

"I'm sorry to hear about your mother," I said. "I've lost both my parents. It's a hard thing."

"It is," he said. "And I need to go to South Carolina for a few days. To make arrangements. My sister is there, but she does not speak English as I do, and it would be difficult for her to handle everything that must be done."

"I understand. Is there anything I can do to help? Make some phone calls or something?"

"There is something. I do not wish to ask it."

"It's all right, Jorge. You've been a part of this farm for a long time. You need anything, you only have to ask."

"I am worried about . . . I do not know what you call it. *Huitlacoche.*"

"Corn smut," I said.

I was familiar with smut—a fungus that invades the corn and swells the kernels into brown and black tumorous nodules. In some quarters people find it a delicacy, but Jorge wasn't in the business of raising delicacies. Most of his crop was destined for either the market or animal feed, and a bout of *huitlacoche* would kill his investment.

"I cannot keep an eye on the corn while I am away. I would be grateful if you would look at it every several days to assure that there are no problems."

"Sure," I said. "Don't worry about a thing. You have enough on your plate right now. I'll see to it nothing goes wrong with your crops."

We talked for another several minutes before Jorge thanked me again and left for his sad duties. I had enjoyed our conversation. For the first time in weeks I had been able to talk about the sun and the rain and the earth and how things grew and bloomed, rather than about killing, drug dealing, and extortion. Despite my own futility as a farmer, I was strongly imbued with the land on which I had been born. I realized I hadn't walked the fields in months, even as I also realized that I missed it.

I limed another Corona, pulled on a pair of soft, battered Red Wing work boots, and set out on a hike across my land. I had clipped a two-way radio to my belt and I carried a fully loaded Winchester lever-action thirty-thirty rifle I had inherited from my father. Even though I believed that my troubles with Kovalenko were over, he had threatened my life, and I didn't know for certain that he was too far away to be dangerous.

I stopped by Jorge's twenty acres of corn and checked a few random stalks. It was still early in the season, not yet the middle of May, but I could already see the pistils forming in the calyxes which would become Silver Queen cobs the size of a rolling pin. Sweat bees and clouds of gnats flitted over the field, fulfilling their own contracts with nature. The smell was a mix of dank and sweet perfumes that elicited memories of a time decades earlier when Sean and I had stolen a few hours from our chores and played rambunctious games of make-believe in the fields and woods around my home.

Thinking of Sean spurred another mystery in my mind. I was pretty certain Bobby Spurlock had killed Boyd Overhultz, and I also had a strong suspicion that it had nothing to do with Kovalenko. Spurlock was simply trying to get back at Over-hultz—and maybe eventually at Sean—for the beating he had taken in the alley behind Shug's Nashville.

I still couldn't figure out Ram-Billy's murder. I didn't see it as some kind of Russian mob–related hit. They did, on occasion, like to leave a messy scene as an object lesson to others who might consider crossing them, but cleaving Ram-Billy's head in two didn't seem like their style. If Ram-Billy had been that big a nuisance, somebody simply would have walked up behind him and parked a couple of slugs in the back of his head. Why all the drama?

At one point, I'd suspected Overhultz, given that his prints were in the house. Now I questioned that. While the neighbor— what was his name? Kincaid?—had recognized Overhultz's Riviera when I described it, he hadn't said he'd seen it in Ram-Billy's driveway recently. Perhaps Overhultz had only been there to deliver a few bricks of marijuana, and everything else was nothing more than coincidence.

And while on the subject of coincidences, I remained troubled by the image on Ram-Billy's computer screen of Natalya Guthrie fingering herself. Without it, I never would have made the connection between Ram-Billy, Natalya, and Bunny Kovalenko.

Sometimes things fall your way. As a cop, I know that most cases are solved not by keen deductive reasoning, but by sheer luck of the cards being dealt in your favor. There is a role for coincidence in the solution of many crimes, but in this case it didn't feel right. Why would Ram-Billy be cruising porn sites at the moment someone split his skull, and—more importantly— why was he perusing *that* porn site, with *that* model? It felt contrived, almost as if I had been intended to see that screen and make the connection.

And then there was the matter of the mystery fingerprints in Ram-Billy's house, the ones that sounded all the alarms in Washington and brought Cantrell down on Don Webb with what was, in effect, a gag order. Who were they from, and why were they so important?

I have maintained for many years that it's the information you don't know that winds up biting you on the ass. It occurred to me that if I knew who those fingerprints belong to, I'd be a lot farther down the line to knowing who killed Ram-Billy Pressley.

The sun began to set as I made my way back around the south forty toward my house. On the way, I passed a barn my grandfather had erected in the 1940s. It had originally been a stable for draft horses he used to plow the fields. Later, when my father bought his first tractor and retired the horses, it had been renovated into a tobacco curing shed. Still later, after my father died and I declared that tobacco would no longer be raised on my land—more on moral than practical principles—I had converted it to equipment storage.

The frame was made of stout, old-growth red oak beams that were impervious to insect and water damage. Years of ammonia fumes from horse urine had interacted with the tannic acid in the oak and had turned it a deep, rich, mahogany brown. The frame would stand for a hundred years after I had long since returned to dust. The exterior was built from painted Carolina yellow pine, and had not borne up as well under the duress of the elements. The red paint had blistered and peeled away years earlier, and the boards themselves had begun to rot and crack. There were some holes in the side of the barn where entire sections of pine had deteriorated and crumbled. If something wasn't done, the entire outer shell would collapse.

I had let a lot of things fall apart on the farm, between my attention to the job and my nine months recuperating from the shooting. It was time to take charge. I carried in my heart a trust endowed upon me by ten generations of Wheelers stretching back to a time when people who wore strange three-cornered hats had cleared and developed and cultivated this land with a fervor that verged on religion. My only child, Craig, was studying to be a lawyer, so it was possible that I would be the last Wheeler to supervise this farm, unless he decided to run it for tenants as I had done for almost ten years. For the time being, if things were going to get done, I was the person responsible for doing them.

I resolved to use the next weekend to restore this barn, as I saw Donna's car turn off the highway onto my gravel drive. It seemed right to turn my attention back to my land and my ancestral home. It seemed to signal a return to normalcy in my tiny town.

The steaks had turned out perfect—charred crispy on the outside and a juicy medium rare in the center. Donna and I had split a bottle of California merlot over dinner, and we lay together in the hammock, watching the Milky Way take shape in the night dome over our heads. The air was crisp but not cold, and the middle spring daytime warmth had brought the tree frogs down by the pond and the katydids in the fields back to life. They sang at one another as we swung lazily and stared at the stars.

"I've been thinking," she said.

"Me, too."

"If this mess with your Russian mobster is over, maybe it would be a good time to take a trip."

"What did you have in mind?"

"How much time could you take away from work?"

"Kind of early to ask the city council for a vacation. I've only been back on the job for a couple of months."

"I think they'd understand. At least that's what Kent told me the other day."

"You've been talking to the mayor behind my back?"

"Sort of. Angry?"

"Hell, no. How long until school's out?"

"Four weeks."

"We could go to the beach."

"Well, sure . . ."

"Not what you had in mind?"

"Not exactly. What's the farthest you've ever been from this farm?"

"Went to New York once on a school trip. I've been to Dallas.

Of course, I lived in Atlanta for a time. That's about it."

"You've never seen the west coast?"

"Never had the inclination. We have a perfectly good coast on this side of the country."

"Damn, Chief, you are some kind of parochial."

"If I knew what that was, would I be angry?"

"I suppose not. I think you'd consider it a badge of honor. I was looking at a brochure today at school. It's for a cruise."

"Like to the Bahamas?"

"No. A cruise of the Mediterranean."

There was a pause that barely exceeded the length of comfort.

"What?" she said, finally.

"Sounds expensive. Wouldn't we have to fly to Italy or Greece or some such place first?"

"Well, yes."

"Haven't done a lot of flying."

"Great time to start."

"So where would this ship go?"

She spent the next fifteen minutes describing all the ports of call, and the sights to be seen there. She sounded as if she had been rehearsing it for most of the afternoon, which was likely the case. Donna does few things that are not deliberate. I listened as she worked through her recitation, and around the halfway mark I started to think it sounded like a good idea.

I wasn't about to let her win that easily. "I don't know," I said. "I hear cruise ship food is fattening, and I kind of like the new slimmer me."

"You *are* pretty hot now. We'd probably burn off all those calories walking on the shore excursions."

"I'll have to think on it. You're talking about a trip of two, three weeks. That's a long time to leave the town unprotected."

"I swear, Judd, sometimes you are more stubborn than a rusty mattock."

As soon as she said the word *mattock,* I experienced an inspired flash of successive logical steps, as if five doors inside my head opened in sequence.

"Oh, my God," I whispered. "I think you just solved a murder."

Chapter Thirty-Nine

Jack Cantrell sat on the bench outside my office when I arrived the next morning.

"No time, Jack. Stuff's happening," I said, as I unlocked the station door.

"Whatever it is can wait. I need you to come with me."

"Not now."

He pulled a leather wallet from his jacket pocket and flashed his badge. "This is official, and as a federal investigator I have the right to order you to comply."

"Going to be hard to do that with your face planted in the gravel," I said. "Whatever you want, we can do it later."

"I have some answers you want, and I've been ordered by my superiors to fill you in."

That got my attention. "Step inside," I said.

He followed me into the station. It was early, much earlier than I typically arrive. Sherry hadn't even gotten in yet. I led Cantrell to my office. He plopped down in the chair across from me. I pulled my Sig from my belt and placed it on the desk, within easy reach.

"Not friendly," he said.

"We're not friends. How quickly after Ram-Billy was murdered did you come across the crime scene?"

I'd never seen a face change color so quickly.

"You'd better explain that," he said.

"Coincidences. Hate 'em. You're a lot smarter than I gave

335

you credit for. I bet you're practically a goddamned chess master. You think five moves ahead all the time, don't you?"

"Not an explanation. Are you suggesting I killed Pressley?"

"No. I know you didn't. I'm pretty sure I know who did, but I don't know *why*. I expect to know that in a few hours. Maybe sooner. When Don Webb's lab tech sent those prints from Ram-Billy's house to Washington, the response was quick and decisive. You showed up in Morgan and told everyone to ignore them. We already knew one set of prints belonged to Boyd Over-hultz, because they were in the state system. Ram-Billy's were easy to identify, because we had him on a slab. There was a set of prints we lifted that didn't come from either of them. When they arrived in Washington, tagged as evidence from a crime scene, it set off a lot of alarms, and I'm betting it's because they were prints that shouldn't *be* part of a crime scene."

He eyed me suspiciously. "Go on," he said.

"They were *your* prints, weren't they?"

"You're way out of line, Wheeler."

"That's *Chief* Wheeler. You're in *my* town. There was no reason for your prints to be in Ram-Billy's house. You weren't part of the original investigation. So how did they wind up there? My guess is that you had some kind of hold on Ram-Billy. The same way I suspect you were using the Guthries to get at Kovalenko, you were also manipulating him. You hoped that Ram-Billy, because of his role as the American agent for Debuchke, Limited, might be able to get you evidence you could use to pin Kovalenko to the wall for his Russian mob activity. I'm about ninety percent certain it has something to do with the white slavery trade, since illegal immigration is a big part of Homeland Security's bailiwick. You showed up at Ram-Billy's house and found him dead. You realized that the scene was going to draw a lot of attention, so you gloved up, but not before you left some prints behind. Maybe you tried to clean them all up, but we both know that's impossible if you can't recall everything you touched. Am I close?"

"Keep going."

"You realized that your best shot at closing your case against Kovalenko had been murdered. You presumed Ram-Billy was killed by Kovalenko, but you didn't have any evidence. You didn't want to trip your hand, in case Kovalenko didn't know you were on his case, which seems likely. At his house the other day, he didn't recognize you, but when I told you about the mean iced tea Barclay made, you said you'd had it. Your true plant inside Kovalenko's operation was Barclay, and you were running him by remote control."

"Let's say you're on the right track. What does this have to do with anything?"

"It's about how I hate coincidences and I hate being used. You knew Ram-Billy lived in Prosperity, and we've knocked heads in the past, so you also knew I don't like to leave untidy crimes unsolved in my town. You also knew I was looking for the Guthries. So, you laid a trap for me. You pulled up the Baltic Babes website on Ram-Billy's computer and made sure Natalya Guthrie's picture was front and center. There was no way I could miss it. Then you wiped the place again, as well as you could, and you left."

"Why?"

"A flanking maneuver. You figured I'd make the connection between the Baltic Babes site and Debuchke. You also figured I'd make the connection between Debuchke and Bunny Kovalenko. And, since you've seen me in action before, you figured I'd rattle Kovalenko's cage, maybe pressure him into making a big mistake so you could swoop in and snatch him up. When I called and asked whether you would object to me investigating the Ram-Billy Pressley murder, I was yanking your chain for giving me shit on the Guthries' disappearance, but you didn't bite. You said go for it, and now that I look back on it I think you wanted me to dive in head first. Like I said, you *used* me. I hate that."

Cantrell picked at a hangnail as he ruminated. "Now you really do have to come with me," he said.

"Why?"

"Because the other option is a week or two in federal detention while I mop up the mess in this town. You know entirely too much for me to let you run around without being fully briefed."

I picked up my pistol. He stiffened, but then relaxed when I slid it into my belt holster.

"Okay," I said. "Let's go."

We took Cantrell's car, since I had no idea where we were going and caravanning didn't sound very efficient.

"I'm not a full-time asshole," Cantrell said, when we were about halfway to Pooler. "Sure, I manipulated you, but it was in a good cause. You're partly right. I did expect you to bang on Bunny's bars, but it wasn't to rattle him and push him to make a mistake. That would have been nice, but it wasn't my ultimate goal."

"What was it?"

"Can't tell you. Not yet. You'll understand in a bit. I *was* working on Ram-Billy Pressley. Did you know he was dying?"

"Carla Powers, the ME over in Morgan told me. Pancreatic cancer, right?"

"Yeah. Nasty shit. It was eating him up from the inside, and fast. He wanted to get right with God or some shit before he kicked, which was about the time I discovered his link to Kovalenko. The Russian is into a lot more than white slavery and dope. A ton more. He's eight kinds of dirty on a slow day. I was trying to find something to offer Pressley that he'd accept in return for rolling over on his boss. I didn't kill him."

"I know."

"You said you know who did."

"I'm pretty sure." I told him my suspicions.

"Not a bad suspect," he said. "Don't see much in the way of motive."

"Haven't figured that part out yet either. Got means and opportunity. That might be enough to get him in an interview room and sweat him."

"Wouldn't mind watching that show. You know Kovalenko was an arbitrageur before tossing in with the mob, which means he knows all about moving money around. That's highly attractive to his gangster buddies. They have a lot of money that needs moving. More than Kovalenko can handle himself."

"So I was right about Guthrie's role. He was helping Kovalenko launder mob money."

"Yeah. You read the folder on Natalya Gromykova from ICE, the one I sent you?"

"Yeah. It was bullshit."

"How did you know?"

"First of all, you told me it was garbage. I knew that before, though. Nothing fit. The girl is a poster child for juvenile delinquency and depravity, but suddenly goes straight and becomes a nice office girl? It didn't read."

"Well, you're right. Natalya was one of the mob's whores in Lithuania. Her handlers faked her folder to make her look like some kind of reformed choir girl. Their original plan was to sell her to Guthrie, but keep her on the payroll as a sex model on Kovalenko's porn sites. Eventually, after a decent interval, she'd divorce Guthrie and leave with American citizenship."

"It didn't work out that way," I said.

"No. Against all odds, she developed a liking for the big lug and actually fell in love with him. He knew what she was doing on the side, but let's face it—she's an eight or nine, and he's a low four on his best day. He was willing to put up with a lot to keep her in the marriage. That worked fine until she really did get a case of the decents and decided she didn't want to do the porn thing anymore. She asked Bunny to let her go, and he told her he owned her."

"And Guthrie made a deal with the devil. He traded his arbitrage expertise for her freedom from the mob."

"You got that part right the other day. He would help Kovalenko launder money, and they'd let Natalya be a one-man woman. And it worked, at least for a while. You know how these guys work. First he only had to work for Kovalenko one or two nights a week, off the clock. Then they started demanding more and more, and before he knew it, Guthrie was spending part of his real work day moving money for Kovalenko. His performance at the bank began to fall off. He couldn't serve two masters."

We had reached the center city of Pooler, where Cantrell drove into an underground parking lot next to a cluster of interconnected buildings called The Metrix, which was supposed to be some kind of mash-up between *Metro* and *Matrix*. It was a mixed-use community of offices, shops, restaurants, hotels, movie theaters, and a couple of high-rise apartment buildings. On the second level, I saw an entire row of parking spaces labeled RESERVED FOR IMMIGRATION AND CUS-TOMS ENFORCEMENT. Cantrell parked in the first empty space.

"Homeland and ICE have their offices upstairs," he said, as he turned off the car. "Got some people who want to have a talk with you."

"What about the rest of the story?" I said, as we entered the elevator.

"So the pressure is getting to Roger. He can't keep up with Kovalenko's demands and those of his job."

"And that's why his supervisor caught him crying at his desk."

"Probably. First time I heard of that was when you mentioned it the other day. Anyway, he calls Kovalenko and starts talking like he's had a set of balls all along. Says he has to back down a little on the laundering, or it's going to fuck up his job. Kovalenko, being a psychopath, couldn't give two shits, and he decides to intimidate Guthrie into getting back in line. So he sends our late buddy Boyd Overhultz to scare some sense into him. Used your buddy Shug Burch as the intermediary. Boyd was supposed to deliver a message. You know, something like 'Get in line or get gone.' That was supposed to turn Guthrie's bowels to water or some such shit. Only Guthrie had taken it up to here with mob abuse, and as soon as Overhultz started his act Guthrie took a baseball bat to him."

"A baseball bat?"

"A goddamned Louisville Slugger. Chased Overhultz off the front porch and all the way back to his car. Took a swing at the headlights as he was backing out of the driveway. I'd love to see film of it. That was the last straw. You suggested the other day that we somehow sniffed out unusual activity in the bank's arbitrage records. Sorry. We aren't that smart, and Roger was really good at his job."

We exited the elevator, and Cantrell led me down a short hallway to what appeared to be a standard office door. The placard next to it read *Flight Attendants' Rights Mediation.* I poked at it.

"What the hell?" I asked.

"It's bullshit. Doesn't mean a thing, but it looks official. Keeps people from sniffing around."

He unlocked the door and held it open for me. I had expected to see a conference room or some kind of office cube farm, but beyond the door was a comfortable and relatively modern apartment. Floor to ceiling windows offered a panoramic skyline accented by the Pooler Pythons football stadium. Two people sat on a couch watching TV. One of them turned off the remote control, and stood to face us. Something rubbed against my leg. I looked down.

"Hello, Kisa," I said. "Mr. and Ms. Guthrie, can't tell you how nice it is to meet you at last."

CHAPTER FORTY

Roger Guthrie insisted on telling the entire story again from his point of view. It was essentially the same as Cantrell had presented it, up to where Roger dispatched Boyd Overhultz from his property with the bat.

"That was the last straw," he said. "I couldn't take any more. I was dealing with gangsters, and I didn't know what to do. A couple of days later, during lunch, I found a pay phone down at the bus station, and I called the FBI. They forwarded my information to Homeland Security, since we were dealing with possible illegal alien activity. That's how I came into contact with Agent Cantrell."

"You engineered the disappearance," I said to Cantrell.

"Nice piece of work, too," Cantrell said. "We pulled it off like a black op. Spirited them out in the middle of the night. Had a med tech on hand to draw a vial of blood from both of them, and dabbed a few spots around to make it look like it was a forced abduction. We had this safe house set up for them. They've been here ever since."

"Can we leave soon?" Natalya asked. Her voice was heavily colored by her Lithuanian accent. "I am getting tired of being cooped up in this place. I would like to go back to my beautiful home."

"We're working on it," Cantrell said, and then he turned back to me. "Roger's been providing us with details of the various accounts he use for Kovalenko's money. It's pretty complicated. At the same time, like I said, I was working on Pressley, trying to get some more juice on Kovalenko. I went to visit him one day, and he was dead. I didn't deceive you to throw Kovalenko into a tizzy and force him into a mistake. Pressley's killing offered an opportunity to take Kovalenko's mind off the Guthries while we built their testimony. You're right. I put Natalya's picture up on the computer screen. We have our differences, but I know you're a good cop. I figured you'd find the connections between Ram-Billy Pressley, the Guthries, and Kovalenko's companies. Knowing how you operate, all up-in-your-face, I figured you'd keep Kovalenko occupied. It worked better than I planned, but not entirely because of you."

"Overhultz getting killed," I said.

"Oh, yeah," Cantrell said. "Icing on the cake. Overhultz getting zagged—and you finding the weed stash in his house—helped a lot. Now Kovalenko had two employees killed, and no idea who killed them. He's been so busy trying to keep all those plates spinning on all those sticks that he hasn't had time to hunt for Roger and Natalya."

"What happens now?" I asked.

"Remains to be seen. Kovalenko's in the wind on a federal beef now. Up to this point, he was flirting with deportation or maybe a prison sentence, but killing Barclay could land him on a gurney with a needle in his arm. Fact is, we don't know where he is. He had access to a small jet, but it's still sitting in its hangar. He hasn't boarded any boats we're aware of, and we've covered the commercial airlines and bus and train lines. For all we know, he hopped in his car and headed for Canada or Mexico."

"Or maybe he's still around, trying to figure out how to put everything right."

"There is that possibility. If it's any comfort, before he went

344

and murdered a government agent, Kovalenko's biggest problems were with his own backers. If I could reel in Kovalenko, I don't think Roger and Natalie would be in much danger. Nobody's been talking about witness protection or anything. The Russian mob hasn't demonstrated a lot of patience with employees who screw the pooch more than once. My goal was to paint him into a corner and then ask for information on his handlers."

"The big fish," I said.

"Guess crime fighting is the same everywhere, big or small."

"I've gone fishing once or twice in my little pond. Not much chance of Kovalenko making a deal now, is there?"

"Killing Barclay made the possibility remote. I guess it would depend on what he could give us."

"He doesn't know that, and you have no way to tell him. That makes him dangerous."

"That's why I wanted to pull you in, let you know what's happening. I couldn't tell you while you were serving your purpose in my plan, but now that Kovalenko has taken his act on the road, it seemed a good idea to bring you up to date. See, it's not just Roger and Natalie who are in danger. Kovalenko has threatened you and pressured your buddy Kramer, and I hear he isn't on the best terms with Shug Burch."

"You're saying we can't totally relax yet."

"I'd advise against it."

I tried to leave three times, and each time the Guthries stopped me to heap their thanks again for whatever I'd done above and beyond seeing to it that their cat was well tended. It was Cantrell who finally got us out the door.

"Want to go with me to arrest Ram-Billy's killer?" I said.

"I'd kind of like to stop on the way for lunch, but sure. Got nothing else to do today."

We took an hour to grab a bite at an Italian chain restaurant, and then drove back to Prosperity, where we switched to my Jeep. Ten minutes later, we pulled into Ram-Billy Pressley's driveway.

Sam Kincaid's garage door was open, and I could see him inside. He wore a denim work apron and a pair of safety glasses, and he appeared to be wrestling a sheet of plywood into position on his table saw. He looked up as we climbed from the Jeep, and removed his glasses. I waved at him and he waved back. Then I hiked up the five steps to Ram-Billy's porch and made a big production of pulling the crime scene tape from the doorway. Cantrell leaned against the Jeep and watched. By the time I stepped down from the porch, Kincaid had doffed the apron and glasses, and stood at the edge of his driveway.

"Find out who killed Mr. Pressley yet, Chief?" he asked.

"I think I have," I said. "Have you met Agent Cantrell here?"

"Can't say as I have," Kincaid said, extending his hand. "Real estate?"

"Homeland Security. Federal government," Cantrell said, without moving.

Kincaid's hand hung in midair before he blushed and let it drop. "Wow. Can't say I've ever met a federal agent before."

"That's good—for you," Cantrell said, and let a smile sneak across his face. He was trying to look friendly.

"What are you working on this time?" I said, as I stepped onto his driveway.

"Saw this guy on TV making a country style kitchen china cabinet. Liked the look of it, so I ordered the plans. I'm starting to make the case out of plywood."

"Got the plans in the garage? My grandfather was a farmer first, but he learned to be a master carpenter. Built the house I live in today. Me, I don't know which end of a hammer you blow into, but I'd be interested in seeing how this kind of thing is built."

"Sure, come on in."

Cantrell and I followed Kincaid into this garage. As it had been the other couple of times I'd seen it, the place was tidy and relatively clean. The spider webs that had been gathering on the wood lathe had been swept away, and despite the fact that he was actively working on a project, Kincaid didn't have a lot of tools lying around on the workbench. It appeared that he was fastidious about keeping things in their place.

"I really should introduce you to this fellow I know," I said, as Kincaid unfolded the plans. "Between the two of you, I think you could open up a furniture store."

"Oh, I'm not that good," Kincaid said. "Besides, since my wife passed, I spend as much time on the road as I do here at home. I spend a couple of weekends at the beach each month, and several weeks each summer."

"Retirement. Sounds like a blast to me," Cantrell said, from the corner of the garage.

"It doesn't suck," Kincaid said.

"I think you're a better craftsman than you give yourself credit for," I said. "Look at this place. Some guy who just bangs a few boards together from time to time doesn't put much effort into shop organization. Looking around, I can tell you went at this place seriously. Good traffic flow, lots of space for each power tool, and I have to hand it to you, Mr. Kincaid. I have never seen a better organized tool wall outside of a professional cabinet shop."

"Well, thanks," Kincaid said.

I walked over to the pegboard wall. "Look at this, Agent Cantrell. Not only has he assigned each tool a specific spot, but he's taken a marker and outlined each tool precisely. That's a great idea. That way, you'll always know where the tool belongs.

Take a tool down, use it, then put it back up where you found it. Mark of a craftsman, wouldn't you say?"

"Don't know a handsaw from a screwdriver myself," Cantrell said. "But I do know order when I see it. Very admirable."

"Just one problem," I said. "This tool here—what is it, a pick?"

"No," Kincaid said. "That's a mattock. A pick has two pointed blades. The mattock is a lot more useful."

"Mattock. That's right. Hey, Cantrell, did I tell you what my girlfriend Donna told me the other night? She said I was stubborn as a rusty old mattock. What do you make of that?"

"Sounds like she knows you inside and out."

"Might be right. *This* isn't a rusty old mattock. It looks brand new. Look here, even has the price sticker on the handle. I don't believe you've had a chance to use this yet, have you Mr. Kincaid?"

"Uh . . . no," he said.

"There was an old one here before, though. You can tell because the outline on the pegboard is a different shape than this mattock. That means you had another mattock here before. I noticed that the first time I talked with you, but didn't make anything of it at the time. I mean, I own a farm. I'm always having to buy new tools. Things break, right?"

"That they do," Cantrell said.

"Except I can't recall ever having to replace a mattock," I continued. "Darn things last almost forever. I bet a good mattock could go through two, three generations before it broke or wore down to the point of needing replacing. Hey, you know what that reminds me of?"

"What's that?" Cantrell said.

"We were talking on the way over here about the weapon that killed Ram-Billy Pressley. You were saying you thought it was a maul. I thought it was an axe. Looking at this bright new—

sharp—mattock, I believe it would have the heft and the cleaving force to split a man's skull. What do you think, Mr. Kincaid?"

As I had spoken, Kincaid's face had reddened, and I could see perspiration forming on his brow. He grasped the edge of his table saw with one hand to steady himself.

"Just a quick question," I said to him. "Whatever became of your old mattock? Looks like you bought this one recently."

"I, ah . . ." He stammered. "I . . . well . . . it was one of the tools that Mr. Pressley borrowed from me."

"He broke it?"

"Well, no."

"Lost it?"

"Not exactly."

"Because I've been in his garage and in that tool shed he had out in his backyard, and I didn't see a mattock in either place."

"Chief Wheeler is being polite," Cantrell said. "He's giving you the opportunity to come clean of your own accord. Me, I don't come from the genteel south. I've got a lot less patience than he does. So, just for the record, what did you do with your old mattock after you parted Ram-Billy's skull with it?"

Kincaid stepped woodenly over to a shop chair next to the workbench and settled into it.

"Don't reckon there's a way out of this, is there?" he said.

"Depends," I said. "Courts always love a good sob story. Why don't you tell us yours?"

"He killed my dog!" Kincaid wailed, tears forming at the corners of his eyes. "The old man was insufferable, always bitching and moaning about one goddamn thing or another. He was going to sue me because he found out my driveway encroached on his property by three inches. *Three inches!* Hell, I didn't even build this house. The driveway was here when I bought it! He said I had to move the driveway or he was going to take me to court and get restitution for the loss of his yard! You ever hear such a thing? I told him to ram it. 'Go ahead. Take me to court,' I told him."

"So he killed your dog?" I asked.

"No. Not then. Dutch was a golden retriever. I'd had him fifteen years, which is really old for that breed. He was sweet as the day is long, but he was old and he wandered. My wife, Allison, gave him to me when he was just a pup, not ten weeks old. She died five years ago, and Dutch was the only company I had. He was a gift from her, and for that I treasured him. But he was old. He used to know to stay in my yard, but I guess he forgot, or didn't realize where he was. I let him out into the yard, and usually he'd stay there, but he sometimes wandered into Pressley's property. One day Pressley banged on my door and said Dutch had taken a shit in his backyard and he wanted to know what I was going to do about it.

"I apologized, and said I'd clean it up. I took a pooper-scooper over and I removed Dutch's mess, and Pressley stood over me and complained the whole time, saying I ought to take Dutch to the shelter and have him put down for a nuisance."

"Mr. Warmth," Cantrell said.

"Well, Dutch did it again a few days later, and this time Pressley went ballistic. He demanded that I keep Dutch inside the house or on a chain in the garage. Goldens are an active breed. They need to run, even really old dogs like Dutch. Putting him on a chain would have killed him. A week or so later, I saw him up on Pressley's front porch. There was a dog bowl up there. I figured Pressley had softened a little, maybe taken a shine to old Dutch. A couple of hours later, I found Dutch lying outside my back door, dead as a mackerel. The dog bowl had disappeared from Pressley's front porch and I never saw it again. I knew what had happened. Pressley, that mean old goat, got tired of my dog fouling his yard and fed him poison. He killed my Dutch."

"So you killed him back," I said.

"No. Not right away. I fumed about it for a while and then decided to cut ties with the miserable old bastard. I went over to his place and I demanded he give me back all the tools he'd borrowed. He pulled them together, and dropped them in the living room. Told me to take them and leave, and then he turned his back on me and sat at that damned computer. The last thing he said to me was, 'Nice mattock. Maybe you can use it to bury your dog.'

"I won't lie, sir. I had been drinking. When he plain as admitted that he'd killed Dutch, I saw red. I lost control. It was over quickly. I don't believe he ever knew a thing that happened. I believe, in my heart of hearts, that his passing was far less painful than Dutch's."

"Where's the mattock?" I asked.

"Tossed it over the bridge into Six Mile Creek."

I pulled the two-way from my belt and toggled Slim's frequency. I asked him to meet me at Kincaid's house. Then I cuffed Kincaid and read him his rights.

That evening after dinner, as the sun was setting, Donna and I took a walk down to the pond on the west side of the farm.

"Killed Ram-Billy over a dog," Donna said, shaking her head.

"The dog his wife gave him. The last living thing connecting him to her. Hard to imagine what I'd do under similar circumstances."

"You'd do the right thing. You always do the right thing. Sometimes it takes you a while to figure out what that thing is, but I do believe you are incapable of doing a thing that wrongly harms another person. I feel kind of bad about Mr. Kincaid. What will happen to him?"

"Depends on whether he gets a smart attorney. If I were him,

I'd ask for a bench trial, keep a jury out of it. Every judge in Bliss County knows what a crotchety asshole Ram-Billy was, and half of them might have paid good money to help Kincaid bash in his head. Might be a lot easier to draw sympathy from a judge than from a jury of people who never heard of the old cuss. The dog story might be interpreted as mitigation, if Kincaid can prove it."

"Kind of wish I'd kept my mouth shut with that rusty old mattock crack."

"It would have come to me sooner or later. Kincaid being the killer makes me wonder about other things."

"Like what?"

"Well, I know Kovalenko didn't kill Ram-Billy. I'm about ninety-five percent certain Boyd Overhultz was murdered by Bobby Spurlock, and it's a matter of time before I run him to ground, which takes Kovalenko out of the picture for that killing too. The Guthries weren't abducted by Kovalenko or his Russian buddies. So, what's this whole last couple of months been all about? If I'd discovered that Kovalenko had engineered the Guthries' disappearance and killed Ram-Billy and Overhultz to cover his tracks, I'd feel a lot better about leaning on him the way I have. It wasn't like that. It's all connected, in a crazy fashion, but not in a cause-and-effect way."

"I seem to recall you saying some time back that crime never makes sense. Half the time it's due to hot blood, and most of the rest of the time it's people making dumb decisions. Maybe you hit some kind of perfect crime storm. Everything fell together the way it did, and you simply found the connections."

"I almost feel sorry for Kovalenko," I said. "In the end, he didn't make any of this happen—not directly—but he's going to carry the water for it. If Cantrell doesn't nail him, the Russians will. Plain bad luck."

"Some good might come of it," Donna said. "Kovalenko being gone will be good for Bliss County. And some real estate agent is going to get ungodly rich off selling that compound of his."

"Silver linings," I said.

"One more good thing happened. These murders brought you out of your funk. I feel like I have my boyfriend back."

I pulled her close and kissed her deeply against a live oak next to the pond bank. She was right. I felt as if I had returned from a long, arduous journey through a dark land where I had been almost—but not entirely—irretrievably lost.

"Tell me more about this trip you want to take," I said. "Nearly getting killed makes me want to see what there is of this world I missed for the first half of my life."

CHAPTER FORTY-ONE

Lily Holder stepped back from the dining room wall in Burch's farmhouse and checked the paint she'd rolled onto it. It looked even, which was impressive considering how long it had been since she'd wielded a paintbrush. Outside, a team of contractors had finished installing the new roof shingles and had begun working on pulling down the warped and splintered shutters on the front porch windows. Through the back kitchen door, she could see Sean manhandling a cultivator, plowing the furrows of a vegetable garden she'd requested.

Lily was happier than she could remember having been in years. After she and Sean had quit dancing around one another and had declared their mutual attraction openly, things had moved along quickly. She had moved to days at Shug's Nashville, and Sean had discovered all sorts of lively places to take her each night, before ultimately taking her to his place. She had found him as energetic and enthusiastic in bed as he was on stage, and she had a feeling she had provided him with a surprise or two to boot. It was as if he awoke each day imagining what new thing they could try together.

Sean had closed on the old Murray farm in record time—paying cash for the place cut a ton of red tape—and had contracted a small army of renovators and repairmen almost before the ink was dry on the deed.

It was strange the way things turned out. On the night Sean picked her up walking along the highway, she had been so

354

distraught over being abandoned by her most recent boyfriend that she had actually contemplated stepping out in front of the next transfer truck that roared around the bend. Instead, by pure random chance, a music superstar had pulled over and yanked her out of one life and into another.

She stepped into the kitchen, pulled a pitcher of iced tea from the new refrigerator, and poured a glass to the brim.

"How about making me one of those, sweetness," Sean said from the kitchen door.

"You got it, Ace."

She prepared a glass for him and they sat on the back porch steps.

"Place is coming right along," he said, as he ran the sweaty glass across his forehead.

"It's beautiful. Does it remind you of the farm you lived on as a boy?"

"No, and that's a good thing. I loved the earth and the crops and the animals, but where we lived wasn't fit to be on this place. Hate to disillusion you, darlin', but you've hooked up with pure trailer trash."

"You're not the place where you came from," she said. "You've risen above that. Whatever hardship you were dealt in your youth prepared you to be the person you are today. This is the last time I wish to hear you disparage yourself."

"Yes, ma'am."

He fell silent and sipped his tea. Lily was surprised by her ability to tolerate the silences between them. It seemed that they did not feel the need to keep the conversation lively. She had never experienced that before, and she believed that it could be attributed to their natural comfort with one another and their shared history of overcoming the boulders in their personal paths.

"You ever been to Paris?" he asked.

"You mean in France? 'Cause I've been to Paris, Texas."

"Good lord, me, too. Don't care to go back. No, I am talking about France."

"Never been there. Never been out of the country. Not to Mexico or Canada or any of the islands off the coast of Florida."

"I hear it's a hell of a place, Paris. Wonder whether a grizzled old ex-con like me can get a passport."

"A grizzled old ex-con can get one if he's Sean Burch. Fame and prosperity open a lot of doors."

"Yeah, might have to look into that. Might want to take you to Paris, show you what real night life is like. How'd you like that?"

"I'd like that fine, but you don't have to lavish things on me. I don't think I've ever met a girl who doesn't like pretty stuff. But you don't have to buy me, Sean. I've already made my decision to be with you for as long as you'll have me."

"Don't see much of an end to that road. Runs off as far in the distance as I can spy. Hey, what do you think of that as a song lyric?"

"Are you going to put our life together to music?"

"It deserves to be. Yeah, I think Paris would be fun. Got some things to take care of first."

She glanced at him and noted that his features had darkened, even in the crystalline light from the sun directly overhead.

"I do not wish to hear about these things," she said.

"I know, but if you're going to be with me, you should know all about me. There are accounts unpaid in my life. Things need to be put right. Debts must be settled, or they will gnaw at my soul like a rabid beast."

"Let the past die, Sean. You have a new life now."

"I have one or two more things to settle, and we'll start a life together they'll write poems about after we're dead."

She shuddered. "Please don't say that. I'm feeling too alive now to contemplate the grave."

CHAPTER FORTY-TWO

The weekend rolled around without a scent of Bobby Spurlock or Bunny Kovalenko. On Friday afternoon I took the farm truck to a contractor's store and purchased a couple hundred board feet of yellow pine one-by-tens. After dumping them and some tools next to the rotting barn, I had lunch with Donna at the picnic table next to the stone barbecue, and she headed off to do some shopping.

We'd spent the evening before poring over cruise brochures she'd picked up at a travel agency. We hadn't settled on a trip yet, but we had narrowed down the possibilities. Before I could think about taking off for a couple of weeks, I needed to finish some neglected maintenance around the farm.

After Donna wheeled down the gravel drive, I pulled on a tee shirt, a faded pair of overalls, and some work boots, and took the Jeep across the hill to the barn. I packed the Winchester— not so much out of fear, but rather as a precaution. The fact that Kovalenko had not been spotted didn't mean he wasn't still around. An old hippie saying occurred to me as I tossed the weapon into the Jeep—better to have it and not need it than it is to need it and not have it.

I set to work pulling the rotting boards from the side of the barn, using a crowbar and a sledge. I needed to replace almost an entire short end of the barn's siding, which meant pulling down twenty or thirty boards. As I worked into the afternoon, the sun began to bear down on me like an unpaid debt. I undid the straps of my overalls and yanked off my soaked tee shirt, and let the bib of the overalls hang so I'd get more ventilation.

I could tell I was out of shape. My hands had softened over the months since being shot, and I could feel blisters beginning to form under the leather of my favorite work gloves.

Then I walked around the corner of the barn and discovered Sean Burch standing by my Jeep with the Winchester in his hands.

"Nice piece," he said. "You planning to do a revival of *The Rifleman*?"

I froze. He wore designer jeans that probably cost a week of my pay and a white pima cotton shirt. His boots were made of ostrich, comfortably broken in. He pulled the lever action on the Winchester and examined the cartridge in the chamber.

"Thirty-thirty," he said. "Interesting. Somehow thought you'd go for maximum punch, maybe a forty-five. Went hunting up in Washington State a few years back—elk, moose, even imagined we might bag a bear, but we didn't. Guy I was with had a fetish for antique weapons. Had himself a Sharps fifty-caliber muzzle-loader he'd inherited from his grandpap. He liked to use it for long distance shots, but when push came to shove he preferred to pull out his lever-action forty-five Winchester. Taught me how to use it. Decided right there and then I liked a carbine. Can't buy one of my own, of course, being a felon, but I did learn to use one. Yes sir. An admirable piece of iron."

I didn't reply. I couldn't take my eyes off the gun.

"Man, you ought to see your face right now," Burch said. "Kinda surprised I could sneak up on you this easy, you being a trained lawman and all."

"What do you want?" I said.

"Seems we've had something hanging between us like a bad smell for too long. I reckon it's time to set accounts straight."

I pointed toward the rifle.

"With that?"

Burch guffawed. "Too easy, man! No, I think our problems likely run way too deep to be settled with this old thing."

He placed the Winchester into the back seat of the Jeep. Then he rolled up his sleeves and started walking toward me. "I've waited for a long time to do this. You've got something coming, and today we're going to put paid all the grief that's built up between us for the last thirty years."

I tensed up as he drew within arm's length, and turned partly sideways, waiting for him to attack. Sean had an inch or two on me, and probably thirty or forty pounds, most of it muscle based on what I could see of his forearms. He also had the advantage of not having had the crap shot out of him in the last six months. If he intended to deliver a beating, I was at a distinct disadvantage. He stopped a foot and a half away, and stared directly into my eyes. Then he raised his hand.

"I apologize," he said. His hand froze in midair just above his waist. "I was a wild, angry person, and I put you in a terrible situation way back then. I know how hard it must have been for you to go to the police and testify against me, because it would have been as hard for me. I didn't realize that until later. A lot later. Will you take my hand and say we'll put it in the past?"

I stared at his hand. I was shocked, and a little ashamed. I had been treating Sean as the same teenager who had violated Lisa Rae Youngblood. I had destroyed our friendship. I had prejudged the man based on behavior that was three decades dust. Almost embarrassed, I took his hand.

"You had a head of steam in my office the other night, so I figured you wouldn't listen to reason. Used to be, that wouldn't have stopped me. Things change. When I came by here the other day and upset your lady, Donna, this was what I intended. I started to tell her all the stuff I've been thinking. Then it occurred to me it would be kind of chickenshit to use her as some kind of messenger. What I need to say should be said directly to your face."

He released my hand, stuffed his hands in the back pockets of his jeans, and looked around the farm. For as far as he could see in any direction, he'd survey Wheeler farm land.

"Nice spread. Always said you had a great place. You know I bought the Murray farm, other side of town?"

"I'd heard," I said.

"It's not as big as yours and it needs a lot of work, but I reckon in five, ten years it might be something to be proud of. Thinking of turning it into a vineyard. Now don't that beat all? Shug Burch a winemaker?"

"Sean Burch, maybe," I said.

"Yeah. It's time to put ol' Shug to bed. So here's what I wanted to tell you the other day. I wish things had been different. I wish I hadn't been raised in a succession of shacks and single-wides, and I wish I hadn't spent the first ten years of my life shittin' in an outhouse instead of a flush toilet. I wish my dad hadn't regarded me as some kind of practice target for his razor strop and his hickory switch. I wish my mama had lived to see me become something in this world, instead of dying with her son sitting in a lousy prison cell. I wish I hadn't been feral and hot-headed. I wish I hadn't ever chucked that rabbit into the incinerator or done a half dozen other things even worse that you never knew about. I wish I hadn't raped Lisa Rae, and I wish you hadn't been there, and I wish you hadn't been forced to testify against me. I wish we were still the friends we were when we were kids. I wish I'd found a good woman twenty years ago, and that I had a fine son in college like you got. Wishes aren't worth the breath it takes to whisper them, and I know that if none of those things had happened the way they did, I wouldn't have had the career I had—still have—and that means it all must have been some sort of huge plan. You believe in that, Judd? Destiny?"

"I believe in being who you are," I said. "I believe in following your beliefs and values."

"Well, that's sort of the point, ain't it, old son? I came back here because I wanted to knock the road dust off my boots and find something with meaning. It's been a fine old trip, but not a happy one. Between the drugs and the booze and the broads and the fights and the shows and recording sessions and awards, it always seemed the only time I was really happy was when I parked my ass in the tour bus and put the last town in the rearview. I found no peace in that life. I been to AA and NA and every other goddamned Anonymous you can name, and every one of them said I ought to take what they call a fearless moral inventory of my life. Well, I finally did. Discovered that I had no center. I had no idea where I really belonged. I'd simply been bouncing from one sensation to the next, and I knew what that meant. I know the word psychopath, and I am completely acquainted with its meaning, but deep down I didn't think it was a word that described me. Not the real me. Maybe the person I seemed to be, or maybe the behavior I engaged in, but not the person I was deep down inside."

"So who is that person?"

"Shit, son, he's nothin' but a ten-year-old kid skippin' out on his chores so he can spend an afternoon sitting by a trout pond with a bamboo pole, a roll of waxed twine, and a bobby pin for a hook, pissin' away a sunny afternoon with the only friend he has in the world."

"Me," I said.

"For years I hated your ass. I won't deny it. I sat in the High Rise up in Morganton and dreamed of what I'd do to you on the day I got out. I blamed you for taking away the only thing I truly treasured in my life—you and me, friends. I contemplated it for years, but after a while the fire burned down, and I could see things for what they really were. It was me. I ruined it by giving in to my anger. It took thirty years, but I finally saw things straight. That's when I knew it was time to come home. I'm here, now, and I'm asking you to forgive me."

In every imagined scenario I had conjured about Sean, this had never happened. I pulled the brute to me and hugged him tight, and I let the years of resentment and self-recrimination flood out of me. When we parted, perhaps a little self-consciously, I realized that all my anger toward him was gone. It had been replaced with the sort of gratitude I believe might have been felt by the father of the prodigal son when he saw his progeny silhouetted by the sun at the top of the hill, ending his long sojourn home.

"So," he said. "I guess that's that."

"No," I said. "There's loss that can never be regained. We can build something new. Bet you wouldn't guess it, but I actually have a couple of your albums in the house."

He grinned, his repaired teeth beaming like ivory in the brilliant sunlight.

"No shit?"

"My son gave them to me. I never told him about us as kids. He had no idea that it might be awkward. I listened to them once or twice, mostly out of some kind of morbid curiosity. You turned into a first class musician."

"Thanks. And, while I never thought I'd say something like this to anyone, you became a first rate cop. Just one thing I need to tell you. You are an idiot, trying to tackle a job like this barn by yourself. Sure as shit you are going to get hurt before the sun sets. How about I lend you a hand?"

We spent the next couple of hours ripping rotted planking from the side of the barn. I was gratified to find that the timbers underneath were sound. I set up a couple of sawhorses behind the Jeep, and we started cutting two-by-tens to length. Sean ruined his shirt not long after we started, and laughed it off as if it had been a free concert tee shirt. As the heat got to him, he first pulled out the tails, and finally yanked if off entirely and tossed it into the back of the Jeep.

"I should probably tell you," I said, as we took a short break to drink bottled tea from an ice chest, sweat pouring off us in rivulets. "Your friend Lily Holder came by my office the other day. She wanted me to know you couldn't have had anything to do with Boyd Overhultz's murder."

"Is that so? Now what do you make of something like that?"

"Sounds like she thinks a lot of you."

"Gotta tell you, Judd. Don't know whether I'd be here today if it weren't for that woman. When I came back to Bliss County, I had no idea how to rebuild my life. It wasn't something I'd had a lot of experience with over the years. When I met Lily, things began to change. It was like she believed in me, even when I wasn't so sure about myself. She saw something in me worth redeeming. Somehow, being worthy in her eyes made me want to be worthy in everyone's eyes. Don't that beat all?"

"It does at that."

He studied my chest, and then he put his hand out and fingered the puckered flesh of the entry wounds where Spud Corliss's bullets had pierced my body.

"Does it still hurt?" he asked.

"It did, for a long time. I think I had always had an abstract belief about what it would feel like to be shot, but I was wrong. At first I thought he had missed. Then, when the pain came, I think there was a part of me that prayed to die just to make it stop. Now, it's mostly scar tissue, and you know scars have no feeling."

"Don't I know," he said. He twisted around and gestured toward triplet scars halfway up his back. "A puke in prison down in Georgia took a shank to me in the dining hall one night because I called him a vile name. Bang, bang, bang, just like that. Felt like wasp stings at first, but then the blood started to flow and I felt a taste like old pennies in my mouth and a feeling like a branding iron hit me so hard that I arched my back on the dining room floor thinking I could escape it. Then it got really bad. Sometimes I dream about it and it wakes me at night. Somehow, little bastard missed my kidneys by a quarter inch and he didn't hit any major arteries. Hey, we survived, right?"

"That we did," I said, holding up my bottle. He clinked it with his and we shared a chuckle.

We finished skinning two sides of the barn not long before sundown, and decided that was enough work for one day. I stowed the tools inside the barn, intending to finish the job on Sunday, and I suggested that Sean bring Lily over for a cookout in a couple of hours. I figured if we were going to try to salvage some kind of friendship from the wreckage of our last three decades, we needed to get on it. We piled into the Jeep and headed over the hill, back toward my house.

As we crested the ridge, Sean shouted for me to stop. I jammed on the brakes. He pointed toward the house. A dark blue SUV was parked in the driveway in front of my porch. Three men were walking around the house looking through the windows.

"Kovalenko," Sean said. "I recognize the car."

I had a pair of binoculars stowed behind the front seat. I grabbed them and quickly focused on the men.

"They're carrying weapons," I said. "Look like some kind of automatic carbines. Maybe M4s."

"That's not good. I didn't tell you, but Kovalenko approached me a week ago and asked me to put pressure on you to leave him alone."

"Yeah, he did the same to Kent Kramer. Do you suppose they're here for the barbeque?"

"Not unless you're the one bound for the spit."

"Looks like Kovalenko is pissed. Probably blames me for snooping in his business, spoiling his nice deal with the Russians. Looks like he wants a little payback."

One of the men peered in my direction and pointed. I saw the others come to attention and rush to take a look.

"We're spotted," I said. "Time to go."

The intruders dashed around and climbed into the SUV, which roared to life and squirted gravel in a rooster tail spray as it skidded around the house in Sean's and my direction. The men were perhaps a quarter mile away and closing fast. I dropped the Jeep into gear and headed back toward the barn, even as I grabbed the two-way from the back. I was about to toggle the SEND button when the right front wheel of the Jeep hooked a deep rut at the bottom of the hill, and sunk into the hole by almost a foot. The momentum of the car lifted the rear, and we began a long slow roll. We had belted in and we landed on the roll bar, upside down. The radio and the Winchester flew out of the Jeep in different directions.

"You okay?" I yelled as the car came to a stop.

"Yeah. You get the radio. I'll grab the gun."

I found the radio maybe twenty feet from the car and switched it to Slim's frequency. It was Saturday, which meant he was on duty. Gunny Sikes wasn't scheduled to be on patrol until the next morning.

"Slim, got your ears on?" I shouted.

"Five by five, Chief. What's up?"

"I'm at the farm. Kovalenko and a couple of his guys are here, loaded for bear. They're after me. I'm going to need some backup."

"On my way." He didn't sign off right away, and I could hear the siren crank up over the radio. Sean, having retrieved the rifle, stepped up to my side.

"One of your officers coming?"

"Yeah. Slim. He's good."

"How long?"

"Maybe five minutes."

"Don't know how to tell you this, but we don't have five minutes. And there's another problem."

He held up the rifle. When it flew out of the Jeep, it landed barrel down in the Carolina red clay. The barrel was jammed with dirt.

"We'll have to clear it as best we can," I said. "Probably have to do it on the run. Need to find a small stick. Let's head for the barn."

He reached out and grabbed me. "Wait! Not the barn. It's not much more than a shell. We need some place more substantial."

"This is a farm, Sean. There isn't much here except for fields and ponds. The barn is the only shelter within a half mile."

"No. It isn't. Remember? When we were kids? The cave down near the pond?"

I hadn't thought about it for years. It wasn't actually a cave, but rather a depression in the hillside probably left over from a natural spring house used by one of my ancestors two centuries ago. Someone had dug it out, maybe ten or twelve feet back, and high enough for a grown man in the nineteenth century to stand in. Over years of disuse, the opening had begun to erode and close again, so that it wasn't much larger than the circumference of a fifty-gallon drum. When Sean and I were children, we'd sometimes hide there to get out of chores. It would be cramped for both of us, but it was a shelter, and it was difficult to see unless you were right on top of it.

The pond was a couple of hundred feet away, on the other

side of the barn. We ran as quickly as we could in that direction. Sean had found a penknife in his pocket, and was digging at the dirt in the rifle barrel with it.

"Think I got it clear," he said, as we rounded the barn and saw the opening in the hillside, barely visible.

"Hand it to me," I said. I could hear the SUV motor as it climbed the ridge. They couldn't see us yet, but they would be able to shortly. Sean gave me the rifle, and we made one more scramble toward the hillside. I pulled out the radio.

"Slim!" I called. "Where are you?"

"Just turned off the Morris Quick Road. Coming in hot and loud."

"We're near the pond, just behind the old barn. There are three men total, armed with assault rifles. Don't know whether they're on full auto, but being the Russian mob, I'd bet on it."

"I've already called Don Webb for backup. He should have a couple of deputies here in ten or fifteen minutes."

"This thing'll be all over by then, one way or the other. Be careful. Keep under cover as much as you can, but if you get a shot, take it."

"You strapped, Chief?"

"I have a rifle. It's full, but that's only six cartridges. Sean Burch is here, and we're looking for a place to hide until you and Don's boys can get here."

"Hunker down. Help's on the way."

I crawled into the hillside depression headfirst. It was dank and smelled of rotting vegetation. The only light was from the opening itself. My face brushed against a spider web, and I shuddered. I wasn't about to run, though. A spider bite, even from a black widow, was infinitely preferable to what awaited us outside the cave. Sean started to climb in behind me, but stopped.

"Just had an idea," he said. "They don't know I'm here."

"They had to see your car when they drove up. Get the hell in here!"

"My Caddy's in the shop. I drove Lily's car. Kovalenko's never seen it. For all they know, you're here alone. So I'm going to the barn. There are tools there I can use as close-in weapons. Here, I'm just more meat. If you can, try to keep an eye out through the opening. Cover me if I need it." Then he flashed a lopsided grin, and it occurred to me that, in a strange way, he was enjoying the situation.

"Wait!" I said, but it was too late. He had backed out and was sprinting toward the barn. I started to follow, figuring it would be easier for two people to make a stand than one, but the SUV crested the ridge just as Sean ducked into the barn. I saw him grab the crowbar and a hammer and slip inside one of the old draft horse stalls.

The SUV stopped just short of the building. The doors flew open and the three men jumped out. From my covered vantage, I could make out Kovalenko and his doorkeeper, Fyodor. Fyodor was carrying the same HK assault rifle I'd made him toss down a few days earlier, and I was immediately sorry I hadn't shot him then. The third man was hard to make out from my angle, but he was carrying a smaller M4-style carbine. He walked with a slight limp.

As if they could tell I was watching, all three turned in my direction simultaneously, and I ducked back into the darkness.

CHAPTER FORTY-THREE

Shug crouched in the horse stall and waited. His grip on the crowbar tightened and he swung it in a short arc once or twice to test its heft. It was off balance, never having been intended as a weapon, but he thought he could control it. The hammer was a standard carpenter's claw type with a fiberglass handle, slightly larger than the kind you'd find in a homeowner's tool kit. Either end could be lethal, wielded correctly, but he knew he'd have to get in really close to use it. At least the crowbar gave him a little extension. Not much, but it might be enough.

He heard the SUV skid to a stop in the grass, and he found a small chink in the wood siding through which he could see it without being detected. He watched as the three men hopped out, and then drew in a sharp breath.

One of them was Bobby Spurlock.

That messed up all his plans. As far as Kovalenko knew, Shug—at least ostensibly—was still aligned with Kovalenko. Shug had intended, though he had no clear idea yet exactly how, to convince Kovalenko that he had come to the farm looking for revenge on Judd, and planned to suggest they might find him down in one of the cornfields. That would give Judd's officers time to get to the farm and prevent a wholesale slaughter.

Bobby Spurlock blew that plan all to hell. It was likely he had already killed Boyd Overhultz over the theft incident in the bar, and he probably had vivid memories of getting the crud kicked out of him in the alleyway. Whether he had signed on with

Kovalenko or not, Bobby wanted a piece of Shug, and would be all too happy to shoot as soon as Shug showed his face.

Shug was still formulating a new scheme when Kovalenko turned to Fyodor and Bobby.

"Fyodor," he ordered, "you stay here by the car. Spurlock, you check out the barn. I'm heading up that rise over there to see if they're still running toward the fields. They can't have gotten far from the Jeep."

Fyodor positioned himself near the front of the SUV as Bobby started walking cautiously toward the barn.

Shit, Shug thought.

CHAPTER FORTY-FOUR

From the cave, I watched Kovalenko give orders to the two men. The one I couldn't see clearly started walking toward the barn. Fyodor took up a sentry position in front of the SUV, and for a moment he seemed to stare right at me. Luckily I was hidden by the cave's shadows. Kovalenko walked right in front of the opening. I scurried deeper into the depression and pointed my rifle toward the light. If he as much as stuck a finger inside, I'd blow him into the middle of next week.

When he walked on past, I allowed myself to breathe, and then I crept back toward the opening. I knew what was in the barn, and what Sean had to choose from for weapons.

Far off in the distance, I heard the first mournful wail of a lone siren. Fyodor heard it too, and stood at attention, straining to make it out.

"Don't worry about it," I heard Kovalenko shout. "Even if it's coming here, we'll have time to get out in the SUV. Keep looking!"

He was right. The dirt road that connected all the fields on my farm terminated in a separate exit that led to the Old Village Road. It was easy to see on any satellite image of the farm, and I favored Kovalenko as a person who didn't leave much to chance. Almost certainly, he had checked the maps and images of the area and knew about both entrances to the farm.

Fyodor leaned back on the hood, but remained vigilant. Every so often he turned his head toward the sound of the approaching siren, and he appeared more worried each time.

From my position, I could easily take Fyodor down with one shot. If I had thought of it sooner, I would have chanced it. Now, the SUV blocked my line of sight to the third man. For all I knew, he was already in the barn. Also, while I could hear Kovalenko barking orders to his crew, I couldn't tell where he was in relation to my cubby. I kept my rifle trained on the easiest target—Fyodor—and hoped that Slim and Don Webb's deputies would hustle.

CHAPTER FORTY-FIVE

The wall of the horse stall and the new siding planks he and Judd had installed that afternoon gave Shug a relatively secure position with no clear visual access. On the other hand, if Bobby were to come around the half-wall that defined the stall, the enclosed space left Shug with no path of escape. If they came face to face in this confined space, it would come down to kill or be killed, and Bobby had more firepower.

Shug heard Bobby's feet shuffle on ancient hay as he stepped into the barn. Shug closed his eyes and tried to determine by sound where Bobby was, but it was difficult because one entire side of the structure was still wide open and the sound wasn't confined to the interior.

As he waited, Shug examined his options. Maybe Bobby wasn't familiar with the military carbine he carried. If he'd never used one before, it might take him time to aim and shoot. Then Shug could take a whack or two at him with the crowbar. That would leave Fyodor at the car, and if Shug could grab Bobby's gun the next step would be to take out Fyodor. Kovalenko wouldn't dare try to take on both Shug and Judd without backup. He might even take off running, which would suit Shug just fine.

There was another shuffle, maybe eight or ten feet from the stall. Still too far away for Shug to make a move. He stole a quick glance through the sliver opening in the barn wall and saw Fyodor still at this station in front of the SUV. Off in the distance, Shug could hear a faint siren.

He heard another shuffle, closer this time. It sounded as if Bobby was moving from stall to stall, in the way a television cop might clear a building. That was good, for a couple of reasons. If Bobby was basing everything he did on TV, he probably didn't know a lot about what he was doing. Also, it meant he was moving systematically through the barn, which meant that Shug could predict exactly when he might reach the end stall.

He clutched at the crowbar, and reassured himself that the hammer was close by his side. The seconds ticked away, and the distant siren grew steadily louder.

Kovalenko shouted, "Don't worry about the siren!" He sounded pretty far off, at least a hundred feet away. That meant he'd cleared Judd's hidey-hole, which put Judd between Kovalenko and the other two men.

Another shuffle, this time in the next stall. Bobby was almost in reach. Shug decided to seize the element of surprise and make his move.

CHAPTER FORTY-SIX

From the sound of Kovalenko's voice, he had moved some distance from my position in the cave. I hazarded a smile. Tactically, that had been a mistake. Putting me between him and his men gave me the advantage.

I decided it was worth taking the chance of removing Fyodor from the equation, as I judged him to be the most dangerous of the trio. I pulled myself into a prone shooting position and centered the barrel on Fyodor's largest body mass. It was possible he was wearing body armor, but even the best vest probably won't stop a thirty-caliber, steel-jacketed rifle round.

My finger tightened on the trigger, just as I heard a short burst of automatic carbine fire from the barn. Fyodor dropped to the ground and crab-walked around the SUV. I heard a shout, and a series of grunting sounds, and then a clang of steel on steel, almost like a swordfight.

Sean was in a battle, and I couldn't help him, but I could try to keep the odds even. As soon as Fyodor reappeared on the other side of the SUV, I squeezed off a round at his head. The carbine barked in my hands, and I was grateful the barrel didn't explode from compacted dirt as the side windows of the SUV crazed and collapsed. My initial reflex was to keep firing until the gun ran out, but Fyodor dropped to hug the earth and I couldn't see him anymore. I had five rounds left, and I wasn't wasting them on a damned SUV.

I heard thudding footsteps outside the cave, as Kovalenko

came running back over the hill.

"What's happening?" he shouted. "Fyodor!"

"Get down, you idiot!" Fyodor yelled, and then he said something in Russian.

Kovalenko was still on the other side of the cave from the SUV. Now I had a problem. What had previously been an advantage had deteriorated into the equivalent of being trapped. Shit! Unless I could somehow take out Fyodor, I was pinned down, stuck in a potential crossfire.

CHAPTER FORTY-SEVEN

Shug took a deep breath, hoping it wouldn't be his last, and launched himself around the stall. Bobby had just stepped into the next stall, and was turned three-quarters of the way around. Shug raised the crowbar and swung for Bobby's head. Bobby, alerted by the sound of Shug jumping into the stall, instinctively rolled away. The crowbar landed heavily on his shoulder. His hand spasmed reflexively and the carbine spat out a quick burst of bullets that peppered the dust of the stall floor.

"Fuck!" Bobby turned, his ruined face mottled with rage. "You!"

He tried to raise the gun again. Shug swung the crowbar, connecting with the gun hard enough to loosen Bobby's grip, but not hard enough for him to lose the carbine entirely. With the gun no longer pointed at him, Shug dropped the crowbar, sprung at Bobby, and grabbed him around the chest, pushing him back until he collided with the barn wall. Shug could hear the air blow out of the boy's lungs with a loud grunt, but he didn't pause. Instead, he swung his fist once, twice, then a third time into Bobby's face. Bobby's eyes began to glaze over, but he kept hold of the gun and tried to raise it for one more shot.

Shug grabbed the crowbar from the floor of the stall and with a single motion swung it overhand, burying the clawed end into the top of Bobby's skull. Without even a whisper or groan Bobby collapsed to the dirt and finally let go of the gun.

Gasping for breath, Shug sat against the half-wall and

watched Bobby's pupils dilate fully. Then he grabbed the carbine and headed for the door.

One down, two to go.

CHAPTER FORTY-EIGHT

Fyodor had heard the same shots in the barn I had, but he could tell that the shot that had missed him and shattered the window of the SUV had come from a different direction. He and Kovalenko kept yelling at one another in Russian, and I could make out the top of Fyodor's head behind the car, swiveling every which way, looking for a concealed sniper.

I saw movement on the far side of the barn. Sean was creeping around the area we had repaired. Because Fyodor was about thirty degrees farther to the left from my position, his view of Sean was blocked by the corner of the building. At the same moment, I heard Kovalenko's feet pound the earth over my head as he dashed to the SUV and ran around to the rear.

I wasn't pinned down anymore. Even better, I could see Sean, and I knew neither Kovalenko nor Fyodor could. I trained the Winchester on the SUV, then glanced back at the barn.

"Spurlock!" Kovalenko yelled.

Fyodor barked at him. I don't speak Russian, but *shut the fuck up* is pretty recognizable in any language.

So, the third man was Bobby Spurlock. I didn't have time to figure out the connection. It looked like Sean had given his old employee a second ass-kicking and had taken his gun.

Sean stopped near the vertex of the two walls, still out of the line of sight from the SUV, and he stared straight at the entrance to the cave and waved. He raised the carbine he'd taken from Spurlock and pointed at it. He was grinning widely. Then he pointed toward the van. He pointed toward me and mimicked shooting.

It took me a minute to figure out what he wanted. He planned to storm the car, but he needed a diversion. I waved at him and pointed toward Fyodor, but by then he couldn't see me. He was taking my compliance on faith. I wouldn't let him down.

I had five shots left in the Winchester. Fyodor was on Sean's side of the SUV, and Kovalenko was at the rear. I couldn't hit either one of them from my position, but I couldn't miss the SUV. I tried to think where the thinnest metal might be on the car, and settled for the front doors. If I hit it right, I might be able to put a round straight through the thin gauge sheet metal. It might not go through both doors, but it would make a hell of a racket bouncing around the inside of the car.

I ripped off one quick shot, and I saw the top of Fyodor's head drop. The bullet must have penetrated both doors, because he crab-walked around the front of the SUV, right into my line of fire. I cranked the lever again, and took a quick pot shot at him. I missed, hitting the radiator, which spewed a cloud of steam that drove him back around to the far side of the SUV.

Sean jumped from the side of the building and ran toward the SUV, firing the M4 on full auto. The bullets struck Fyodor's midsection and spun him to the right, back into my gun sights. I took careful aim, squeezed the trigger, and blew the entire top of his head onto the hood of the car. His body slumped over the fender and twitched once or twice as it hit the ground.

I cocked again and swung the rifle around, hoping that the gunfire would drive Kovalenko back into my view.

Kovalenko stood, raised his M4, and laced Sean from hip to shoulder with a full automatic burst.

I wanted to scream, but that wouldn't have done any good. Instead, I scrambled from my hiding place, rose to my feet, and planted a thirty-caliber round at the base of Kovalenko's neck.

It went through, and he staggered and dropped the automatic and raised his hands to his throat as if he might be able to stanch the flood of life that cascaded from the wound. He leaned against the SUV. I took careful aim and parked my last round in his brain pan. He was dead before his knees buckled.

I ran to Sean's side. There were six different splotches on his white cotton shirt, and they quickly grew and spread toward one another. I yanked my tee shirt over my head and crumpled it to apply pressure, but the wounds were too spread out to cover more than two at any given point. I could hear Slim's siren now as he turned into my driveway, far too late to help either of us.

"Shit fire," Sean said, his eyes already glazing. "Damn if that don't hurt something awful."

"Just hang in," I said. "We'll call a medevac chopper in here just as soon as Slim gets up the hill."

"Think I'm gonna miss that flight, old son." His words were wet and sputtered. "Saved your ass, didn't I?"

"That you did, Sean."

He grinned as a small rivulet of blood began to collect at the corner of his mouth.

"Don't be sad," he said. "It was always gonna end this way. Ain't no easy finish for people like me. Woulda been nice to see Paris. Did I . . . redeem myself? Would Lily . . . be . . . proud?" The last words were fluid and raspy.

"Finest kind," I said, as my eyes moistened. He was staring off into space, observing some spectacle no living man can understand. I don't think he was seeing the real world anymore, but he tried to keep talking.

"Hell of a song . . . the farm . . . left to Lily . . ."

"I'll take care of whatever needs doing," I said.

He coughed weakly twice, and I could feel his pulse ebb and become erratic through the hand I clasped in my own, just as

Slim skidded over the hill in the new cruiser.

"Good . . . friend . . ." Sean whispered. Then the breath went out of him and he fell slack.

CHAPTER FORTY NINE

Hours later, after the ambulances had hauled off the bodies, and after the crime-scene folks ripped up half my farm collecting evidence, and after I killed three beers trying to slow my heart, and after I held Donna close for what seemed like forever as she cried on my shoulder from fear that she had nearly lost me and relief that she hadn't, and after I showered and shaved and dressed in my khakis and my blue oxford cloth and my brogans and my jacket and my cream Stetson, I drove over to the old Murray farm, where I found Lily Holder sitting in a rocker on the front porch, staring off at the stars that speckled a crystal clear night and dabbing at her eyes with a linen handkerchief.

"Sheriff came by a few hours ago," she said, as I stepped up to the porch and removed my hat. "Can you believe that? The actual sheriff himself. He told me what happened."

"Sheriff's a good man," I said. "I wish I could have gotten here sooner. I'd prefer to have been the one to tell you."

She held the handkerchief to her nose and snuffled a little. I could tell she had been crying nearly nonstop since she'd gotten the news. She was almost cried out.

"Was he brave?" she asked.

"None braver. He saved my life. At the end, he asked me if he'd redeemed himself. I believe he did. I believe he became everything you saw him capable of being."

"That's good," she said, and as if to emphasize the point she said it again, "That's good."

"You might want to know. Before we were attacked, Sean and I settled our differences. I was planning to have the two of you over for dinner tonight. Start things fresh."

"He wanted that so badly," she said, and the tears flowed again.

I pulled another rocker next to her, and I sat and held her hand as she wept. Her palm was rough and dry from years of hardscrabble work at God knows how many menial jobs. I realized how good a fit she had been for Sean, and I reflected on how sad it was that he should find that perfect match on the eve of losing his life, and also how wonderful it was that he hadn't died without finding her, and I got a little weepy myself. After a spell, she regained control.

"I got a call an hour ago," she said. "A lawyer. Said his name was Minor Levine."

"I know the man."

"He said Sean visited him several days ago and drew up some papers. A will. He said the club and farm go to me."

"That's how he felt about you. He saved my life. I think he felt you had saved his."

"I don't want the club. It's too much. I wouldn't know where to start."

"So sell it. Let it go."

"I was thinking in that direction. There's money, too. A lot. More than I ever dreamed of. What in hell will I do with that? I have no idea how to deal with wealth."

"I'll put you in touch with some people I know. I told Sean, just before he passed, that whatever needed to be done, I'd see to it. I keep my promises."

"I like the farm. I think I'll stay here. I think maybe my wandering days are over."

"That's good."

"Sean had a wild scheme about planting grapes and starting a winery. What do you think? Can this land grow wine grapes?"

"Hell," I said, "it's grown corn and tobacco and soybeans and snap peas and damned near every other thing that sprouts from a seed for over two hundred years. Can't imagine why it wouldn't grow grapes."

"A vineyard. That sounds nice. Guess I'll have a lot to learn."

"You'll have friends who can help. There's me, and there's Donna, and farmers help one another. You put down roots here in Prosperity, make this place your home, the people will come."

"Home," she said as a meteor streaked brilliantly across the Milky Way. "I like the sound of that. Home. I do believe, for the first time in my life, I have found a place I can truly call home."

We didn't talk for a long time. Instead, we rocked and gazed at the stars and reveled in our private thoughts and memories of a man who rose from a shanty on the edge of a tobacco field to the top of the music business, and who nearly lost his soul until he returned to the land that had spawned him and, at long last, discovered the sense of peace and purpose that came from loving a woman who saw only the nobility in his heart. Sean had buried the hostilities he'd carried since his youth like an anchor chain around his shoulders. In the final moments of life, he achieved the highest level of heroism a man can aspire to by laying down his life to save another.

Lily mourned the love she had known all too briefly. I mourned the friend I had abandoned and neglected for all too long.

For decades to come, we would remain the breathing tribute to a life so fervently lived and so tragic that the world was wholly inadequate to contain it.

ABOUT THE AUTHOR

Richard Helms retired in 2002 from a quarter-century career as a forensic psychologist to become a college professor in Charlotte, North Carolina. He has been nominated four times for the PWA Shamus Award (2003 for *Juicy Watusi*, 2004 for *Wet Debt*, 2006 for *Cordite Wine*, and 2014 for *The Mojito Coast*), four times for the SMFS Derringer Award, and once each for the MRI Macavity and ITW Thriller Awards. He is the only author ever to win the Derringer Award in two different categories in the same year (2008), and he won the ITW Thriller Award for Best Short Story in 2011. The parents of two grown children, Richard Helms and his wife, Elaine, live, as he refers to it, "Back in the Trees" in a small town in North Carolina.

Older than Goodbye is his seventeenth novel.